Plaidy   Apr87
The prince and the quakeress

1
LF MY19'88
LP JY 2'87
SE 8'87
DE
AL AG 24'89
FO NO 19'87
ME SE 19'88
BK1 JE 13'89

2
BU MR 11'88
EB NO 21'88
AN JA 05'87
RO AP 6'89
WP OC 26'89
BR FE 3'89

The Prince and the Quakeress

JEAN PLAIDY HAS ALSO WRITTEN

BEYOND THE BLUE MOUNTAINS
(A novel about early settlers in Australia)
DAUGHTER OF SATAN
(A novel about the persecution of witches and Puritans in the 16th and 17th centuries)
THE SCARLET CLOAK
(A novel of 16th century Spain, France and England)

Stories of Victorian England {IT BEGAN IN VAUXHALL GARDENS
LILITH
THE GOLDSMITH'S WIFE
(The story of Jane Shore)
EVERGREEN GALLANT
(The story of Henri of Navarre)

The Medici Trilogy MADAME SERPENT
Catherine de' Medici THE ITALIAN WOMAN } Also available in one volume
QUEEN JEZEBEL

The Lucrezia Borgia Series MADONNA OF THE SEVEN HILLS
LIGHT ON LUCREZIA

The Ferdinand and CASTILE FOR ISABELLA
Isabella Trilogy SPAIN FOR THE SOVEREIGNS } Also available in one volume
DAUGHTERS OF SPAIN

The French Revolution Series LOUIS THE WELL-BELOVED
THE ROAD TO COMPIEGNE
FLAUNTING EXTRAVAGANT QUEEN

The Tudor Novels KATHARINE, THE VIRGIN WIDOW
Katharine of Aragon THE SHADOW OF THE POMEGRANATE } Also available in one volume
THE KING'S SECRET MATTER
MURDER MOST ROYAL
(Anne Boleyn and Catherine Howard)
THE SIXTH WIFE
(Katharine Parr)
ST THOMAS'S EVE
(Sir Thomas More)
THE SPANISH BRIDEGROOM
(Philip II and his first three wives)
GAY LORD ROBERT
(Elizabeth and Leicester)
THE THISTLE AND THE ROSE
(Margaret Tudor and James IV)
MARY, QUEEN OF FRANCE
(Queen of Louis XII)

The Mary Queen of Scots Series ROYAL ROAD TO FOTHERINGAY
THE CAPTIVE QUEEN OF SCOTS

The Stuart Saga THE MURDER IN THE TOWER
(Robert Carr and the Countess of Essex)
Charles II {THE WANDERING PRINCE
A HEALTH UNTO HIS MAJESTY } Also available in one volume
HERE LIES OUR SOVEREIGN LORD
THE THREE CROWNS (William of Orange)
THE HAUNTED SISTERS (Mary and Anne)
THE QUEEN'S FAVOURITES (Sarah Churchill and Abigail Hill)

The Georgian Saga THE PRINCESS OF CELLE
QUEEN IN WAITING
CAROLINE, THE QUEEN
THE PRINCE AND THE QUAKERESS
THE THIRD GEORGE
PERDITA'S PRINCE
SWEET LASS OF RICHMOND HILL
INDISCRETIONS OF THE QUEEN
THE REGENT'S DAUGHTER
GODDESS OF THE GREEN ROOM
VICTORIA IN THE WINGS

The Queen Victoria Series CAPTIVE OF KENSINGTON PALACE
THE QUEEN AND LORD M
THE QUEEN'S HUSBAND
THE WIDOW OF WINDSOR

General Non-fiction A TRIPTYCH OF POISONERS
(Cesare Borgia, Madame de Brinvilliers and Dr Pritchard)

The Spanish Inquisition Series THE RISE OF THE SPANISH INQUISITION
THE GROWTH OF THE SPANISH INQUISITION
THE END OF THE SPANISH INQUISITION

The Prince
and the Quakeress

JEAN PLAIDY

G. P. Putnam's Sons
New York

G. P. Putnam's Sons
Publishers Since 1838
200 Madison Avenue
New York, NY 10016

Library of Congress Cataloging-in-Publication Data

Plaidy, Jean, date.
   The prince and the quakeress.

   Bibliography: p.
   1. George III, King of Great Britain, 1738–1820—
Fiction.   2. Lightfoot, Hannah, b. 1730—Fiction.
I. Title.
PR6015.I3P68   1986   823'.914   86-91468
ISBN 0-399-13191-4

Printed in the United States of America
1 2 3 4 5 6 7 8 9 10

Author's Note

THE story of George III and Hannah Lightfoot is admittedly one of the mysteries of history. No one can be absolutely certain of what took place. There are even some who declare that Hannah Lightfoot never existed. There is, in my opinion, too much evidence from various directions for this to be likely. I believe that Hannah Lightfoot not only lived but was the mistress of George III, as Prince of Wales. There is even a report that Queen Charlotte at one time believed that the King had made a previous marriage and insisted that a second marriage ceremony should take place between her and the King, and that this was done 'under the colour of an evening's entertainment'. There is also the Reynolds portrait at Knole. I have based my findings on the available evidence and the character of the King; and I think my version has as good a chance of being the true one as any other.

J.P.

CONTENTS

Encounter in the Rain   11

The Family of Wales   23

The Face at the Window   48

The Quakeress of St. James's Market   64

Journey in a Closed Carriage   77

The Elopement   95

Marriage Plans   109

A Slight Case of Blackmail   133

Visit from a Blindfolded Doctor   155

'The Butcher's' Disgrace   164

Joshua Reynolds Calls   175

Rule Britannia   188

The Secret Wedding   195

The Grave at Islington   208

A Sad Farewell   239

George, the King   248

The King's Courtship   271

The Face in the Crowd   312

BIBLIOGRAPHY

George the Third	J. D. Griffith Davies
George III	J. C. Long
George III: As Man, Monarch and Statesman	Beckles Willson
Farmer George	Lewis Melville
The Four Georges	Sir Charles Petrie
The Four Georges	W. M. Thackeray
History of the Four Georges and William IV	Justin McCarthy
The House of Hanover	Alvin Redman
Memoira and Portraits	Horace Walpole
The Lovely Quaker	John Lindsey
The Fair Quaker	Mary Pendered
Mystery of Hannah Lightfoot	Horace Bleackley
Hannah Lightfoot	W. J. Thoms
A Short Political History of the years 1760 to 1763	Henry Fox, 1st Lord Holland
The Life and Letters of Lady Sarah Lennox	Edited by the Countess of Ilchester and Lord Stavordale
History of the Reign of George III	R. Bisset
History of the Reign of George III	W. Massey
Memoirs of the Reign of George III	W. Belsham
History of England	William Hickman Smith Aubrey
British History	John Wade
England under the Hanoverians	Sir Charles Grant Robertson
The Dictionary of National Biography	Edited by Sir Leslie Stephen and Sir Sidney Lee
Eighteenth Century London Life	Rosamund Baynes Powell
Notes on British History	William Edwards

Princess Augusta

Encounter in the Rain

THE Princess Augusta was well satisfied with life. She was Princess of Wales, she had been married for eleven years to an amiable husband—unfaithful of course, but all German wives were brought up to accept that inevitability and she thought nothing of it. She was handsome, complacent and fruitful, this last asset being the most important.

The Prince was uxorious as his father had been with Queen Caroline and all were aware of how *he* had expected *her* almost to take a part in his affairs with other women, expressing her approval, doing all she could to help him as he would say to 'his pleasure'. It was a Court joke. Not that Frederick went as far as that—in fact he was an improvement on his father. He never flaunted his women under her nose; and he was without that irascible temper which was so amusing when directed against others and so alarming when turned on oneself. After all, the little man was the King—and the bombastic strutting, dapper, choleric creature would never allow anyone to forget that.

'A pox on him!' murmured Augusta pleasantly. *And* on that Walmoden woman whom he had wasted no time in bringing to England; and while he publicly wailed that no one would ever replace his beloved defunct spouse he was sporting with Walmoden in private. But the son of that union—Monsieur Louis whom Madame Walmoden had brought with her to England (no doubt seeing high honours for him there)—should never be recognized, if Augusta could help it; and she might well be in a position to decide for the King, in spite of his high colour—or perhaps because of it—did not seem to her a healthy man; and when he had followed his dear Caroline to the grave it would be the turn of Frederick and Augusta.

King and Queen of England! Oh no, Monsieur Louis, there will be no place for the old King's bastards when his son and daughter-in-law come to the throne. Louis was about two years older than her own George.

She was mildly sad when she thought of George. Such a puny little fellow he had been when he was born—a seventh-month child arriving so unexpectedly on that hot June day instead of waiting for August which was his allotted delivery date.

'And I never thought we should rear him,' she murmured. But one of the gardeners had an accommodating wife. What a woman! What a chest! What milk! Why were those people always so much more lavishly supplied? She had been a good woman who took to the child as though he were her own and suckled him and guarded him so that in a few months he made up for that early arrival.

George Frederick William! He would be Prince of Wales when the old man went and Frederick became King. Perhaps it would have been better if Edward had been the elder. George was so *meek*. That was it ... meek. And he could not learn. It was not that he did not try. George tried very hard, for George was a good boy. He would do everything he was told; that was why it was so necessary to watch him for fear the wrong people might do the telling; Princess Augusta was determined that only one person should; and that was herself.

She smiled and decided to visit the nursery. Frederick was probably already there. He liked to be with the children and was a good father to them in as much as he showered them with affection and they in return adored him. People might laugh at Frederick but he was a good parent. Queen Caroline, who was reputed to have been a wise woman, had said of him: 'My dearest firstborn is the greatest ass, the greatest liar, and the greatest *canaille* and the greatest beast in the whole world, and I heartily wish he were out of it.'

German candour! But although the English laughed at it—and one had to admit laughed at Fred—they did not admire it. Perhaps they would have been disappointed if there were not quarrels in the royal family. Who knew? But at the same time they cheered wildly when she appeared with the children and they approved—outwardly—of a pleasant family life. Fred at least was not quarrelling with *his* son as his father had quarrelled with him and his grandfather had quarrelled with his father. Quarrelling in German families seemed the natural thing to do. But Fred was different; he loved his sons and his sons loved him.

Yes, Fred was doubtless paying a visit to the nursery before they set out for the races.

Augusta rose from her dressing-table where her women had been attending to her toilette and declared her intention of looking in at the children.

*   *   *

Cliveden, the country home of the family of Wales, had been rented by Frederick from Lady Orkney. Here the Prince and Princess of Wales could entertain lavishly and at the same time shut themselves away from the King's Court. In fact they could build a little Court of their own, and their friends were only too ready to encourage them in this. The house was charmingly situated, being set on a terrace which stood high above the river. The gardens were cultivated to appear natural and thus supply the maximum charm. Daisies and buttercups mingled with lilies and roses; and because of his love of the theatre Frederick had ordered that a stage be built near the river. This spot was shut in by yews which formed a natural theatre, and it was greatly appreciated by visitors to Cliveden;

and as Frederick shared his family's enthusiasm for music it was most frequently used for concerts, when orchestras would be brought from London to Cliveden to entertain the guests. The children were encouraged to take part in these theatrical entertainments and when they performed, the Prince and Princess would make it a gala occasion.

Frederick was very popular in the district, living simply with his family, mingling with their neighbours and even playing the cello in the local musical group.

Life at Cliveden was not devoted entirely to these diversions. Ambitious men found their way to what was called the Prince's Court in opposition to that of his father. William Pitt came often, Chesterfield, Stair and Bolingbroke—men with their eyes on the future, for choleric George was well past his youth and it was believed that one of these days he would not survive a particularly violent outburst of rage. It was wise therefore to attach oneself to the rising star and this appeared to be the resolve of these ambitious men.

The King considering his son's activities would grow purple with rage. 'Impudent puppy,' was his frequent comment; but nothing he could say would alter the fact that Frederick was the Prince of Wales.

Augusta was right. Frederick was with the children. None could have doubted who he was for a moment. He bore the Hanoverian stamp: blue eyes and fresh complexion. He had been a good-looking boy, but the appearance of all members of the family was marred by the heavy sullen jaw and the almost vacant expression. Frederick differed from the King on account of his easy-going temperament. Now he looked his most genial, listening to his two elder sons telling him about the next play they intended to perform.

'Elizabeth wants to play a part,' Edward was saying. George had opened his mouth and was about to have spoken—to say the same thing, Augusta supposed. Why did he always allow Edward to get there before him!

'So she shall,' replied their father. 'We will ask Mamma's opinion.'

She joined them, embracing them all in turn—her dear, dear children.

'Yes, Elizabeth my dear, you shall play a part,' she told the six-year-old girl, going over to her chair and bending over to kiss her. Poor child, she was deformed and unable to stand owing to her weakness. Augusta was very worried about Elizabeth.

The two little boys William and Henry had toddled over to her; she lifted baby Henry on to her lap. He was only two and cuddling him against her she put out a hand to fondle William's golden hair so that he should not feel he had been ousted by the baby.

'Well, you will have some fun, I am sure.' Frederick smiled fondly at her. He could not have had a better wife, he was thinking now as he did so often. She was always good-natured and never murmured when Lady Archibald Hamilton was a little arrogant—as all mistresses will be if merely to assert themselves—and when Lady Middlesex tried to show her superiority with her Latin quotations and her proficiency in painting and music. 'It is very clever, my dear,' Augusta would say placidly. 'My duties as Princess of Wales would not allow me the time to acquire such accomplishments.' A gentle reminder that although they might have their place in the Prince's bedchamber, she was his wife and the mother of the royal line.

'Now we will talk of this play.' Her accent was German and of course the children were being brought up to speak in perfect English. In spite of an early youth spent at Hanover, Frederick spoke tolerably well—his mother in the early days of his life before she had first forgotten him and then despised him, had been wise enough to give him an English tutor—and far better than his father, who had never bothered to perfect himself in the speech of the country of which he was King, although even he was an improvement on George I who could not speak, and refused to learn, a word of English.

'Now, George, my son,' went on the Princess. 'You shall tell me what play you wish to perform and what part *you* wish to take.'

He was silent, a little flushed, thinking hard. Oh dear, he was a little backward. 'Come, George.'

'I have not yet thought, Mamma.'

'I will tell you what *I* want, Mamma,' cried Edward.

'One moment, my dear boy. George first ...'

'Oh, *George* never thinks anything ...'

'Now, Edward. Come, George ...'

Prince Frederick came to his son's rescue by announcing that he had no doubt that George would soon decide what he wanted to play; and it was time they left for the races. The children could discuss among themselves which play they would perform and most certainly there must be a part for Elizabeth.

*   *   *

On the way to the races Augusta discussed George with her husband. He caused her some anxiety, she admitted.

'He is a good boy but too meek and he makes no progress with his studies. I thank God that you will be there to guide him so that when his time comes ... which I pray may not be until he is an old man and strong in wisdom ... he may be ready.'

'George is a good boy,' Fred told her, and laid his hand over hers. 'You fret too much.'

'But he can scarcely write his name.'

'All in good time. All in good time.'

'I am anxious on his account.'

'Forget your anxieties. All will be well with the boy. Ayscough is a good man and I have decided to send for James Quin.'

'An actor!'

'Who better to teach the children elocution?'

'You mean to teach them how to act!' she laughed. 'I believe you wish to make actors of them above all else.'

'It is not so. But George must learn how to speak English if he is going to please the English. Do you not agree?'

'You are right, of course,' she told him.

And they laughed together, being, as usual, in such harmony.

Such a cloudy day, thought Augusta. There would be rain before it was over. How she hated to get wet. She wished they had not come, for how was she to know at that stage what an important encounter was to take place and what part the rain was to play in it. Often she was to think of this day and the effect that gloomy weather had had on her future. Life, she was to muse, reflecting on it, was full of chance and surprise.

In the meantime here was Bubb Dodington in attendance, his enormous body encased in the most elaborate brocade although several buttons were missing and his clothes gaped in most inconvenient places. He always gave the impression of bursting out of them and as though their purpose was not so much to cover his body as to proclaim his wealth to the world. It was the same with his mansions, particularly La Trappe at Hammersmith and his place in Pall Mall into which he had crammed as much costly furnishing as was possible. But he was a clever fellow—very learned, he could quote the classics lengthily and—to Augusta—boringly; and he was so rich that Fred said he could not afford to do without him because whenever he, Fred, was in particular financial difficulty, Bubb would obligingly lose a few thousand to him at the card table. Bubb was a man with his eyes on fame—and he had the fortune to buy it. So he was naturally ready to pay dearly in order to claim the friendship of the Prince of Wales.

Augusta yawned her way through the races; she was not as devoted to gambling as Fred was. Fred was fascinated by it; it was almost as important to him as women. So while she watched the races she was thinking of George and wondering whether they should consider finding a new tutor for him, for the boy must be made to understand that one day he would be King of England. He was such a *good* boy; there was no trace of wildness about him; yet he must learn to be a King.

The rain had started. Oh dear, now they would have to wait until it was over.

Bubb was fussily conducting them into the tent. It would soon be over, he said; and perhaps their Highnesses would like a game of cards to while away the time?

Fred declared that he fancied a game of whist but they needed a fourth, of course.

Bubb put his finger to his lips in that rather vulgar way of his and declared that His Highness could safely leave the finding of the fourth member of the party to him.

Fred sat down in the tent, yawning. 'A pox on the rain,' he said. Poor Fred, his conversation was obvious; small wonder that wags and wits thought him a little dull. Augusta was content with him the way he was, for she herself was not considered brilliant. She never raised her voice in contradiction to her husband, and from her first coming to England she had made it a point to agree with everything he said. That did not mean that she was not aware of what was going on about her, that she did not see Fred's failings. The fact that she had so successfully hidden her own ambitions during the years she had lived in England might suggest that she was by no means stupid. She had seen Queen Caroline appear to bow down to her husband's wishes; she had seen her meekly accept humiliations from the King; but everyone except the King had known that it was she who ruled the country. She, Augusta, had dutifully hated her mother-in-law because her husband did, but that did not mean that she could not admire her and imitate her as far as her own abilities would allow her. So while she echoed Fred's words she could be thinking that Fred was ineffectual, that he was a little dull and that if he were not the Prince of Wales he would have been a nonentity.

And then Bubb came into the tent with Lord Bute.

There are moments in one's life when the whole pattern of one's existence can change. Augusta recognized this as one.

As soon as he entered the tent she was immediately aware of the shortcomings of all other men. Frederick seemed inane as he never had before and Bubb more vulgar than ever.

'May I present Lord Bute to Your Highnesses?'

She was very ready to be presented. Surely, she thought, he is the most handsome man at Court. Why have I never seen him before? If he had been there, I must have noticed him. Who could fail to do so?

He was tall and his dignity was overwhelming. How much more kingly then Frederick! His manner was grave yet courteous; respectful yet admiring; and he had the finest pair of legs she had ever seen.

'Lord Bute,' she said, 'I am surprised that we have not met before.'

'I have only recently come to London, Your Highness.'

She knew whence he had come. His accent betrayed him. Surely it must be one of the most charming of accents. She had never thought it so before. Like all the family she had hated everything from beyond the Border, that stronghold of the Jacobites, for Scotsmen had never taken kindly to the Hanoverians. The recent '45 had started up there, and it was they who had harboured their Bonnie Prince Charlie. But Lord Bute was not of that kind. She was sure of it. He would be loyal to the crown. Bubb would never have brought him into the tent if that were not so.

'You're welcome,' Fred told him. 'Come now, Bubb, the cards.'

Your Highness.' While fussy Bubb produced the cards and dealt, Augusta watched the newcomer's strong hands. His calm expression betrayed nothing. She refused to admit to herself that she was unduly excited. An interesting man, she thought, whose conversation would surely have been more diverting than the cards.

They talked between games.

He had come down to London, he said, soon after the '45. He had felt that he no longer desired to stay in Scotland after that.

'Perhaps you should remain there to guard our interests,' she suggested gaily.

'There is no need for that, Madam,' he replied gravely. 'The Battle of Culloden showed the Pretender what happens to those who threaten the throne.'

'I see you are a loyal Scotsman.'

He took her hand and kissed it. It was very courteous and gallant and very bold, but they were in a tent and it *was* an informal occasion. Never had she felt so informal in so short a space of time.

Frederick wanted to get on with the game and was raising the stakes. Bubb was his reckless self and Augusta noticed that while Lord Bute did not betray any anxiety he played cautiously so as not to lose. How wise!

She waited for the game to finish, that conversation might be resumed. Then Lord Bute mentioned the theatre and it emerged that he was very fond of the play and since he had come to London it had been his great hobby to organize masquerades in his own house where he had insisted that all his relations join him and form a company to perform for their own pleasure.

Now Fred was interested. What plays? Lord Bute explained. Nothing was too comic, nothing too tragic. He himself was actor-producer and stage-manager. Even Frederick had laid aside the cards now; Augusta was leaning forward, her cheeks flushed. A fascinating subject made doubly so by such a fascinating talker.

'You could be useful in our productions,' Augusta pointed out. 'I am sure the Prince will agree with me on that.'

The Prince did.

'The Prince will wish you to visit us and see our theatre at Cliveden.'

The Prince thought that an excellent idea.

It turned out that Lord Bute had lived for nine years on the Island of Bute where he had amused himself studying agriculture, botany and architecture, which, Augusta declared, sounded quite absorbing. The Prince thought so, too. Only Bubb was a little bored but he never liked them to show too much interest in other people, being afraid that he might be ousted from the Prince's favour.

Augusta sat back in her chair listening to Lord Bute's musical voice with the accent which had suddenly become so attractive, and the sound of rain pattering on the tent. Such a pleasant sound she would think it ever after. She hoped it would go on because when the rain stopped this pleasant *tête-à-tête* was likely to do the same.

But the elements were favourable and although Bubb went to the door of the tent and scowled up at the darkening skies, the rain persisted.

So in that tent she learned the background of this most fascinating man. He was thirty-four years old—six years younger than Fred—and had been born in Edinburgh. He was his father's elder son and his mother had been the daughter of the Duke of Argyll. He had come south to Eton for his education and while there had met that gossip Horace Walpole; eleven years before this meeting in the tent he had married the daughter of Edward and Lady Mary Wortley Montague. Augusta, who was conscious of such aspects, immediately thought that he would have married a pretty fortune there. His wife and family were in London now with him; and he had been driven to the races in a carriage which he had hired from his apothecary.

It was a stroke of good fortune, he remarked, that he *had* come and been so honoured as to have been invited into the tent.

Augusta was delighted to note that Fred was as interested in Lord Bute as she was—perhaps not quite so much, but then Fred was superficial by nature.

She believed that he, like herself, was a little dismayed when Bubb announced that the rain had stopped and they could now start on the homeward journey.

Lord Bute took his leave.

'The Prince will wish you to call on us at Cliveden,' Augusta reminded him; and Fred endorsed this.

Never, declared Lord Bute, had he received a command which gave him more pleasure.

'We shall look for you ... soon,' Augusta reminded him.

He bowed.

'And where is your apothecary with his carriage?'

'Madam, he left an hour ago. That was the arrangement we made as he had business to which he must attend.'

'And what shall you do now?'

'Find a means of getting back to London.'

'My lord!' She was looking at Fred who was never one to fail in hospitality.

He was laughing. 'We invited you to Cliveden, my lord,' he said. 'There's no time like the present.'

What a pleasant journey. The rain had freshened the countryside, bringing out the sweet scents of the earth as they rode along, Lord Bute entertaining them on such subjects as architecture, botany and agriculture which had suddenly become quite fascinating.

But Frederick soon led him back to the theatre and that was the most interesting topic of all.

And so they came to Cliveden. What a pleasant day! thought Augusta, looking at the tall handsome Scotsman—and all due to the rain!

The Family of Wales

GEORGE was in the schoolroom with his brother Edward. He was dreaming idly as he often did when he should be studying. He knew it was wrong; he knew he should work hard, but lessons were so tiring, and try as he might he could not grasp what his tutors were talking about. He was watching the door, hoping his father would come in, breezy and affectionate, with a new idea for a play, for George preferred acting to learning lessons. Mathematics were a bore, but history had become more interesting because his mother was constantly reminding him that he, too, would one day be a King, and this brought the aspirations of Henry VII, the villainies, in which he did not altogether believe, of Richard III, the murders of Henry VIII and the tragedy of Charles I nearer home. These men were his ancestors; he could not forget that.

But the lessons he really cared for were those of the flute and harpsichord. Edward enjoyed them, too. And their father was anxious that they should have such lessons; even that old ogre, their grandfather the King, loved music. This love was inherent, and it was said that they had brought it with them from Germany. Handel had been the very dear friend of several of his relations. George was not surprised.

Unfortunately lessons other than music had to be learned, and they were not so congenial.

'Some persons agreed to give sixpence each to a waterman for carrying them from London to Gravesend, but with this condition: that for every other person taken in by the way threepence should be abated in their joint fare. Now the waterman took in three more than a fourth part of the number of the first passengers, in consideration of which he took of them but fivepence each. How many passengers were there at first?'

Oh dear, sighed George. This is most complicated.

Edward scowled at it and demanded to know why the future King should have to worry about such matters. Was he ever likely to travel in such a way, and if he did would he be so foolish as to make such a bargain with a waterman?

George explained painstakingly that it was not an indication that they should ever have to face such a problem in real life. It was a lesson in mathematics.

At which Edward laughed at him. 'My dear brother, did you think I didn't know that?' Whereupon George's prominent blue eyes were mildly sad and his usually pink cheeks flushed to a deep shade.

George was a simpleton, thought Edward. But at least he would work out the problem and tell Edward the answer, no matter how long it took him to do it. It was his duty to *try* to learn, George believed; and he would always do his duty.

George had hoped his father would come to the nursery accompanied by Lord Bute, the tall Scots nobleman who had become part of the household.

George shared the family's enthusiasm for Lord Bute, who was always so kind and understanding to a boy such as he was. He explained everything in such a way that George never felt he was stupid not to have grasped it first time. His father was kind but sometimes impatient with him, and now and then laughed at his slowness, comparing him with Edward, who was so much brighter. It was not done unkindly, but in a bantering affectionate way; yet it disconcerted George and made him fumble more. Lord Bute seemed to understand this. He never bantered; he was affectionate and kind and ... helpful. That was it. Whenever Lord Bute was near him, George felt safe.

In the family circle his father never behaved as though he were Prince of Wales; he would take his sons fishing on the banks of the Thames; and they played cricket in the Cliveden meadows. The Prince was very good at tennis and baseball, and he enjoyed playing with his own children. Lord Bute would join in the games; he was so good that he was a rival to the Prince; and the Princess Augusta would sit watching them with a little group of ladies, applauding when any of the children did well—and also applauding for the Prince and Lord Bute. George noticed that his mother applauded even more enthusiastically for Lord Bute than for the Prince of Wales.

George preferred being at Cliveden rather than Leicester House; as for those rare occasions when he was commanded to wait on the King, he dreaded them. His grandfather was an old ogre—a little red-faced man who shouted and swore at everyone and insisted on everyone's speaking French or German because he hated England and the English, it seemed. The old man was a rogue and a tyrant. Papa and Mamma hated him, so, of course, George did too.

But even at Cliveden there were lessons to be learned, and now he must attend to this stupid affair of the waterman.

Edward was looking out of the window. Clearly he would not help. So George sighed, and after a great deal of cogitation he came up with the answer.

'It's thirty-six,' he told Edward.

'Sure?' asked his brother.

'I have checked it.'

Edward nodded and wrote down the answer.

George picked up the next problem but at that moment the door opened. Eagerly the boys looked up from their work; but it was not one of their parents nor Uncle Bute. It was their true uncle, the Duke of Cumberland, their father's younger brother.

Edward was delighted by the diversion, George to see his uncle. They saw little of him, and George presumed it was because he was on the King's side, which he concluded judiciously, was what one would expect in view of the fact that he was the King's son.

The Duke of Cumberland was dressed for hunting—a large man inclined to corpulence, at the moment beaming with affection.

'I was hunting in the district and thought I'd come and see my nephews.' He embraced George first, then Edward.

Come to see his nephews! thought George. Not his brother or his sister-in-law?

'Papa and Mamma are here,' said George.

'Not in the house,' replied their uncle. 'Doubtless in that theatre of theirs with my Lord Bute.'

George detected a certain contempt in Uncle Cumberland's voice. He hoped Papa would not come in and quarrel with him. He hated quarrels.

'And here are you boys sitting over your books on a sunny day like this.'

'It's a shame,' agreed Edward.

'We have to learn our lessons,' George reminded him primly.

Uncle Cumberland pulled up a chair and sat down heavily. He laughed. 'What do you learn, eh? What's that?' He picked up the waterman problem and scowled at it. 'Much good that'll do you.'

'Mr. Scott thinks we should be proficient in mathematics.'

'Well, I'm not a great mathematician like Mr. Scott. I'm only a soldier.'

Edward had leaned his elbows on the table and was propping up his face as he stared intently at his uncle. 'Mathematics are a bore,' declared Edward. 'So are French and German.'

'Mr. Fung does his best to teach us, but we are a trial to him,' George explained.

'I like dancing with Mr. Ruperti,' declared Edward.

'But music is the best of all,' put in George. 'It is the only subject at which we seem to make much progress. Mr. Desnoyer is pleased with us.'

The Duke sat smiling expansively at his nephews.

'You boys should be learning to become soldiers, not prancing about with Mr. Ruperti and scraping violins.'

'We play the flute and the harpsichord,' George explained.

'You should learn how to command an army; you should study the niceties of strategy. Wouldn't you like to be a general?'

Edward said he would, but George was silent. He hated the sight of blood and did not care to think of men dying. Dying was not a noble glorious thing; people did not merely fall down dead; they suffered. He hated to think of people's suffering, and worst of all, himself suffering or inflicting it.

All the same Uncle Cumberland was a fascinating figure and as they rarely saw their relations from the King's Court a visit like this was an event.

He was a good talker and even made war sound fascinating. He drew his chair up to the table and said he would explain to them what had happened at a certain battle, the result of which had put their family firmly on the throne.

'For, nephews,' he said, 'we came within danger of losing the throne. Your grandfather was ready to fly to Hanover; he had his valuables packed, and with his friends was ready to leave. And the rebels had come as far as Derby.'

'To Hanover!' cried Edward. 'Do you mean, Uncle, that the people would have sent us away?'

'Aye, sent us packing and put the Stuarts back on the throne. Our enemy the King of France had sent Bonnie Prince Charlie over to drive us away, and they were as far as Derby. Think of that. All the way from Scotland. Here, where are your maps? Now, I'll show you. This is where the rebels were. It was November. I advanced to Stone, hoping to meet them. They were soon on the retreat.'

His big hands were on the maps; his voice was low and intense; he glorified war himself, and his very single-mindedness fascinated the boys.

'Now ...' The hand, big, brown, powerful, ranged over the map. 'I drove 'em back here ... right to Penrith ... right over the border. This had taken time and it was now December. I attempted to cut them off at this point, but there were too many for us. I had good men...' His face softened. George could believe that he had good men. He would see that they caught his enthusiasm, his passion for war. It was apparent as he talked that this was a man who would know no fear ... and no mercy. His eyes glowed; he was reliving that occasion all over again, and George had the impression that he was hoping the Pretender would come back or that someone else would give him an opportunity to save the crown for the House of Hanover.

'We were all that winter in Scotland,' he said. 'Can't do battle in the winter, boys. It's cold up there. Spring's the best time for battle. But there are bigger problems for a commander than battle. Ah yes. How he's going to feed his men? How's he going to get them where he wants? That's the nightmare, boys. The battle ... that's the glory.'

'Many die ...' began George.

'Do you know how many they lost at Culloden, boy?'

George shook his head.

'Good God, and they're supposed to be educating you! Two thousand rebels! And our losses? You must always set one beside the other. That's how you calculate the extent of your victory. Three hundred and forty loyal English gentlemen lost their lives at Culloden, boys. But we got two thousand of them. It'll be long before that scum raise a standard against our King, I can tell you.'

George was silent. 'What is it, boy?' demanded his uncle.

'George doesn't like people being hurt,' explained Edward.

That made Uncle Cumberland rock with laughter. 'So that's the way they're bringing you up, is it? Dance with Mr. Ruperti! Music with Mr. Desnoyer! French and German with Mr. Fung! By God, what you boys want is to learn to be *men*. I'll teach you a few things about living.'

'But this is dying,' interrupted George.

That made Uncle Cumberland laugh louder. In breathless tones he told the story of Culloden and how the bloody battle had gone. Even George was caught up in the excitement, and Cumberland looking from one to the other of the flushed faces was well pleased.

'I'm going to get Sir Peircy Brett to tell you how he encountered the *Elizabeth* on the high seas. That's a story well worth hearing. You'll learn what it means to defend your country and that's what you'll have to do, boy, when you're King, which will be one day. Now the *Elizabeth* ... she was a French ship. She was convoying the small frigate with their Prince Charlie on board and she was carrying the ammunition. Sent by the King of France, boys, to defeat good Englishmen, he hoped. Much chance he had.'

'When there was a Cumberland to defend us,' cried Edward, and received a warm look of approval from his uncle.

'And not only a Cumberland, boy. There are men like Peircy Brett in England too. He was in command of the *Lion* ... sixty guns. *Elizabeth* she was a ship of twenty-four. And *Lion* sighted *Elizabeth* and went into the attack.'

'And sank her?' cried Edward.

'Hey, wait a minute, boy. You want it too easy. It was a bloody battle...' George saw the gleam in Uncle Cumberland's eyes. 'What slaughter! It was indeed a bloody battle. *Lion* was a wreck when it was over. Forty-five killed and one hundred and seven wounded.'

'But that was *our* ship.'

'Yes, you have your losses in battle. But *Elizabeth* was fit for nothing. She couldn't go on. She had to limp back where she'd come from ... *and* she was carrying supplies. So ... their Bonnie Prince Charlie landed in Scotland, an impoverished adventurer ... not the well-equipped young conqueror the King of France sent out. That's battle, boys. That's war. We lost *Lion,* but the purpose was achieved. I can tell you this: the loss of *Elizabeth* was as important to our victory as Culloden.'

George was thinking of the battle at sea; the shrieks of

dying men; the blood .... there would be blood on the decks ... on the cold cruel water. No, he did not like it, although he was fascinated.

'I'll get Brett to tell you the full story one of these days,' went on Uncle Cumberland. 'It's a tale you boys should know. I'll take you with me to camp. You, George, should know how to defend your crown. Now...' He had pulled the map towards him. This was the map of Europe. He was going to tell more stories of battles and blood. This was living, he was thinking; the boys' education was being neglected; battles were of more importance than hypothetical problems about non-existent watermen.

He had the map spread out before him when the Prince and Princess of Wales came in accompanied by Lord Bute and Lady Middlesex.

'Ha, ha, brother,' cried Uncle Cumberland, getting up and kicking his chair back. 'And my sister...' He took Augusta's hand and kissed it. George, watching, saw that his father was displeased and as his parents were always in agreement, so was his mother.

Cumberland ignored Lord Bute and ran his eyes swiftly over Lady Middlesex. He liked women; in fact, gambling and women were what he enjoyed next to making war; he had never married; and had no desire to; but that had nothing to do with his fondness for the opposite sex. Lady Middlesex he knew was a favourite of Fred's—a clever woman but too short, too dumpy and her skin was as brown as a walnut; someone had once said she was as yellow as a November morning and by God, they were right. Fred, like his father and grandfather could not be said to choose his mistresses for their beauty.

'We did not know that you were here,' said Frederick mildly. He disliked his brother, but was too good-natured to show it. 'We should have been advised.'

'I wanted no ceremony. So I slipped into the schoolroom and gave my nephews a lesson.'

'They look as if they've enjoyed it,' said Lord Bute.

The Duke raised his eyebrows; he was surprised that an

attendant should have expressed an opinion. He disliked the fellow in any case. He had heard he had a great influence with the Prince of Wales and that he accompanied them everywhere. The Prince commanded him to attend on the Princess while he enjoyed the company of Lady Archibald Hamilton, Lady Middlesex and Lady Huntingdon. It made a cosy foursome, a little bourgeois community. Frederick liked to live *simply* at Cliveden. It would have to be different when he ascended the throne, which Cumberland hoped would not be for a long time. Fred as King was a project which did not appeal to him.

Augusta was clearly pregnant, so Frederick was doing his duty in spite of the ladies. She looked well content with the arrangement, too. A stupid woman, thought Cumberland; but a docile one. She never raised her voice against Fred. She was very different from their mother. Cumberland was sad, thinking of the Queen's death. She had doted on him and had done her best to have Fred passed over for him. He was the son both his father and mother would have liked to see mount the throne. But Fred was the eldest, and although his parents had done their best to keep him in Hanover and had not allowed him to come to England until he was twenty-one, he was Prince of Wales, and nothing was allowed to interfere with that.

Well, Fred could keep his yellow-skinned mistress; he could keep his docile wife; but the education of the boy who would one day be King of England was surely a matter with which the family should concern itself. George was doubtless a good boy, but he was obviously a simpleton. He should be taught something about life. They should try to make a soldier and a man of him. Cumberland would speak to his father about the boy and if King George said his grandson must be educated in a certain manner, then so it would be.

Cumberland turned away from Lord Bute as though he had not spoken and said he would like to have the chance of teaching the boys something about the strategem of war.

Frederick replied that the boys had the best tutors in the

country and he and the Princess were very pleased with their progress.

Cumberland nodded ironically and replied that he was sure of that—that the Prince and Princess of Wales were pleased, he meant.

Then Frederick suggested that as the time set for his sons' lessons was not yet at an end, he and the Princess should show the Duke the gardens at Cliveden, as he was sure he would find something there to interest him.

*   *   *

Trouble in the family. It was distressing. George wished that they could all be friends together and that his grandfather did not hate his father, and that when an uncle called it could be an occasion for rejoicing rather than for anger, for he was well aware of the indignation this impromptu visit had aroused.

His mother talked of his uncle. He was a crude man, a brutal man. He liked bloodshed. When she spoke Uncle Cumberland's name she did so with loathing. He loved war, this uncle. It was not so much that he wished to save the crown as that he wanted to kill ... for the sake of killing. He liked the sight of blood; he liked to see men suffer. The people called him The Butcher.

The Butcher? George shivered at the name.

The Butcher, repeated his mother. That was when they heard of all his cruelty at Culloden. Oh, when he had returned from that battlefield they had shouted for him in the streets. They had reverenced Duke Billy, as they called him; but when they heard what had really happened, the cruelty he had delighted in practising they called him 'Butcher'.

'It is a hateful name to be given to a man,' said George.

'Hateful indeed,' replied his mother. 'Why, when it was proposed that he should be elected an Alderman of the City ... this was after Culloden, one of the aldermen said: "Let it be of the Butchers." So you see that is how the people think of him. Once when there was a disturbance at the Haymarket Theatre he lost his sword and the people started to sing: "Billy the Butcher has lost his knife." That is what the people think of your Uncle Cumberland. How different he is from your father. Did he tell you that your father wanted to take command of the forces that went against the Pretender? Of course, your grandfather wouldn't hear of that. He wanted all the glory for the Butcher. How different it would have been if your father had obtained the command. There would have been victory just the same—but glorious, not shameful victory. Did your uncle tell you that your father obtained the release of Flora MacDonald, that your father is a kind, human man, who is tolerant in his ideas?'

'He did not,' said George. 'He did not mention that lady. Who is she?'

'She is a brave woman. She is mistaken, of course, because she supported the Stuarts. But then, she is Scottish and knew no better.'

'Uncle Bute is Scottish.'

A soft look spread itself across the Princess's face. 'You should not mention his name in the same breath as that woman's. His loyalty to us is all the more to be admired because he is Scottish.'

'Oh yes, yes, Mamma.'

She was a little embarrassed under his gaze. She said quickly: 'I was telling you of Flora MacDonald. She helped Charles Edward Stuart to escape and was captured and brought to the Tower. It was your father who pleaded for leniency for this woman; he pointed out that she was a simple creature who was led astray. He obtained her freedom. He is a good tolerant man.'

'I'm so glad Papa did that.'

'You should be glad you have such a good kind Papa. And I can tell you this, your Uncle Cumberland is no friend to him. His great desire is to take the throne from him. He hates your dear kind Papa simply because he was born before he was and so is Prince of Wales. What do you think of any man who can

hate your dear kind Papa? Must he not be a rogue to do so?'
George agreed. Only a rogue could hate dear kind Papa.

*   *   *

Augusta was brought to bed of another boy—her fifth.

He was christened Frederick William and it was decided, to
George's consternation, that he was to be one of the sponsors.
It was his first public duty and he was terrified that he would
make a fool of himself. It was easy to confide his fears to Lord
Bute who did not laugh at him but told him that there was
nothing to fear, and actually explained the whole ceremony to
him. It was very simple, said Lord Bute, and if there was anything George feared at any time he would be honoured and
delighted if he would come and tell him about it.

'I will,' declared George.

His father would have been kind, but Lord Bute always
seemed to *sense* his uncertainties and be ready with his comfort
before it was asked. And his mother was so pleased when Lord
Bute offered his advice. 'It is as though you had two kind
fathers,' she would say. 'You are a fortunate Prince.'

Fortunate indeed, thought George, when he remembered
the stories of how his grandparents had left his father in
Hanover when they came to London and how he had had to
threaten to elope with his cousin before they would bring him
to London. What disaster if that had happened! He would not
then have married Mamma. And what would have happened
to him and Edward, and William and Henry, and Augusta
and Elizabeth, to say nothing of this newest arrival to whom he
was to act as sponsor.

Grandfather had given his permission which it was necessary
to receive, but fortunately he was away in Hanover, where he
so often was.

'Long may he stay there,' said Papa, and Mamma echoed his
words as she always did.

So fortunately the old King would not be present at the
ceremony; and with kind Papa to help him—and, of course,
dear Uncle Bute—it might not be such an ordeal.

'You will have to get used to ordeals like that,' his sister Augusta, who was a year older than he was, told him brusquely, and he knew she was right.

But it passed off well. He did what was expected of him and no one remarked that he was shy and gauche; and his voice was quite steady when he pronounced that his little brother was to be called Frederick William.

*   *   *

That year they played the tragedy of Lady Jane Grey in the theatre of Cliveden. Nicholas Rowe had written it very appealingly and there were tears shed when the lovely Jane was led to the executioner's block.

There was the excitement of rehearsals and learning one's part; and Uncle Bute was so very good at anything concerning the theatre.

He was constantly with the family and Edward and Augusta whispered that many unkind things were said about him, but George could not believe that anyone could find anything unkind to say about Uncle Bute.

Papa was as fond of him as Mamma was. He was always saying, 'Where's Bute?' And when he said he wanted to walk in the gardens with Lady Middlesex he would tell Lord Bute to accompany the Princess. Papa and Lady Middlesex would disappear for quite a long time, 'walking the alleys' as Papa called it. Mamma seemed very happy at such times because she did so enjoy walking with Uncle Bute. Although Papa and Lady Middlesex disappeared for a while Mamma and Lord Bute could be seen together in the gardens, always talking and laughing together, Mamma's voice a little higher, a little more German as it was when she was pleased or excited. And then after a very long time if Papa appeared with Lady Middlesex the four of them would be very contented together.

Once when Uncle Cumberland called to see them he came to the nursery as he had on that other occasion and George had shrunk from his embrace because he could not stop thinking of him as The Butcher. He was aware of the sword at his uncle's side, and in his imagination George saw it dripping with blood.

Uncle Cumberland was aware of this change in his nephew. He drew back in dismay. He said: 'Oh my God, what have they told you about me?'

And he was too sad even to talk of wars.

George was sorry, for he hated trouble in the family.

When his father heard that the Duke had gone away he said: 'Good riddance. We don't want him here.'

Yet George could not believe his uncle was such a villain when he saw him face to face and he continued to think of him for a long time ... sometimes as the Butcher with the sword dripping blood and others as the jolly uncle who was one of the most generous members of the family.

Papa was, he said, becoming a little anxious about their educations, and busied himself drawing up an account of how their lessons should be regulated.

They were to get up at seven o'clock and be ready to read with Mr. Scott from eight until nine. Then they must study with Dr. Ayscough from nine till eleven; from eleven to twelve Mr. Fung must take over and from twelve to half past Mr. Ruperti would be in charge. After that they could play until three, when dinner was taken. Mr. Desnoyer came three times a week at half past four to instruct them in music; and at five they must continue the study of languages with Mr. Fung until half past six. At half past six until eight they must be with Mr. Scott again; at eight they took supper and must go to bed about ten o'clock. On Sundays George and Edward would be instructed by Dr. Ayscough, with their two sisters, on the principles of religion.

This was a rigorous timetable and one which was not closely adhered to. It was typical of Frederick that having drawn up a list of stern rules he could feel he had done his duty, and when he decided that a game of tennis or cricket would be good for the boys, or it was time they performed another play, he happily interrupted the curriculum he had so carefully arranged.

At this time he introduced Francis, Lord North, into the royal nursery to take charge of his sons.

One bright March day George, with some of the family, went to watch his father at tennis. It was a most exciting game but it was brought to an abrupt end when one of the balls struck Frederick in the eye. There was immediate consternation. In dismay Augusta hurried to her husband, and George stood staring, not knowing what to do. But in a short while Frederick was telling them that it was all right. 'Just the shock of the moment,' he said.

However, he did not want to continue with the game, and went to his apartments to lie down for a while.

Augusta accompanied him, and Lord Bute took Frederick's place on the tennis court.

* * *

That blow from a tennis ball seemed to affect Frederick adversely. In the first place he developed an abscess and he was so low in health that he had a bad attack of pleurisy. From this he recovered and was well enough to go to the House of Lords. It was a cold day and hot inside the chamber; when he returned to Carlton House he changed into lighter garments and lay down to rest on a couch in a room which opened on to the gardens. As a result he caught a fresh cold, and this undermined his health still further. The abscess flared up again and he declared himself to be in great pain.

He was taken to Leicester House and there Augusta called in the doctors. The Prince was suffering from the abscess, they said; and he had a touch of pleurisy; they expected he would recover shortly.

Frederick seemed contented to have Augusta beside him, but he whispered to her that he was uneasy about George.

'George!' cried Augusta. 'He is well.'

'He is young,' replied Frederick, 'and my father is an old man.'

Augusta cried out: 'Do not speak so. It will be many years before George comes to the throne.'

But Frederick was obsessed by a premonition that it would not be long.

He said: 'I have a paper for George. It is in my desk. I wish you to give it to him if I should be unable to do so myself.'

'But of course you will give it to him.'

But Frederick shook his head. 'You have been a good wife to me,' he said. 'Bute will advise you.'

He saw the tender smile touch her lips and he was pleased. He had not been faithful to her. Let her find some consolation if she could. It had occurred to him lately that there was a great deal in Augusta which neither he nor others appreciated. Perhaps Bute did. She was not the gullible fool many believed her to be.

'The paper for George is in my desk,' he said, and even as he spoke a spasm of pain crossed his face.

'Augusta,' he said, 'send for Desnoyer ... I'd like him to play a little for me. He has a way with a violin which pleases me.'

Augusta sent for the children's music master and when the man came Frederick smiled at him and bade him play.

In the Prince's bedchamber the candles guttered; the Prince lay back on his pillows, his face drawn and yellow; Augusta watched, telling herself he would soon recover. It is a good sign that he asked for the music. In the shadows the doctors waited: Wilmot, Taylor and Leigh, with Hawkins the surgeon —some of the best medical men in the country.

He'll soon be well, thought Augusta, soon taking 'little walks in the alleys' with Lady Middlesex while she herself enjoyed one of those stimulating and most delightful sessions with Lord Bute.

The Prince began to cough; the violin stopped; the doctors were at the bedside.

Frederick put his hands on his heart and said: 'I feel death close.'

Augusta rose in her chair and snatched up a candle.

'My God,' cried Wilmot, 'the Prince is going.'

As Augusta held the candle high and looked at her husband,

she saw the glazed look in his eyes as he sank back on the pillows.

He lay still; she stood staring aghast, and it was some time before the numbing realization came to her that she was a widow.

*   *   *

There was gloom in Leicester House. Everyone was shocked. Frederick was only forty-four years of age. His father was still alive and looked as if he were good for a few more years. And Frederick was dead. His eldest son was but a boy—thirteen years old. Who would have believed this possible, seeing Frederick on the tennis court, acting in plays, fishing with his children, sporting with his mistresses. It was incredible.

The Princess Augusta remained stunned. She would not move from her husband's bedside. She sat in her chair there and no persuasion could move her. It was as though she believed that by remaining there she could by the very force of her desire to bring him back breathe some life into him.

'Frederick...' she murmured, from time to time. 'It can't be ... You must be here. What will become of us ... of George, the children ... of me?'

In the background of her mind was that grim shadow, that old ogre, the King. Who would protect her from him now? What would he decide to do? What if he determined to take the care of the children out of her hands! This was like a nightmare.

She covered her face with her hands, hoping that when she uncovered it she would see Fred lying there in bed smiling at her, telling her she had had a bad dream.

But there he was, still, unlike himself. Oh, the horror of looking at the dead face of a loved one! The terrible realization that he will never speak again, that he has gone out of this life for ever!

'No, Fred ... *no!*'

She felt the child move within her ... Fred's child. In four months time that child would be born. Only five months before this man had begotten the child and now he was dead!

And the future? It was dark and menacing.

A hand lightly touched her shoulder. She turned sharply. Lord Bute was looking down at her, tenderly, lovingly.

'Your Highness will make yourself ill,' he said.

She shook her head and placed her hand rapidly over the one which lay on her shoulder. Hastily she removed it. One must be careful. The very thought of the need for care started to lift her out of her misery. John was here, dear John Stuart, Earl of Bute.

She rose and with him left the death-chamber.

*   *   *

George walked up and down trying to fight back his tears. It was easier walking, he found; if he threw himself on to his bed he would break into wild sobbing; and he must remember that to give way to his grief would be childish.

Dear kind Papa was gone! He could not realize it. He had known Papa was ill; he had been present when the tennis ball had hit him and that had started the tragic business. But to die ... never to see him again! It was more than he could bear. This was the first real sorrow. His father had died in pain, and he could not bear the thought of people in pain. When two workmen had fallen from the scaffolding at Kew he had been overcome with horror and had been affected for days. But this was his own dear Papa.

What would become of him, what would become of them all?

His grief was overpowering; there was nothing but his grief.

Then it was invaded suddenly by another emotion—one of stark terror.

Now that his father was dead he, George William Frederick, was Prince of Wales.

*   *   *

The King came to Leicester House, setting aside enmity at such a time.

The children were summoned to his presence and he stared

at them all, but chiefly at George. He was a terrifying old man—little, it was true, but with a red face and prominent blue eyes, and he spoke in broken English.

'Vere is the Prince of Vales?'

And George must stand before him for scrutiny. 'Don't be a frightened young puppy. Prince of Vales now ... How old are you, eh? Thirteen ... Remember now you are the Prince of Vales.'

But there were tears in his eyes, for he was a sentimental old man for all his high temper; he saw that Augusta was genuinely grieved and tried to comfort her. The woman was a fool. Caroline had said so ... his own dear wife, Caroline (and there was no woman fit to unbuckle her shoes) had said so. But fool as she was, she had been fond of Fred and any woman who could have been fond of that villain (mustn't speak ill of the dead) of that ... *puppy*, must be a meek woman. She'd need help in looking after the children and he'd see she got it. By God, she should do as she was ordered in that respect. But in the meantime she was a woman grieving for her husband and he knew what it meant to lose a spouse.

'Do not cry, my dear,' he said. 'Try not to grieve. I know how you suffer. I lost my own vife. Your mother-in-law ... the best voman in the vorld. Ven I lose her I lose heart...'

Augusta thought: Yes, you old hypocrite, and all the time you were mourning for her you were thinking of how you could bring Madame Walmoden to England, and all the time you were pretending to be so fond of her you were deceiving her with other women. As Fred was ... but Fred was kinder ... and Fred was dead.

The King patted her knee comfortingly, and beckoned to his grandsons.

'Come here, young fellows. Be brave boys now. Obey your mother and remember you are the grandsons of a King.'

Augusta said quickly: 'Your Majesty will, I know, out of your goodness of heart not take my children from me. I have lost my husband ... to lose my children would be unendurable.'

She was on the verge of tears and the King's eyes were swimming too. Augusta was alert in spite of her grief. Now was the time to get this important matter settled, she was well aware, while he was in a sentimental mood. Once he had gone away and remembered that Fred was a villain whom he had hated, that she had always been her husband's ardent supporter, he would set some plan in motion to take her children from her. Now was the moment then, while he was in a sentimental mood and could not in all decency deny such a request to a grieving widow.

'Your Majesty, who understands my loss as few others can, will grant me this. Your Majesty, you will leave me guardian of my children. It is the only thing which can console me now.'

The King nodded.

'So it shall be,' he said.

Augusta sighed with relief and was aware of triumph. Fred was dead, no longer there to overshadow her. Now was the time for the true Augusta to emerge.

*   *   *

Augusta sent for her eldest son. She was seated at her table and there were papers before her; when she saw George she rose and held out her arms.

He ran into them and she embraced him crying: 'My poor fatherless boy.'

George wept with her and as he did so thought of his father lying dead in his coffin and the pain he must have suffered before his death. He wept bitterly for the loss of that kind man and the fact that his passing had made him Prince of Wales. There was a difference in being Prince of Wales and the son of the Prince of Wales. He had sensed it immediately. He was expecting a summons hourly to appear before his terrifying grandfather.

Augusta dried her tears. She had lost dear Fred, but there were compensations. There was power and there was Lord Bute.

'Your dear kind Papa left a paper which he would have

given to you on your eighteenth birthday had he lived. But now that he has ... gone ... he would wish you to have it at once, for, my son, you will have to grow up quickly. You will have to learn to be a King. You understand full well what your father's death means to you ... what changes it has brought in your position.'

'Yes, Mamma,' said George mournfully.

'Then we will read this paper together, shall we? We will see what instructions dear kind Papa has left you.'

'Yes, Mamma.'

She opened the papers and spread them on the table, and together they read:

'Instructions for my son George drawn up by myself for his good, that of my family and for that of his people, according to the ideas of my grandfather and best friend, George I.'

Augusta looked at her son significantly. 'You see, he did not trust his father, our present King, *your* grandfather. Ah, his grandfather was always a good friend to him. How different it would have been if he had been his father ...'

'It was a pity they had to quarrel,' George said.

'Anyone would quarrel with the King,' replied Augusta fiercely. 'We shall have to be very careful to avoid trouble now we no longer have your dear Papa to care for us.'

George read what his father had written:

'As always I have had the tenderest paternal affection for you, and I cannot give you stronger proof of it than in leaving this paper in your mother's hands, who will read it to you from time to time and will give it to you when you come of age or when you get the crown. I know you will always have the greatest respect for your mother....'

'I hope it too,' said Augusta. He took her hand and kissed it.

'You know it, Mamma.'

'Bless you, my son.' She glanced down at the paper with him. 'Your father was always a man of peace,' she said. 'It was only

when the need arose that he would take to arms. He was very
different from his younger brother, the Butcher Cumberland.'

'If you can be without war let not your ambition draw you
into it. A good deal of the National Debt must be paid off
before England enters into a war. At the same time never
give up your honour nor that of the nation. A wise and
brave Prince may oftentimes without armies put a stop to
the confusion, which ambitious neighbours endeavour to
create.'

Reading these instructions George began to have a deep
sense of responsibility. Before he had always believed that
there was plenty of time for him to learn. He had never before
seriously thought of being King of England. It was something
for the very distant future. His father had been a compara-
tively young man with at least twenty years to live, and twenty
years in the opinion of a thirteen-year-old boy was a lifetime.
And now here he was with an ageing grandfather, given to
choleric rages, who could die at any moment—the only barrier
between young George and the throne. It was an alarming
prospect.

He must learn all he could as quickly as possible. He must
study these papers. He read feverishly; he must balance the
country's finances; he must understand business; he must seek
true friends who would not flatter him but tell him the truth.
He must separate the thrones of Hanover and England and
never attempt to sacrifice the latter for the former as both his
grandfather and his great grandfather had done. Uppermost in
his mind must be the desire to convince Englishmen that he
was an Englishman himself, born in England, bred in England, and an Englishman not only through these matters but
by inclination. Never let the people of England believe for a
moment that he saw himself as a German whose loyalties were
first for Germany.

Frederick finished his injunctions by recommending his
mother to his care and also the rest of the family, his brothers
and sisters.

'I shall have no regret never to have worn the crown if you do but fill it worthily,' he ended.

George lifted eyes swimming with tears to his mother's face.

'But, Mamma, it is almost as though he *knew* he were going to die.'

'Sometimes these revelations come to us,' she answered. 'You see how he loved you, how he loved us all. You will want to do all that he wished, I know.'

'Yes, Mamma,' answered George fervently.

'He would have wanted me to guide you, my son, for he had more faith in me than in anyone.'

'I know it, Mamma. I feel so young, so ... so unworthy.'

'Trust in me, my son. Rely on me and all will be well.'

'It is what I want to do above all else.'

She kissed him warmly; he was hers to mould; and he was the future King.

*   *   *

It was characteristic of the King that his resentment towards his son should not end with the latter's death. In the presence of the widow and children he allowed his sentimentality to get the better of him; but he was not going to change his attitude now.

Frederick was a young puppy who ought to have remained in Hanover. He would have liked to see William, Duke of Cumberland, King of England, and if it had been possible to make him so, he would have done it. It was what dear dead Caroline would have wished. Perhaps it was not too late now. That boy George was a simpleton. Prince of Wales indeed! When there was William, a fine figure of a man, the hero of the '45, and people could say what they liked, it was William who had saved the throne and driven that Stuart puppy yelping back to his French masters. William was the man who should take the throne, not a young puppy scarcely out of his nursery, son of that impudent rascal who ought never to have been brought to England.

Of one thing the King was certain—there should be no fine

funeral honours for Fred. No grand ceremonies was the order. Let no one forget that although he was the King's son and Prince of Wales he was no friend of the King's. A simple funeral, then, with none of the nobility—who considered themselves the friends of the King—to attend. There would have to be some lords to carry the pall and attend the Princess, he supposed, but let it rest there. He wanted everyone to know that he considered the death of his eldest son no major calamity.

So the funeral of Frederick was less of an occasion than it was expected to be; and as when the cortège came out of the House of Lords it was raining there were not many who cared to stand about in such weather to see it pass on its way to the Abbey.

Bubb Dodington was indignant. Bubb was like a man demented. The Prince should have had better medical atten-ton, he declared; the Prince should have had great funeral honours. Poor Bubb! He was worried as to what the future held for him. He had been the Prince's ardent supporter and friend, so it was hardly likely that the King would look with favour on him. And what else was there? A young boy Prince of Wales, thirteen years old, and a Princess Dowager who had never opened her mouth except to agree with her husband.

His only hope was to attach himself as speedily as possible to the Princess Dowager, to seek to advise her, and if possible to keep the rival Court alive which could form a nucleus about the new heir and guide him in the way he was to go.

It was a sad state of affairs.

The indifference of the people showed clearly that they did not share Bubb's views. Frederick Prince of Wales was dead. Just another of those Germans, said the people. The whole lot of them were not much use, and it was a pity they had ever come here. If Bonnie Prince Charlie had not been a Catholic ... But he was, and at least the Germans were Protestants, and they were comic enough to provide a little amusement now and then.

The people were laughing at Frederick's epitaph which delighted them so much that it was spoken and sung in every place where men and women congregated; in fact, it made Frederick more popular in death than he had been in life.

> *'Here lies Fred*
> *Who was alive and is dead.*
> *Had it been his father,*
> *I had much rather;*
> *Had it been his brother,*
> *Still better than another;*
> *Had it been his sister,*
> *No one would have missed her;*
> *Had it been the whole generation,*
> *Still better for the nation.*
> *But since it's only Fred*
> *Who was alive and is dead,*
> *There's no more to be said.'*

George II

The Face at the Window

THE King received the Duke of Newcastle, his chief minister, who was immediately aware that His Majesty was not in the best of moods.

He had just officially created his grandson Prince of Wales and Earl of Chester; and he was wishing, as he had so often, that William had been his eldest son instead of Frederick; then this rather vacant young boy would not now be heir to the throne.

William would have been so much more suitable. A strong King; a man who could lead his army against the country's enemies. He was not very popular at this time, it was true. But that was because the Scots had spread evil stories of his savagery at Culloden; but he would win back their favour. It had always been dear Caroline's wish ... because it was *his* wish, and he and Caroline had always seen eye to eye, he believed.

He continued to mourn her. He would never forget her. He loved her more now that she was dead than he had when she was alive. Or so he believed. It was easier to in any case, for now he need not be continually watchful that she was not appearing to be cleverer than he was. She had been something of a blue stocking, his Caroline; or she would have been if he hadn't kept her in order.

His thoughts were straying from that young puppy George to discuss whom he had summoned Newcastle.

The King did not greatly like Newcastle. Sir Robert Walpole had been the minister he had loved—although when he had first come to the throne he had dismissed him ignominiously, only to take him back immediately; and he had always refused to admit that it was the clever scheming of his Queen Caroline which had brought about this most satisfactory state of affairs. But the days of Sir Robert were over and here was Newcastle.

Thomas Pelham-Holles, Duke of Newcastle, was an ambitious man and one of the richest in the country. He had inherited his title at the age of twenty-two and through his marriage great wealth. He had attained his ministerial post largely through his wealth, for he was by no means brilliant and his habits made him appear ridiculous. He rarely walked, but trotted as though in a great hurry to arrive at his destination; he appeared restless and uncertain; he rarely finished what he intended to; he was continually fussing without achieving his goal. One of the Court wits had remarked: 'The Duke of Newcastle always loses half an hour in the morning which he is running after the rest of the day without being able to overtake it.'

As a young man he had supported the House of Hanover, even before the death of Queen Anne; and George I had selected him to be godfather to a son of George II, who because he was a friend of his father's had hated him and had picked a quarrel at the baptismal ceremony. This had resulted in starting the famous quarrel between George I and George II, who was at that time Prince of Wales. The King had never liked him. Still, in spite of his faults, he was more honest than most and if he irritated the King, so did most of those who surrounded him.

Now he was saying in his ridiculous squeaky voice: 'Your Majesty, it will be necessary to offer some guidance in the Prince's education.'

This was exactly what the King himself was thinking, so he

was slightly less irritated by Newcastle than he usually was. He grunted.

'It would be well ... er ... to er ... remove His Highness from his mother's care, to bring him here and to have him under Your Majesty's surveillance.'

'Yes, yes, yes,' said the King. 'But I promised his mother she should keep him.'

'If we could bring him under Your Majesty's surveillance ...'

The King hammered the table violently and the veins stood out at his temples. 'I've told you, Newcastle. I've promised the voman. She'll have the puppy ... I've told her. Could do nothing else ven she was crying for her husband. She's to keep him vith her and the rest of them, too.'

'Yet, Your Majesty ...'

'Oh, be silent, you fool. The boy stays with his mother.'

'Then if Your Majesty would consider appointing new tutors ... tutors whom Your Majesty would choose ...'

'Ah, that's a different story. If his grandmother vere here ...' The King looked mawkish. 'There was a voman. I could trust her. I can trust no one else ...'

Newcastle thought: She would have led you by the nose while she told you she was following you. Wasn't that always her way?

'She vould agree vith me that ve couldn't take the boy from his mother.'

'North should go, Your Majesty. Perhaps Your Majesty would consider substituting Lord Harcourt for North.'

The King considered the point, heartily wishing that he had not promised the Princess that she should have charge of the Prince.

'Yes,' he said, 've'll send the present lot packing, Newcastle, and appoint new ones. The boy struck me as being ignorant, Newcastle. Ignorant!'

'It's to be expected, Your Majesty, in the care of a woman.'

'Bring your suggestions to me, Newcastle. Talk vith your council. Then ven you have them I'll acquaint the Princess vith the names of the Prince's new tutors.'

When Newcastle left the King the Duke was congratulating himself.

Very soon he would have the Prince surrounded by those whom he could trust to support him. If the King should die suddenly, the new King must have been imbued with the right ideas, which meant that he must have been brought up to respect the excellence of the Duke of Newcastle.

* * *

George was disturbed by the changes in his household. Dr. Ayscough had been dismissed and his place taken by Dr. Hayter, Bishop of Norwich. He did not dislike Hayter whom he considered sensible; he was the illegitimate son of the Archbishop of York, a very merry man, who enjoyed the company of women and did not allow his calling to interfere with his pleasure. George knew nothing of this; he would have been horrified if he had. Not that he knew much of the world; he was an idealist and was innocent enough to believe that his grandfather's Court was full of people with similar ideas.

Lord Harcourt had taken the place of Lord North whom Frederick had appointed shortly before his death; he was proficient in little except hunting and drinking—neither of which accomplishments were of much use to the young Prince nor of any great interest to him. His sub-governor was Andrew Stone, a brother of the Archbishop of Armagh; and George Scott remained as sub-Preceptor.

The Princess resented these changes and George was aware of her dissatisfaction as he struggled manfully to learn but without much success.

Augusta expressed her disquiet to Bubb Dodington who was constantly in attendance on her.

'They teach him nothing,' she declared.

And Bubb did not suggest for one moment that the Prince's ignorance might in some measure be due to his inability to learn.

'Oh, the difficulties of bringing up a Prince without a husband to help one!' she sighed.

But even as she spoke she was conscious of warm satisfaction. She was not so desolate as she liked people to think.

She had her friends. And there was one ...

Their relationship had progressed since the death of Frederick, as indeed it was natural that it should.

He was discreet but purposeful; and she had no wish that he should be otherwise. From the first moment he had entered that tent on a certain rainy day she had never wished him to be any different from what he was.

When she had been mourning for Fred, on that first day when she was stunned by the terrible shock and had not yet begun to realize all it implied, she had been conscious of him close to her.

He had waited for her to recover a little, only betraying by a touch of the hand, the softest caress, the meaningful glance that he was standing by waiting.

And then as the days passed he had become a little more daring, taking those little steps nearer and nearer towards complete intimacy—a state neither of them would have considered while the Prince lived. Fred might have his mistresses, but a Princess was different. She had been solely Fred's wife until the end; even now she was carrying his child.

When that was born ... then she would consider herself free.

Bute knew it even as she did. There was in the air a delicious awareness of the future. This little bridge to be crossed to ... paradise.

So she allowed herself to be angry with George's new tutors, knowing that very soon there would be one who not only would be closer to her than the husband she had lost but would also be guide and father to her son.

*   *   *

Four months after the death of Frederick, Augusta's child was born; it was a daughter and she named her Caroline Matilda. As Augusta lay in bed, the child beside her, she reflected that this was the end of a phase; and in some measure it was like stepping out of captivity. Already in the last four months she had begun to feel alive as never before. She was a person of importance; she could form her own opinions; no need now to wait until her lord and master voiced his views before she declared her own. Now she could think as she liked, speak as she liked.

This would be the last of her children. That saddened her a little. She liked children; and she was pleased with her brood. They should be hers, entirely hers, she thought passionately; and no one—no King on Earth—was going to take them from her.

They might say that children in such a position needed the guiding hand of a father. They should have it; for she knew of one who would be to them all that a father could possibly be. He would be waiting now ... As soon as she was well; as soon as she was able to receive him ... The time to which they had both looked forward with such intense longing was very close.

It was perhaps a little unseemly to be thinking of that now, while she lay abed with the Prince's child. So she would direct her thoughts from such imminent joys and think as the parent of fatherless children should.

George! Her thoughts could always come uneasily to him. She did not like his tutors. And why should she tolerate those she did not like? Why should she allow the boy's grandfather to dictate to her? She was his mother; she cared for him as his grandfather never could care for anyone except his silly strutting self. No, she was going to take charge of George's upbringing, and no one was going to prevent her.

She thought of George's father, grandfather and great-grandfather. Women! That was their chief pleasure and occupation. There was a strong streak of sensuality in the family; and George must be protected from it.

George at the moment was an innocent boy who knew little of the world. It was true he was just entering into his teens, but he was exceptionally innocent. She was going to keep him like that. He should not mingle with the boys of his own age who inhabited his grandfather's Court. That place was a sink of iniquity. How long would George keep his innocence there?

No, George was going to be protected, and she his mother would protect him.

What a glorious future! She was free to make her own life. She had done with childbearing and she had a fine family to show for the arduous years. She had cast off her yoke and now she would do what she wished. And one thing she wished was to control her son, the Prince of Wales, so that when the time came for him to be King of England his mother would be beside him—the true ruler of the country.

There might be one other to stand with her. He was coming to see her now. A little unorthodox. Oh, but he had been such a friend of the Prince of Wales!

His presence filled the bedchamber—such poise, such authority, such looks.

His smile was tender.

'I trust Your Royal Highness will soon be restored to perfect health.'

'Thank you, my Lord Bute. I am sure this will be so.'

Lingering looks, full of plans for the future.

This was living as she had never lived before, thought the Dowager Princess of Wales; this was freedom.

*   *   *

It would have been a pleasant enough household but for the dissensions among his tutors, thought George. But there was continual intrigue in the schoolroom. This was one of the penalties of being Prince of Wales.

He and his brothers and sisters never met people of their own ages because their mother was afraid that they would be contaminated. She wanted to keep her children pure and innocent, she said, and saw no reason for bringing to their notice the unpleasant side of life before they need be faced with it.

She wanted George to confide in her—her and dear Lord Bute who was in constant attendance. No one could have the children's welfare more at heart than dear Lord Bute and she wanted them to know it. But George knew this very well; his adoration for Lord Bute almost equalled that of his mother for the noble lord. Every problem he discussed with his dear uncle; and no one had ever been more kind; never did he show the slightest exasperation when George failed to grasp a point; he would explain it in several different ways to make it clear. George was contented as long as he had his dear Mamma and dear Uncle Bute close at hand. He was aware though of the trouble between those dear people and his tutors. Lord Harcourt and Bishop Hayter always seemed to be putting their heads together to annoy Mamma and Lord Bute. He was conscious of the way these two ignored Mamma—and Lord Bute—when they came to the schoolroom and how they always tried to denigrate or shrug aside as worthless anything either Mamma or Lord Bute suggested.

George sometimes felt that he was like a bone between growling dogs. He knew very well whom he wanted to care for him.

'I don't know what those men are doing here,' said Mamma again and again. 'I should like to know what they teach you. Stone is a sensible man and so is Scott, but they are in subordinate positions and cannot raise their voices against those two.'

George said mildly that Lord Harcourt was always pleasant to him, to which his mother replied that this was doubtless because the man knew his pupil would one day be King and he felt it expedient to be, but she did not trust him; and she feared that what he wished to teach George above all else was to distrust his own mother.

'That he could never do, dearest Mamma,' cried George.

'I know that, my son. You may not be clever with books but you have the good sense to recognize your friends. And there are two on whom you can always depend—your mother and dear Lord Bute.'

'I should indeed be a fool not to know that.'

'You are my own child. Your mother would always be your best friend ... and Lord Bute too.'

'Lord Bute is as a father to me. I love him dearly.'

'It pleases me to hear you say it. What a wonderful man he is! What should we do without him? It was a fortunate day for us when the rain brought him into our tent.'

'Mamma, I often think of Lady Bute.'

'Why should you do that?'

'She is his wife, and wives and husbands are usually together ... sometimes.'

'Oh, she is happy enough. She lives in London. I doubt not he visits her now and then. She is a fortunate woman. Did you know he has given her fourteen children in as little time as it takes to have them?'

'I always thought,' said George fervently, 'that he was a wonderful man.'

'So you see,' said the Princess firmly, 'Lady Bute has nothing of which to complain.'

* * *

Newcastle, watching the situation in the Prince's schoolroom with close attention, was well aware of the growing influence of the Princess Dowager and Lord Bute. It was dangerous, he decided. Each week the future King grew more and more devoted to those two; and when he stepped out of the schoolroom, possibly to the throne, he would be completely conditioned, a puppet of theirs. What Newcastle desired was that the boy should be a puppet of his, and it was the task of the tutors, Harcourt and Hayter, to bring about this desirable state of affairs.

But they were not succeeding.

Summoned to his presence for consultation they declared that the odds were against them. The Prince was constantly in the company of his mother and the man everyone now believed to be her paramour. It was too strong an influence to be easily broken. Moreover, Scott and Stone were on the side of the Princess and Bute.

'Then,' said Newcastle, 'as we cannot get the Princess out of her son's household, and while she is there so will her lover be, we must at least rid ourselves of Scott and Stone.'

This presented a problem, because neither Harcourt nor Hayter were greatly concerned with the studies of the Prince. They left that to the professors. Scott and Stone were the learned gentlemen.

'There are other learned gentlemen,' declared Newcastle. 'Get rid of those two and we will find them.'

Hayter said that Stone read strange books and was constantly preaching tolerance. It might not therefore be difficult to pin on him a charge of being a Jacobite.

'There you have it,' said Newcastle. 'There's your chance. Use it.'

* * *

The people of England—and in particular London—had an inquisitive attitude towards their royal family. They jeered, they sentimentalized, they took sides. A young and innocent Prince had their sympathy and interest. He was a charming figure, fatherless, in all probability destined to be their King when a young man. They wanted to know how he was being treated; they wanted fair play for George; and surrounded by such a set of villains as his family were, they believed the situation needed their watchful attention.

The old King was a rogue. The sooner he died the better. He was a German, a little red-faced man without charm, and only happy when in Hanover. He had even brought a mistress over from Germany, implying that English women weren't good enough! Of course he had his share of them, but to bring a woman from Germany and make her Countess of Yarmouth and set her up as his mistress-in-chief ... it was simply not patriotic. He was old—and who ever wanted an old King? Oh yes, they were waiting impatiently for young George. A good boy by all accounts. And not bad-looking. He was tall—not like his little grandfather; fair skin, blue eyes, rather vacant expression and sullen-jawed; but he couldn't help that, being a German. A pleasant boy on the whole, and the old fellow couldn't die quickly enough for the people.

But he was young and there would be jostling for power. The rumours about the Princess were interesting. This Lord Bute seemed to be in constant attendance on the lady. For what purpose? They could guess, and whether it was true or not they were going to believe it was because it was more amusing that way. Bute and the Princess on one side—Newcastle and his henchmen on the other. There was going to be conflict; and this was what the people found amusing.

In the coffee and chocolate houses the latest gossip was discussed. The Whig writers vied with the Tory writers and the witty results of their labours brought great pleasure to all who read them.

So the conflict round the Prince was common knowledge and everyone waited to see who would be triumphant—Newcastle or the Princess Dowager.

The storm broke when Hayter came in and found George reading.

George was not a great reader. He was slow; but he was painstaking and if he took a long time to get through a book, at least he had read every word.

Scott and Stone had encouraged him to read. He should read history they assured him; the subject most necessary to Kings. He should have a good knowledge not only of his own country's affairs but also those of his neighbours.

'Your Highness is absorbed,' said Hayter pleasantly.

George looked up, trying to bring his mind from the book's subject to the Bishop.

'It is an interesting book,' said George. 'Mr. Stone recommended it and I am glad he did.'

'May I see?' asked Hayter.

'But certainly.'

Hayter looked. 'My God,' he said. '*Revolutions d'Angleterre!* It's by a Frenchman!'

'It makes it doubly valuable ... improving my knowledge of the language at the same time.'

'At the same time as imbuing Your Highness with Jacobite sympathies?'

'Jacobite sympathies...' George stammered. 'But ... I could never have sympathies against my own family.'

'Unless they were presented to Your Highness so cleverly, so attractively, that you felt them to be the truth.'

'But...'

'Your Highness says that Mr. Stone gave you this book?'

'Yes, but he thought...'

'I must ask Your Highness to allow me to take this book.'

'I have not finished...'

'Nevertheless my duty impels me to take it.'

'I...I...'

'With Your Highness's permission...'

George was always unsure how to deal with a situation of which he had had no experience, so he allowed the Bishop to take the book from him; he sat staring before him wondering what fresh trouble was about to break.

*　　*　　*

On his way to his mother's apartment he met one of her maids of honour, Elizabeth Chudleigh. He blushed as he always did when he met her; she seemed to him such a wonderful woman. She must be about eighteen years older than he was, but he felt more at ease in the company of women older than himself than in that of younger ones. And Elizabeth seemed to possess the qualities he most admired. She was one of the most self-possessed persons in his mother's entourage; she was flamboyant and beautiful, always resourceful, not caring a jot for all the scandal that surrounded her, and there was plenty of that. Only recently she had appeared at a ball at Somerset House as Iphigenia for the sacrifice, and her gown—or lack of it—had caused such a stir because it had appeared that she was naked. In truth she had been clad in flesh-coloured silk so tight that it gave the appearance of being a skin and this was decorated in appropriate places by fig leaves. She had laughed at the storm such an appearance had aroused.

There were many scandals about Elizabeth and George often wondered why he liked her so much. He did not usually care for people who were talked of. It was his grandfather perhaps who had brought scandal to Elizabeth's name, for he had been taken with her when she first came to Court and had presented her with a watch which had cost thirty-five pounds. Whether she had been his mistress or not George was unsure. There were many women who did refuse the King's attentions; and although this irritated him, it did not necessarily result in their being banished from Court. Long ago the Duke of Hamilton had been greatly enamoured of her and they actually became engaged before he was sent off by his family on the Grand Tour. That romance came to nothing—it was foiled, some said by a maiden aunt of Elizabeth's who had intercepted their correspondence and withheld it so that they both believed the other had broken the promise to remain faithful. Exciting events would always circulate about Elizabeth. She was doubtless engaged in some secret adventure at this time; but all the same she had time to spare for an uncertain boy.

'You look disturbed, Your Highness,' she said, with that charming concern which was half flirtatious, half motherly.

He told her about the book he had been reading and how Hayter had taken it from him.

She snapped her fingers. 'He's out to make trouble. Don't give him another thought.'

'But he is accusing Mr. Stone of trying to make a Jacobite of me. Of me, Miss Chudleigh! Why how could I possible be a Jacobite?'

'I'll tell Your Highness this: Hayter and Harcourt are only trying to make trouble. Just laugh at them ... that's all.'

'I wish I were like you, Miss Chudleigh. Everything seems so easy for you.'

That made her laugh. 'If only Your Highness knew,' she whispered. Then she was motherly again. 'Don't worry. If you're in any trouble, just let me know. You do understand, don't you, that I'd put all my worldly wisdom at Your Highness's disposal?'

'Oh, Miss Chudleigh, I am sure you would.'

He meant it. It was comforting to think that he had the support of his mother, Uncle Bute *and* Miss Chudleigh.

* * *

The trouble came quickly. Hayter and Harcourt lost no time in laying their complaint against Mr. Scott and Mr. Stone before the Duke of Newcastle, who immediately took it to the King.

'Young puppy,' growled the King. 'Ve should look into this. Vat does he think he is doing? Trying to drive himself off the throne before he's reached it!'

The Dowager Princess was indignant. Because the Prince had read a book which put forward the case for James II it did not mean that he must agree with it.

'If we are going to be accused of supporting every opinion of which we read we are going to be in difficulties. Does my lord Harcourt and my lord Bishop believe that we must read only one set of opinions, then? My son is heir to this throne. I should like him to study *all* opinions; only thus will he have a clear understanding of history.'

Newcastle was nonplussed. There had been too much shouting about the whole affair. Many men had read *Revolutions d'Angleterre*. Were they all going to be accused of harbouring Jacobite tendencies because of that?

Harcourt and Hayter believed themselves to be in a very strong position and declared that unless Stone and Scott were immediately dismissed, they would resign.

'Dismiss Scott and Stone!' cried the Princess. 'But who, then, is going to *teach* my son? He learns little from my lord Harcourt or my lord Bishop. It is Mr. Scott and Mr. Stone who are the teachers.'

Too much notoriety had been given to the affair and in the coffee and chocolate houses the conflict between the Prince's tutors was being discussed. To dismiss the Prince's tutor simply because he had been discovered reading a book was going to arouse ridicule and criticism so the matter was shelved. But Harcourt and Hayter had sworn they would resign unless

Scott and Stone were immediately dismissed. The tutors were not dismissed because there was no one of the academic ability to replace them.

Nonplussed, yet clinging to their dignity, there was only one thing Harcourt and Hayter could do. Resign.

Their resignation, much to their chagrin, was accepted; and in their places came Lord Waldegrave and Dr. John Thomas, Bishop of Peterborough.

While these matters were coming to a head and reaching a settlement, George's attention had wandered away. He had not disliked Harcourt and Hayter; he did not much care whether they left him or not; he did not greatly take to Waldegrave but Dr. John Thomas seemed charming.

His thoughts, though, were far from the schoolroom. George was growing up; he was no longer a child.

For the last few months he had begun to notice the young girls of the Court—never of his own age, usually those much older like Elizabeth Chudleigh. They seemed to him entirely delightful. He would like to chat with them, perhaps to kiss their hands and tell them how pretty he found them. That would be very pleasant, but there must be nothing sordid in the friendship. George wanted an ideal relationship. It would be wonderful to be happily married.

Yes, that was the idea. To be happily married as Papa and Mamma had been, as Lord Bute and his wife were ...

This thought made George pause and frown a little. But Papa and Mamma *had* been happy; they had said so many times. Papa had had lady friends. Just friends, George supposed. And although Uncle Bute had a wife—he had been most punctilious in supplying her with children—his Court duties naturally kept him in attendance on the Princess of Wales.

Yes, these were ideal relationships and only such a one could satisfy George. He could never reconcile himself to doing wrong.

He wanted a wife, a home and children. He was not quite sixteen but he was tall and physically well developed; he was man enough to desire a woman and the only way he would wish to satisfy such desire was in marriage.

Marriage! he thought of it constantly. While his mother and Uncle Bute talked earnestly about the scheming Harcourt and Hayter, he thought of marriage. He could see his bride quite clearly. Very beautiful and older than he was because there was something so comforting about older women.

And gradually his picture of the woman he wanted for his wife took shape. He had seen her when he rode in his carriage from Leicester House to St. James's. She was sombrely dressed in a grey Quaker gown; she was demure; and she was the most beautiful woman he had ever seen.

She would be sitting in the upper window over a linen-draper's shop in St. James's Market so he always commanded his chairman to take that route. As his chair came level with the linen-draper's window he would raise his eyes and flush; and she would look at him with wide-eyed innocence and after a few such occasions she too took to flushing. It was clear that she was as conscious of him as he was of her; and this fact delighted him.

His mother might rage about the fiends who wanted to take her son from her; he would always answer her mechanically. Even when Lord Bute spoke to him he scarcely heard. His thoughts would be occupied by the beautiful young woman in the linen-draper's shop.

ᑲ Hannah Lightfoot ᑕ

The Quakeress of St. James's Market

HANNAH LIGHTFOOT had been about five years old when she
and her mother had come to live with Uncle Henry Wheeler in
St. James's Market. Memories of life before that were vague,
something to dream of with horror, to awake from shuddering
in the comfortable bed in the room she shared with her
mother, for her father's shoemaker's shop in Wapping had
been very different from Uncle Henry's prosperous establishment in St. James's Market.

She could not remember her father; perhaps life had been
easier when he was alive; she had been two when he died. Her
mother told her of how her family—the Wheelers, always
spoken of with awe—had not been very pleased with the
marriage. Matthew Lightfoot had not been a good Quaker and
it had been against the advice of her family that she had
married him; they were not surprised that she had lived so
poorly in Wapping.

But Matthew had died and Uncle Henry being a deeply
religious man and a Quaker had, after giving his sister Mary
three years in which to struggle on in expiation of her folly,

come to her rescue and offered her a home in his linen-draper's establishment.

So as a child Hannah would lie in the big bed beside her mother and listen to the sounds outside the shop which never failed to delight her—the voices raised in bargaining, the lowing of cattle brought to the market for sale; the grunting of pigs, the reedy voice of the ballad singer; the shouts of the pie-man; the street traders songs.

> *'Won't you buy my sweet blooming lavender*
> *Sixteen branches one penny . . .'*

Or:

> *'Three rows a penny pins,*
> *Short whites and middlings.'*

She would sing the songs to herself—quietly because singing was frivolous—as she dressed in the warm sun of summer or the cold of winter, for it was bitterly cold in winter. It was not that Uncle Henry could not have afforded a fire; but he believed in the Spartan life. In spite of prosperity they must live simply.

In the bad dreams—which grew less as the years passed—she would hear the scrape of a boat against the stairs; she would smell the slimy, tarry smell of the river; she would hear men whistling tunes or singing river songs, shouts of abuses, the voices of men and women raised in anger as they fought each other. She would remember the vague empty feeling which was hunger; the numbness which was cold—not the healthy cold of Uncle Henry's house but the cold which came of insufficient covering, insufficient food. They had stepped over a bridge it seemed to Hannah from hunger and poverty and want to the well-being which came from righteous living—thrift and piety. Uncle Henry was like a beneficient god—a knight of old who had rescued them from dragons, and carried them away from the dungeons of despair into the castle of comfort.

Her mother shared her pleasure, she knew. Mary Lightfoot could not do enough for her brother.

Uncle Henry had been a bachelor of thirty-one when Mary

and her daughter came to live with him. Mary therefore could
be of use to him, for she was an excellent housekeeper and she
began to transform his house into a home as no servant could
do. Henry was fond of his niece, for she was a charming girl
and indeed grew prettier every day. Not that as a Quaker he
believed in stressing those charms. The dark curls should be
severely strained back from the oval face and neatly braided.
The child should be attired in a simple gown of grey cloth.

'Clothes are meant to keep the child warm, sister,' said Uncle
Henry, 'not to adorn her.'

'Oh yes, brother,' Mary agreed fervently.

But as Hannah grew a little older she found a great pleasure
in beautiful things and when one of the flower-sellers in the
market gave her a rose she carried it up to her room and
pinned it on her dress. Her great dark eyes seemed to glow
more brightly; the pink of the flower toned perfectly with the
grey cloth and seemed to bring out the delicate pink in Hannah's own clear skin.

Uncle Henry cried out in dismay when she came down to
dinner wearing the rose.

'What is that thou art wearing, Hannah?' he asked, and she
thought that the devil must have changed the beautiful flower
into a toad or something horrible since that was the only way
she could account for Uncle Henry's horror.

She looked down at it. 'It ... it is a rose ... Uncle.'

'A rose. And what is it doing there?'

'It is just there ... Uncle.'

'How didst thou come by such a thing?'

She was bewildered. She had been so pleased to be given the
rose; she enjoyed its scent; and the contrast of colour it made
on her dress; she had felt happy wearing it. And now it seemed
she had done a dreadful thing.

'Old Sally the flower-seller gave it to me.'

'Thou shouldst not have taken it.'

'She wished it, Uncle.'

'The place for flowers is in gardens. God put them there. He
did not mean them to be worn for vanity.'

She had flushed and although she was unaware of this, her beauty was startling. It alarmed Uncle Henry as well as her mother. They would have preferred to see her insignificant.

'Thou are guilty of vanity, niece,' said Uncle Henry. 'I think thy mother will agree with me.'

'Indeed yes, Henry,' whispered Mary Lightfoot.

'This is a sin in the eyes of the Lord. Thou wilt go to thy room. Take off that flower. Give it to me ... now ...'

She felt the tears in her eyes. For a few seconds she hesitated, almost ready to defy him. Then she was aware of her mother's terror; and she pictured them being turned out of this comfortable house ... back to Wapping ... the cold, cold room, the smell of boots and shoes ... the smell of the river and the vague lightness of hunger. Then with trembling fingers she handed him the rose.

He took it and said to her in a voice that thundered with indignation so that she was reminded of Moses returning from the mountain to find his people worshipping the golden calf: 'Go to thy room. Pray ... pray long and sincerely for God's help. Thou hast need of it.'

She walked slowly up the stairs. The feeling of sin weighing heavily on her.

In the cold room she knelt and prayed until her knees were sore. Then her mother came in and they prayed together.

When they rose from their knees and Hannah's mother appeared to think she had gained God's forgiveness for her wickedness, she ventured to say as though excusing herself: 'But it was such a pretty rose.'

That gave Mary an opening for one of those lectures which were so much a part of Hannah's upbringing.

'Sin often comes in the guise of beauty. That is why it is so easy to fall into temptation.'

*   *   *

When she was alone Hannah would stand at the window and watch the ladies and gentlemen pass through the market on the way to the theatre. They were so beautiful but so sinful, for they wore more adornments than a single rose. Hannah feared it was probably sinful to *watch* such people. There was so much sin in the world that it seemed one must constantly be on the alert for it. There they were, the ladies in their Sedan chairs, and surely their complexions could not have been naturally so brilliant as they appeared; ornaments flashing in their hair; feathers, diamonds ... What a load of sin they must carry on their persons if a simple rose could be so full of iniquity.

But how Hannah loved to watch them! Gentlemen with brocade coats and elegant wigs; footmen running ahead of their chairs to clear the way and while some in the crowd gaped at their magnificence others were too accustomed to the sight to pay much attention, unless it was a person of some note. Then the crowd would cheer or boo, however the mood took them; but they would almost always laugh. There seemed to be such a lot that was gay, amusing, interesting and such fun going on down there. Fun? It was sin. But Hannah was conscious of a quiet rebellion within her. If one sinned in ignorance could one be blamed? She thought not—at least it could not be quite so wicked to sin in ignorance. Therefore how much better it was to remain in ignorance.

She would tell no one of the pleasure she derived from looking down on the noisy excitement of St. James's Market.

*   *   *

Hannah was ten years old when Uncle Henry decided to marry. What consternation there was in the room she shared with her mother. Mary Lightfoot feared the cosy existence might be at an end. Henry was good to them; but what of Henry's wife?

Five years of living comfortably—at least as comfortably as one could live in such close proximity with sin—had softened them. Mary was disturbed—not that she believed her brother would see her go hungry, he was too good a man for that; but a strange woman in the house would be sure to change something and Mary trembled for the future.

She need not have feared. Aunt Lydia proved a meek and docile wife—a true Quaker, a virtuous woman who would no more have thought of turning out her sister-in-law and her fatherless child than she would of taking a lover.

After the first mild difficulties of settling down Mary and Hannah adjusted themselves to the new *régime*. Uncle Henry was the head of the house—good but stern, anxious to care for those under his roof—his sister and her child, no less than his wife and his own children. The children began to arrive in due course; George three years after the wedding, Rebecca two years later, Henry two years after that and Hannah two years after Henry. Mary and her daughter Hannah soon found new ways of being useful in the house and Mary realized that their position was yearly becoming more secure. Hannah was nurse to the children; Mary helped her sister-in-law in the house. It proved to be a very satisfactory arrangement.

In spite of having three able-bodied women in the household Henry Wheeler could afford to employ a servant and he took into his household a young woman of Hannah's age.

They called her Jane, and Jane's coming made a great deal of difference to Hannah. Jane was not a Quaker; she liked to laugh and enjoy herself; she remarked to Hannah that she could see no harm in that. Neither could she for the life of her see why it should be more sinful to laugh than to look glum. Hannah listened half fearfully. Jane's attitude to life was everything she had been taught to fear. Yet she did enjoy laughing with Jane when they were making the beds together or taking the children for their airings. Being so much older than her cousins—she was thirteen years older than George the eldest—meant that Hannah had no choice of a friend except Jane. So it was natural that they should be often together.

It was Jane who caught Hannah at the window. She was not in the least shocked; she came to join Hannah and pointed out the elaborate chair which was being carried through the market. Did Hannah know the gentleman who was being carried? Hannah did not know. Oh, but Hannah knew very little of the world because everyone should know the gentle-

man in the chair. It was Lord Bute himself. And they said that
the Princess of Wales was very partial to him. Had Hannah
ever heard that? Hannah had not and she thought that must
make the gentleman very happy, which set Jane rocking with
laughter.

'It makes them both happy, so they say, Miss Hannah. But
whether the Prince is so happy about it ... that's another
matter. Not that he would complain, considering...'

Hannah was nonplussed and fascinated. It was interesting to
learn from Jane that every household was not run like Henry
Wheeler's, and that there were scandals even in the royal
family.

Jane was surprised by the ignorance of Hannah; and enjoyed enlightening her.

So Hannah began to learn something of the world outside a
Quaker household and she could not help it if she were
fascinated by it, and secretly she longed to be part of it. If
Uncle Henry had had a house in the country where they never
saw any life other than their own it would have been different;
but it was not so. Here they were in the midst of a noisy, bustling, virile world and yet not of it. St. James's Market with its
haggling and bargaining was a strange place for a Quaker to
live; yet Quakers could be good businessmen and Uncle Henry
was undoubtedly that, and if it was unsuitable in some ways it
was profitable in others; for as far as trade was concerned it
was an ideal spot. In the middle of the Market was the large
Market House inside which were the butchers shambles and
outside were the butchers' stalls. Market-days were Mondays,
Wednesdays and Saturdays; and on these days the noise of the
buyers and sellers filled the house. Then there was The Mitre
tavern to which even on those days when there was no market
the people flocked in from St. Martin-in-the-Fields.

It was not easy to turn one's eyes away from the busy world
when it was one's doorstep.

'It's no life for a girl, Miss Hannah,' said Jane mournfully.

Hannah might tell of how Uncle Henry had rescued her and
her mother from the dire poverty of Wapping, but Jane still

insisted that it was no life for a girl. Better to be a servant-girl than the master's niece, Jane reckoned. She wouldn't change places with Miss Hannah. There was a mysterious person to whom she referred as Mr. H. who was very interested indeed in Jane. At first Hannah had not believed in his existence; he was a dream figure, something to talk about when they were alone together; but it seemed that he was no phantom. Once when they were out with the children Jane took Hannah down Cockspur Street past Betts the glass-cutters and as they passed a young man slipped out and talked nervously to them.

It turned out that he was Mr. H. and he was really 'far gone' on Jane.

On the way home Jane said it was a shame that Hannah had not got a beau. Yes, with her looks it was a *crying* shame.

And when she returned to St. James's Market Hannah surreptitiously looked into the mirror and could not help being pleased with what she saw there. She was a beauty. She only had to look at Jane's pert and pretty face to know that she had something which the serving-girl lacked; and she felt a little sad to think of passing all her days in her uncle's house making beds, looking after the children, and growing as old as her mother without ever having been part of the gay and bustling life which went on under her window every day and in particular on Mondays, Wednesdays and Saturdays.

There was great excitement when the King, the Prince and Princess of Wales and other members of the royal family were going to the theatre, the back door of which was in Market Lane; to reach this, the procession would have to cross the Market; and to see them a crowd would undoubtedly gather, for in view of the strained relations between the King and his elder son, it was rarely that they were all seen together.

Uncle Henry was disturbed. One never could be sure what the crowd would do. What if they became wild. 'I think,' he said, 'we will take the linens out of the window. It will be better so.'

'If the linens are taken out the children might perhaps sit in the window on our chairs to see the procession pass,' suggested Lydia.

Uncle Henry considered this, but really he could see no harm in it.

As the children were growing excited at the prospect, Uncle Henry added a little homily about the worthliness of outward pomp and the difference between the shadow and the substance. But he believed they should be there because loyalty to the throne was something the children should be taught; and there were always intolerant people who could work up emotions about those whose opinions were different from their own.

Yes, they should all sit in the window and watch the royal procession to the theatre.

Hannah was delighted with an opportunity to enjoy something without secrecy.

Lydia had placed chairs in the window in place of the bales of linen. Little George and Rebecca were dancing up and down with excitement and Hannah put a finger to her lips to warn them lest their father decide that too much pleasure must indeed be a sin. Young Henry was clutching his mother's skirts and Hannah's mother was holding in her arms the newest arrival—Hannah after her cousin. Mary Lightfoot placed the chair for the master of the house and discreetly took her place at the back of the window.

The Market was full of noise and bustle on that day, for people from Jermyn Street, Charles Street and Pall Mall were all hurrying in to see the royal family pass by.

And so they came: the King himself, small and testy, looking neither this way nor that, his face deep red tinged with purple, taking no heed of loyal greetings nor abuse. He gave the impression that he was not interested in any of these people who had come to see him; *he* had come to see the play and if he had to pass among his people to do so, so much the worse.

And now the Prince of Wales. Frederick was like his father, but much more pleasant; he smiled and acknowledged the people's greetings as he passed in his chair; but he had the same colourful complexion, the same prominent eyes, the same heavy jaw; but this was less apparent when its owner smiled as Frederick did frequently. And in her chair the Princess, not beautiful but amiable, and a good wife and mother, everyone said, even though there were murmurs about her friendship with Lord Bute.

And then ... Prince George, a pleasant, modest-looking boy; the same prominent blue eyes, clear complexion, not yet grown too ruddy and no tinge of purple apparent; the same heavy jaw, but he was young and his expression held not the slightest trace of arrogance. The people cheered Prince George who, when the old King died—which could not be long—would be the Prince of Wales.

Prince George's chair passed very close to the linen-draper's window and as it did so he looked out and his eyes met those of Hannah.

She thought: The Prince is looking straight at me!

That is the most beautiful woman in the world, thought George soberly.

He smiled with pleasure; she found that she was smiling too. Some understanding—neither of them were absolutely sure what—had passed between them.

*   *   *

Hannah thought a great deal about the Prince. The smile had been for her alone, she was sure of it, although no one else had noticed it. Had she been wrong? Was he bestowing such smiles all along the route? Was it part of the royal duties to smile indiscriminately?

Perhaps Jane was right and she was a simpleton. But she had glowed with pleasure and she was going to allow herself to go on thinking he had smiled especially for her.

A few days later she was confirmed in this belief, when the Prince's chair passed through the Market close to the linen-draper's shop, and from her window Hannah looked out at precisely the same moment as the Prince looked from his chair.

Once more their eyes met and once more the understanding flashed between them.

Hannah was distrait. Could it really be that she was beginning to be caught up in the world outside her uncle's Quaker household?

*   *   *

The interest of a boy who could not have entered his teens could not be expected to change her life; and yet she was at the window whenever possible in the hope of seeing him pass. He did not come often. How could he without attracting attention? He was always surrounded by important-looking people, but whenever he did pass that way he never failed to look up at the window for her and when he saw her his face would lighten and he would smile with pleasure.

How strange! thought Hannah. What could it mean? She thought him charming, beautiful in his innocence. He was like a child—untouched by the world, perhaps as she was. She must be many years older than he was—six, seven, eight even—but there was a bond between them, a bond of unworldliness. They were like two children looking at life through a glass door, aware of it, yet ignorant of it. She had been warned of lascivious men; in fact their glances had often come her way. Her uncle could not protect her from that; she was so attractive and he could not shut her up in a lonely tower until he found a Quaker husband for her.

This was different. This was the pure adoration of an innocent boy, years her junior—and he was a Prince. More than that, one day he would be a King.

It was small wonder that she was bewildered.

*   *   *

When Jane married and went to live in Cockspur Street with her husband, Hannah was desolate. As Mr. H. was still an apprentice the only way in which Jane could join him in his master's house was by going into service there. Thus she left her employment in the Wheeler house to join that of Mr. Betts the glass-cutter of Cockspur Street.

They did not need another servant, decided Mr. Wheeler. Rebecca was old enough to perform small duties about the house and it was good for her to be useful; George could do minor errands for the shop; there were three able-bodied women in the house, Lydia his wife, Mary his sister and Hannah his niece. Therefore what did he want with serving-maids?

So there was no one now for Hannah to chat to in that frivolous but enjoyable way. She heard, of course, that the Prince of Wales had died; and that brought home to her the astounding fact that the young boy with whom she believed she had a secret understanding was now the Prince of Wales. That made the affair so fantastic that she began to believe she had imagined the whole thing. The Prince seemed to have ceased his visits to the Market and life had become very drab indeed. Her days were lightened only by her shopping expeditions to Ludgate where she sometimes lingered in the grocery shop talking to the grocer's son, Isaac Axford. The Axfords were Quakers like themselves; so naturally they did business to-gether. Isaac was half in love with her, she believed; he was three years younger then she was and not in a position to marry, but she had no wish to marry him. There had been a time when she supposed a marriage would be arranged for her by her uncle, and Isaac had seemed a likely partner; after all, being only the niece of the prosperous linen draper, she could not expect a dowry as enticing as that he would give to his own daughters.

Hannah thought of married life in the grocer's shop at Ludgate Hill and it did not attract her. She liked Isaac but only mildly. Yet, but for the penetrating glances of a young boy she might have been contented enough to accept him.

Jane came visiting from Cockspur Street and the two young women sat in Hannah's room and looked over the Market-place together.

Married life was a disappointment, Jane admitted. She was no better off than she had been on her own. Mrs. Betts was a good-natured mistress, easy-going and not unfriendly, but there was little money.

And living in the heart of London, seeing the fine ladies and gentlemen in their carriages and chairs, going to balls and banquets and the theatre did make a young woman discontented with her lot, particularly when she was prettier than some of those painted, bedecked creatures in their silks and brocades and glittering gems.

Jane tossed her pert pretty head and said she was a fool to have rushed into marriage. She fancied she could have had other opportunities and she feared Mr. H. would never be anything but an apprentice, for he had no money to set himself up in business.

And what of Hannah—Hannah who was beautiful? Was she going to spend her days dressed in a Quaker bonnet and gown, never having a chance to display her charms?

Hannah smiled at Jane's petulance. It was good to be able to chat with her friend again.

Journey in a Closed Carriage

THE Dowager Princess of Wales was where she liked to be best in the world; in the company of her dear Lord Bute.

So handsome! So clever! What should she do without him? Now even more than ever, for she was by no means old, and since poor Fred was dead there was nothing to keep them apart.

Her lover and her children—they were her life.

'Dearest John,' she was saying, 'I was just asking myself what I should do without you.'

'What a monstrous thought. Why should you?'

'Because we are always fearful of losing what we most value.'

'If you lose me it will be of your own choosing, for it will never be mine.'

'Ah, dearest John. What happiness you give me! Is there much scandal about us, do you think?'

'Whatever we did there would be scandal, so . . .'

'We may as well earn it?'

They laughed and embraced.

'The old man could scarcely complain of us,' she said.

'His Majesty complains of everyone, so what would it matter if he did?'

'At his age! You would think he were past such adventures.'

'Perhaps he is, and won't admit it.'

'I remember when my mother-in-law was alive, how he used to write to her about Walmoden from Hanover. How should he proceed with the seduction? And his father with those two grotesque women of his—one tall and thin, the other short and fat. They were a laughing-stock. John ... I am afraid for George. I am afraid he will take after them and if he gets a fondness for women ...'

'It will be natural enough. He'll soon be thinking of taking a mistress, I'll swear.'

'But George is different. He is not like his father, his grand-father or his great-grandfather. Frederick ... well, you knew Frederick as well as I; and George I always had his women, plenty of them. Our present King has always been chasing them, even when in fact he preferred his wife he felt it neces-sary to his dignity as a King to have his mistresses. George I was a dour man and people were afraid of him—even his women. George II is irascible and a silly little man easily deceived, but his women fear to offend him. George III will be different.'

'There is an innocence about him,' admitted Bute.

'Yes, I fear what would happen to him in the hands of some scheming woman.'

'He is a boy yet.'

'Fifteen! His father, grandfather, and great-grandfather were already experimenting in sexual adventure at that age.'

'But not our George.'

'No, not our George. He is an innocent boy. I want to keep him so. I want to make sure that he does not mix with people of his own age at the Court. The young are especially dissolute nowadays. I want to keep George and his brothers and sisters *innocent*.'

'For a while, but they must learn something of the world. Although as you say, they are young yet.'

'I do not care for the behaviour of some of your young people.'

'We will keep our eyes on him,' said Bute, 'together . . .'

'Together,' she murmured smiling at him.

*   *   *

Bute had left her. Augusta yawned contentedly. There was no one in the world like him, no one whom she could trust to help her with the bringing up of her family—and particularly George.

Dear George. Poor George. She thought almost as much of him as she did of dear Lord Bute. Nobody was going to take her son from her. She was going to guide him and make sure that he was protected from the world.

One of her women had come into the apartment. It was Elizabeth Chudleigh, a handsome girl but one who had, according to rumours, lived rather more recklessly than a young unmarried woman should. Elizabeth was not so young, being round about thirty. She was gay and amusing, and at one time everyone had thought she would make a brilliant marriage with the Duke of Hamilton. That had gone wrong, however. Why, Augusta was not sure; but of one thing she was sure, and that was that Elizabeth Chudleigh was a very experienced young woman indeed.

'Elizabeth,' she called.

Elizabeth came and stood before her. 'Your Highness wishes for something?'

'I feel, Elizabeth, that I should warn you. There are some unpleasant rumours going about the Court concerning you.'

'Oh, Madam, I have heard it said that a woman should only worry when there are no rumours about her. Then it means that the world has lost interest in her.'

'Rumours are not becoming when attached to a young unmarried woman.'

'Do they say of me that I have another lover?'

'I hope, Elizabeth, that that is not true.'

Elizabeth lowered her eyes and looked very demure.

'Ah, Your Royal Highness knows *chacun à son But.*'

The Princess was astonished. She could find no words. Elizabeth said: 'Did Your Highness wish me to perform some task?'

'No, no,' said Augusta shortly, 'you may leave me.'

*   *   *

Now, thought Elizabeth, that is the end of me. And all for the sake of a *bon mot*. It was pretty good, though. I would never have dared if it had not been so good. Did she get the *But*? Or did she think I was merely quoting the French proverb? However, she was too flabbergasted to reply ... just then. But that does not mean there will be some riposte. And when it comes ... Goodbye to Court, Elizabeth.

To hell with the Court! And what would happen if she were dismissed? She should have thought of that before she allowed her tongue to run away with her. She was a fool at times. Hadn't she allowed herself to be carried away by her feelings before? If she had not been so foolish as to believe Hamilton had deserted her, if she had tried to find out why he did not write, she would have discovered the perfidy of Aunt Hanmer and waited for him. Instead she had allowed herself to be carried away by pique and had made the mésalliance with John Hervey. Thank Heaven she had kept it secret, even the birth of their child who, alas, had died when she had put him out to nurse. If Madam Augusta knew the dark secrets of her lady-in-waiting she would have been dismissed from Court long ere this. That secret she believed was well guarded and the King was pleased enough with her to have made her mother housekeeper at Windsor—a pretty profit in that; and he had helped them to acquire a farm of a hundred and twenty acres. So she had not done too badly at Court and if Augusta should decide to dismiss her no doubt there would be a place for her in the King's Court.

Oh well, Madam Augusta could not be too high-handed—not when she herself could so easily be steeped in scandal. Her passion for my Lord Bute was a little too obvious for secrecy. One could hear it vibrating in her voice when she spoke to him or even of him; and her expression betrayed her whenever he appeared.

So perhaps the Princess who was proving to be a great deal wiser than many had thought her to be while her husband was alive, would not act rashly even where an impertinent maid-of-honour was concerned, when that maid-of-honour happened to be rather a favourite with the King.

In any case, thought Elizabeth, she and Bute are trying to keep the Prince of Wales tied to her apron strings. They treat him as though he's a baby, both of them. It's clear enough they want to be in command when he's King—and he could be tomorrow. Poor old George can't last much longer and poor young George is such a baby. It's time someone opened his eyes, helped him to become a man, let him see that he is no longer in the nursery, that he only has to assert himself and need not blindly obey everything fond Mamma Augusta and Papa Bute command.

It was not long afterwards that she had an opportunity of speaking to George. He was calling on his Mamma and she encountered him in one of the anterooms.

She curtsied decorously and said: 'Your Highness is in good spirits today. There is a change in you.'

George blushed and stammered that he hoped it was for the better.

She laughed in an intimate way. If she could banter with the Dowager Princess, how much more readily she could do so with the Prince of Wales.

'I believe you are in love,' she said.

She was astonished at the effect of these words. The faint flush in his cheeks deepened to scarlet.

'It's true,' she cried.

'Oh, please, please ... you must tell no one.'

'Your Highness may trust me. Not a word outside these walls. Who is the fortunate lady?'

'Oh ... I cannot tell. She does not know ... but I assure you she is ...'

'The most beautiful at Court?'

'Not ... not at Court.'

'Oh?'

'I must not burden you with my affairs.'

'Your Highness.' Her beautiful eyes were wide with sincerity. If there is anything I can do to help ...'

'There is nothing to be done ... It is impossible.'

'Nothing is impossible, Your Highness, and something can always be done.'

'I cannot speak of this.'

'Oh, Your Highness ... not to me!'

'You are kind, but it is no use. And someone comes...'

'Your Highness, I want to help you. I would do anything to help you. Could you give me an audience ... In the gardens ... Later.'

He looked at her appealingly, so worldly, so knowledgeable, so wise.

'Yes,' he said, 'please.'

*   *   *

Elizabeth walked beside the Prince. He said: 'I have never spoken to her.'

'Oh, why not?'

'I have seen her only at a window.'

'What window?'

'Of a shop ... a linen-draper's.'

'Where?'

'In St. James's Market when I have passed in my chair on the way to the theatre. I go there often ... whenever possible ... without attracting attention. It has not been so easy since my father's death.'

'Too many in attendance on the Prince of Wales! But there is no reason why you should not meet this young lady.'

'Oh, there is every reason.'

'Your Highness is wrong. She will be immensely honoured and Your Highness will be immensely gratified. It is the way of the world. Your Highness is the Prince of Wales, the heir to the throne. You are not a child as some would appear to think.'

'She is a Quaker, I have discovered that. And she sits in the window of Mr. Wheeler's shop. I think she must be his daughter. She is very beautiful, in fact I have never seen any to compare with her. Her gown is so simple, and yet all the ladies in their silks and brocades, their glittering jewels cannot compare with her.'

'I can see Your Highness is deeply affected. But do you not wish to speak with her, to make your admiration known?'

'I could not speak to her. She is a Quaker. I fear she would be displeased.'

'Is it enough, then, to look?'

'Yes, for the rest of my life I would be content if only I might look at her.'

'Perhaps she would wish for something more from Your Highness than looks?'

He was startled. 'You think she would?'

'I am sure of it. I suspect that this young lady is hurt and disappointed because you have made no attempt to speak to her.'

'Hurt! Disappointed. Oh, but I would not hurt her for the world.'

'Then you should show your devotion by arranging to meet her.'

'How could I do that? I could not call at the linen-draper's.'

'No, certainly you could not do that. But she will know that you are the Prince of Wales and she will believe that because you do not seek a means of speaking to her you feel yourself too far above her to wish to.'

'She could not think that.'

'How could she think otherwise? Do you really wish to speak to this young lady?'

'It is what I long for.'

'Perhaps it could be arranged.'

'Who could arrange it?'

'I have friends...'

'You would ... Oh, Miss Chudleigh!'

She curtsied and raised her mischievous eyes to his face. 'Did

I not tell Your Highness that I wished to serve you. Now you tell me all you can and I will see what can be done. Only this must be a secret. If you told your mother ... Heaven knows what would happen to the young lady.'

'I fear my mother would not wish me to meet her.'

'Ah, mothers! It is the same with my own. Do you know she regards me as an infant in arms even now. But we have to remember that we are grown up, although it does no harm to let our mothers go on believing we are babies if it pleases them. Why shouldn't everyone be pleased?'

'That is what I want ... to please everyone.'

'Let me discover what can be done. I think I can promise you that very soon you will have been able to tell your beautiful Quakeress how much you admire her.'

'And you will tell no one?'

'Trust me. As soon as I have news I will give it to Your Highness.'

'I do not know how to thank you, Miss Chudleigh.'

'It is *I* who should thank *you* for giving me a chance to be of service.'

* * *

Elizabeth was enjoying her part in the Prince's first love affair. Intrigue fascinated her; and it was quite right, she assured herself, that the poor boy should be cut free from his mother's apron strings; and who more able to do that than a mistress.

He was young, but not too young. It was a man's desires which decided for him when he should begin his love life; and George's had evidently decided for him. Let him have a mistress or two and the Princess Dowager and her paramour Lord Bute would find they could not guide their little Prince as easily as they had hoped. It would be fun to watch the breakaway.

In the meantime the rendezvous with the fair lady had to be arranged. It was not so easy as she had at first imagined. The girl was a Quakeress and therefore it would be impossible to call at the linen-draper's and explain the Prince's interest in the fair inmate of that establishment. First of all she must sound the young lady's inclinations. If she were agreeable it would be so much easier; not that Elizabeth would entirely dismiss the possibility of abduction. After all it was for the Prince of Wales; and reluctant ladies could become willing ones in certain circumstances.

This was a project after her own heart. She paid a visit to the linen-draper's where she was treated with great respect. These Quakers were good business-folk and Mr. Wheeler paid due homage to ladies of quality in his shop no matter how he might disapprove of them in his back parlour.

His wife was present and it was easy to indulge in a little conversation with her about her children. They all seemed so young. Then she made the discovery that the young lady in question was not a Miss Wheeler; she was Miss Hannah Lightfoot, niece of the linen-draper who had been sheltered under his roof from an early age. Fortunately before she left Hannah came into the shop. She was a beauty; there was no doubt about that. George had chosen well. He had better taste than his father or grandfather—as for his great-grandfather, every man in England had better taste than he had! But Hannah was indeed a beauty. What luminous dark eyes, what grace! Even the austere Quaker gown could not hide her charms. Worthy ... indeed worthy to be the mistress of the Prince of Wales.

Elizabeth spoke to her. Her voice was low and soft; yet, thought Elizabeth, there was sparkle in her; she might well be ready for adventure. And why not? This sombre shop was no place for a beauty like that.

It's my duty, Elizabeth told herself, to bring her out of it. If I needed to salve my conscience, which I don't because I don't possess one, but if I did, I should have a very good reason for proceeding with this most amusing affair.

She graciously took her leave.

What next? There was a man of whom she had heard who kept a house in Pall Mall; he had worked for several people at Court and she had heard that he could supply certain services as efficiently as any. He could arrange meetings in the most secret and unlikely places; he was discreet; ready to help any in need of help. He was expensive, but this after all was the Prince of Wales.

Masked and cloaked she called on Mr. Jack Ems of Pall Mall—an assumed name doubtless, which added to the excitement. Not that she would give her name. He received her in a beautifully furnished apartment and she told him that she wished to arrange a meeting between two people.

Nothing could be simpler. Was the meeting to take place in London?

Most decidedly. The gentleman concerned was very young and of very high degree. Mr. Ems would be surprised if he knew how high.

Very young and very highly placed. Her ladyship could rely on Mr. Ems' discretion.

'I must,' said Elizabeth. 'If I could not this could cause consternation in very high circles, in roy ...' She pretended to stop herself in time and Mr. Ems was duly impressed. A man of his alertness would know that she was referring to the Prince of Wales; and he would bring forth all his ingenuity to execute this commission with all his power and skill.

'The difficulty is the lady. She must be sounded. Not even the exalted young gentleman has an idea of how she will receive this proposal.'

'I am to ... er ... sound her?'

'You are to find some means of sounding her.'

'I will do it.'

'Don't be too optimistic. She is a Quakeress, very sternly brought up. You will have to go to work very carefully.'

'Ah.' He was shaken. He could deal with most difficulties, but this was a big one. 'If your ladyship will give me all particulars I will do whatever is possible and I can tell you this: if Jack Ems can't bring about the desired result, then, my lady, no one can.'

'I am sure of it. She is Hannah Lightfoot, niece to the Quaker linen-draper of St. James's Market.'

He nodded grimly.

'Do not attempt to approach me. I will call on you in three days time and I hope that by then you will have something to tell me.'

* * *

Jack Ems was in a quandary. He had visited the linen-draper's and made some purchases, for his wife, he explained, who was unable to leave her home. The linen-draper himself served him. Jack Ems knew the type. Stern, upright, moral; if he made the sort of proposal he had come to make to such a man he would promptly be shown the door. No bribes would suffice. If the King himself commanded Mr. Wheeler to hand over his niece Mr. Wheeler would firmly refuse. A weighty problem, and Mr. Ems was searching his mind to find some way out.

He had walked far, he said, having come from Hammersmith. The roads were so bad and the mud of Piccadilly was unbelievable. Might he sit down for a moment? He was given an opportunity to observe Quaker hospitality when Mrs. Wheeler brought him a glass of ale.

He sat sipping it, listening to the conversation of Mr. Wheeler and his customers—ladies from Knightsbridge and Bayswater who had been dealing with Mr. Wheeler for years. They enquired after the family. And how was Miss Rebecca's toothache? Little Hannah was growing fast...

Little Hannah! Jack Ems pricked up his ears and hoped for some comment on that other Hannah. None came.

If she would appear in the shop, if he had a chance of seeing her ... He went on sipping his ale, desperately seeking to form a plan.

Good luck was with him. A young woman came into the shop, and he was immediately alert. She was pretty and young, and being a student of human nature—as his business demanded he should be—he detected a certain petulance about her.

'Good afternoon, Jane. Hannah is sewing in her room. Thou mayest go up.'

Mrs. Wheeler came over to him to ask if he would like more ale.

'You are most kind, but no thank you. That will suffice. I have been listening to the enquiries after your children. You are fortunate to have a family. My wife and I .... alas, we have no children.'

Mrs. Wheeler was all compassion. That was sad, very sad. Yes, they had a full household, and she counted that a blessing from God. Two boys and three girls.

Surely not the young lady who had just gone in. Mrs. Wheeler could not possibly be the mother of a girl of that age!

Oh no, that was Jane. She had worked for them and had left to be married. A good girl but a little flighty, so it was well she was married.

And married well?

Mrs. Wheeler put her head on one side. 'She married an apprentice to a glass-cutter in Cockspur Street. My niece misses her. They were of an age.'

'So you have a niece living here too?'

'Oh yes, my husband brought her and her mother here before our marriage. Hannah is like a daughter to us.'

Jack nodded and said they were singularly blessed indeed. And so, he believed, was he, to have gained so much information. He was pinning his hopes on the flighty servant.

*   *   *

It was not difficult to strike up a conversation with Jane. Jane liked to go about the streets of London and Mrs. Betts gave her plenty of free time. She would shop for her mistress and enjoyed conversing over the counter with the younger and gayer shop assistants. Sometimes she met Hannah in Ludgate Hill and they would go into Axfords together—Hannah to shop for the Wheelers, Jane for the Betts.

It was in a shop that Jack Ems made Jane's acquaintance. It was very easy to knock into her, upset her purchases, apologize profusely, pick them up and that gave the opportunity.

What was such a pretty girl doing as beast of burden? Would she allow him to carry her purchases for her?

'As far as Cockspur Street?'

'To the ends of the earth.'

Jane was enjoying herself. Her apprentice was a good man but unexciting. He would never be able to provide the laces and ribbons she saw in shop windows. It was a pity, because they were so becoming. Jack Ems summed up her frivolous nature and decided that she would be ready to go a certain way for a little reward and some excitement, so he lost no time in coming to the point.

She had a friend, Miss Hannah Lightfoot, the niece of her old master.

Jane was a little disappointed that the man she had thought was her admirer was after all interested in Hannah; but she was practical enough to realize the inevitability of this and there was a strong streak of kindness in her nature. If she were dissatisfied with her own lot she believed it to be an improvement on Hannah's. So she thrust aside her disappointment and was ready to tell all she could of Hannah.

Hannah was beautiful ... anyone could see that. It was a shame that she should be shut away in the Quaker's shop. Hannah was twenty-three years old ... no longer so young. And Hannah had never had a chance.

Hannah was soon going to have a miraculous chance. If Jane would help him.

Jane would like to help him, but she would have to be careful.

It was also a shame, he pointed out, that Jane did not have the pretty things she craved for. If she helped she would be so well rewarded that she could buy some of them. What would Jane have to do? First she must find out from Miss Lightfoot whether she would be prepared to make an assignation with a very important young gentleman who had fallen in love with her.

'She never would,' cried Jane. 'It is against everything she has been taught.'

'You could explain to her...'

'She wouldn't listen. There'd be terrible trouble if they found out. Suppose Hannah told her uncle? He might consider it his duty to speak to my husband...'

'Your husband is an apprentice, is he not?'

'Yes.'

'Suppose your husband had a chance of setting up his own business.'

'*What?*'

'I can see you are a sensible girl. The young gentleman involved is of very high nobility. If you would help me and if together we were able to bring about the desired result I can see no reason why there should not be big rewards in this for you. Not just a pretty gown or two ... which your beauty deserves and which you shall have in any case ... but I see no reason why, if we are successful in this affair your husband might not be in business on his own.'

Jane's eyes were sparkling. No longer to be a servant! To be mistress in her own house, ordering her own servants ... and all for helping her dear friend Hannah to escape from that dreary linen-draper's shop.

'I'll do it,' she said.

'Then it's a bargain. But you do understand the need for secrecy, don't you? Not a word to anyone. And you must be discreet. First find out how Hannah feels about this young man. She will know to whom you refer, because although they have not spoken he has made his interest clear.'

'She never told me.'

'So you will have to tread carefully. Remember what is at stake.'

Jane nodded; and after having made an arrangement to call on Mr. Ems at an early date, bemused, she went into the glass-cutter's.

* * *

Hannah was astounded. The Prince of Wales wished to speak to her! No one had mentioned the Prince of Wales, but she knew. He was the young man ... the boy ... who had looked at her so earnestly as he had passed in his chair. He had been so moved by the sight of her that he had wanted to talk to her.

'Thou art making it up,' she accused Jane.

Jane swore that she was not. 'There can be no harm in it. Why shouldn't you meet him? You only have to talk to him.'

'But where ... how ...?'

'You don't have to worry. You only have to go out with me ... we're supposed to be shopping ... In Jermyn Street a closed carriage is waiting for us ... We get into it and together we go to this address. There you will speak to this young nobleman and together we come back to Jermyn Street. What harm can there be in that?'

'There could be great harm.'

'Really, Hannah, you are a coward. Are you going to stay in your uncle's shop all your life, or possibly marry Grocer Axford and go on and on through life never having any fun.'

'Isaac Axford would be a good husband.'

'I've no doubt but you owe it to this young gentleman to see him.'

'How can I know what will happen when I get to this house?'

'You have seen the gentleman. You could trust him.'

Yes, thought Hannah. I have seen him—an innocent young boy. Of course she could trust him. He was no lecherous roué out for a new sensation with a prudish Quaker girl. She knew she could trust him. So since he so desired to see her, she must go to him.

'I will come,' she said.

Jane was jubilant. She could scarcely wait to call on Mr. Jack Ems to tell him that the first step had been taken.

*   *   *

George left the Palace for the Haymarket where Miss Chudleigh had engaged a suite of rooms for him. As his chair was carried to its destination no one glanced at him as he was travelling incognito, just an ordinary gentleman with his private chair, his chairmen and his footman.

He was very excited. He had been daring. It was the first time he had acted without the approval of his mother or Lord Bute, and he did wonder very much what they would say if they knew what he was doing. Miss Chudleigh had warned him not to betray his actions, for his mother and Lord Bute would surely try to stop him if he did.

'I should not really go against their wishes,' said George. 'Everything they do is for my own good.'

'And for their own,' retorted Miss Chudleigh.

'But mine is the same as theirs,' replied George.

How well they have trained their little tame pet, thought Miss Chudleigh. Well, there were going to be some surprises in Court circles when it was discovered that little George had suddenly become a man.

'Everything,' Miss Chudleigh said quickly, 'will depend on Miss Lightfoot.'

'Oh yes, everything must depend on her.'

George's heart was beating wildly as he opened the door of the suite. A man was waiting to bow him into a room which was pleasantly though not luxuriously furnished. With him was a young woman, obviously Hannah's servant.

'My lord, the young lady will stay for half an hour and then she must be gone.'

'It ... it shall be as she desires,' stammered George.

'If your lordship will excuse me ... the lady will be here immediately.'

For a few seconds George was alone in the room; his throat constricted, his sight blurred. Nothing like this had ever happened to him before; it was like something he had dreamed. And it was all due to clever Miss Chudleigh.

The door opened and she stood there—the beautiful vision from the linen-draper's window. He gasped and she came towards him, serene—she would always be serene—and only the faint colour in her cheeks betraying the fact that she was excited.

'I ... I trust you are not displeased,' he stammered.

She curtsied. 'Your Highness must forgive me. I have never been taught how to behave with royalty.'

What simply charming words! How graciously spoken.

Some impulse made him kneel before her.

'Oh no,' she said. 'Thou must not.'

Thou must not. What a delightful manner of expression. It suited her. He wanted to kiss her hand, but he felt that he should not touch her yet. She might object and he did not want her to go away before he had had a chance to speak to her.

He rose to his feet rather clumsily. 'You are more beautiful close than in the window.'

'Your Highness is very kind to me.'

'I want to be. I wish I knew how.'

'Shall we sit down and talk?'

Everything she said seemed to him so wonderful, so wise.

They sat side by side on a sofa; he was careful not to sit too close for fear she should object. 'I have never talked much to ladies,' he said.

She was moved by his sincerity and honesty. Nothing could have charmed her more. He was incapable of pretence; he was charmingly innocent. And he was the Prince of Wales!

She said: 'I know thou art the Prince of Wales.'

'I hope that does not displease you.'

'No, but it makes it difficult for us to be friends.'

He was alarmed. 'I feared so. But Miss ... er ... a friend of mine has told me that it is possible for us to meet.'

'As we have now.'

'I hope that this will be the first of many meetings.'

'Is that what thou wishest?'

'I wish for it more than anything on earth. I have never seen anyone as beautiful as you are. I would be happy if I could look at you for the rest of my life.'

She smiled gently. She was almost as inexperienced of the life as he was; and it was pleasant to sit beside him and talk.

She talked more than he did for he was so fearful of offending her. She told him of how she had come to the linen-draper's shop and of her life there. He listened avidly as though it was a tale of great adventure. They could not believe that the half-hour was over when Mr. Ems scratched discreetly on the door.

George seized her hands; he could not leave her without her assurance that they would meet here again ... within the next few days.

If it could be arranged, Hannah said, she would be there.

Jane looked at her curiously as they jolted back to Jermyn Street in their closed carriage. She seemed more excited than Hannah; but Hannah had changed; there was a quiet radiance about her. She knew she was loved, devotedly and unselfishly by no less a person than the Prince of Wales.

The Prince of Wales

The Elopement

THE meetings were taking place regularly. The closed carriage, the journey with Jane, the ecstatic reunion in the Haymarket ... they had become a pattern of life. George loved her. He had said so. He admitted he knew little of life, but one did not have to learn about love; it came to one and there it was the meaning of one's existence.

They talked of love; of their adoration of each other; it was enough to be sure of their meetings, to touch hands and occasionally kiss. Each was aware of the barriers which separated the niece of a linen-draper and a Prince of Wales; but they did not discuss this matter.

All they asked was to be together.

*   *   *

Hannah had changed. She did not realize how much. When one of the children spoke to her she was absent-minded; she forgot to perform those household tasks which had been second nature to her; moreover, her beauty had become so dazzling that even the linen-draper noticed.

'What is happening to Hannah?' he asked his wife.

Lydia and Mary had been aware of the change before he

had, and Lydia replied that she wondered whether Hannah was in love.

'She goes often to Ludgate Hill,' went on Lydia. 'I suspect that she goes to see Isaac. Perhaps it is time to arrange a marriage.'

'Isaac is younger than she is and scarcely in a position to marry.'

'Perhaps if she had a fair dowry . . .'

'We have our own daughters to think of. Hannah has beauty. Perhaps that should be considered dowry enough.'

'Well, she is twenty-three years of age and that does seeem old enough for marriage. It is our duty to see her settled even as our own daughters.'

Henry agreed that this was so and that although Isaac was young and it would be many years before he inherited his father's business, the Axfords were a good Quaker family and Hannah must of course marry into the Society of Friends.

Henry decided to walk over to Ludgate Hill to have a word with Mr. Axford about his son and Hannah. He talked to Mr. Axford who said that Isaac was somewhat young for marriage but that he was no doubt taken with Hannah and as she was a good Quaker he would have no objection to the match. A dowry would be helpful. Grocery was not so profitable as linen-drapering, and Isaac would need to put a little money into the business.

Mr. Wheeler explained that he was not in a position to put up a large dowry for a girl who was after all only his niece when he had daughters of his own to think of. But the young couple were clearly attracted. Hannah was constantly making excuses to call at the grocer's.

'She comes here rarely,' said Mr. Axford. 'Only to order the grocery, and then she is in and out in no time.'

Mr. Wheeler replied that he had been mistaken in that and doubtless Hannah spent the time at the glass-cutter's with her friend Jane.

But he was disturbed.

*   *   *

A few days later he was more than disturbed; he was alarmed. He had followed Hannah and Jane and seen them get into the closed carriage; he had gone into a coffee house and sat watching the house in the Haymarket. He had seen Jane and Hannah emerge and get into the carriage; he had waited in the coffee house and seen a young man, little more than a boy, come out of the house. He knew that face. He had seen it many times.

It could not be. It was impossible. But such things had happened before. The closed carriage; the secrecy. Only someone in a high place would make such arrangements. In a high place indeed!

Here was ... disaster. Here was scandal. His niece Hannah was clandestinely meeting the Prince of Wales. For what purpose did Princes make assignations with humble girls?

This was disgrace such as had never befallen the Wheeler family before. Death was preferable to dishonour, and Hannah was bringing dishonour to their household. A Quaker girl a Prince's mistress. Something must be done at once.

But what? Mr. Wheeler was a shrewd and cautious man. There was no sense in shouting their disgrace to the housetops. If he did, Hannah's conduct would bring disrepute to the entire community of Quakers. It was never comfortable to be members of a minority religious group. Such groups were always open to persecution. The essence of the Society of Friends was simplicity, chastity, devotion to duty; and when their members strayed from virtue, when a Quaker girl became a harlot, that was a far greater crime than when a woman who was not a Quaker behaved in such a way.

But there was no sense in publicizing Hannah's crime.

No one should know of what he had discovered but himself, Lydia and Mary.

*   *   *

Mr. Wheeler sent for his wife and sister, and when they arrived he shut the door of his sitting-room and bade them be seated.

'I have made a terrible discovery,' he said. 'We have a sinful woman under this roof.'

Mary's heart began to leap about in the most uncomfortable manner. Hannah! she thought. What has she done? She is with child. That is why we have seen this change in her lately. This is the end. We shall be turned away.

Lydia was equally alarmed. 'Pray tell us, Henry,' she said.

'It is Hannah. She has a lover.'

Mary moaned softly, and Lydia put her hand to her mouth and cried: 'No. No.'

'It is true,' said Mr. Wheeler. 'She leaves this place in a closed carriage with that wanton Jane who has no doubt led her into this. She goes to a house in the Haymarket to meet her lover.'

'This is terrible,' cried Mary. 'I could wish to die of shame.'

Lydia said: 'They must be married. It is the only way to rectify the wrong.'

Mr. Wheeler's lips twisted into a grim smile. 'Marriage is impossible.'

'A married man ...' whispered Mary.

'Unmarried.'

'Then ...'

'His position prevents his marrying Hannah.'

'Hannah can read and write,' said Mary almost indignantly. 'She is so very beautiful. What man considers himself too good for her?'

'The Prince of Wales, Mary.'

There was a deep silence in the room; then Mary whispered: 'The Prince of Wales!' And there was a note of reverence in her voice.

'The sin does not grow less because of the exalted position of one of the sinful,' said Mr. Wheeler sternly. 'All men are equal in God's eyes.'

'Amen,' said Lydia.

'Amen,' echoed Mary.

'This has caused me the gravest concern,' went on Mr.

Wheeler, 'and I see only one way out of it. Hannah must be married without delay ... to Isaac Axford.'

'The dowry ...' began Lydia.

'That is not my least concern, but I must find it. I must satisfy Mr. Axford. For of one thing I am certain. There must be no delay.'

There was silence in the room; then Mary began to weep quietly.

'That I should bring this disgrace to thee, brother, who hast put the bread in our mouths and the roof over our heads ...'

Mr. Wheeler said softly: 'Everything is in God's hands, Mary. Let us pray for His guidance.'

They knelt there in the sitting-room, while above them Hannah, unaware of what was being decided, sat at her window singing softly under her breath and looked out on the sights of the Market.

*   *   *

It was hardly likely that George could keep his secret. He had said nothing of the wonderful thing which had happened to him but his looks betrayed him, and it was very clear to such an observant man as Lord Bute that something had changed George and he guessed that it was a woman.

He was hurt that George had not confided in him; he was alarmed too, for his hold on the young Prince was obviously not as firm as he had believed it to be. It was imperative that Bute did not lose his influence with the Prince. His whole future depended on it. Augusta was his, and he would continue in her favour; he was sure of that. But Augusta was, after all, only the boy's mother; and her power rested on her ability to keep her influence over him. There was one way of losing it; and that would undoubtedly be through a woman. If George transferred his affections to a mistress and if she were a woman of strong opinions, Bute and Augusta could be powerless. And George was just the kind to become completely enamoured of a clever woman.

Bute therefore set out to discover who it was who had wrought this change in George.

It was not long before he heard of the closed carriage which arrived at the house in the Haymarket; he had even caught a glimpse of the occupants of the closed carriage. Two women— one obviously a servant, the other a woman of outstanding beauty; and a woman too, not a girl. That was the alarming part. There was a serenity about her which suggested intelligence. Such a woman could completely command George.

There was not a moment to lose. When he told Augusta what he had discovered she could not believe him. George, her little George to so deceive her!

'He is a man, my dearest. We forget that.'

'But my George ... such a baby! He has never looked at women.'

'He may have done so when you were not present, my love. In any case, he has looked at this one, and more than looked, I'll swear. He would not need to hire rooms in the Haymarket just to look. I have found out that he commanded Elizabeth Chudleigh to engage those rooms for him.'

'Elizabeth Chudleigh! That girl ... she is too saucy.'

'But a woman of the world, surely. It may be that she knows something of this affair.'

'That's more than likely. Shall I send for her, John, and question her?'

'We will question her together.'

When Elizabeth was summoned to the Princess's presence and heard what she wished to talk about, she believed her dismissal was near. She tried to feel philosophical, but she was alarmed. It would be dreary if she were banished from Court; and perhaps old George would have nothing to offer her. She would go to him, though, with a tale of Bute and the Princess which would amuse him, although, of course, the old hypocrite would pretend to be shocked. But the King disliked Bute heartily, and she would trust to her luck and she would come through.

'You engaged rooms for the Prince of Wales in the Haymarket,' said the Princess. 'I wonder why?'

'Because, Your Highness, the Prince commanded me to do so.'

'And you knew of his ... er .... friendship with a young Quaker woman.'

'I did, Your Highness.'

'And you thought it incumbent on you to find the Prince rooms for this purpose.'

'I thought it incumbent, Madam, to obey the orders of the Prince of Wales.'

'H'm,' said the Princess. 'And here is a pretty state of affairs!'

'Your Highness is a fond mother and attaches too much importance to a perfectly natural affair, perhaps.'

'I shall be the best judge of that, Miss Chudleigh. The Prince is very young to indulge in such adventures. I am displeased that you should have aided him in this matter. Tell me what you know of this young woman.'

'That she is very virtuous, Madam. She is a Quaker.' She was smiling appealingly from Bute to the Princess. 'I am sure Your Highness and you, my lord, will understand...'

'Miss Chudleigh,' said Lord Bute, 'can you see any way of extracting the Prince from this delicate situation? If you can, I should advise you to tell the Princess of it.'

Oh, thought Elizabeth. Conditions! Help us or ... dismissal. Could she rely on old George?

'Miss Lightfoot is of a very respectable family. Quakers, Your Highness. And Quakers marry with their own kind. There is a young man who has been chosen for Miss Lightfoot. A grocer ... More suitable than the Prince of Wales ... but...'

'Miss Chudleigh,' said the Princess severely.

But Lord Bute put in: 'You mean the young woman's family are arranging a marriage for her with this grocer?'

'I think he would need a considerable dowry ... considerable to a grocer, my lord, but a *bagatelle* to Her Highness and your lordship ... if he were to be hurried into marriage.'

'Hurried into marriage!' cried the Princess.

'The young lady's new husband would scarcely allow her to visit a young gentleman ... even the Prince of Wales, Madam.'

'Miss Chudleigh,' said Lord Bute quickly, 'it might well be that you could be of service in this matter. If you were, I am sure Her Highness would overlook your fault in helping the Prince to find this lodging in the Haymarket.'

'I should be honoured to be of the smallest service to Her Highness,' murmured Elizabeth.

*   *   *

Mr. Wheeler was not altogether surprised when he received a visit from an unknown gentleman who told him that he had a matter of considerable importance to discuss with him.

As soon as Mr. Wheeler ushered him into his private sitting-room he whispered that he came from my Lord Bute, of whose position at Court Mr. Wheeler was doubtless aware. Perhaps Mr. Wheeler could guess on what mission he came.

Mr. Wheeler solemnly declared that he was aware of certain trouble which connected his household with the Court.

'Your niece, Mr. Wheeler, is a very beautiful young woman, and these things will happen. Our desire is to repair any damage as quickly and with as little noise as possible. I am assured that you will wish the same.'

'It is my heartfelt wish.'

'You are in a position to arrange the immediate marriage of your niece with a young and respectable grocer, I believe.'

'Perhaps not immediate,' replied Wheeler. 'This matter has been broached between our families and Mr. Axford is naturally asking a dowry for his son's bride. Hannah is my niece and has been brought up in my house, but I have daughters of my own for whom I must provide in due course.'

'My dear sir, it is precisely on this account that I am here now. It is the desire of everyone who wishes that your niece be happily placed in life to see her married to this worthy young man. I am here to offer him a dowry on your daughter's behalf of five hundred pounds. Do you think that he would be persuaded to agree to an immediate marriage? That, I must insist, is part of the bargain.'

'Five hundred pounds!' cried Mr. Wheeler. 'I am sure there will be no difficulty.'

*   *   *

Hannah was in despair. The Axford family were dining with the Wheelers for it was an occasion for celebration. Hannah was betrothed to Isaac Axford and the marriage was to take place in two day's time. In view of the haste it would not be advisable for the young couple to marry at the Friends' Meeting House. There would be too much talk of the haste and the reason for Isaac Axford's sudden affluence. The family would have to resort to Keith's Chapel in Curzon Street where it was possible to marry speedily, no questions being asked.

It was a sorry business, Mr. Wheeler reckoned. Dr. Keith was a marriage-monger who would marry anyone for the sake of his fee; his method was similar to that of the notorious Fleet Marriages when people were married in the prison without licence or banns. This was a pernicious trade because it enabled scoundrels to go through a mock ceremony with innocent young girls, who had believed themselves to be truly married, and these men could, when they desired, abandon their 'wives' with the utmost ease and legality. Dr. Keith had begun in this way, but being a shrewd businessman he had prospered so much that he had been able to buy land in Curzon Street, Mayfair, and there erect a chapel.

He had become famous; he still married people in the Fleet Prison while he officiated at his chapel and he even advertised in the papers that people who desired matrimony could achieve it at his chapel in Mayfair with a licence on a common stamp and a guinea.

Dr. Keith, it was true had been excommunicated by the Church for these practices; this was an added virtue. Those who did not wish to take marriage seriously declared that since the Doctor was excommunicated the marriage was not legal; and those who wished the marriage to be binding declared that it was so since it had been performed by a priest. Earlier he had been in prison, and in June of this very year the Marriage Act had been passed which declared that banns must be published on three Sundays preceding the ceremony in the church or chapel where the prospective bride and groom lived; that the true names of the parties concerned should be delivered in writing together with their addresses to the ministers one week before the first reading of the banns; that though either party be under twenty-one a minister would not be considered guilty of an offence if parents and guardians of the parties had given no notice of dissent to the proposed marriage. But where they did dissent, the publication of the banns should be void.

When Mr. Axford reminded Mr. Wheeler of this new law which would mean the delay of the marriage for at least three weeks, Mr. Wheeler--who had this special information from his ministerial visitor—was able to assure Mr. Axford that although the Bill had been passed and had received the Royal Assent it had not yet been embodied in the Statute Book and it would not actually be law until the following year. There was nothing therefore to delay the marriage; it should take place in Keith's Chapel two days from now; there should be little fuss; there would be a quiet celebration at the bride's home, and after that Isaac could take her to her new home in Ludgate Hill.

*   *   *

Jane came to see Hannah and slipped up to her room unseen by the Wheelers, for she had become unpopular in that household. Hannah was sitting by the window, a figure of melancholy.

'Jane!' she cried.

'Yes,' said Jane. 'Here I am. They didn't see me slip up.'

'They will be angry if they know you are here.'

'Oh yes, I am blamed, I know.'

'What am I going to do Jane? I am going to be married ... married to Isaac Axford!'

'Yes, I know,' said Jane. 'But don't despair. Mr. Ems has been to see me.'

'What!'

'Now listen. The Prince refuses to lose you.'

'He is but a boy ... the dearest best boy in the world but only a boy.'

'Nonsense! He's a man. He must be ... because he is determined to keep you.'

'But how can he. He is romantic. They will never let me out except to go to Dr. Keith's Chapel. Oh, Jane, it is all over.'

'It is just beginning,' said Jane.

'Do you realize that I am going to be married to Isaac Axford in two days from now?'

'Yes, you are.'

Hannah shivered.

'There's nothing to fear. It's better for you to be a married woman, because the Prince can't marry you, can he?'

Hannah laughed ruefully. 'He will be King of England.'

'That's so. It is why he can't marry you, though he would if he could. So you are going to marry Isaac ... but you are not going to Ludgate Hill.'

'What dost thou mean?'

'You are going to a place he has prepared for you.'

'Jane, what art thou saying?'

'It's all arranged. Mr. Ems, Miss Chudleigh ... the Prince himself ... they're going to see that you don't go to Ludgate Hill ... instead you are going somewhere else ... with the Prince. Oh, it's wonderful! You are the luckiest woman alive. Loved by a Prince! Now listen. This is what I've got to tell you. You'll go to Keith's Chapel. You'll be married to Isaac and then you will all come back here for the wedding celebrations.'

'Yes,' said Hannah.

'A man will come into the Market ... you must listen for him. He will be playing a pipe and a tabor.'

'Yes ... yes ...'

'The children will run to the window to watch him. Doubtless there will be a juggler with him. The children will want to see it. The elders too. While they are looking, you slip out the back way to Jermyn Street. You will find a carriage there ... waiting for you.'

'Jane. Is it true?'

'You didn't think the Prince would leave you to Isaac, did you?'

'No, I did not.'

Hannah threw herself into Jane's arms. 'I thought I would have rather died,' she said.

'Don't talk of dying. You're just beginning to live.'

'Jane, how can I thank thee for all thou hast done?'

'Don't worry about me. I'm safe enough. We're setting up in the glass-cutting business ... on our own, think of that. That's my reward. Half already paid, and the rest when you're safely with the Prince.'

'Jane ... I'm so happy for thee.'

'And I for yourself too, I should think. What a happy day when you decided to sit in the window and watch the Prince go by.'

*   *   *

The ceremony was brief. Hannah was Mrs. Isaac Axford. The Wheelers were a little ashamed that it had had to be such a hole and corner affair, but the Axfords were delighted. Five hundred pounds dowry! Isaac was a lucky man—all that, and a beautiful bride into the bargain!

The bride was clearly nervous, but that was to be expected.

The brief ceremony over, the guinea paid, the certificate declaring Isaac Axford of St. Martin's, Ludgate, to be married to Hannah Lightfoot of St. James's, Westminster, signed by Dr. Keith's representatives; and the entry was made in the registers of the Mayfair Chapel. The little party came back to the linen-draper's shop in St. James's Market and there Mary and Lydia busied themselves in the kitchen.

Hannah went to her room to take off her cloak. She looked about it; it might well be the last time she would see it, if it happened as Jane said it would. If the player and juggler came into the Market.

What if they did not? That was more than she could bear to contemplate. He must come. The Prince must be waiting to carry her away.

He will come, she told herself. She thought of those conversations in the Haymarket, that adoration he had shown her, that wonderful respect. How could she endure Isaac Axford when she thought of her Prince!

But he was only a boy and he was governed by great men. They would never allow him to take her away ... she had been a fool to imagine it was possible ... a fool to hope!

Yet how could she endure a life with Isaac in the grocer's shop on Ludgate Hill? I shall never never know happiness again, thought Hannah, unless the miracle happens.

'Hannah, where art thou?' It was her mother's voice strained and nervous, yet somehow proud, proud because she had brought Isaac such a dowry and had been admired by the Prince of Wales.

She would have to leave her mother, but she could not help it. She would leave not only her mother but her cousins and the good home which had been hers for so many years, for the sake of the Prince.

In the big sitting-room which overlooked the Market they were all assembled. Hannah joined them, her eyes straying to the window, as she listened for the sound of a pipe or a tabor.

He will not come, she thought. It is all a dream. It is hoping for a miracle. He is only a boy without power. I shall have nothing for the rest of my life but the memory that he loved me.

'Listen.' It was little four-year-old Hannah. 'Oh, Papa, listen. The pipe.'

She was at the window. Henry was beside her and Rebecca was calling out with pleasure.

There was the man with the pipe and the tabor; there was the juggler.

'Papa, Papa, look!'

The dream was coming true. They were at the window ... all of them.

She was out of the door, down the back stairs; she did not feel the cold December air, although she was without her cloak. She ran as fast as she could and there in Jermyn Street, as Jane had said, was the carriage waiting.

The door was open and she stepped in.

He was there. The Prince in person. For the first time he took her into his arms.

The door was shut; the carriage started up; and the sweetest music in the world to Hannah was the sound of horse's hooves on the cobbled streets.

Marriage Plans

'I FEEL,' said the Princess Augusta, 'that nothing will ever be the same again. That George ... *my* George ... could behave in such a way!'

'It is natural,' replied Lord Bute. 'The Prince of Wales has a mistress. It has happened before.'

'But at his age!'

'Oh come. He will soon be sixteen.'

'It is not so much the fact that he has a mistress. It is the manner of his doing it. Abduction, no less.'

'The lady apparently went willingly.'

'But to set her up ... to have planned such an enterprise.'

'No doubt he has had help.'

'That's what worries me ... that he should have had help from anyone ... not ourselves.'

Lord Bute comforted her. 'We have perhaps been careless. We thought we knew him. We believed him to be the innocent boy. But nature asserted herself. He fell in love and so he grew up suddenly.'

'My dearest, what *shall* we do?'

'We shall simply be more observant in future. We shall keep

a close watch on George and his fair Quaker. In the meantime
we should perhaps congratulate ourselves. How much better
that he should have fallen under the spell of a woman like this,
not of the Court. It could have been some scheming woman in
our midst. Imagine that!'

The Princess shuddered.

'As it is there is this harmless woman,' went on Lord Bute.
'No, we should rejoice that it is who it is. Although, of course,
we have had our little lesson. All to the good. We will learn
from it. We have been warned. George is not the child we
thought him. He is capable of taking strong action. It is good
we learned that ... in time.'

'You are such a comfort to me, my dear.'

'It is my purpose in life ... to please and comfort you.'

*   *   *

The tall house in Tottenham was an ideal setting. It was
surrounded by gardens—completely isolated. It was furnished
luxuriously; cared for by many soft-footed servants, well paid,
all aware that their high wages were the reward of discretion.

There was a sewing-woman to make beautiful dresses for the
mistress of the house. There was a music teacher; there were
books for her to read. She had her carriage—a closed one—in
which she could ride out when she wished. Everything had
been planned with care.

When she had first arrived here Hannah had been bewildered. For twenty-three years she had lived more quietly
than most girls and then, since a young boy had smiled at her
as she sat in her uncle's window, she had been swept into an
adventure so romantic, so incredible, that when she awoke in
the night she had to convince herself that she had not dreamed
it all.

When she had stepped into the carriage and found the
Prince waiting for her she had been too overcome by joy for
anything else. She and the Prince had clung together as they
rattled along, assuring each other of their undying love. She
asked nothing more; nor did he. Both of them refused to look

beyond the immediate future. They were in love; they were alone; Hannah had successfully escaped to him; they asked nothing more.

He took her to the house. 'It is planned for you.'

'It is a palace ... It is an enchanted place.'

'Your being here makes it so,' he told her.

They went through the house together.

'It is so large for one.'

'But I shall be here often, as often as I can.' He turned to her suddenly. 'I intended to marry you. It is only if I married you that I could be completely happy.'

'Thou—marry me! The Prince of Wales marry me ... the linen-draper's niece!'

'I wanted to marry you. It was what I planned.'

She embraced him tenderly. He was a child after all. He really believed that the Prince of Wales could marry the niece of a tradesman.

'Once we were married,' he insisted, 'they would have had to accept it.'

She shook her head. They never would. Unworldly as she was, she knew that. Did he really think that he could make her Queen of England?

'But they married you to that man Axford.'

Perhaps, she thought, it was as well, otherwise what folly would he have been prepared to commit?

'I had to save you from that ...' he went on.

She kissed his hands. 'How can I thank thee ...'

'No ... no,' he cried. 'It is I who should thank you. Oh, Hannah, they were too quick for us. I should never have let them marry you to Axford. Now, you see, *we* cannot marry.'

She felt old and wise; she led him to a sofa and drew him down beside her. She held his head against her breast as though he were indeed a child.

She said tenderly: 'My love, marriage is impossible, so we must needs do without it. It was no fault of ours. The intention was there. I had no love for Isaac Axford, so I count it no marriage ... nothing but a few words spoken before a priest who in a short time will have no power to marry people in this way. We will call it no marriage. Thou stood beside me in spirit ... it is to thee that I consider myself married this day.'

He lifted his head to look at her wonderingly.

'Oh, Hannah,' he whispered, 'how wonderful you are!'

* * *

She went about the house like a young married woman in her new home. She sang as she never had before. She was happy. She had thrown aside her old beliefs. Uncle Wheeler thought that we were not put on earth to be happy and that if one felt an excess of happiness one should be wary and ask oneself if the devil was not looking over one's shoulder. Well, Hannah was happy. And she no longer believed in Uncle Wheeler's doctrines. She had come to a new and glorious understanding that human beings were put into the world to find happiness and the ones that did so should remember this and do all in their power to keep it.

The Prince came regularly. He was now the lover—no longer the boy. He was turned sixteen, but he seemed several years older than the boy who had brought her here. He was a husband—for that was how he saw himself. Nothing else was possible to him. He told her that there was much profligacy at his grandfather's Court and it shamed him. When he was King he would set up a new standard of morals. He would see that the sanctity of marriage was respected.

Hannah did not look as far as that. She wondered what would happen when he became King and his ministers insisted on his marrying; there would have to be a Queen of England and it would not be Hannah Lightfoot. But that was a long way off. In the meantime she was happy; she must stay happy; and happiness was here in the present not in the vague and distant future.

He wished that he could live here. What fun it would be. Mr. and Mrs. ... Guelph. Or perhaps Colonel and Mrs. George. That was the name in which he had taken the house: Colonel George. Guelph was too dangerous.

He was happy. There was only one regret, that he could not have been legally married to Hannah and could have told the world so.

However, as Hannah said, they had so much. They had each other, the chance to meet frequently; they had love; and they knew that their intentions were honourable; they could rely on each other's fidelity; and they were married in the sight of God.

They must not ask more. If they did, Fate would consider them greedy and perhaps decide to deprive them of some of their blessings.

They must be happy. And while they could be together, safe from discovery, she was happy; she asked nothing more.

* * *

A carriage came to the door of the house.

Hannah was horrified. It was not her lover. Then who? No one called at the house. She must shut herself away, refuse to see any visitors. What if it were her uncle come to take her away ... or her husband!

From behind a curtained window she saw a woman get out of the carriage; she was veiled, but she was relieved to recognize her as Jane.

She rang for her servant. 'There is a lady below,' she said. 'Please bring her to me without delay.'

Jane came into the room, throwing back her veil, and they embraced affectionately.

'But it's magnificent,' cried Jane. 'Oh ... it's quite magnificent. You lucky creature!'

'Jane ... what brings you here?'

'To see you, of course. And ... to warn you.'

'To warn me of what?'

'Let me sit down. And what about a dish of tea? I'm thirsty.'

Hannah rang for the maid and gave an order, while Jane looked on with admiration.

'Different from the Market, eh?'

'Jane tell me of what thou wishest to warn me.'

'They are searching for you. There's a great stir among the Society of Friends.'

Hannah grew pale. 'They may have followed thee here...'

'Not they! I was careful. Never fear that I would lead them to you, Hannah. I was questioned: "Where is she?" "What do you know?" Mr. H. came to my rescue. He swore I knew nothing ... and they couldn't go against a girl's husband, could they? He knows which side his bread's buttered. We shall soon have our own shop, think of that. And all due to Mr. H.'s clever wife. So you can rely on him ... and me ... me for friendship, Hannah, as well as the money. That's why I came to tell you that you must be careful. I'm to be the go-between ... and I'm to be careful, they tell me. If there's anything you have to know, I shall be bringing you news of it. And now I've got to tell you, Hannah, that they are all searching. Isaac, he was near demented. "Where is my wife Hannah?" he kept asking, and he was running through the streets looking into carriages.'

'Oh dear,' cried Hannah aghast.

'You have become important,' shortled Jane. 'A *cause célèbre*. Where is the fair Quaker of St. James's Market? everyone is asking.'

'They must not find me, Jane. They must not.'

'Of course they mustn't. And they never shall.'

Jane sat contentedly sipping her tea.

'My, how I've come up in the world,' she murmured. 'Tea with a *cause célèbre* and my own mistress and all because of you, Hannah.'

Hannah could not share Jane's pleasure. She was very uneasy.

*   *   *

Although the search went on and in the St. James's Market area there was constant speculation about the disappearance of Hannah Axford, Lightfoot that was, Hannah continued to live without disturbance in her tall quiet house, visited frequently by her lover who became more and more devoted as the months passed.

George was happy: he constantly reminded himself that he considered himself married to Hannah, which was the only way in which he could enjoy such a connection. He had intended to marry Hannah; he would be faithful to Hannah; and she to him.

There were very few people in the secret, but these he could trust. Elizabeth Chudleigh was one; she had been of great help to him and had shown him how to make this liaison possible. It had changed him from a careless boy to a man of responsibilities and if he still had to sit in a schoolroom and learn history and mathematics, in one phase of his life he was a man and this gave him confidence. There were two others with whom he shared that confidence and who in the family circle were closer to him than any other; this was his brother Edward and his sister Elizabeth. Edward had declared that in George's place he would have done exactly the same; in fact, Edward had applauded his brother and swore he would always support him.

So while George sat in the schoolroom and wrote his account of English history he was thinking of Hannah.

'Charles I did not regard the laws of the land,' he wrote, 'but violated them when they thwarted his interest or inclination.' It was no way to rule; and Charles I had discovered that too late. It was something to remember.

George understood that he must prepare himself for kingship. The old King was growing more feeble every day, more irascible. It was said that one of these days the old man would go off when he was in one of his violent outbursts of temper; and when he does, thought George, I shall be King.

His mother was anxious about him. He loved her dearly; he admired Lord Bute as much as any man he knew; and both of them were constantly telling him: 'You must learn to be a King.'

It was comforting to ride out to Hannah, to tell her of the ways of the Court, of the trouble in his household, of his mother and Lord Bute pulling against the tutors the King had chosen for him.

'I have two ambitions,' he told Hannah, 'to be a good King and to be a good husband to you.'

* * *

George was delighted to find that his dear friend Lord Bute did not blame him for his affair with Hannah.

'It is natural that Your Highness should have a mistress,' he explained. 'You should feel no sense of guilt.'

'But Hannah is not a mistress. I do want to make that clear.'

'Of course not,' soothed Lord Bute. 'Do you not realize that I understand your feelings ... *perfectly*.'

'I knew you would if I had an opportunity to explain.'

'Your Highness can always explain everything to me. Have I not always assured you that any skill I may have is at your disposal.'

'You have ... no one more.'

'Then when you are in any difficulties I can expect you to come to me. Now that you are no longer a boy I can talk to you freely. There are two people whom you can trust: one is your mother; the other is myself.'

George nodded. 'And fortunate I am to have you.'

'I think of this nation and I can see no one who can care for you as your mother does. You have this delightful lady, your beautiful Quaker. She loves you as a wife but she knows nothing of the malice and intrigues which always surround a Court. Your mother does; and she is here to protect you. She wishes you well for your own sake. Others have interested views; they wish for riches or honours; they are ambitious not for your good or that of the country but for themselves. The advice they give you will be contaminated by these considerations. So her advice alone is the advice you should follow, for you will know it is given with your own good in mind solely, and for no other reason.'

'I do know it; and I thank God for her care.'

'I too care only for your good. You will find many to speak against me. They will try to represent me to you as a villain.'

'I would not believe them.'

'You say that now; but some are skilful. I am certain that in the future, when you are King of this realm, attempts will be made to vilify me. They will use all their arts to win you over. If they do you will be ruined.'

'I know this. I know it well. I am young. I am without experience and I want advice now and shall in the future. I trust you as I trust no other man.'

'If you failed to trust me I should contemplate leaving the country.'

'I beg of you do not speak so. I need your friendship. I am so young and I know so little.'

'If you married you would not feel the need of my friendship so strongly.'

'I am married ... and I still feel it.'

'There will come a time when you will have to make a state marriage...' began Bute tentatively.

'How can that be when I am married already?'

'When you are King it will be necessary for you to marry a Princess, to give the country heirs...'

George shook his head and looked stubborn. Trouble here, thought Bute; but he is only sixteen. Give him a chance to grow weary of the Quaker adventure.

He spread his hands. 'It will be for you to decide,' he said comfortingly. 'And you know that I shall always be ready to advise in any problem. I trust that you will always come first to me, Sir, or to your mother.'

'I shall. I shall insist that everyone accepts you as the Friend of the Family. My dear friend will always mean more to me than the crown itself. I need you now, but I shall need you more when the crown is mine. You must never think of leaving me.'

Bute took the Prince's hand and kissing it, swore he would not.

Shortly afterwards he was repeating this conversation to the Princess.

'I feel we have lost nothing through this affair of the Quaker,' said Bute.

'But I shall never forget that he acted without consulting me,' replied the Princess.

'It was natural that he should not consult his mother about his mistress. Rest happy. He is more devoted to us than ever before; and as long as we do not try to separate him from his mistress he is ours to command. Trust me, my dearest, this little affair of his is no bad thing.'

The Princess nodded. She could always rely on dear Lord Bute to comfort her.

*   *   *

George, the King, was in a testy mood. Nothing was going well in the country—discord at home and defeats abroad. He was beginning to suspect that Newcastle was not the best man for his post and that Pitt would be an improvement. Pitt was a man of war, but perhaps what the country needed at this time was a man of war. Pitt ... an outsider and a master of oratory! His brilliance in that direction had caused Robert Walpole some misgivings. Oh, the days of Sir Robert, when Caroline was alive and the three of them had conferred together! Everything was so much easier then. Sir Robert was a man of genius and he, the King, had known how to bring out the best in that genius; and Caroline was always there to support him. No woman worthy to unlatch her shoe, thought the King sentimentally, forgetting to remember that he loved her so much more since she was dead than he had when she was alive. He had always been so devoted to her when he was away from home; he had regularly written to her letters twenty or thirty pages long, quite often about his affairs with other women, asking her advice, explaining their particular accomplishments in the bedchamber. She had never shown any resentment. A remarkable woman. No one worthy to buckle her shoes.

But now she was dead, and there was Newcastle making his insufficiencies apparent every day and Pitt clamouring to take office and Henry Fox standing by, cunning as his name implied. Pitt and Fox ... good men both. Pitt had integrity; he knew that; and men of integrity were as rare as they were

valuable; and Fox, well since he had married Richmond's
daughter he was wealthy and he did not have to rely on his
position in politics. Security could make a man honest. Perhaps
Pitt and Fox provided the answer.

And there was one other the very mention of whose name
made the veins stand out at the King's temples: Bute. But one
could not ignore him because of the power he wielded at
Leicester House. Was it true that he was the Princess's lover?
Of course it was true. One only had to see the pair together to
know that they were cooing like a pair of turtle doves. The
Princess doted on Bute as she never had on Fred. He didn't
blame her there. Married to Fred, poor woman; anyone who
married Fred would have his sympathy. And Fred was gone
and she was free, so let her have a little fun, poor woman. But
she was not going to put Bute into his government while he
lived. And when he had gone ... Ah, then Bute would be
there; she would see to that. He was installed there in her
household as though he were young George's father—and he
behaved as such, by all accounts. And young George accepted
him!

And what was all this talk about a Quaker? The young
puppy must have a mistress, one supposed. But why couldn't
he choose one from his own or his mother's household or even
the King's household come to that? Why must the young fool
go sniffing round Markets.

It was because he was concerned about his grandson that
the King had sent for him, and the boy had come down to
Hampton and was waiting to be called in. All right, let him
come.

The King was standing with his back to the door looking out
of the window at the craft on the river when the Prince
entered.

The King turned slowly. So this was his grandson, Fred's
boy. The King frowned. He was tall, and George II had always
disliked tall men because they reminded him of his own lack of
inches, something which all his life had irritated him. Now the
Prince of Wales stood there, tall and gangling, not making the

most of his height which irritated the King as much as his having it.

'Well?' barked the King.

'You ... Your Majesty sent for me.'

'Don't stammer. Never could abide it. Now ... what's all this, we hear. Abducting Quaker girls from Markets. By God, what do you think you are? A dashing young gallant, I suppose. But let me tell you this, you young puppy, you are the Prince of Wales and are not expected to behave like some ninny on a theatre stage.'

This was spoken in French so fast that the Prince could scarcely keep up with it. He realized to his dismay that he was expected to reply in the same language.

'Well,' went on the King, 'what have you to say for yourself? Young Quaker girls! Why can't you find a girl in one of the households? Why do you have to go prancing round Markets. Do you know there has been trouble. Enquiries made. Good respectable tradesmen looking for their girl. There has been a note delivered to the Secretary. Did you know that? Of course you didn't, you young puppy. Not your job to know, you say. Yours is only to go sniffing round Markets.'

'Sire ...' stammered George, and could go no farther.

'So you're dumb, are you? It's time I took a hand with your education. That mother of yours ... Women are no good at this sort of thing ... except your grandmother. She was a woman who could do anything. No one worthy to unbuckle her shoes. I'll speak to Waldegrave. This won't do, you young puppy. It won't do. Do you hear me? Then say something. Don't stand there like a ninny!'

'If Your Majesty would speak in English...'

A further offence. The Prince spoke perfect English. The King was not going to display his very imperfect brand.

'Don't tell me what to speak.'

'Sire, I ... I did not tell you ... I ... I ...'

'Stuttering ninny! Now what's this about the Quaker girl? You send her back to her family and find a woman in your mother's household ... better there than your own.'

'I ... I must ask Your Majesty not to speak of ... of ... this lady in this manner.'

'So you are telling me how I should speak of my subjects, are you?'

'Your Majesty does not understand...'

'Not understand. Look, you ninny, I had mistresses when I was your age. Don't think you're the first. But there are whores enough about you. You don't want to go to Quakers for them.'

The Prince had turned pale. 'I must ask Your Majesty not to speak of this lady in this way.'

'I speak of my subjects as I please, boy.'

'N ... not of this one.'

If George had not drawn himself up to his full height the King might have laughed at him; but he did and he towered above his little grandfather so that the King had to look up to him.

'Infernal puppy!' shrieked the King, and bringing up his hand slapped the Prince so violently across the face that he reeled backwards. 'Get out of my sight, whelp, idiot, *puppy*! Get out before I set the guards on you.'

The Prince stared at his grandfather, but the King, his face purple, shaking with rage, was on the point of calling the guard.

George stumbled out of the room, humiliated and angry. He never wanted to see the old man again; he never wanted to see Hampton again.

The guards smiled at each other as they watched the Prince stalk out of the palace to the river stairs and take boat to London.

Only the King quarrelling with the Prince of Wales ... an old Hanoverian custom.

* * *

The King sent for Lord Waldegrave; he wanted to speak to him he said about that young puppy, the Prince of Wales.

Waldegrave looked sad and the King nodded grimly.

'I can see you have no great opinion of your pupil.'

'I fear I shall never make a scholar of him, Sire.'

'Scholar! Who wants a scholar? Don't want the puppy bleating poetry all over the place. But the young fellow doesn't seem to have any sense. That's what I complain of.'

'He is very slow, Your Majesty. I suppose he tries to learn, but it's not easy for him.'

'Lacks the intelligence, I suppose.'

'Not a very good brain, Your Majesty.'

'I know ... I know. Takes after his father. A stupid ass, that was Fred. And it seems this one's the same. Fred's mother ...' The King's eyes were glazed with tender memories. 'How different she was. I used to say to her: "You're more like a schoolmarm than a Queen." If she were here now. There's not a woman worthy to unbuckle her shoes, Waldegrave.'

Waldegrave successfully managed to stifle a yawn. The eulogy on the late Queen—whom the King had delighted to humiliate during her lifetime—would go on for precisely five minutes and Waldegrave knew it almost off by heart. One virtue the King possessed was his precision. He was always accountable. He was as regular as a clock in his habits. There were people at Court who remembered how he used to walk up and down outside his mistress's door, his watch in his hand, so that he could call on her at precisely the time he had set himself to do so. He would leave at the arranged time also. The joke at Court was that he made love by the clock.

So Waldegrave waited while he delivered his speech on the virtues of the Queen. The King wiped his eyes at the end as he always did. Waldegrave wondered mildly whether Madame Walmoden had to listen to a recital of the late Queen's virtues before getting into bed with her lover. He hoped so. Caroline deserved that small consideration after all the accounts she had had to listen to of his affairs with other women.

The King had finished with his Queen and was now ready to get to the business for which he had summoned Waldegrave.

'So you find the young puppy no good at his lessons?'

'He's not lazy, Sire, perhaps it's an inability to learn. Sometimes I think he tries.'

'H'm,' grunted the King. 'He's a brainless whelp. And, of course, his mother keeps him under her thumb—and that prize stallion of hers too, I doubt not. Between them the pair hope to turn out a nice little wooden doll, who'll nod when they say nod and shake when they say shake. That's it, eh, Waldegrave?'

It was not the sort of agreement one gave even to the King, so Waldegrave contented himself with smiling at His Majesty.

'Oh, I know, I know. And now I hear the boy has a mistress. A young Quaker, they tell me.'

'There is a rumour to that effect, Sire.'

'Quakers,' mused the King. 'Their women are thin. I never fancied thin women, Waldegrave.'

No need to mention that, thought Waldegrave. Your Majesty has made that perfectly obvious.

'And he's not content with choosing a nice plump woman of the Court. He must go for this thin Quaker and snatch her from her husband almost at the altar. What do you think of that, Waldegrave? I'd never have believed it of the puppy, that I wouldn't.'

'It is said that His Highness was aided in the matter.'

'Some interfering scoundrels, I am sure. Ha! And that mother of his none too pleased—nor the Scottish stallion either, eh? I hear they knew nothing about it until it was over. Is that true do you think, Waldegrave?'

'I think so, Your Majesty.'

The King was in a sudden good humour at the thought.

'Well, well,' he went on, 'it's time we mated the puppy. That much is clear.'

'Your Majesty has someone in mind?'

'When I was last in Hanover I looked around. The Duchess of Brunswick-Wolfenbüttel brought her two girls to see me.'

'And Your Majesty liked what you saw?'

The King licked his lips significantly. 'So much, Waldegrave, that if I'd been twenty years younger I'd have married the elder of the girls myself and that would still have left the younger for my grandson.'

He shaped the outline of a generously formed female shape with his hands.

'Charming young girls, Waldegrave. Charming.'

'Well then, Your Majesty, since you feel the time has come...'

'How old is he? Sixteen, seventeen? In a year or so, I think, Waldegrave.'

'Your Majesty will wish the Princess Dowager to be informed.'

'H'm. Wait a bit. But I think we should give thought to these matters. It's time the young puppy was mated. Quakers!'

*   *   *

When the Princess Augusta heard of the rumours she was infuriated.

She paced up and down her apartment and her lover had difficulty in pacifying her. 'Do you think that old scoundrel would dare bring one of those Wolfenbüttel girls over here without consulting me?'

'Surely not,' soothed Bute; although he believed the old scoundrel capable of doing anything.

'I will not have one of those girls for my daughter-in-law. I detest their old mother. She is the most unattractive woman I ever knew, and the girls will take after her. George is too young to marry. And I will not have one of those girls here.'

'You might find that you liked the girl when you met her. She might not take after her mother; but of course I agree that George is too young to marry.'

'He will come of age when he is eighteen and that is not far off. He will have to marry then; but it will not be one of those Wolfenbüttel girls. Their mother is the most meddling, intriguing woman you can imagine. The father was all right ... but like as not the girls will take after their mother. When George marries I should like him to choose someone from the Saxe-Gotha family—my own.'

'It would be ideal, of course.'

'Well, since the old scoundrel has his eyes on Wolfenbüttel perhaps he could be looking towards Saxe-Gotha.'

'Our best plan would be to make George understand that he must never accept one of those girls whose mother you so dislike. Shall I sound him? Perhaps you could follow on from there.'

She pressed his hand. 'As always you provide the answer.'

*   *   *

Bute found George in the schoolroom, his brow furrowed as he tried to understand the different methods of taxation which had been applied through the various preceding reigns and the measure of their success. He was very pleased to be interrupted.

'I thought you would wish to know that the King is thinking of marrying you off.'

George turned pale. 'It cannot be!'

'Certainly not to the woman of the King's choice.'

'So he has chosen?'

Bute nodded slowly. 'He has decided on either Sophia Caroline or Anna Amelia of Brunswick-Wolfenbüttel. You are to pick which you prefer.'

'I cannot marry.'

'So your mother thinks. She has the strongest objections to either of these young females.'

'It would not matter who they were. I consider myself married already.'

Bute nodded sympathetically. So the boy was still held in the Quaker web. But give him a little time.

'Do not be unduly alarmed. I am sure that if you firmly decide not to be forced into marriage by your grandfather you will stay free.'

'You will help?'

'Have I not sworn always to do so?'

'Oh, thank you ... thank you. I don't know what I should do without you.'

'Why should you?' Bute laughed breezily. 'When you are

King all you will have to do is to make me your chief minister and I shall always be at your side.'

'Of course, that is what I intend to do.'

Oh, triumph! thought Bute. If you could hear that New-castle ... Pitt ... Fox ... you would shiver with apprehension. The old man cannot last much longer surely. And then this boy will be King and that means that I and the Princess will in fact rule this land. What a dazzling prospect for an ambitious man!

'I shall keep Your Majesty to that.' Spoken playfully to hide the sealing of a promise beneath a jocular guise.

'Oh hush! Remember the King still lives.'

'God save the King!' cried Bute, and whispered: 'And in particular His Majesty King George III.'

George smiled faintly and was immediately anxious. 'So you understand that I could not consider marriage ... any marriage. I am morally bound to Hannah. I want no one else.'

'I understand. But have no fear. The King may attempt to force this marriage on you, but we will stand firm. He needs the consent of Parliament, and members will be afraid to give that consent, if you are firm enough. They remember that his star is setting and yours is about to rise. You must remember it, too. Do not give way easily to anything. Stand firm. Remember that any day you could become King.'

'I do not like my grandfather. He is a disagreeable man and since he struck me I fear I can never feel what I ought towards him. But I do not care to speak of him as a dead man when he is still alive. He has as much right to live as I have ... that is how I see it.'

'A right and noble sentiment worthy of Your Maj ... Your Highness. But I am warning you. Stand firm. Declare your refusal to take one of these girls and your grandfather is powerless.'

'How can I thank you!'

'Oh,' laughed Bute. 'Don't forget the promises you have made to me.'

'I swear I never will.'

Bute was able to tell the Princess that he had persuaded the Prince to stand out against the Brunswick-Wolfenbüttel proposition.

'We have nothing to fear from St. James's Palace. The King will see that he cannot rule the Prince from there. We are his guardians—and we must see that it remains so.'

* * *

The King's face was purple with rage.

'So the puppy won't be bewolfenbüttled, he says. I'll teach him whether to defy me. I say he shall be bewolfenbüttled, and like it. I'll have him yelping to me to hurry on the marriage, I promise you, Waldegrave. He doesn't want to marry? Well, it is his duty to marry, and I am going to see he does his duty.'

'Your Majesty, the Prince would have some support in Parliament.'

'Support! What support?'

'He is the Prince and he has his following. His mother's friends would be ready to uphold him.'

'Who is she? Fred's widow. *I* am the King of this country and I'll be obeyed.'

This was a difficult task, Waldegrave realized; and he secretly thought that the sooner he was released from his position of tutor to the Prince of Wales and chief King's spy in the Princess's household the better.

'If a vote were taken on the matter of the Prince's marriage the result might well be in his favour.'

'But I say he shall marry the girl. He's no longer a boy. He's proved that, hasn't he? Sniffing round Markets! If his grandmother were alive. Ah, there was a woman . . .'

Waldegrave allowed his mind to wander for five minutes. The King must be made to see that he could not force the Brunswick-Wolfenbüttel marriage just yet. The Prince was only seventeen. It was another year before he would officially come of age. The old King was well over seventy; everyone had expected him to die at least ten years ago. He could not last

much longer; in fact, when he went into one of his frequent
rages they expected him to have an apoplectic fit on the spot.
With the purple colour in his cheeks, his prominent eyes
bulging and veins knotting at his temples he really looked as
though he were on the verge of a stroke. And there was young
George, seventeen years old, with his fresh pink skin and his
blue eyes almost as prominent as his grandfather's but placid,
and the same heavy jaw, though in his case, sometimes sullen,
where the King's was more likely to be bellicose.

How could Waldegrave explain to the King that ambitious
ministers would be more likely to support the young man who
must certainly ascend the throne in a few years time rather
than an old one who must most certainly soon leave it.

But perhaps the King saw that, for when he had finished the
five minute eulogy on the dead Queen, he said: 'I heard a
rumour that that woman has her eyes on Saxe-Gotha. I tell you
this Waldegrave, there'll be no Saxe-Gotha woman for my
grandson. I'll not have our family tainted by that lot. And I'll
tell you this too, Waldegrave: there's madness there. I shall
stand firmly against any of her plots in that direction. No Saxe-
Gotha here. Do you understand?'

Waldegrave replied that he understood His Majesty perfectly.

No Saxe-Gotha! And no Brunswick-Wolfenbüttel either.

The marriage of the Prince of Wales was satisfactorily
shelved for a while.

* * *

The King was alarmed. Foreign affairs were at a very low
ebb. England's place in the world was insignificant. There was
one man who railed against this with a passionate fury so
intense that it had impressed the King. He thought a great
deal about William Pitt. There was a man who impressed him
deeply. Pitt was a man of words—the finest orator of his day.
He could turn a phrase and bring tears to the eyes; he could
present an argument and convince.

When he had been young and lusty the King had preferred

to live in Hanover rather than England; but when he had been a still younger man he had professed a great love for England but that was only because his father had hated it and he automatically loved all that his father hated. In the days when he had first come to England with Caroline he used to say: 'If you vould vin my favour call me an Englishman.' He had always spoken in English then—with a marked German accent, of course—but that was because his father George I had refused to learn a word of the language. But when he became King he felt it undignified to speak a language which his subjects spoke so much better, and everyone about him had to speak in French or German. Then, of course, he had made several attempts to sacrifice England to Hanover which Sir Robert Walpole had prevented.

But that was the past. He was an old man—he was a vain old man—and no King, particularly one who has always made a semblance of virtue, wanted to leave his country in a worse state than that in which he found it.

'If Valpole vere here,' he mused, lapsing into English. 'If my dear Caroline vere here ...'

Those days were past and Newcastle was no Walpole. But there was Pitt.

He thought of Pitt. The orator, the man of war, who deplored the desultory state of Britain's arms. Pitt had grandiose schemes. He talked of Empire—and by God, how he talked! No one could talk like Mr. Pitt. He could make people see a country astride the world, leading the world, in wealth, in commerce. That was Mr. Pitt's dream of England, and he wanted a chance to make it become a reality.

He was called a war-monger. Such men always were. Did any man think that great rewards could be gained without effort. If so, that man was a fool.

The King decided to send for Mr. Pitt.

In the presence of such a man even a King must feel insignificant. George usually hated to feel insignificant; that was why he never liked tall men. But this was different. George was not thinking so much of the King of England as of England itself. Some instinct told him that Mr. Pitt was the man; and if he were tall of stature, imposing in personality, on this occasion, so much the better.

His manner was deferential—almost servile—another quality which pleased the King. There was nothing arrogant about this man in the presence of royalty, although he could be haughty enough with those whom he considered beneath him. He was vain in the extreme; he held himself erect; he had a little head, thin face and long aquiline nose, heavy lidded eyes ... hawk's eyes. He was like an actor on a stage, thought the King; he might have steped right out of a play; and when he spoke it might have been Garrick or Quin speaking; the beautiful cadences of his magnificent voice filled the apartment and demanded respect.

There was greatness in this man, the King believed. I could work with him as I used to with Robert Walpole. I wish the Queen were here. She would agree with me—or I would soon persuade her to.

She had always believed that England should be great; she and Walpole together and himself, of course. What a triumvirate. And now it should be Pitt and the King.

The King begged Mr. Pitt to be seated, and for a few moments he exchanged pleasantries with the minister. Pitt had only two or three years before married—rather late in life, for he was now close on fifty. He had married well, of course, everything Mr. Pitt did would become his dignity—Hester Grenville whose mother had been connected with the Earls of Temple. Pitt seemed happy in his marriage and had a daughter, Hester, at this time.

The King came to the point and they discussed the affairs of the Kingdom. Now Pitt glowed with purpose.

He believed in expansion—in Empire. England was a small country. His Majesty would be aware that the population of Great Britain in this year 1757 was somewhere in the region of seven million persons; now they must compare this population with their great enemy France which had one of twenty-seven millions. The difference appalled Mr. Pitt. But Great Britain was two small islands, and the whole world was open to us, and we must go out and make it ours.

These sentiments uttered in that deeply sonorous voice, with those magnificent gestures echoing round the audience chamber thrilled the King. He believed Mr. Pitt; he was inspired by Mr. Pitt; and he wanted Mr. Pitt to bring such glory to this country, of which for so many years he had been a reluctant ruler, that on his leaving it, it would be the richest, the most powerful, the most formidable in the world.

'There have been defeats both on land and sea,' said Mr. Pitt. 'Defeats to make an Englishman shudder. We have been at fault. We have lacked leadership.'

The hawk's eyes were studying the King's face. This could be touching on a dangerous point. Cumberland, the King's son, and the one of his offspring he came as near to loving as he could anyone, had been appointed commander of the Army not because of his military genius but because he was the King's son. Culloden, where he had scored an undoubted victory, was a blot on English military history; and the Duke's record in the field had not been conspicuously successful since. If he was to achieve his purpose he wanted the right man doing the right job irrespective of his position; a soldier from the ranks who was a true leader should have as much chance as a King's son who fancied playing at soldiers.

Mr. Pitt had no intention of stating this to the King at this moment but it was one of the rules he would adhere to—and he would have his way. He was not dedicating his talents to the service of a royal family but to the greatness of England.

'It is a state of affairs which will have to be carefully overhauled ... without delay,' said Mr. Pitt.

'You know why I have summoned you here, Mr. Pitt,' said the King. 'It is to offer you the post of Secretary of State.'

'Your Majesty is gracious to me and I accept the post.'

'Newcastle continues as First Lord of the Treasury. This is agreeable to you, Mr. Pitt?'

It was agreeable. Pitt had not a great deal of respect for Newcastle but provided he obeyed orders—and he would get orders from Pitt—he would be, the new Secretary decided, a good man to deal with administration. No, he had no objection to serving ostensibly under Newcastle, for in point of fact, he himself would be the leader.

'Your Majesty,' he went on, 'rarely has this country been in such a dire state. Our sole ally, the King of Prussia, is laid low. We must give aid to Prussia. It is against my principles to support other countries but the position is vital. The French will be in command of America if we do not take care. Sire, we should turn our eyes to America. Our expansion lies outside these islands.'

The King said: 'I am in agreement with what you say, Mr. Pitt.'

'Canada must be ours ... we have subjects in North America. We cannot allow the French to oust us. This is one of the important periods of our history. It is in our hands now to make or lose an Empire. It is up to us to decide.'

'Then we will decide to make an Empire, Mr. Pitt.'

'So say I, Your Majesty. But it has to be won, Sire. It has to be won. Have I Your Majesty's permission to seek out and promote those men who can do the best work for their country?'

'You have, Mr. Pitt.'

'I have already consulted Sir John Ligonier, who has given me some names of men whom he believes should be promoted. I believe these men should be entrusted with commands of the utmost importance. Colonel Jeffry Amherst, Major-General Henry Seymour Conway and Colonel James Wolfe.'

'I have never heard these men's names before,' complained the King.

'No, Sire. You have heard the names of men who have so far led this country to disaster.'

Mr. Pitt was rather an uncomfortable gentleman; but the King still believed in him. He said he would consider his minister's proposals; and when Mr. Pitt had left he began to think of Caroline; he was sure she would have approved of Mr. Pitt.

A Slight Case of Blackmail

In the house in Tottenham the years passed pleasantly. George's visits were perhaps less frequent but that was explained by the fact that as Prince of Wales he had many duties; he was watched and could not easily slip away, and both he and Hannah lived in daily terror that their hiding-place would be discovered.

Jane visited Hannah from time to time and told her that she was still remembered in St. James's Market and that Isaac still professed to be looking for her. There were continual alarms. Someone had called on the Wheelers and told them that they had met Hannah somewhere in the country; someone else professed to have seen her at Wapping. Every Quaker girl who had any pretensions to good looks was suspected of being Hannah Lightfoot, the girl who had disappeared on her wedding day.

She longed for George's visits and while waiting for them occupied herself with working in the house, for she had been brought up to believe it was sinful to be idle. She had her stillroom and her garden, enclosed by a tall wall, and she had her needlework. But it was not really enough.

She longed for a simple country house with a husband who was always with her. Yet she would never love anyone but George. She would tell herself that although her life was not entirely satisfactory she was happier living in this way shut away from the world than she could ever have been with anyone else.

George was a little sad, too. He was very conscious of their position. He was essentially respectable and conventional and wished above all things that they could have been married. They were living in sin, he once said; and it was like a shadow between them. If he had been born someone other than the Prince of Wales, if they could have been respectably married, he would have asked nothing more of life.

He talked of his life at Court to her so that she felt she had lived there herself. Poor George! He was not meant to be a King—and a King he must soon surely be. Being a simple young man, he did not want power or glory; he only wanted to be happy in a respectable conventional way.

But life was not all one hoped for.

She looked forward to Jane's visits. Jane was growing more and more prosperous, for the glass-cutting business was doing well. Mr. Jack Ems had sent customers to her and she had connections with the Court through Miss Elizabeth Chudleigh. It brought good customers and their business was going to prosper as Mr. Betts never could have done.

Jane, seated on a chair, her silk skirt spread around her exuding prosperity and enjoying freedom.

When Hannah went out it must be in a closed carriage; her exercise was taken mainly in the garden; and the great days of her life were when her lover came to see her.

Still, she would not change.

She was in the garden tending the first spring flowers when a servant came to tell her that Jane had arrived. Jane followed the maid into the garden and embraced her friend.

'Thou hast news?' said Hannah, who had never quite learned to drop the Quaker form of address and used it now and then.

Jane nodded.

'Good? Bad? You don't say.'

'I don't know how you'll take it, Hannah. If it were me I'd not care a jot. You're expelled from the Society of Friends. What they call a Testimony of Denial.'

'I know,' said Hannah.

'Now you're not going to mope about that!'

'Oh no, I shall not mope.'

'You've been away from them for a long time now. You're not going to tell me you want to go back to them.'

'Never.'

'There's a great notice about it. It says you've disappeared and they no longer consider you one of them.'

'This means that they will stop searching for me, Jane.'

'I don't think that. They'll go on looking and people will go on talking. But they say you're out ... not one of them any longer. But you won't worry much about that.'

'Oh no.'

'It says something about their being afraid some of your sin will come off on them. That's why you're disowned ... until such a time as from a penitent mind and a true contrition of heart you will confess sorrow for your sins.'

'That I shall never do.'

'No. I thought not. Oh well, here you are and the garden looks pretty and that's a new gown. It's lovely. And you're beautiful Hannah and I'm not surprised there's been all this stir about you. Now, how do you like my new silk.'

Hannah liked it very well and as she smiled and chatted with Jane she was thinking: Cast out. Disowned. And when Jane had left she sat down and thought about the room over the linen-draper's shop and all the kindness Uncle Wheeler had shown to her and her mother when they had had nowhere to go.

George found her a little melancholy.

'You look sad,' he said, 'but so beautiful. I'd like to have a portrait of you just as you look now.'

She tried to throw off her melancholy but she could not and

at length she confessed that she had been cast out by the Society of Friends.

George embraced her, swore eternal devotion and tried to cheer her.

But he too was a little sad, wishing as fervently as she did that they could marry and put an end to this feeling of sinfulness which was constantly between them and their happiness.

* * *

It was a comfort to be able to talk of his affairs with the brother and sister he loved dearly. Edward was only a year younger than he was, and although Elizabeth was three years his junior she had a wisdom which neither of her brothers possessed, for she had read a great deal more than they had, and although shut away from the world in common with her brothers and sisters, reading had given her some knowledge of it.

George loved Elizabeth tenderly; she aroused in him the deepest pity; she was very deformed, one shoulder being higher than the other and she limped painfully so that it was impossible for her to dance or run or even walk very much. She was good-natured and seemed to accept her disabilities philosophically, never complaining. Their mother and Lord Bute seemed scarcely aware of her existence. Poor girl, she would be at the Court for the rest of her life; there would be no marriage for her, so she would be useless as a bargaining counter; she would just be there, evidence of one of the Princess Augusta's less successful examples of child-bearing.

She aroused all the chivalry in George's nature. He told her: 'You and I will be together all our lives. Perhaps it is wrong of me to be glad about that, but I can't help it.'

Whereupon Elizabeth smiled her gentle smile and said: 'You mean, brother, that because I'm deformed and what people kindly call "homely" I shall never be commanded to marry and leave home. I, too, rejoice that I shall never leave you. So you see good cometh out of evil.'

Now it was pleasant to tell these two of his difficulties.

'I am a husband and yet no husband. How I wish I were truly married to Hannah!'

'I'll swear Hannah is very happy to have you at any price she has had to pay,' suggested Elizabeth.

'Shut away in that house! Never knowing when the Quakers will ride up and take her away. What an adventure,' cried Edward.

Elizabeth smiled. 'You speak as though Quakers were the French army, Edward. They are a mild people. They don't believe in taking life. I have been reading about them. In fact, since George and Hannah have been together I have been reading everything I can find about them. The Society of Friends! Don't you think that it is a pleasant way to describe themselves?'

George sat back in his chair, his eyes half closed. The next best thing to being with Hannah was to be with Elizabeth, to know that she followed every phase of his life; that she was always beside him, his very dear friend and sister who would be there until the end of his life.

'I have been reading about George Fox who founded the Society. Oh, he was a great man—the son of a weaver in Leicestershire. "None are true believers but those who have passed from death to life by being born of God," he said. "God does not dwell in temples made by hands, but in human hearts." I think that is a wonderful sentiment. And it's true.'

'Oh yes, it's true,' cried George. 'I should like to be a Quaker.'

'That,' retorted Edward, 'would be quite impossible, for when you are crowned King of England you will have to swear allegiance to the Church of England—the Reformed Faith.'

'It is not so different,' protested George.

'Oh, George, you must not think of it,' said Elizabeth. 'If you told Lord Bute or Mamma that you wished to be a Quaker they would be truly alarmed. You don't know what they would do.'

'What could they do?' demanded Edward.

Elizabeth was silent. She looked at George—dearest of

brothers, kindest of friends—and she was afraid. He was so good, and being simple in his goodness George was inclined to believe that everyone was as good as he was. What were they thinking now of his connection with Hannah? They deplored it, of course. If he had a mistress ... two or three mistresses ... about the Court, if he had behaved like a lusty young man in an immoral society where he, on account of his position could enjoy special privileges, they would have shrugged their shoulders and smiled. But George was not an immoral young man; he was a good young man who had fallen in love and believed it was for ever; he wanted his union sanctified by marriage and that was something these worldly people about him could not understand.

George needed protecting and who was she ... the poor deformed 'homely' member of the family, of no account at all ... who was she to protect the most important one of them all—George who would one day be their King.

'They could not take me from Hannah,' cried George. 'I would never allow that. If they attempted to I ... I would marry her and ... join the Quakers.'

'She is married already to Mr. Axford,' Elizabeth reminded him.

'I heard,' put in Edward, 'that marriages conducted at those marriage mills are not considered legal.'

'That is true now,' agreed Elizabeth, 'but when Hannah married Mr. Axford such marriages were legal.'

'It seems rather ridiculous,' said George, and there was a hint of excitement in his eyes which made Elizabeth apprehensive, 'that what is illegal now was once legal. It is the same thing, yet now it is wrong and then it was right. It seems to me that if it is wrong now it was wrong then.'

'Hannah married Mr. Axford,' said Elizabeth, plucking at the rug which covered her knees. 'And, George, please don't mention to my Lord Bute that you would like to be a Quaker.'

George smiled at her blandly. 'He would listen sympathetically. He is a wonderful friend to me ... the best I have.

Oh, I don't mean better than you two ... but you are my
family. Well, so is he in a way. I think of him that way. But he
is a statesman and a politician. I should be terrified of becoming King but for Lord Bute. But if he is there I know everything will be all right.'

'You will soon learn to govern without relying too much on
one minister,' Elizabeth assured him.

'All kings must have ministers,' put in Edward. 'Our grandfather had Sir Robert Walpole ... though they say our grandmother was the real ruler ... she and Walpole between them.
Grandfather didn't know that, though.'

'Grandfather is an ... objectionable old man,' said George,
remembering the blow he had received at Hampton Court.
'I'm not surprised that Mamma and Lord Bute dislike him so
much.'

'Quarrels ... quarrels,' sighed Elizabeth. 'I wonder why there
always have to be quarrels in this family!'

'Perhaps we are quarrelsome by nature?' suggested Edward.

'George, you must not quarrel with your son when you have
a Prince of Wales. But of course you will not. You will be a
kind King; you will put an end to this silly chain of quarrels.'

'Well,' George reminded them, '*I* didn't quarrel with our
Papa.'

'There,' Elizabeth pointed out. 'Didn't I say that you were
far too good-natured to quarrel with anyone?'

'Of course I was very young ... too young to quarrel perhaps.'

They all laughed and were sober suddenly, thinking of poor
Papa who had died so suddenly and the cruel verses that were
sung about him in the streets, as though he were of no consequence.

Elizabeth was thinking that perhaps he had been of no
consequence. There was still the same King on the throne;
George was nearly eighteen, and at eighteen he would come of
age. Eighteen was old enough to ascend the throne. And even
Mamma had not been rendered exactly desolate by Papa's
death—at least after the first shock had subsided and she had

begun to grasp her new power. And then, of course, there was Lord Bute to comfort her.

Our mother's lover, thought Elizabeth, whom George so reveres because he treats him as a son. George is too trusting, he is unaware of the schemes of ambitious men.

'Well, what are you thinking now?' asked George.

'How glad I am that I shall always be with you ... no one is going to want to marry me. I'm glad. I shall stay at home living close to the King. I shall be your most devoted subject ...'

George's eyes filled with tears.

'I wish,' he said, 'that you two could meet Hannah. You would love her and she would love you.'

'Why do you not have her portrait painted?'

George's eyes lightened with pleasure. 'It's a wonderful idea. I will do it. I will engage the best artist in England. Of course it must be done. How is it, Elizabeth, that you always know what I want before I do myself.'

'I should set about discovering how best it can be done,' suggested Edward.

'And, George,' murmured Elizabeth, 'do remember not to mention to anyone that you would like to be a Quaker. It would never be possible ... and you can never be sure what would come of it.'

'Not even to my Lord Bute? He has asked me to tell him everything ...'

She leaned forward and laying her hand on his arm looked at him earnestly.

'Don't mention it to anyone ... but Edward and myself, George. It could be dangerous. To please me.'

George kissed her forehead tenderly. 'You know I would do anything to please you, little sister.'

'So it's a promise.'

'A promise.'

Elizabeth was relieved. George could always be trusted.

*   *   *

Elizabeth Chudleigh daringly offered to give a ball in

honour of the birthday of the Prince of Wales. 'It was a great occasion,' she said, and one which should call for celebration. So she, who had a very particular fondness for His Highness, would beg the honour of his attendance at her ball.

'Impertinence,' said the Princess Augusta to Lord Bute. 'I have never known a woman so ... so blatant.'

'It would be well for George to attend,' pointed out Bute. 'She knows a great deal about the Lightfoot affair. In fact, she may know more than we do. We must be careful with Miss Chudleigh.'

'What harm can she do? The Prince keeps a mistress in Tottenham. That is going to please rather than shock the people.'

'George is not like other young men. Let us remember that. He is too serious ... too sentimental. We must watch this Lightfoot affair. I had not thought it would go on so long. We must be very careful and I do not think it wise to offend Miss Chudleigh.'

'It seems ridiculous that we must consider this ... maid of honour.'

'She is no ordinary maid of honour, my love. There is much we do not know of Elizabeth Chudleigh, I am sure. And while this is so I believe we should go very carefully with that young woman. What harm can there be in George's going to her ball? In fact, he will have the chance of meeting there some beautiful young women. I should be happy to see him lured from his fair Quakeress.'

'Well, we will raise no objection then, and George shall accept her invitation.'

*   *   *

Life was very amusing, Elizabeth Chudleigh told her mother, and had been more so since the Lightfoot affair.

'Do you know,' she declared, when she visited her at Windsor, 'I do believe Madam Augusta is afraid of offending me.'

'You be careful,' warned her mother. 'The old King could go at any minute. Then where would you be?'

'This isn't the old King's doing, my dear Mamma. It is my own. I helped George to enjoy his little Quaker girl and Mamma Princess knows it. The fascinating point is that she doesn't know how much I know and that is causing herself and her dearest Bute some anxiety.'

'I repeat, be careful.'

'Oh, I shall be careful, never fear ... careful to keep this happy state of affairs just as it is.'

And now the ball. Every lady of fashion should come; it would be a ball worthy of the occasion. A Prince's coming of age—and a Prince of Wales at that.

She asked for an audience with the Prince to thank him for honouring her by accepting the invitation.

He received her in his simple way which she found charming. He was quite unspoilt, this Prince. It remained to be seen how long he would stay like that once he was King and my Lord Bute began teaching him how to govern, for Elizabeth was sure that was Bute's intention. Bute was going to make George what he would call 'a real King'. They would be hearing about the Divine Right of Kings before long if my lord Bute had his way—and Madam Augusta, of course.

Oh well, life was very amusing for Miss Chudleigh and the deeper she was in her intrigues, the more she enjoyed life.

'Your Highness, I am overwhelmed by the honour you do me,' she told him.

He flushed and stammered. 'I ... feel *I* should be overwhelmed. Such a beautiful lady, to go to such trouble to celebrate my birthday.'

'Your Highness's birthday is a day we should all celebrate and there will be many to come and wish you well. You will find some of the loveliest ladies in England at the ball, Your Highness.'

His expression was a little prim. Oh dear, thought Elizabeth, he's still enamoured of the little Quaker.

'How I wish,' she went on quickly, 'that I could invite the most beautiful of them all. I often think of Your Highness's happiness and rejoice in it. I would wish you to know if at any time you need my help...' She paused and added 'again', for there was no harm in reminding him how useful she had once been to him ... 'you should not hesitate to ask me.'

His expression had changed. How easy he was to read! 'I shall never forget your kindness to me at a time ... at a time when I most needed it.'

'I count myself fortunate to have been of service to Your Highness.'

'And I to possess such good friends.'

It was very agreeable. She could be sure that if any fresh contretemps arose she could count on his keeping her informed.

'May I ask a special favour?'

'I beg you to.'

'Will you give her my respects when you next see her. Tell her I think of her often and rejoice in her happiness.'

'I will. I will.' Face flushed with emotion; eyes alight with sentimentality.

So matters have not changed at Tottenham for our little Prince, thought Elizabeth.

*   *   *

That was clear at the ball. There were many young ladies who had come in the highest hope. The Prince was eighteen years old—time he began to amuse himself—and any week now might see him King. Could the old man go on much longer? King's mistress. What an enviable position! And with such a King as George—a simple boy, weak, malleable—great power would be in the hands of his mistress.

All eyes were on him. He was really a very handsome young man. Hanoverian, of course. German to the fingertips, but not as *unpleasantly* German as his forebears. He was very tall for one thing. How different from dapper little George II! And charming, modest. Different in that way too. His eyes were blue and clear; there was nothing debauched about this one; he seemed gentle, eager to be on good terms with everyone.

He danced, not exactly with grace but not unskilfully. His mother and Lord Bute were watchful; and it was not difficult to guess what they were thinking. His indifference to any particular young lady seemed to affect them deeply. Did they want him to take a mistress? Or was there something in that rumour about a woman he kept at Tottenham.

However, one fact was made apparent at Miss Chudleigh's ball: the Prince of Wales was not very interested in young women, and it seemed hardly likely that he would take a mistress at Court.

*   *   *

The King could not ignore his grandson's coming of age and sent for him.

George obeyed the summons reluctantly. Ever since his grandfather had struck him he had not wanted to go near him. The King had forgotten the incident. His temper went as quickly as it arose and as he forgot it he expected everyone else to do the same.

This grandson of his was a bit of a ninny, he was thinking, but after all he was his grandson. The boy would be King one day and it was time he started to learn something about kingship. They should be together more. The Prince of Wales might *not* take after his father; and the King guessed that that mother of his and her lover, that insufferable Scotsman, were trying to poison the boy's mind against him. It was time he put a stop to that, and the best way to do it was to have the young fellow under his roof. They could take walks together; they could discuss affairs together; in fact, he could prime his grandson so that he would be ready to take his place when the time came.

'Well,' the King looked almost benignly at young George, 'so you're of age now.'

'I came of age on the fourth of June, Sire.'

'Yes, yes, well so you did. And you're a man now, eh? Time you broke away from your mother's apron strings.'

'I do not understand, Sire . . .'

'You don't understand much, do you, George? Time you stood on your own. Not a baby any more, you know. Why, when I was your age ... Now listen. I'm going to be generous. I'm going to make you an allowance, £40,000 a year, and you shall have your own apartments in St. James's Palace. How's that.'

'I thank Your Majesty. The income will be most welcome. My mother was saying I should need to enlarge my household now that I am of age. But I am happy where I am ...'

'What do you mean?'

'I ... enjoy being with my mother and my brothers and sisters ...'

'Enjoy! You can come to St. James's and enjoy, boy. You shall have your own apartments here, and I'll have time to see you now and then.'

'Sire ... I have no ...'

'That's all right. No need to splutter your thanks. You can go now.'

'Sire, I wish ...'

'All right. I know. You're grateful, but you're the Prince and these things are expected.' The King had turned away, leaving his grandson to stare helplessly at his back.

*   *   *

'£40,000 a year!' cried Augusta in anger. 'How dare he! Why the Prince of Wales should have £100,000 from the King's income. It is a custom. The government voted the King £800,000, and £100,000 of that was for the Prince of Wales.'

'Worse than that,' pointed out Bute, 'he wants George under his roof. You can guess what that means. He is going to take him away from us.'

'We shall never allow it. We had better send for George.'

'Do you think it would be better if I spoke to him alone?'

Augusta was thoughtful.

'Let us speak to him separately,' suggested Bute, 'and perhaps our arguments will have a double impact. He may be forced to accept the £40,000 a year, but I am convinced that he should never agree to live under the same roof as the King when this means that he is away from us.'

'Let us do this,' said Augusta.

George listened to Bute's account of the schemes of those who were seeking to separate them. They knew that the Prince's only true friends were his mother and Lord Bute, which was why they could not bear for them to live together.

If the Prince really loved his mother, if he had any feeling for Lord Bute, he would decline the King's offer of apartments at St. James's; he would insist on living under the same roof as his mother.

'I see you are right,' agreed George. 'On no account must we be separated.'

'You should, of course, increase your household and should live in the state of a Prince of Wales. You will need a Groom of the Stole. Shall I tell you something? It is a position I covet. If it were mine I should always be near you. We should have opportunities which we have so far lacked. I was wondering how Your Highness felt about granting me this favour.'

'I desire it more than you do. It shall be yours.'

'Unfortunately it will be necessary to get the King's consent.'

'I will ask it.'

'At the same time as you decline his offer of accommodation at St. James's. I fear he will be a little displeased. But before you make any decision consult your mother. We will abide by her decision. I beg of you listen to her. Take her advice. Remember that she—and I—are the only two people here who have your real interest at heart. I beg of you ask her whether she thinks I should have the post of Groom of the Stole. If she feels it would be unwise, think no more of it.'

'My dear friend, I am certain that she will wish it, even as I do.'

'Speak to her and when you have done so, write to the King. That would be better than asking for an audience. Write and tell him that you accept the income—it should be more but this is not the time to ask for it—but that you cannot consider leaving your mother. Then you might suggest that you wish to appoint a Groom of the Stole...'

*　　*　　*

The King raged up and down his apartment.

He'll have a stroke if he doesn't take care, thought Waldegrave.

'This letter from that impudent puppy! I know who has put him up to this. It's that mother of his. Sly-faced cow. And that Scottish stallion. A pox on the pair of them. He will take the money. By God, he will. But he prefers to live with his mother. Baby! Cannot leave Mamma! You know why? Tied to her apron strings, that's why. And Bute has tied the knots. Never trust a Scotsman, Waldegrave. They're the ones to make trouble. All the trouble starts across the Border and this fool of a daughter-in-law of mine has to keep a warm place for one in her bed. Here's a nice state of affairs. I'm flouted in my own Court. He'll take the money but he'll stay with Mamma. By God, he won't. If he stays with Mamma he gets no money from me. If his grandmother were alive...' Sentimental tears in the blazing blue eyes, incongruous when his anger blazed in his purple cheeks and the veins were knotted in that dangerous way at his temples. 'No, I'm glad she's not alive. That's how I feel sometimes, Waldegrave. I'm glad she's not alive to see what an ungrateful puppy she'd have for a grandson. A Prince of Wales! A ninny who can't leave Mamma. And this is the whelp who asks me for £40,000 a year and he'll graciously accept it as long as we don't untie the leading rein Mamma and Mamma's bedfellow have tied about his silly neck. I tell you this, Waldegrave: If he does not come here he'll get no money and that's my word on it.'

Waldegrave waited a few seconds for the worst of the anger to subside a little.

Then he said mildly: 'It may well be that Your Majesty's ministers will think that the allowance is the Prince's due.'

'So my ministers are on his side, eh? My ministers will work for the puppy against me?'

'I can only suggest that this may be so, Your Majesty.'

'We'll see. If my ministers cannot serve me, Waldegrave, they can get out.'

Waldegrave was silent. The King would doubtless have to give way. He must remember how unpopular his own father had become when he quarrelled with his Prince of Wales, George II himself. Did the old King know how unpopular he was and how the people were all waiting for this blue-eyed boy to step up to the throne.

Perhaps he did. Perhaps he gave way to these spasms of rage out of habit. He had always been a man of habit.

'And there's something else, Waldegrave, something which makes me wish I had that puppy here so that I could kick him round this room till he yelped to be let free. There's something else.'

'Your Majesty?'

'He asks a favour for Bute. "Groom of the Stole," he says. "I know of no one who could better fill the role, nor one whom it would please me better to have about me." No, I'm sure he doesn't. Who's put him up to that, do you think? Mamma! Let's have him Groom of the Stole to the Prince as well as Stallion in Chief to the Princess. This is my witless nincompoop of a grandson, Waldegrave.'

'Sire, I doubt not your ministers would decide the Prince should choose the members of his own household.'

'But he has to come to me for the key, eh. He has, in fact, to have my assent. I'll tell you this, Waldegrave, I'd meant this office for you. You've done good service and it was to be your reward.'

'Sire, I shall be happy indeed to retire from the Prince's household.'

'Well, that's what it will mean, Waldegrave, that's what it will mean. He's of age now. No place for a tutor. He's a man at last ... so they tell me. But I fail to see it.'

'Your Majesty, I beg of you have no regrets on my account, for I shall retire from the Prince's household with none.'

'I know well your opinion of the boy.'

'He is not a bad boy, Your Majesty, but by no means bright. He is not ill-natured; he simply cannot apply himself.'

'In other words, he's a fool. Don't mince your words, Waldegrave. He's my grandson, but he takes after his father. Fred was the biggest fool in Christendom and a rogue into the bargain. This young whelp is not that ... yet. But, believe me, that mother of his and her Scot will make him so. Depend upon it. Depend upon it.' The King looked at the watch which was hanging on his coat. 'In five minutes I must call on the Countess of Yarmouth. Never fear, though. I shall have something to say to young George.'

Waldegrave took his leave. Still making love by the clock. Those rages of his were alarming. One of these days ... thought Waldegrave, and surely that day not far distant ... then young George!

Not a very hopeful prospect, thought Waldegrave; but he must be thankful that at last he was free of his duties with the Prince. He had never wanted them; and was delighted to find they were at an end.

Groom of the Stole indeed! Let Bute have it. His own idea was to put as big a distance as possible between himself and that uninteresting young man.

*   *   *

The King was angry. Newcastle and Henry Fox had just left him. He must, they had told him, respect the wishes of the Prince of Wales, and if the young man decided he preferred to live with his mother, then he should do so. The people would not be pleased if the King tried to interfere with his grandson's domestic arrangements.

'And *I* am not pleased that he defies my wishes.'

'Your Majesty will remember your own case, and the feelings of the people. They were with you against your father. They would be with the Prince of Wales now.'

'If he can't be gracious enough to accept my offer of apartments he can forget about his allowance.'

'It is a matter for the government, Your Majesty.'

'A pox on the government!'

Silence for the outburst to subside.

'So I am to have that puppy dictate to me?'

'It would be the wish of the people and Your Majesty's government. The custom is that when the Prince of Wales comes of age his allowance is increased. That sum has been set aside ...'

'So he is to dictate to us, is he?'

'It is the custom, Your Majesty.'

'So be it, then. Give him the money. Let him go his own way. I hear he's an ignorant young fool and knows nothing. I was giving him a chance to learn ... a chance to acquire an understanding of state matters ...'

The ministers were silent. The King faced them, his rage subsiding suddenly; his voice breaking with emotion.

'I thank God his grandmother is not here to see this day.'

*   *   *

The King summoned the Duke of Grafton.

'You're a member of the Prince's household.'

'Yes, Your Majesty.'

'I have something here I wish you to pass on to a man I have no wish to see here.'

Grafton murmured in surprise: 'At Your Majesty's service.'

The King went to a drawer and took out a golden key—the badge of office for the Groom of the Stole.

'The Prince wishes to bestow this on a certain gentle ... on a certain person. It is against my wishes that it should be bestowed on this *person*. But, my ministers inform me, it is for the Prince to choose the officers of his own household, so my wishes in this matter are ignored. Ignored, I say.' His voice rose to a shout; and Grafton lowered his eyes. 'Hey,' went on the King, 'take it, Grafton, and give it to the person for whom the Prince intends it.'

'That is, Your Majesty?'

'Lord Bute. I don't want that Scottish fellow in my presence. My ministers inform me that he is to have the key. Very well, he shall have it, but by God, I'll not give it to him. Here, take it. Give it to him. Tell him it comes to him with my displeasure. I'll tell you this, Grafton, if that Scotsman came within a few inches of my foot I'd be ready to kick him so hard he'd go hurtling back across the Border where he belongs.'

'I will see that the key is delivered, Your Majesty.'

*   *   *

On his way from the Prince's apartments where he had been to congratulate him on the success of their firm stand against the King, Lord Bute met the Duke of Grafton. Grafton was looking rather uneasy as he paused, exchanged a few words and muttered that he had just come from the King.

'And he was in his usual humour by the look of you.'

Grafton lifted his shoulder and slipped something into Bute's pocket.

'Don't be put out,' he said. 'It was ungraciously given but at least it is yours and he could not withhold it.'

'What...' cried Bute putting his hand into his pocket and drawing out the gold key.

'It is yours since you are to be the Prince's Groom of the Stole.'

'But the King...'

'Would not present it to you himself. He asked me to slip it to you.'

'But ... it is an insult.'

'My dear fellow, George is insulting someone every minute of his life. He always has. It's a habit. And you know his habits. Don't take it to heart.'

'Do you mean to say he wouldn't even *see* me to hand me the key?'

'That's it. However, you have the key and that's all that matters.'

'Yes,' said Bute slowly. 'I have the key.'

But it was an insult none the less.

There was another shock ahead of him. Miss Elizabeth Chudleigh was waiting to have a word with him. He was surprised. He wondered why she should wish to see him and for a moment he thought she had come to give him some news of George's Quakeress.

She was a very beautiful woman, Miss Chudleigh—beautiful, bold and brazen. He was certain that she had passed through many adventures, and wondered why she had not married. Not still mourning for Hamilton surely; it was years since he had married the famous beauty Elizabeth Gunning.

'It is good of you to call on me,' said Bute, and she smiled her very bold smile and he wondered whether it held an invitation. He would have to let her know that there was no place in his affection even for such an exciting woman. He could consider no other mistress but the Princess Augusta. 'I am glad that you did. I wanted to congratulate you on the very excellent entertainment you gave for the Prince's birthday. His Highness was delighted and felt it was so good of you to take such pains to please him.'

'It was a glittering occasion, was it not? And how gratified I am that the Prince and you, Lord Bute, enjoyed it. I trust the Princess did also.'

'We were all delighted. I can assure you that.'

'Such a costly entertainment! Ah, my lord, you doubtless would not think so. But I am not as rich as you are.'

'You are a very fortunate young lady to be able to afford such entertainments.'

'That is the trouble, my lord. I can't.'

'That hardly seems so on this magnificent occasion.'

She laughed light-heartedly but there was a steely quality in her flashing eyes. 'Well, my lord, I knew I had good friends.'

'You mean you are in debt?'

She lifted her hands and raised her eyes to the ceiling in mock dismay.

'I am sure the Princess will be displeased. You know that she disapproves of the members of her household becoming involved in financial difficulties.'

'But for the sake of the Prince of Wales...'

'I do not understand you, Miss Chudleigh.'

'We are all concerned for his happiness, I know. I think he is at times a little anxious. He thinks a great deal of his little Quakeress tucked away in Tottenham.'

'I do not think you should talk of such matters, Miss Chudleigh.'

She was smiling at him slyly. She was a woman who could convey a great deal by a look, by a gesture, by the emphasis she put on a word.

'In view of your position in the household, my lord, I felt sure you would agree with me that we should help to make the Prince happy. If this affair of his were brought into the open ... Oh, there are rumours now of a lady of Islington, but people are not sure and there are always rumours; I think for the sake of the Prince we should keep it ... just a rumour.'

Oh God, thought Bute. The woman is blackmailing me. She is a menace. She is going to spread rumours of myself and the Princess. Not that there were not rumours already; but a woman who had lived in the Princess's intimate circle would be able to supply details ... any details she liked to invent and she would be believed. If she whispered to the Prince, that prim young man would be horrified. It seemed incredible that he had no idea of the true relationship between his mother and Bute, but it was the case. And if he knew ... And worse still if the woman started to talk of his affair with the Quaker; if she put out her highly coloured version ... oh, disaster!

She was watching him obliquely.

'I believe that your lordship will wish to help me in this little matter of the Prince's entertainment. I know how fond you are of the Prince ... and the Princess. And His Majesty is so difficult. Oh, not with me ... in fact, the old gentleman is rather fond of me ... If His Majesty heard certain facts ... on which he could rely ... Oh, what an unhappy time for the Prince and, as you and the Princess are so devoted to him, for you also. In view of all that I felt a little entertainment to cheer him up would be welcome ... and I was certain that you would agree with me.'

'How much do you owe?'

'Your lordship really wants to know? Oh, how generous of you.'

'I should warn you, Miss Chudleigh, that in future before you engage yourself in such expense you should first decide whether you can meet it.'

'Oh, Lord Bute. You are an angel! This is a lesson to me, I do assure you.'

Lord Bute was very uneasy. He could not get the memory of that beautiful sly face out of his head.

Visit from a Blindfolded Doctor

THE Prince of Wales was unrecognizable as he slipped out of Leicester House. To some young men adventure like this would have been the spice of life. George hated it. Intrigue, subterfuge, romance that lacked the blessing of the clergy were abhorrent. He believed passionately in love and marriage. One of the things he hoped to do—he had said it to Edward and Elizabeth and to Lord Bute—when he was King was to restore morality to the Court. His grandfather and his great-grandfather had been a disgrace to the family. A King, he knew, set the morals of his Court. That was what he intended to do. And yet here he was, living in sin with his beautiful Quakeress. Of course we are married in the sight of God, he had told her. But those were empty words. God would demand the certificate, the signature, the written evidence that two people had decided to live together in holy matrimony.

Hannah was the wife of Isaac Axford; there was a certificate to proclaim this to the world. If only I had been a linen-draper! sighed the Prince. Or a grocer like Isaac Axford, how happy we might have been!

And yet his future was beginning to excite him. As the carriage jolted on its way to Tottenham he was thinking of conversations with Lord Bute and his mother. They were making him see what an important destiny lay before him. There was great work for him to do, work which no linen-draper or grocer could hope to achieve.

Oh no, how much better if Hannah were a Princess—a German Princess preferably because that would please his mother and he loved her so dearly that he wanted to please her—then he and Hannah could be married and live happily ever after.

The carriage turned in at the private drive. Hannah would be waiting for him as she always was, peeping out from behind the curtains watching as the carriage drove up. Poor Hannah, she never knew when a carriage would turn in this drive or the main one—or perhaps not a carriage ... but some sinister figure would come creeping in ... Isaac Axford, her husband, who had discovered her at last.

It was a life of subterfuge for poor Hannah, shut away from the world, never sure from one moment to another what the day would bring.

He strode into the house. She was standing on the stairs waiting for him. He always felt in those first moments of reunion that everything—all the fears and alarms, all the subterfuge, even the *sin* of all this—was worth while.

She threw herself into his arms.

'Hannah, my little Quakeress...'

She smiled. Quakeress had become a word of endearment between them. She did not look like a Quakeress now. Gone were the sombre grey garments. Her seamstress was constantly engaged on devising new gowns for her. Today she wore one of rich claret-coloured velvet and looked regal, for she had a natural grace.

She is fit to be a Queen, thought George angrily. Why could they not accept her? Why should everyone make life so complicated when it could be simple. If they could marry now they could be completely happy, completely at peace. They could repent their sin in forestalling their marriage vows and live in respectable bliss for the rest of their lives.

What of Mr. Axford? George had temporarily forgotten him. But perhaps he would die. People did die. They caught the smallpox. Almost everyone caught the smallpox. One of Hannah's greatest charms was her clear unblemished skin—so very rare when almost every other woman was pockmarked. If God saw fit to remove Mr. Axford from the scene ... if Hannah were a Princess ... how happy they could be.

'It seems long since we were together,' said George.

'I have waited long for thee.'

George was always moved by the Quaker form of address. It was part of her charm for him; it set her apart from Court beauties like Elizabeth Chudleigh.

'And I have waited too. I have thought of you constantly. My grandfather sent for me because of my birthday.'

'Yes, your birthday ...' She smiled secretly. She had a gift for him. It would be something wrought with her own hands, something he would treasure for always. An embroidered waistcoat perhaps; she was so clever with her needle, but always careful not to prick her fingers. 'Thou woulds't not wish me to be as a sewing-woman in thy mother's palace.' He had laughed and told her that he would not care how she pricked her fingers. When she talked of his mother's palace he was always tenderly amused, for she had no notion of what a Court household was like, and George was not fluent enough to describe it so vividly as to make the picture clear. She doubtless had visions of a Sultan's Palace of the utmost magnificence and the King walking about in a golden crown.

Sometimes he wished he could show her his grandfather in one of his rages, his wig awry, his face scarlet, spitting as he roared and shouted at this ninny or that puppy. A very different picture from Hannah's King, he was sure.

He linked his arm in hers and they went to her rooms on the ground floor. The heavy curtains obscured the windows ... it was a luxurious prison, thought George.

When he kissed her, when they made love, he thought there was something changed about her. He was not sure, for he was neither very sensitive nor observant. But she seemed remote, more ethereal than usual.

It was later that she told him.

'George, we are to have a child.'

His emotions were great but mixed. He would be a father. It was a matter over which any man must rejoice. A child ... his child. How strange! How wonderful! He wanted to tell everyone—his mother, Lord Bute, his brothers and sisters ... even his grandfather. Oh yes, he even wanted to tell his old grandfather. 'You call me a ninny, a baby tied to his mother's apron strings, a puppy—but I'm man enough to be a father.' But how could he tell anyone. This was another secret. No one must know. The birth of the child would have to be kept secret for ever ... Now he was aghast. What had they done? It was all very well to sin oneself and be prepared to take the consequences. But this was involving others ... This was involving a child.

'I see thou art disturbed,' said Hannah.

'It ... it is wonderful ... We are to have a child! But ... I think ...'

'I know. I think, too. This child will be without a name. It will be a bastard.'

'Oh, don't call our child that, Hannah.'

'But it is what the child will be. We must face the truth, George. We cannot hide from truth.'

'We will love this child, we will cherish it ... we will plan for its happiness. It shall be happy as no child ever was before.'

'But in time it will know the truth, George, that we brought it into this world when we had no right to do so. I am a sinful woman and I fear for this child.' She turned to him and her face was radiant. 'Yet I rejoice. I cry "My spirit doth rejoice in God my saviour." I do not know what has happened to me, George. I am steeped in sin and yet I am so happy.'

'We will find a way,' he said. 'Hannah we will find a way of pleasing ... God.'

She looked at him tenderly and shook her head. 'Perhaps I

should go away. Perhaps I should return to my people ... repentant and contrite.'

'Return to Isaac Axford?'

'Oh ... no ... never, never ...'

'That is what they would call repenting. To live with him, to bear his children ...'

'To stand up in the Steeple House, to confess my sin. That I could do ... but return to him ... never.'

George said: 'I shall be King of this country. When I am, I shall know what to do. You must think of nothing but the child. It would be bad for it if you fretted. Remember that. And leave it to me. I will think of what we must do.'

On his way back to Leicester House he could not suppress his excitement.

I am about to be a father. I, George, Prince of Wales!

This would be the most wonderful thing that has ever happened to me if only ...

Recently he had gained confidence. Everyone paid homage to him. His mother listened to him with more attention than she ever had before. Lord Bute was respectful. And even the King could not command him to do what he did not want.

He must not forget that he was the Prince of Wales and that one day he would be King. Kings were meant to govern, so said Lord Bute and he was a very wise and clever man.

Surely it was within the means of a King to discover a way round a situation like the one in which he found himself.

*   *   *

He wanted to talk to someone about it and whom could he trust but his favourite brother and sister.

He called Edward and together they went to Elizabeth's apartment. Poor Elizabeth, it was one of her bad days and she was unable to leave her bed. She looked very wan propped up with pillows, but at least one did not see her deformity in this position.

'I have some news for you,' said George. 'I don't know what you will think of it.'

'Well, let's hear and we'll tell you,' retorted Edward.

'I am going to be a father.'

He looked from one to the other. Edward's mouth had opened in surprise; a faint colour touched Elizabeth's cheeks, making her look almost healthy.

Elizabeth spoke first: 'So Hannah is with child.'

George nodded.

'What are you going to do about it?' asked Edward.

'Do? What can I do?'

'Is Hannah happy?' asked Elizabeth.

'She is both happy and sad. She is happy because she longs for the child and unhappy because of the circumstances.'

'Poor Hannah! And you, George?'

'I wish to God I could marry Hannah.'

'They would never allow it.'

'No. And there is Mr. Axford.'

'It was a marriage mill,' said Elizabeth. 'So perhaps if it were possible it could be proved that the marriage was not legal and that Hannah was free.'

'Oh, do you think that could be.'

'Marriages like that are illegal,' said Edward. 'If you married Hannah, and if this child is a boy it could be a King of England, think of that.'

'Children can be made legitimate, I believe, even if the parents were not married at their birth,' said Elizabeth.

George's blue eyes were shining with purpose. 'I shall not rest,' he said, 'until I have righted this.'

'George,' cried Elizabeth, suddenly fearful, 'will you promise never to do anything ... that might be considered rash ... without first telling me about it.'

George was at his sister's bedside; he took her thin hand and kissed it.

'I swear that I will consult you first.'

She seemed relieved.

'It is most exciting,' said Edward. 'George, I never thought you'd have it in you. When we used to sit in the schoolroom while we cogitated over those ridiculous problems and I copied the answers I used to think Old George will always be the good and respectable member of the family.'

'I always wanted to be good and respectable,' George admitted. 'It is strange how fate seemed to decide against one's own decision and make one what one is not.'

'We always have the chance to go our own way,' Elizabeth reminded him.

'It's true,' put in Edward. 'If you had taken one look into that linen-draper's window and then looked away and forgotten all about the girl you saw there this would not have happened. You would have been cosily married either to one of the Wolfenbüttels of Grandfather's choice or the Saxe-Gothas of our mother's. Perhaps you would have been about to be a father. You see it is in our own hands.'

Elizabeth was watching her elder brother anxiously. But he had promised to let her know before he did anything rash.

* * *

The Prince was not subtle enough to hide his feelings and Elizabeth Chudleigh recognized the change in him and guessed its cause.

'A natural and not unexpected result,' she chuckled. 'What now?'

Whatever it was she decided to have a place in the centre of affairs.

As soon as she had an opportunity of speaking to him alone she told him that she was sure there was something about which she should congratulate him.

He looked startled. 'How ... how did you know?'

'Oh ...' she smiled wisely and with the utmost affection. 'Perhaps it is knowing Your Highness so well, having Your Highness's welfare at heart. I sensed that something of importance has happened.'

The Prince had unconsciously pressed his lips together.

'Your Highness should not imagine that I wish to pry. I only want to tell Your Highness that if at any time you should need my help ...'

'You are very good, Miss Chudleigh. I shall never forget how good.'

'Then if there is anything I can do at any time . . .'

'Oh yes, yes, indeed. I know I can ask you because I know I can trust you.'

As she had guessed, it was not long before he was confiding in her.

Hannah was going to have a child and he naturally wanted the best attention for her. He believed that a lady might help him best in this matter.

He was right about that, Elizabeth assured him. In fact she had some knowledge of these matters. Some of the maids of honour . . . Oh, the Prince must not be too harsh in his judgment of these giddy young girls. They were careless, thoughtless and they found themselves in this kind of trouble. She had helped more than one.

'But how?'

'Taking them away from Court . . . perhaps some servant's house . . . and there taking a doctor to them.'

'I should want this to be very secret.'

'It could be arranged so that even the doctor did not know whom he was attending.'

'But this would have to be a very *qualified* doctor.'

'Naturally. Has Your Highness anyone in mind?'

'Y . . . yes. Dr. Fothergill.'

'The Quaker!'

George nodded.

'Well, it is natural that she should wish for one of her own sect.'

'Being a Quaker he may not consent to . . .'

'Not a bit of it, Your Highness. I know Dr. Fothergill well. He is not a very *stern* Quaker. He will wish to serve Your Highness.'

'But he is not to know.'

'Of course not. I will tell him it is a person in a very high place. I will accompany him in the carriage and when we reach a certain point he must consent to be blindfolded.'

'Blindfolded!'

'It is an old method, Your Highness. Doctors have attended ladies in extraordinary circumstances before. You may safely leave this to me. I will approach Dr. Fothergill. I will tell him his services are needed; and then when the time comes I will take him to Tottenham, but before we reach the house I shall blindfold him, and the bandage will not be taken from his eyes until he is actually in the room with the patient. Then he will do what is necessary, we shall blindfold him again and then ... when we are back in London the bandage will be removed from his eyes. He will be well paid ... paid a little extra, of course, Your Highness ...'

'Of course.'

'And that is an end to the matter. You have had the doctor you wished for; he has delivered the child safely; and he cannot be sure where he has been or whom he has delivered.'

'It sounds very clever.'

'But I do assure Your Highness that it has been done many times before.'

'I shall pass on this information. I am sure it will give great relief. And when the time comes ...'

'When the time comes, you can count on me, Your Highness.'

* * *

So, when Hannah's time came, Elizabeth was there with Dr. Fothergill, the not-too-stern Quaker, who was delighted to act as instructed. Such commissions were always very profitable and he had undertaken them before and he was becoming known throughout the Court for his discretion ... not the least important quality in such a doctor's reputation.

He rode out to Tottenham in the company of that fascinating, mysterious and rather wicked young woman, Miss Chudleigh, allowed himself to be blindfolded at the appropriate moment, and entering a house, the destination of which he could not be sure but could vaguely guess, he delivered a very personable young woman, whom he quickly discovered to be of his faith, of a healthy girl.

'The Butcher's' Disgrace

CUMBERLAND was coming home to England ... in disgrace. The King strode about his compartment, wig on one side, cheeks scarlet with rage.

'Hanover!' he moaned. 'Hanover in the hands of the French! And he calls himself a son of mine. Was ever a father so cursed by his children? I thank God the Queen has not lived to see this day.'

Mr. Pitt had called to see the King. Mr. Pitt, the man who believed that England's glory lay overseas. Here was a pretty state of affairs, a good beginning to Mr. Pitt's grand schemes. Hanover, the home of the Kings of England, the sacred spot, loved by this royal family as St. James's, Windsor, Hampton, Kensington had never been ... and now it was in the hands of the French!

'Mr. Pitt, sir, you find me low ... very low.'

'Your Majesty is grieved by the loss of Hanover, I know.'

'It is the home of my fathers, Mr. Pitt. I was brought up in Hanover. As you know, I have never let long periods of time pass without visiting it.'

'I know it well, Sire.'

'I was happier at Hanover, Sir, than anywhere else in this world.'

'Your Majesty's subjects have been made aware of that fact.'

'And now it is lost ... lost by that fool of a son of mine. Why did I ever put him in charge of my armies...?'

'An old custom, Sire, to keep the plums of office in the family.'

'Eh ... eh, what's that?'

'Not always a wise one as Your Majesty is now perceiving, but is Your Majesty being entirely fair to His Royal Highness?'

The trouble with these geniuses, thought the King, was that they believed they had some prerogative to speak their minds. They gloried in it. They boasted of it. These honest men! The unpleasant truth was that a King could not do without them. Mr. Pitt was such a one.

'The puppy was caught asleep, I heard, at Hastenbecke ... The French surrounded him and he would have been taken but for the prompt action of Colonel Amherst.'

'One of the officers I recommended to Your Majesty, you will remember. Yes, he did good work. The Duke's position was not a happy one at Hastenbecke, Sire, and I dareswear you knew that some compromise would have to be made. Bremen and Verden had to be saved and the troops brought out of danger. It was the loss of the duchies and all those men ... or Hanover.'

'Hanover,' wailed the King. 'It has a special place in my heart, Mr. Pitt. I spent the first years of my marriage there, you will remember.'

Aye, thought Pitt, and courted Madame Walmoden there too, and sent the Queen accounts of your courtship in that delectable spot.

'You will, then, understand my feelings.'

'Indeed yes, Sire.'

'So that is why I can't wait to get my hands on that ... puppy.'

'Sire, Hanover is temporarily lost. It is a small electorate. I believe Your Majesty penned your signature to the orders which were sent to the Duke to sign the convention.'

'I thought the Duke would make a stand.'

'Against orders from home, Sire?'

'The Duke calls himself a soldier, Mr. Pitt. I had not thought he would lose Hanover. I believed that he would have fought to the last man to save Hanover.'

'But, Sire ...'

The King glared at his minister. 'That was my belief, sir.'

Mr. Pitt despaired. What could one do with a man who believed what he wanted to believe, who twisted the facts to suit his own taste. Bremen and Verden had had to be saved at the cost of Hanover ... why did he not admit it? Because he could not face the fact that Hanover was lost, and that he had agreed to its loss. Why? Because he was sentimental about Hanover. Because there he had lived in the first days of his married life, because there he had courted Madame Walmoden.

Pitt despised the little man, but shrugged aside his duplicity. There were more important matters ahead than the assessing of a King's character—which would doubtless prove not worth the trouble.

'It is a small electorate, Sire,' he repeated, 'and there is Canada and America ... needing our attention.'

*　　*　　*

Hanover lost! It was terrible. It was unthinkable. The King wept with emotion, thinking of the Alte Palais where he had lived in his boyhood; the old Leine Schloss where assassins had murdered his mother's lover, the Count of Königsmarck, Herrenhausen where his grandmother had lived for so long and dreamed of becoming Queen of England. In the hands of the French!

I cannot bear to think of it, he mourned.

He had given his consent that it should be signed away. It was like betraying his family. He could imagine Caroline's eyes regarding him sorrowfully. What would she have said could she have been here? He could hear his father's voice cursing him in German.

George II of England who had lost Hanover to the French! He would not admit it ... even here in the seclusion of his own apartments. It was not *he* who had lost it. It was that block-head ... Willie ... who had been Caroline's favourite son. Her Duke of Cumberland whom she had said so many times she wished had been the eldest of the family instead of Fred. They had agreed that Willie would have been the better King. Willie had been brought up in England; he spoke English like an Englishman. He had always wanted to be a soldier. Willie had been their darling as a child. So bright ... so loving. Different from the *canaille* Fred—Caroline had declared. And now William was the one who had sold Hanover to the French. But the fault was William's, for no one was going to blame him, the King.

He had already forgotten that he had agreed with his German Council to save Bremen, Verden and the armies. The English had known nothing of this. None of their business, snorted George. But Mr. Pitt had known. Mr. Pitt was one of those men who were aware of everything.

It was a false step. He saw that now. Willie should have fought. He should have ignored the instructions of the German Council backed by his father.

It was true that after his agreement with the Council the King had had his misgivings and had even drafted a letter to Willie telling him to fight to hold Hanover at all costs.

He rummaged in a drawer and found a draft of the letter. It had never been sent, but its existence seemed to exonerate him, since it was a command to the Duke of Cumberland to fight and hold Hanover.

'I wrote that,' cried the King triumphantly. 'I told him to fight.'

* * *

The Princess Augusta was secretly delighted. 'Hanover lost!' she cried. 'This is Cumberland's doing.'

'It will be interesting to see His Majesty's reactions to Billy the Butcher now,' replied Bubb Dodington who was often in her company and that of Lord Bute.

'This is the son he would like to have seen King,' added Bute.

'Constantly comparing him with Fred,' agreed Bubb. 'I remember Fred could not stand the sight of him.'

'And I don't blame him. The Butcher! He would like to get our George under his wing.'

'And teach him how to be a soldier, I don't doubt,' retorted Bute with a sneer.

'And throw away his kingdom to the French,' put in Augusta.

'It strikes me,' said Bubb, 'that we're well rid of the place. It was constantly draining the exchequer and was not much good to us.' He shrugged and changed the subject. 'The Prince seems to have grown up lately.'

'Grown up!' cried the Princess, alert. 'What do you mean, sir?'

'I thought I detected a change in His Highness. A certain dignity ... which wasn't there before. He seems to carry his head higher ... Pleased with life and yet ...'

'And yet, sir?'

'Well,' said Bubb 'he seems a little preoccupied with his thoughts.'

'George never has any thoughts,' said the Princess sharply. 'At least, if he has any misgivings he would bring them at once to one of us.'

'Then I daresay he has already told you of his ... cares.'

'He confided in us,' said the Princess shortly.

'In everything!' added Bute.

*   *   *

When the Duke of Cumberland arrived at Court he was dumbfounded to find the cold reception which awaited him. He did not expect the welcome of a conquering hero naturally, but he had acted on orders and had obeyed the King's command, although it was contrary to his own inclinations. He was no coward; he had never been one to withdraw from a battle, even when the cause was hopeless. And in this instance he believed there had been a chance.

Baron Munchausen, the Hanoverian Minister in England, was so incensed by the loss of Hanover that he wanted to call a council and have the Duke's behaviour examined. He declared he had copies of the letters he had sent to the Duke. These would show that in surrendering Hanover the Duke had used his own initiative and that there had been no orders from St. James's to do so. But Mr. Pitt—a man who had little friendship for the Duke—was the one to defend him. Hanover was temporarily lost, was Mr. Pitt's reasoning; the Duke had surrendered it on orders from London; there was no point in denying this just to save some people's faces. The deed was done; Hanover was lost; the best way of dealing with the matter was to face up to the truth; and the truth was that the Duke had acted on orders; England had for the time being lost a small electorate of little account; and her prospects on the American continent were promising.

'Bury the past and over its grave build up the future; in that way it will soon be forgotten there is a grave there.'

But Baron Munchausen could only cry: 'But this is Hanover!'

Mr. Fox had known of the Duke of Cumberland's arrival and had come in readiness to greet him. Fox and Pitt were of one mind on this matter. The Duke was being used as a scapegoat and they, being men of honour, were offering him their support. Pitt was against nepotism which he saw as the downfall of the army and therefore of the country, and was firmly opposed to the appointment of a commander because he was a King's son; but Cumberland was a brave soldier, and he was being unfairly treated in this instance, albeit by his own father. Mr. Fox agreed with him in this matter—so Fox was there to support the Duke.

Fox was a politician of brilliance, though he lacked Pitt's eloquence; in fact he was a poor speaker, hesitant and unable to express himself with grace; but he had a sharp mind and was a match for any orator, even Pitt, by his calm reasoning powers. He never attempted to rely on rhetoric; reason was his weapon. He and Pitt admired each other; they were two ambitious men, tremendously envious of each other's success; and Fox was more popular than Pitt, whose affectations irritated many. But they recognized the other's talents and in this affair they stood eye to eye.

The Duke thanked Mr. Fox for being at Kensington to meet him when he was informed of the reason why the minister had come.

'I am well in mind and body,' the Duke told him; 'and I have written orders in my pocket for everything I did. And now, Mr. Fox, you should take your leave as I do not wish it to be said that I have taken the advice of anyone on what I plan to do.'

Fox understood this and retired, but the Duke must have been extremely comforted to know that he had powerful men on his side.

*   *   *

The King hearing that his son was in Kensington Palace became more irascible than usual. He had to see the fellow, the fool who had lost Hanover. But in his heart he knew that the reason why William had not fought to save Hanover was because he had been commanded to give it up. George would not admit it. He could not face the fact that he was the King to have lost Hanover. It had to be someone else's fault. Caroline had always shielded him. She had let him believe that suggestions were his when they were hers or Walpole's. It had been such a comforting way of life. And here he was an old man ... without Caroline—and Hanover lost.

'A plague on them all,' he muttered. He wanted to be young again ... in Hanover, with Caroline his young wife. The happy days, he thought of them, letting memory skilfully paint them in bright colours for him. Caroline ... Caroline ... no woman worthy to ... Amalia Walmoden was a wonderful woman ... his Countess of Yarmouth ... she would offer him some comfort for the loss of his Caroline.

But now there was this fellow ... this Cumberland ... this Willie come home ... in disgrace. 'Yes, sir, disgrace, I say. You lost Hanover ... the home of our fathers ... and you lost it.'

It was the only way he could bear to look at it. Though it

had seemed the only alternative they had had to save Bremen and Verden. They had had to save the army. It was either that or Hanover.

'Yes, yes ... but *I* could not have lost Hanover, Caroline, could I? You would see that. Didn't you always see everything.'

He looked at his watch. He was to go and play cards with the Princess Amelie, his daughter as he always did. If he did not hurry he would be late. Unthinkable. He was never late.

Amelie ... Emily as they called her in the family ... she was getting old now, and she was sour. She had wanted Grafton. It had caused her mother some concern the way Emily had run after Grafton. Perhaps they should have found a husband for her. It was difficult with Princesses ... not much royalty left abroad and it had to be Protestant royalty, which limited the choice. Either that or someone at home. The girls ought to have been given Englishmen. Why not? That would have been better than letting them go unmarried and turn sour like Emily.

She greeted him with a show of affection when he reached her apartments. The cards were ready.

'Come,' he said, 'let us play.'

'We are ready, Father,' Emily replied.

He said quietly: 'Your brother is in the palace.'

'I know, Father.'

'He'll be coming to cards tonight. Don't leave me alone with him.'

'No, Father.'

'It's an order.'

'Yes, Your Majesty.'

The game began and when the Duke of Cumberland came into the room the King did not look up, but he was aware of him, for he muttered: 'Here is my son who has ruined me and disgraced himself.'

The Duke of Cumberland was scarlet with mortification, but he could not approach his father unless given permission to do so and after that remark the King gave no sign that he was aware of him but stolidly went on playing cards. Nor could the

Duke leave the assembly until the King rose and dismissed the company by his departure.

It was eleven o'clock and as soon as the King had left the card-room the Duke went at once to the apartments of the King's mistress, the Countess of Yarmouth.

The Countess was an inoffensive woman whose main purpose was to please the King and keep her position; she made few demands on him and this was why she held her place. She was a little avaricious, but apart from trying to make money by selling honours she had few vices. She therefore received the Duke kindly for she was eager to help him, knowing that he had been unjustly accused.

'Madam,' said the Duke, 'I have come to ask a favour of you.'

'My dear Duke,' she replied, 'you know I will do everything in my power to help you.'

'My father will listen to you. I want you to break this news to him as agreeably as possible that I am resigning my post as Captain-General and the command of my regiment.'

'Oh no, you cannot. It is too much.'

'In the circumstances, Madam, there is nothing else I can do.'

'I pray you don't make this decision so hastily. Give yourself time to think.'

'Begging your pardon, Madam,' he replied, 'I have not come here to ask your advice, though it is kind of you to offer it. I merely wish you to pass on this news to the King in the manner less likely to disturb him.'

'I wish to help ... and since you ask me this ... I can only do it. But I think perhaps you are over hasty.'

'I have been falsely accused, Madam. I have no alternative but to resign.'

'Then there is nothing I can do but obey your wishes.'

*   *   *

The King arrived at his mistress's apartments at the appointed time.

He saw at once that she was distressed and that did not please him. He had come to her for comfort, not to be fretted. He frowned but she said: 'I must tell Your Majesty at once that the Duke of Cumberland has been to see me.'

'The puppy!'

'Sire, he is determined to resign his post. That is what he has asked me to tell you.'

The King's face grew purple. 'This will be a nice scandal. He must be stopped.'

'He seemed determined,' said the Countess, her face puckered with anxiety. 'But Your Majesty has had a trying day. Should you not shelve the matter until you have ... rested.'

The King looked at his watch. He did not intend to spoil this meeting with his mistress.

'The puppy will have to be brought to heel,' he said.

'I am sure Your Majesty will soon have him where you wish him to be.'

This was her most attractive quality: she always made him feel a wise and great man. In fact he felt more comfortable with her than he had with Caroline, although he would not admit that now.

'I'll deal with him,' he said; and shelved the matter as she had hoped he would.

What a soothing, tender creature she was. He was lucky to have found her!

*   *   *

The King wanted no trouble. He demanded that 'secret papers' be brought to him and he feigned to study them. He then announced that he thought better of the Duke of Cumberland than he had, and he believed that there was no need to continue with this farce of a resignation.

But the Duke was determined. He would treat his father with the respect due to a King, for he was a royalist by nature; and having seen the ill effects of quarrels on the royal family's prestige he did not want to add to that.

He had nevertheless made up his mind that he could no

longer take a command in an army in which he was obliged to obey the orders from the Council and his father, and then take the blame when they were unsuccessful.

He had been deeply wounded; he saw only one course of action open to him: resignation; and nothing was going to prevent his taking it.

*   *   *

The Duke of Cumberland had resigned. The hero-villain of Culloden was no longer in command of the army.

His passion in life had been the army and now he was no longer of it. The action of his father had made it impossible for him to retain his position. But this was no family quarrel. The Duke robbed of his position, of his career through the action of his father, continued to pay him the utmost homage in public.

He now turned appealingly to his nephew. He hoped that the Prince of Wales would allow him to bestow on him that affection which he yearned to give.

The Princess and Lord Bute told themselves that they must watch the Duke of Cumberland.

Joshua Reynolds Calls

THE Prince of Wales was very proud of having a daughter and could not resist talking of her to those in the secret.

'How I wish I could see her!' sighed his sister Elizabeth.

'And how I wish you could. Perhaps I could take you one day.'

'Everyone would recognize my poor body if I attempted to call on her.'

'If she met you she would love you as I do.'

'I hope that one day I shall.'

'I see no reason why *I* shouldn't see her,' declared Edward.

The Prince of Wales considered this. 'No ... I suppose not. Hannah might be a little reluctant. She is very retiring.'

'Tell her I would not harm her. I should only love her ... since you do.'

George beamed on his brother and sister with the utmost affection.

'Have you ever thought of having that portrait painted?' asked Elizabeth.

'Who would paint it?'

'Anyone would ... if you asked them.'

'Wouldn't it be dangerous?'

Edward said: 'If one is going to be afraid of danger one will never arrive at anything. It would not be one half as dangerous as abducting a Quakeress at the altar.'

'I ... I scarcely did that.'

'Oh, come, brother, you are too modest.'

'I have seen the work of Joshua Reynolds,' said Elizabeth. 'It is quite miraculous.'

'I do not understand painting much ...' began George.

'Elizabeth is right,' corroborated Edward. 'I have heard it said that he is the greatest living painter. None but the best would be good enough for the Prince of Wales.'

'I should like her portrait to be painted,' mused George.

'Hush,' whispered Edward. 'Here comes our sister Augusta.'

Elizabeth began talking hastily about a piece of embroidery on which she was working. Augusta looked suspicious. A strange subject, she was thinking, for Elizabeth to discuss with her brothers. These three were always together, always seeming to share secrets, and Augusta had been told by her mother to try to discover what George talked about to his favourite sister and brother.

But, of course, they were silent as soon as she appeared. It was always so.

But George had something on his mind. It was obvious that he had some secret. She wondered what. It would be a triumph if she could discover it and report to her mother and Lord Bute. They would be so pleased with her.

George smiled at her absently. He had never greatly cared for his sister who was a year older than he was and apt to be resentful that she had not been born a boy, in which case all the honours which were his would have been hers.

George was thinking: Joshua Reynolds, why not?

*   *   *

A portrait, thought Hannah, as she dressed with the help of her maid. Thou hast become a vain and empty-headed woman Hannah Lightfoot.

She would not think of herself as Hannah Axford, and preferred to regard herself as a single woman rather than as that. She dreamed sometimes that Isaac Axford came to claim her, that he crept into this bedroom while she slept and that she awakened to find him standing over her.

The bedroom was becoming more and more ornate as the years passed. In the early days she had tried to keep it simple, for every now and then her upbringing would assert itself; then she would suffer terrible feelings of guilt and see the gates of hell yawning before her.

Had her marriage to Isaac been a true marriage? Sometimes she liked to think not. On the other hand, sometimes she must believe it was a true marriage when it seemed less shocking for a woman who had been through the marriage ceremony to have a lover, to be a mother, then for one to experience these things who had never been married at all. Then the thought of Isaac as a husband horrified her.

One fact was clear to her: she could never be truly happy. She loved her Prince; he was charming, never failing in his courtesy to her, giving her the respect he would have given to his Queen—yet the load of sin was on her, and she could never shift it.

And now a portrait.

She could imagine her uncle's stern face if he knew. To dress herself in satin, to sit *idly* while her face was reproduced on canvas. What vanity. What sin.

But my sins are so many, she thought. What is a little vanity added to them?

In her nursery lay her daughter—her idolized child. Born in sin, she thought. What will become of her? But all must go well with her, for was she not the daughter of the Prince of Wales?

She had a suspicion that she was again pregnant. She had not told the Prince yet. She understood him so well and he was so good that their sin worried him as much as it did her, although he was not a Quaker and had lived his life at a Court which in Quaker circles was another name for debauchery.

What a beautiful gown this was! She thought of the day the seamstress had brought in the material and how it cascaded over the table in the sewing-room ... yards and yards of thick white satin.

'Oh, Madam, this will become you more than any of your gowns.' And the woman had held it up to her and draped it round her and Hannah had swayed before the mirror, holding the stuff to her as though it were a partner in a dance. Then she had caught sight of her flushed face in the long mirror. Even such a mirror would have been considered sinful in her uncle's home. And she though: What have I come to?

But even so, she could not help being excited by the white satin and when the sewing-woman had made those enchanting blue bows with which to adorn it she had expressed her delight.

And now she was going to be painted in this gown by a great painter.

Her maid had slipped the white satin gown over her head and stood back to admire.

'Oh, Madam, this is truly beautiful. The most beautiful of all your gowns.'

Hannah's gaze returned to the mirror. I am always looking in mirrors, she told herself. Yet she could not look away.

She had changed since the child's arrival; the hunted look was less apparent in her beautiful dark eyes. She was more serene. Odd, she thought, for the sin is greater now. I have passed on the sin to an innocent being and that my own child.

'You like this dress?' she said to the maid. She must remember not to use the Quaker thee and thou which slipped out now and then.

'Oh, Madam, it is a miracle of a dress. But it needs a beautiful lady to show it off ... and you are that.'

'Thank you.' She smiled gently. Yes, she thought. I am glad I am beautiful. And if I were meant to live humbly all my days in a linen-draper's shop, why was 1 made beautiful?

It sounded like one of Jane's arguments.

'Tell them to let me know,' she said, 'immediately Mr. Reynolds arrives.'

*   *   *

The painter's carriage turned in at the private drive which led to the back of the house and was completely secluded. This was the drive George used when he came.

Some secret woman, mused Mr. Reynolds, but he was not very interested in whose mistress this was, only whether she would be a good subject. He supposed she would have beauty of a kind, but he did not seek a conventional beauty. Nor did he wish to turn some woman, plain in the flesh, into a canvas beauty, which was often the expectation. He hoped for a subject who had something to offer, something on which his genius could get to work, so that he might reproduce her as a Reynolds portrait which would be apart from all other portraits which might be painted of her.

He was here because of the notorious Elizabeth Chudleigh. From what he could discover she was involved in almost every Court scandal, while she took care to keep her own past—which he suspected must be lurid—well hidden.

Not that he was interested in Court intrigues but he was interested in Miss Chudleigh. He had a special reason for this. As soon as he had seen her he had recognized her as a perfect subject for his art. There was a great deal more in Miss Chudleigh than met the eyes, and the artist in him itched to get something of that on canvas.

It must have been eighteen or nineteen years ago when he had first met her. He was visiting his native Devonshire and Miss Chudleigh would have been sixteen or seventeen at the time. To all she must have appeared as a ravishing beauty; to Joshua Reynolds she was a girl he must paint.

He soon made the acquaintance of Miss Chudleigh and asked her permission to paint the portrait. Miss Chudleigh's permission was very readily obtained and during sittings he learned something of her background. She was the daughter of a Colonel and Mrs. Chudleigh, she told him. 'Papa was an

aristocrat ... but a penniless one. Mamma was not an aristocrat but she had all the spirit. He was Lieutenant-Governor of
Chelsea Hospital and I was born there.'

He liked his subjects to talk; it brought out their character.
He liked to watch the emotions flit across their faces as they
discussed this or that incident from the past. It told him so
much that he wanted to bring out in the portrait.

'Papa married for love ... an extremely foolish and incon-
siderate thing to do—in the eyes of his relations.'

'They disowned him?'

'Not exactly. I believe if we could get back to London we
might find ... friends.'

If we could get back to London! This girl had been obsessed
by the idea of getting back to London. She had been like a
tigress in a cage, pacing up and down ... imprisoned by the
green fields and winding lanes, longing for the freedom of the
London jungle.

'Why did you come to Devonshire?'

'It was all we could do. Papa died. He was rather fond of ...
strong waters ... rather too fond. It was bad for his heart ... his
liver ... I forget which ... in any case it was bad. I was too
young to remember him ... but I remember London. I remember riding with my parents through the streets. The City ...
the sedans, the carriages, the fine ladies in their carriages and
masks ... I particularly remember the masks ... and the gentlemen with their elegant snuff-boxes and quizzing glasses. I was
young when we came here but I wept and wept for the ladies
and the gentlemen and the snuff-boxes and the quizzing
glasses, and the noise and mud of the streets. And it is where I
must be sooner or later for I do assure you, Mr. Reynolds, the
country is no place for me.'

He had nodded encouragingly. What a wonderful sitter! He
would never forget her. How could he when that picture had
meant so much to them both.

'No one would help us ... My mother was without the means
to stay in London. It is cheaper to live in the country ... and
rightly so, for who would live in the country from choice?'

He smiled, remembering that his friend Dr. Johnson had expressed the same sentiments often enough. 'Sir, the man who is tired of London is tired of life.' There was a world of difference between Miss Chudleigh and the venerable doctor, but at least they thought alike on this point.

'We have an income of two pounds a week. Country folk think that a fortune, Mr. Reynolds. We are ladies here. But how could we live in London in befitting manner on two pounds a week?'

There were many living on far less, he might have reminded her, but he understood Miss Chudleigh's viewpoint perfectly. When she came to London she would live in Court circles; she would make a stir in her surroundings. Of course she would. Miss Chudleigh was the girl to make a stir wherever she might be.

He had proceeded with Miss Chudleigh's picture and each day he looked forward to those sittings; as he painted he listened to her colourful conversation—her scorns and hatred, her desires and ambitions. They were all there in the portrait for anyone who had the discernment to recognize them.

When the portrait was finished he was almost satisfied with it; she was entirely so.

'One of us, Mr. Reynolds,' she observed, 'is very clever. Or perhaps it is both of us—you for painting this picture and myself for giving you such an opportunity to show your talents.'

He was amused. It was one of the best pictures he had painted to that date.

'I want to exhibit it in London.'

Her smile was dazzling.

'My dear Mr. Reynolds, it is exactly what I hoped you would do.'

And he had; and it had been acclaimed. His name was made. Everyone wanted their portrait painted by Joshua Reynolds. Moreover, everyone wanted to know who was the outstandingly lovely subject of the portrait.

'Miss Elizabeth Chudleigh of Devonshire,' he told them; and he wrote to her.

'Your picture has created tremendous interest here in London. I think there are many who would be delighted to see the original.'

Elizabeth needed no more than that. She and her mother packed their bags and within a short time Elizabeth was in London; it was the starting-point of her extraordinary career, for she was an immediate success. Several men wanted to marry her; she selected the Duke of Hamilton as the most agreeable suitor; that romance went wrong; but Elizabeth was launched and soon had a post of maid of honour in the household of the Princess of Wales.

What had happened since then, why she had not married, was her own secret affair.

But Joshua Reynolds could imagine that it would be a startling story if it ever came to light.

And now she had been instrumental in bringing him to this strange house.

'Mr. Reynolds, sir. Will you step this way.'

A pleasant house, comfortable, luxurious even, just the sort of house in which a wealthy nobleman would set up his cherished mistress.

He was ushered into a room, a room with a high vaulted ceiling and big windows, heavily curtained he noticed. We shall have to let in the light, was his first thought.

And she was rising to greet him. Tall, beautiful, dressed in white satin adorned with blue bows.

Charming! he thought. Beautiful ... and certainly not conventionally so.

He approached her and bowed; his artist's eye took in the oval face, the large dark eyes—some brooding secret there. The dark hair was drawn back from a somewhat high brow and she wore a cap; her dress was low cut but there was a vest of fine lace which covered her neck and ended in a frill under her chin.

Mrs. Axford, he thought. Who is Mrs. Axford?

He could not recall ever having heard the name; but that was unimportant. He knew now that he wanted to paint her.

*   *   *

Hannah looked forward to the visits of Mr. Reynolds. On those days when he came she would awake with a pleasurable feeling of anticipation. It was always a joy to slip into the white satin dress and she could never resist studying her reflection in the mirror and comparing it with the portrait which was rapidly growing on the canvas.

Did she really look as Mr. Reynolds saw her? She hoped so, for the effect was pleasing. She had not wanted George to see it until the portrait was completed and she was longing to show him the finished picture—yet she would be sorry, for that would be the end of the artist's visits.

She was stimulated and perhaps a little apprehensive during sittings. Although that was not what he desired. He was always begging her to be relaxed, to imagine she was chatting with an old friend ... about herself.

An old friend. She thought of chatting to Aunt Lydia or her mother. Her mother! She could never think of her mother without feelings of unbearable guilt. What a wicked daughter she had been! She pictured them now, praying for her in the dining-room where they had prayed incessantly, before all meals, first thing in the morning, last thing before going to bed.

'Save Hannah from her wickedness. Let her repent, O Lord.'

Little Hannah would be lisping her prayers now and so would baby Anne; and she had heard from Jane that there was another baby boy named John.

Mr. Reynolds said: 'Now you are looking too sad. We do not want sadness in the portrait, do we? At least not much. Just a little ... but that is something we cannot avoid. But you are not sad all the time, Mrs. Axford?'

'Oh no. I am very happy ... sometimes.'

'When memories don't intrude?'

She was silent and he looked up from the canvas intently.

'Now, Mrs. Axford, hands in lap. Have you lived long in this house?'

'N ... no. About five years ...'

She would have been just past twenty when she came here. Who was the lover? Some nobleman. She was not of the Court, he knew that.

'It is a pleasant place and not too far from London.'

'No ... not too far.'

'I'll warrant you visit the capital often, Mrs. Axford.'

'No ... rarely.'

'That is strange. Most ladies cannot resist it. There is so much of interest. The theatre for one thing, do you like the theatre?'

'I do not know. I have never visited a theatre.'

He was silent. He could not place her. There was an air of serenity about her, an air of refinement. Who was she? Who was her lover? It was necessary for him to know if he were going to paint her as he wished to. But was it? Why should he not paint her with her air of mystery, for that was how he saw her.

'We will rest awhile, Mrs. Axford. Come and see what you think of the progress.'

She came and stood beside him.

'Thou art a very clever artist,' she said.

He was quick to notice the form of address. A Quakeress, he thought. Of course! Why did I not realize it before? From then on he began to think of her as the beautiful and mysterious Quakeress.

*   *   *

He could not tempt her to speak of herself when she so clearly did not wish to do so. Instead he found himself talking of his own life.

She was very interested and as he talked she became animated. She was living the scenes he described as surely as though she had been present when they had happened; it brought a new animation to her face.

He told her about his home at Plympton Earl in Devonshire. He talked of the beauties of Devon, the coast, the wooded hills and the rich red earth ... all exciting in the artistic eyes.

'But it was always portraits which fascinated me ... *people.* Landscape is exciting but people are *alive* ... They present one face to the world, but there is another which is perhaps truly themselves. One other? There are a thousand. A thousand different people in that one body. Think of that, Mrs. Axford.'

'Are we all so complex, then?'

'Every one of us. Yourself, for instance; you are not solely the charming hostess to a painter, are you. You are many things beside.'

'Yes, I see. I am good and I am wicked. I'm a truthful and I lie. My life is beautiful and hideous...'

'And you live here in this comfortable house, a lady of fashion...'

'Never that. How could I be when I don't...'

He waited hopefully, but she merely added: 'Never a lady of fashion.'

'Yet not a Quakeress?'

'Why did you say that?'

'You were once a Quakeress, were you not?'

'Yes. I betrayed it?'

'Don't forget I am an artist. I try to discover all I can about a sitter so that I can see her not only as the world sees her but as she really is. You look alarmed. There is no need. I am sure that I should never see anything of you, Mrs. Axford, that was not admirable.'

'You flatter me.'

'I never flatter. That is not the way to produce great art.'

She fell silent and to bring back her serenity he talked about himself.

'I always knew I wanted to be an artist. My father was a clergyman. He was master of the grammar school too. I had a religious upbringing.'

Her eyes glowed with understanding. He pictured the austere Quaker household. Poor girl, she must find it difficult to escape from such an upbringing. And what courage she must have, what a deep love she must have felt, to have risked eternal damnation—for that would be what she would have been led to expect—by setting up house with a lover.

'But I wanted to paint,' he went on, 'and at last my father understood there was no stopping me. So he sent me to London and apprenticed me there to Thomas Hudson. He was a Devon man settled in London.'

'And you learned to paint?'

'I learned to paint and I was happy. And when I had served my apprenticeship and thought myself a fully fledged portrait painter I came back to Devon, settled at Plymouth Dock and started to paint portraits. But it was no use. I had to return to London. It is the only place for a man of ambition.'

'Thou wert ambitious.'

She was interested in his progress and had not noticed that once more she had slipped into the Quaker form of address. He found it charming on her lips. How I wish I were painting her in Quaker gown and bonnet. She does not need white satin and blue bows, with beauty such as hers.

'I was ambitious, so back to London I came, where Thomas Hudson introduced me to many artists. I joined their club ... the Artists Club. It meets at Old Slaughter's in St. Martin's Lane. You know the place?'

'I saw it often when I used to go ...'

He waited. 'So you lived near there?'

'Yes, I lived near.' She was shut up again. He wondered where the nobleman had found his little Quaker girl.

'It was my painting of Captain Keppel which brought me many commissions. Then I went to Italy. All artists must go to Italy. Have you even been, Mrs. Axford?'

She had never left England, she told him.

'Ah, you would love Italy. Perhaps Mr. ... Mr. Axford will take you one day?'

A faint shiver touched her, and he was aware of it. It was no use trying to make her talk; he must rouse the animation he wanted to see in her by talking of his own life. So he talked of

Minorca, Rome, Florence, Venice ... and she was enchanted by his description of these places. He described with the artist's eye ... in colours, and she seemed to understand. Then he told her of his friends, Dr. Johnson, Oliver Goldsmith, the actor Garrick.

'There is not much support for the arts from the royal family. Let us hope young George will have a little more artistic sense and responsibility than his grandfather when his time comes.'

'I ... I think he will.'

'They say he is not very bright, and, of course, Bute and the Princess have him in leading strings.'

'Is that what they say?'

'And it happens to be true. I have friends at Court. Oh well, they tell me he needs these leading reins. He's only a boy ... simply brought up ... in fact, a simpleton. I wish they would teach him a little about art. I suppose they think that an unnecessary part of life. They're wrong, Mrs. Axford. A nation's art and literature are a nation's strength. We need a monarch who understands this. I wish I could have a talk with the young Prince. The King is too old now, but I had heard that he had a great contempt for poetry. Poor man. I pity him. Let us hope the new King will be different. For his own sake I hope so. Being a King is something more than marrying and producing children. I dareswear they'll be marrying young George off soon. He's of age. Time he had a wife.'

She was sitting very still and it was as though all the life was drained from her.

She was a woman of moods, he decided. And he wondered whether he had succeeded in getting what he wanted.

When he finished the picture he called it 'Mrs. Axford, the fair Quakeress.'

He received his fee through the ubiquitous Miss Chudleigh; and after a while he ceased to ponder on the strangeness of the mysterious Quakeress.

Rule Britannia

HANNAH had presented George with a son. He shared her delight and her fears. 'If we were only married,' he said, 'I would be the happiest man alive.'

And she the happiest of women, she told him. But perhaps she did not deserve happiness. She thought often of her mother and the sorrow she had caused her; her uncle, too, but particularly her mother. She wondered if they still searched for her, mourned for her, prayed for her.

Dr. Fothergill, blindfolded as before, had delivered the child; but she was not so well after this second confinement as the first; and when she was less well she was apt to brood more on her sins.

George had been delighted with the picture. He told her that Joshua Reynolds was the most fashionable painter in London and people of the Court were clamouring to have him paint their portraits.

'I doubt he will ever paint a picture so charming as that of the fair Quakeress,' said George gallantly.

She had two children, and visits from a lover whose affection never wavered; she could have been completely happy if their union had had the blessing of the Church.

It would be all I asked, she told herself.

*　　*　　*

George had to curtail his visits, for there was business to keep him occupied. Lord Bute scarcely let him out of his sight.

'The King cannot last much longer,' he told George. 'Oh, my Prince, I want you to be ready when the time comes.'

'I shall be, if you are beside me. Without you I should fail. I often think of what a dreadful situation I should be in if I ever had to reign without your assistance.'

Bute was delighted with such reiterated trust. It was worth the tremendous effort he had put into engendering it.

Pitt was the man of the moment. Bute pointed this out to George. The man was a giant. They had to remember that, and although they would relegate him to a minor position— Bute was determined to lead the government, that being the ultimate goal—they would continue to use Pitt.

'Oh yes, we will use him,' agreed George.

He was beginning to look forward to power. It would be pleasant never to have to suffer the humiliation of visits such as that one to Hampton which so rankled in his mind. He would be the King, and when he was no one would dare behave towards him as his grandfather had.

Great events were afoot. Mr. Pitt was a brilliant war leader and under him England was going to be the leading country of the world. Mr. Pitt believed it; and he was a man who always achieved his end.

But he was a just man and he was thundering in Parliament now over the execution of Admiral Byng for which shortly before the people had been clamouring; but now the deed was done they were mourning for him, calling his execution murder.

'You perceive the unreliability of the mob,' said Bute.

'Hosanna, Hosanna ... and shortly after crucify him,' said George.

Bute smiled with approval. George was beginning to think for himself.

'It is always difficult to do what the people want,' went on

Bute, 'for their wants are rarely constant. Mr. Pitt rails against the injustice.'

'He is a good man, Mr. Pitt. I remember how he defended my uncle Cumberland for being unjustly accused over Hanover. He was no friend of my uncle—and I doubt he was of Mr. Byng's.'

George was sad thinking of Mr. Byng. Death and suffering always depressed him. He told Bute so.

'I do not like thinking of it,' he said. 'It makes me feel very uneasy and in fact ... quite ill. I think of Mr. Byng facing his execution. They told me how it happened. He was unafraid and he said he would not allow them to bandage his eyes. He would look right into the face of those men who had been commanded to shoot him. And then he was told that those who had been commanded to the task—for which they had no stomach—would be reluctant to do their duty while he looked on at them, so he answered: "If it will frighten them, let it be done. They would not frighten me." So then his eyes were bound and they fired and killed him. I dreamed of him sinking to the ground ... in his own blood.'

'You should not allow yourself such morbid thoughts.'

'He was my grandfather's subject. He might have been mine had he lived longer or my grandfather died ere this. I do not think I should have agreed to his execution. I hate death.'

'It does Your Highness credit. But admirals cannot be accused of cowardice.'

'Was he a coward? Was he in truth obeying orders from home ... as my uncle Cumberland was. Is he the scapegoat as my uncle was?'

'I can see,' said Lord Bute, 'that you have been studying these affairs with the greatest interest. You are following your mother's advice, which is to be a King. Look at this letter which I have written to Mr. Pitt and tell me what you think of it. From now on, you and I should have no secrets from each other.'

George felt the flush stain his cheeks. He was thinking of the house in Tottenham, the two children Hannah had given him.

What would his dear friend say if he knew that his Prince was a father?

Bute was aware of the Prince's confusion and guessed that it had something to do with the Quakeress. It was time that affair was finished. When they had him married, which would be soon, he would have to desert his Quakeress, for it was difficult to imagine George with a wife and a mistress. At the time of his marriage, at any rate, he must stop seeing the woman. Was this the time to warn him? Perhaps not. Bute was a little displeased about the Quakeress, for George had not confided in him, preferring to do so in that Chudleigh woman. Oh, what a fool he was! The idea of betraying himself to a woman like that and keeping his affairs secret from Lord Bute and his mother.

No, this was not the time. It would only make him withdraw further. But they must keep him busy, give him little time to spare for his Quakeress.

He thrust the letter he had written into George's hands.

'Oh, my dear friend, Mr. Pitt, what dreadful auspices we begin with. And yet, thank God I see you in office. If ever the wreck of this crown can be preserved to our amiable young Prince, it will be to your efforts, my dear Pitt, that he must owe it. I have the greatest confidence that you will rise above all adversity, my dearest friend.

Most affectionately, Bute.'

'Wreck of a crown . . .' repeated the Prince.

'These affairs do us no good, Your Highness. Cumberland's disaster . . . Byng's . . . We are low . . . low . . . low. But I have an idea that we shall soon begin to see changes.'

'And it will be due to Mr. Pitt.'

'Mr. Pitt is a clever man. But he is a commoner. The Great Commoner he may be, but a commoner none the less. He needs guidance . . . our guidance, but he is a great man for all that, and there is no harm in letting him know that we appreciate him.'

'Your letter will tell him that.'

'In a few days time I intend to put a suggestion to him ... with Your Highness's consent, of course.'

'What is that.'

'I am going to ask him to give me Newcastle's place when the King dies.'

'That is First Lord of the Treasury!'

'And Your Highness does not think me capable of holding such a high post?'

'On the contrary, I think no one will do it such honour.'

'None could do it much less than Newcastle has done.'

'You must have it, my dear friend. Nothing will satisfy me than that you have it.'

Bute clasped George's hand and shook it warmly. 'I knew I could count on Your Highness's support. First he shall receive this letter. We will give him a chance to consider it ... then I shall take an opportunity of seeing him and getting a promise from him.'

'I shall feel so contented if you do, for then I shall know that you will be with me when I mount the throne.'

Let that day be soon, prayed Lord Bute, for when it comes I shall be ruler of this land.

*   *   *

Mr. Pitt was no respecter of persons. Although he was almost servile in the presence of the King and the Prince he made no effort to please anyone else.

Bute! Who was Bute? A man who owed his position to the favour he found in the Princess Dowager's bedchamber. Unfortunately that gave him easy access to the Prince of Wales, a boy ... who knew nothing of affairs. If the Prince thought he was going to govern Mr. Pitt he was mistaken.

Bute was ingratiating.

'I have watched with growing admiration, sir, your work in the government. England has need of men such as you at this time.'

The hawk's eyes looked down the long aquiline nose and

Mr. Pitt's hand lightly touched his tie wig. His expression was very haughty.

'You know, sir, of the Prince's regard for me,' went on Bute. 'I have his word on this. When he should attain the throne he wishes me to have Newcastle's place.'

The eyebrows shot up. 'That, my lord, would not be possible.'

'Not possible! How so ... if it were the King's wish?'

'You lack the experience.'

'Experience is something one gains in office. I have watched affairs...'

'Watching is not enough, my lord. Moreover, you are a *Scottish* Peer. Long residence here in the South has allowed this to slip your mind.'

Lord Bute was angry. He said: 'I suppose you would consider the *King's* command must be obeyed.'

'That might be so.'

'So if I tell you that the Prince has given his approval, what then?'

'My lord, I would never bear the touch of command. If I were dictated to, I should resign. So, my lord, I could not give you the post you ask for and if you were to receive it, it would not be my place to give it to you, for the fact of your receiving it could only mean that you would not have it from my hands.'

Lord Bute was furious, Mr. Pitt determined. The perfect actor—as he was on most occasions and never more than in circumstances such as this—he swept off the stage; dignified as ever, holding the advantage because, vain as he was, delighting in pomp and ostentation, he was a man of honour and would never allow his personal promotion to interfere with his principles.

But Bute was his enemy from then on.

He sought the Prince and told him that on the day he became King he would have to find a way of ridding the government of that arrogant Pitt.

*   *   *

Pitt was triumphant. He had persuaded the King that it was to the country's interest to provide Frederick the Great with a subsidy that he might fight England's battles in Europe.

'We have a small island, Sire, a small population; we need an Empire. Let Frederick take care of our commitments in Europe and we will turn the Frenchman out of Canada and India. These territories will be of more use to us than anything in Europe which is too costly to hold and will never be worth the money and effort we spend on it.'

The King was loth to send money to Frederick, but he saw Mr. Pitt's point; and he was with him.

So very soon was the country.

The tide was turning. Victory was in the air. Clive was going ahead in India. Amherst and Wolfe were doing well in Canada.

This was Mr. Pitt's plan and it was working. Englishmen were proud of their country. In the streets they were singing Dr. Arne's *Rule Britannia*. Men congregated in the taverns to talk of great victories and Britain's growing power beyond the seas.

In a few years the position had changed. England was no longer fighting hopeless wars on the Continent of Europe; it was building an Empire. This little island was on the way to becoming the greatest world power.

It was a great year. God save the King ... and Mr. Pitt. Britannia was preparing to Rule the Waves.

The Secret Wedding

IN the drawing-room in which Mr. Reynolds had painted her picture Hannah sat sewing. She no longer embroidered—a pastime she had learned from the sewing-woman, for in Mr. Wheeler's house she had never wasted her time in such a frivolous occupation. But how she had enjoyed it once she had learned! She would sit for long hours, her ears alert for the sound of carriage wheels which would announce her lover's arrival, while her needle plied the cambric, and the reds and blues, the purples and whites grew under her hands. Now she was making clothes for her children. She had a family of two and another was on the way. She had become a fertile woman; she loved her children, but more than anyone on earth she loved the Prince.

Perhaps she had built up this love through her great need of it. She needed more than physical contact, more than constant declarations of loyalty and enduring affection; she needed to prove to herself that love such as she had could not be denied. It was her only excuse.

She spent long hours on her knees. 'Oh God, show me how I can expiate my great sin. I will do anything, Thou knowest ... save one thing. I will never abandon him until he abandons me. And if he does abandon me I shall go forth into the world uncomplaining. I have loved deeply; I have been loved and my love has been fruitful. If my children are cared for, if he, my love, is happy, I would willingly sacrifice my hopes of earthly joy.'

Was it true? Vehemently she assured herself that it was; but equally vehemently she trusted she would never be called upon to prove it. Yet, she could not rid herself of her early training. She did not believe she could go on living comfortably as she had for the last five years. Reckoning would come.

'The sins ye do by two and two, ye pay for one by one.' She could hear Uncle Wheeler's voice droning on in the room behind the shop where they had eaten and prayed. She could feel the roughness of the rush mat on her knees; she could see the faces of the family, palms together, eyes closed, as the candlelight flickered across their faces.

'Vengeance is mine,' saith the Lord. Uncle Wheeler had always pronounced such utterances with particular relish.

Love, forgiveness, were words scarcely heard in the Wheeler household. She remembered that now.

Why was she morbid today? Because she was with child again? Because George's visits were less frequent than they used to be? She must be reasonable. He was a Prince ... a Prince of Wales and had now come of age. At any time he might be King. Naturally he was kept busy. There was so much to learn, he had told her.

She remembered that once he had mentioned these matters with regret; now he did so with excitement. George was changing. Was that what frightened her? George was no longer a shy boy; he was fast learning to become a ruler; and he had recognized it as his destiny. He no longer wished that he were not the heir to the throne. He was waiting ... almost impatiently for the crown.

In one clear flash of understanding she saw the position clearly: George had changed and she had not.

A light scratching on the door. 'Come in.'

'A visitor, M'am. Your lady friend.'

It showed how few visitors she had when Jane could be so introduced. My lady friend, thought Hannah. She might have said your only lady friend.

Jane was growing plump. She was a mother now and undoubtedly the head of her household. Hannah wondered how often she reminded her husband that he owed his good fortune to her astuteness in helping to pass Hannah Lightfoot over to a very important young gentleman.

She enjoyed Jane's visits—the one link with the old days. When Jane sat sprawled in a chair, her fingers reaching for the dish of sweetmeats which Hannah always ordered to be placed beside her, Hannah could almost believe they were back in the bedroom over the shop, talking together while they looked down on the Market.

'I've brought you news ... such news,' announced Jane. 'I wonder what it means. I've been wondering since I heard.'

'I pray thee tell me.' She slipped naturally into the old way of speech with Jane.

'It's Isaac Axford.'

Hannah sat up gripping the arms of her chair; she felt the child moving within her, as though uneasily.

'What ... of him?'

'Don't look so scared. It's good news really. It means he's given up the search.'

'Jane, I pray thee tell me. Do not keep me in suspense. I believe you enjoy that.'

Jane smiled. 'He's married again.'

'Isaac ... married! But how can that be? He is married to me.'

'It's five ... nearly six years since that marriage, Hannah. It's clear he thinks it is a marriage no longer.'

'Art thou sure of this?'

'You don't think I'd come here with a tale like this if I wasn't. I've even talked to her ... the wife I mean. I went into the shop when Isaac wasn't there and had quite a talk with her ... she's pleased with herself. Bartlett her name was ... before she changed it to Axford. Then I talked around ... you know how easy it is. But you don't, of course, but believe me it is for me. One goody to another. All master's wives together. Oh yes, I heard Isaac Axford's done well for himself. He's married an heiress ... Miss Bartlett she were, and she's bringing him in all of one hundred and fifty pounds a year. Very well-to-do she is and not proud with it.'

'But he is not truly married ...'

'Oh come, now, you can't expect a man to go without a wife for five or six years just because the first one deserted him at the altar.'

'But even so ... we were married. Does this lady know?'

'That I did not discover. And if she did ... I'll dareswear Isaac had a good story. Marriage with the disappearing lady? Well, was it a true marriage? It was in Dr. Keith's Marriage Mill which is illegal in any case; and then the bride never was his wife in a manner of speaking, was she? And then she deserted him. Oh, I reckon Mr. Isaac's got a case all right.'

'It is not that I blame him. I am solely to blame. He was ill-used. I wish him every happiness.'

'He's been searching for you ... or pretending to ... for a long time.'

'Pretending to ...!'

'Oh, don't ask me! There's a lot of queer business been going on in this affair. I reckon Mr. Isaac Axford was a bit smug. Perhaps there was some as made it worth his while not to search too diligently. Isaac's a man to look to the main chance. You see, now he's found himself a very comfortable wife. One hundred and fifty pounds a year ... very nice. I doubt not he's been well paid for all his trouble.'

'And ... my mother ...'

'Oh, I never see her,' said Jane uncomfortably. 'I never get my nose in that door, you can be sure.'

'I think of her often. I hope she is not too sad.'

'She'll have got over it all by now, Hannah. Besides she's got the pleasure of knowing ...'

'Of knowing what?'

'That her daughter is in *royal* hands.'

'Oh, Jane, Jane, I sometimes wonder what will become of us all.'

'You'll be all right. Nothing for you to fret about. Whatever happened you'd be all right.'

'Whatever happened ...'

'Well, he's the Prince, isn't he? They're saying in the streets that he's going to be King soon. When it's his birthday there's quite a to-do. Bells ringing and all. And when I hear them I think: "That's Hannah's friend ... my friend Hannah's friend." And I'm proud, Hannah, I'm really proud.'

'There is really nothing to be proud of.'

'You're getting soft in the head, Hannah.'

'I am dishonoured.'

'Nonsense. Not when it's a Prince. That makes all the difference. Now if it was a grocer ... or a linen-draper or a glass-cutter ... well that would be different, but this is a Prince, Hannah—and not just an ordinary Prince. This one could be a King.'

'There is no difference in the sight of God, Jane.'

'Oh, I was never religious like you, but I reckon Kings are special ... to everyone.'

Hannah smiled. 'Oh, Jane, thou art blasphemous.'

'Well, whatever that means it makes you laugh, so it can't be such a bad thing. No, Hannah, you're too serious. You weren't put here to be miserable ... but to laugh and enjoy yourself. Else why were things put here to make us enjoy them?'

'For our temptation perhaps.'

'Temptations my aunt Jane ... only I ain't got one. No, I reckon it's better for my children to have warm clothes to keep out the winds and good food inside 'em and a fire to sit by, and to laugh and play together ... I reckon it's better for them to be happy like that than cold and miserable and always on their knees asking God not to let them have too good a time because it's sinful. If being well fed and happy is sin ... then I'm for sin.'

'Thou art wilfully misconstruing my words, Jane.'

'Oh well, let's talk of something interesting. You aren't *so* again?' Hannah nodded. 'Well, I knew it. Still, you like them, don't you? Mind you, you want to take care of yourself. You're looking a bit peaky. Still it's often that way. To my way of thinking everything's turned out wonderful. Hannah, let's have a look at the picture.'

Jane stood before it and gazed at it in awe.

'It's beautiful, Hannah. Oh, it's really beautiful! And this Mr. Reynolds ... he really is an important man. A lady mentioned him in the shop. She said no one could paint quite like Mr. Reynolds, and that she was trying to persuade her husband to have her portrait painted.' Jane assumed a haughty expression and went on: ' "Anyone ... just anyone who *is* anyone ... must be painted by Mr. Reynolds." And I laughed to myself and I thought: Well, I know someone who has been painted by him. It was an order ... a royal command. "Go and paint that lady..." And, of course, he had to go.'

'Jane, you talk too much.'

'I always did, didn't I? I was the talker, you the listener. Well, don't you fret about Mr. Isaac Axford. I'd say this is good news. He's not going to go sniffing about for his first wife, is he, when he's got a second?'

After Jane had left, Hannah sat looking at the picture. Mrs. Axford, the lovely Quakeress, by Joshua Reynolds.

Mrs. Axford no longer.

Change was in the air. Isaac no longer considered her his wife. The Prince's visits were less frequent. At any time now she might hear that he had become the King of England.

Was this a premonition she felt—or was this sense of doom due to the fact that she was with child and feeling less well than she usually did at such times?

*   *   *

When George next called at the house he was alarmed by the sight of her.

'Are you ill, Hannah?' he asked fearfully.

'It is nothing ... nothing,' she hastened to assure him, for she could not bear to see him anxious. 'Perhaps this time it is a little more difficult than usual.'

'I must send for Fothergill.'

'It is not necessary. All is well. Thou must not worry.'

'But I shall if you are ill. And I know all is not well. Do not think you can deceive me, Hannah.'

'Jane has been here. She has news of Isaac Axford. He has recently married a Miss Bartlett.'

'Married!'

'Yes, Jane is certain. She has seen the lady. She has brought him a little fortune so ... perhaps that is why ... But he is no longer searching and what strikes me is that he has either committed bigamy or ... he does not consider himself married to me.'

George was silent. He was beginning to be apprehensive. For the first years of his liaison everything had gone well and smoothly. But since his eighteenth birthday, when he had begun to realize what would be expected of him as King, he was realizing too what a difficult position he had put himself —and Hannah—into.

It was all very well for a young Prince to have a mistress living in secret in a house in Tottenham—well, not all very well but it was accepted as a not too unusual affair—but for the King it was another matter. Kings had their mistresses. Indeed they did—and none more blatantly than his own ancestors, but they were recognized as mistresses, they lived at Court; it was considered as natural as marriage. But could a King make periodic and secret journeys from St. James's, Kensington or Kew to a house in Tottenham and not expect to be discovered? Certainly he could not.

Like Hannah, he could sense change in the air.

Yet he could not imagine Hannah at Court, living as the Countess of Yarmouth did, or Miss Chudleigh...

Then, of course, he would be expected to marry. One of the first duties of a King was to provide the country with heirs. He had evaded the ladies of Brunswick-Wolfenbüttel and Saxe-Gotha ... but how could he go on avoiding marriage? It would come ... inevitably, and then he would have to accept it, and he would have to make some plans about Hannah.

What could he do? Consult Bute or his mother? He knew in advance what their answer would be. He must bring Hannah to Court, a place could be found for her in his mother's household doubtless, the children would be cared for by people who could be trusted; and he must marry a woman of their choice and do his duty by his Queen and country. There was one other alternative; part from Hannah. That he declared vehemently to himself, he would never do.

But something had to happen soon. Each day that was becoming clearer to him.

He said slowly: 'It is well that Axford has married this woman. Now he will no longer search for you.'

She nodded and they went to the nursery and played with the children, but he was deeply aware of her melancholy, and he was concerned for her health.

'You must hide nothing from me,' he told her gently. 'You are troubled. Tell me why.'

'It is nothing. Thou hast enough with which to concern thyself. Tell me of thy dear Lord Bute's care for thee. I love to hear that thou hast such a good friend. And of thy dear mother who loves thee so tenderly.'

He talked of Mr. Pitt and his ambitions and how everything was going well abroad, but that Mr. Pitt was an arrogant man who would have to be watched. Lord Bute had said that when he came to the throne he would be King of a great expanding Empire.

'I mean to be a great King, Hannah. I mean to be a good King.'

'Thou wilt, George, because thou art a good man.'

'But now I am uneasy about you. There is something on your mind. Pray tell me. Are you having dreams?'

'Oh, I dream, George. I wake in the night trembling with fear. Last night I dreamed I was at the Judgment seat with my load of sins on me. They were heavy. They weighed me down and I knew that there was no place for me in Heaven.'

'There is no happiness for me unless you share it,' he told her soberly.

She seized his hands and kissed them; and after that she made a great effort to be gay. Temporarily they forgot the gloom which thoughts of the future must arouse in them both; but when he had gone back to Kew he remembered, and so did she, alone in the house in Tottenham.

* * *

His solace was to be found with his sister Elizabeth and his brother Edward. Elizabeth looked very wan; her health did not improve as time passed and she was particularly sympathetic when she heard that Hannah was not well either.

'What can I do?' demanded George. 'I am afraid for Hannah. Soon she will be delivered of our child and there is a melancholy about her ... a sadness. Do you think people can die of melancholy?'

Elizageth thought they could. She believed that if people desperately wanted to live they could often overcome illness and even face death and triumph; but if a person wanted to die, if he ... or she ... held out welcoming arms to death ... then death came quickly.

'I know how her mind works. She believes that this affair can bring no good to me. She thinks only of me.'

'Nor can it,' Edward said practically. 'It is clear, brother, that soon you will have to take some action.'

George looked helplessly from his brother and sister. Then he said almost defiantly: 'After I left Hannah, I came to a decision.'

'Yes?' they asked simultaneously.

'I ... I am going to marry Hannah.'

'Marry her,' breathed Elizabeth. 'But that is not possible.'

'It is possible. I do assure you. All we have to do is get a priest to marry us.'

'Secretly?' cried Edward.

'How else?'

But, George, think ...!' begged Elizabeth. 'How can you possibly marry Hannah?'

'Merely by taking our oaths before a priest.'

'I know. But ... it would never be permitted.'

'You cannot imagine that I intend to publish my intentions to the world.'

'Oh ... George ... have a care.'

'I have thought and thought about this and I see only one way out. Hannah is broken-hearted. I have a terrible fear that she will not live long. She believes she has sinned ... and that she is condemned to eternal damnation. There is only one thing which can save her in the eyes of God. Marriage. There is only one way to salvation.'

'Remember that soon you will be the King, George.'

'I know it. But that is no reason why I should deny her salvation. I love Hannah ... as I shall never love another woman, and I fear she is close to death. She feels it too. Do not ask me how this can be so. I only know it is. And she is afraid. Her soul is in torment ... because she cannot face her Maker with this load of sin upon her.'

'And you think that only marriage to you can save her?'

'I know it.'

'But, George, what will this mean to *you*?'

'It is not time to think of myself. I must think of her.'

'You say she is near death?'

'She feels it. If I lost her I should never be happy again, but I think I should find some comfort if I could clear her conscience. If I could think of her through the years ahead as happy in paradise I shall have some modicum of comfort. Then I shall devote myself to doing my duty.'

'George,' said Elizabeth earnestly, 'why has this feeling suddenly come to you?'

He looked at her strangely. 'I do not know. I have a feeling that Hannah will not be long with me. She is to have a child again and I sense that all is not well. It is like a great burden on my shoulders. I think that if Hannah died ... in sin ... I should never know peace as long as I lived.'

'Has Dr. Fothergill seen her?' asked Edward.

'No. She does not wish to see him. He will deliver the child as usual when the time comes.'

'And that time will be soon?' asked Elizabeth.

George nodded. 'I have made up my mind about this. Edward, I need your help.'

'You know that I will do all in my power.'

'You must be a witness of our marriage.'

'But,' cried Elizabeth, 'have you thought deeply enough of this? Have you considered all it will mean?'

'I have considered everything.'

'If you married Hannah she would be ... Queen.'

'And none more fitted.'

'Oh, I am sure of that, but ... will your ministers think so? What of the *people*? George, dearest brother, you have your duty to the crown.'

'I have my duty first to Hannah.'

Elizabeth looked at Edward and then at George, who cried out: 'Would you have me send Hannah to the Judgment seat with this sin upon her?'

Elizabeth interrupted: 'I cannot believe that a sin is expiated so simply in God's eyes.'

'Oh, Elizabeth, you do not see. We have sinned, both of us. I should never have taken her away from her people; she should never have come. We must pay for our sins. Her payment could be to go to her Maker in sin; mine is to marry, no matter what are the consequences. It is the only way we can right that wrong we did when I took her away from her people and she came. Edward, will you come with me? Will you witness our wedding?'

'Certainly I will, George, when you decide to make this marriage.'

'I have decided.'

Edward looked at Elizabeth and lifted his shoulders helplessly.

'Wait,' cried Elizabeth. 'Let us send the best doctors to Hannah, let them cure her ... then there will be no immediate need for marriage. Everything could go on as it is then for a while, until we have planned what would be the best thing to do.'

'And if you married Hannah on her death-bed ... then ... that would not matter for you would be unmarried on her death and could make another marriage ... the one which was chosen for you.'

'Please do not talk of Hannah as though she is dead. Hannah is not going to die. She is going to live and I am going to marry her.'

*   *   *

'Can he mean it?' whispered Elizabeth.
'I am sure he does,' answered Edward.
'Oh, Edward, what will happen?'
'Trouble, great trouble. Unless, of course, she is married on her death-bed. Then he is left free. That is what we must hope for.'
'Hope for Hannah's death?'
'My dear sister, how else can our brother marry this woman except on her death-bed. It would be disaster to do so.'
'You must persuade him against it, Edward. And I must do the same.'
'Dear sister, George is slow to come to a decision, but when he has reached it he is as stubborn as a mule. I have seen something in his face tonight.'
'And that was?'
'A determination to marry Hannah Lightfoot.'

*   *   *

The closed carriage rumbled out of the private drive. In it sat a lady well muffled up in a concealing cloak and hood; she was heavily pregnant. Beside her sat her maid, anxiously glancing at her from time to time, for it was clear that the lady was ill.

The carriage stopped in Curzon Street and the occupants alighted and hurried into the chapel there.

There they were greeted by the Prince of Wales and his brother, Edward, Duke of York.

The young Duke bowed and looked with wonder into the beautiful face of the woman who had so deeply affected his brother.

'Are you well?' asked the Prince anxiously.

'I am at peace,' answered Hannah, 'but I fear for you.'

'All will be well. Fear not.'

He had never looked so handsome as he stood there before Dr. Wilmot whom he had commanded to perform the ceremony. Resolute, determined, he believed he was acting in the only manner possible to an honourable man. Whatever the consequences he would no longer be tormented by his conscience. He had sinned and this was the only way in which he could expect forgiveness in God's eyes.

So, with his brother as witness, on that day in the year 1759, the Prince of Wales was married to Hannah Lightfoot.

The Grave at Islington

ELIZABETH CHUDLEIGH had been to Winchester on a very special mission so it was not until later that she discovered what was happening at Court.

A wise woman, Elizabeth told herself, must keep her eyes open for advantages and when they came seize them; she was a wise woman, and the folly of one day could by a strange turn of fate become the wise action of another.

She lived dangerously; she expected to and she liked to; of one thing she was certain and that was that Elizabeth Chudleigh would draw the utmost advantage from life. Elizabeth Chudleigh! She was Elizabeth Hervey now; and there was going to be no secret about that.

It was many years since she had married the Honourable Augustus John Hervey; she had been piqued at the time because she believed the Duke of Hamilton, whom she had hoped to marry, had deserted her. She had met Augustus at the Winchester races whither she had gone when she was staying at the house of her uncle and aunt, Mr. and Mrs. Merrill, in Larnston, Hampshire. Knowing that Augustus came from a good family—he was a grandson of the Earl of Bristol—the Merrills had encouraged the match and she had agreed to marry him.

She soon was under the impression that she had acted rashly; and deciding to keep her marriage a secret did not mention it when she returned to Court. Augustus, who was a sailor by profession was not in England for long spells but when he was, he expected to live with his wife. Elizabeth's plan had been to spend her time between the Court and her mother's house in Conduit Street; and when she was there Augustus would be with her and insist on his conjugal rights. Elizabeth was nothing loath; the only condition she had demanded was that the marriage should be kept a secret.

In her heart she always believed that one day some great opportunity would come along. She intended to be a Duchess at least and when that opportunity came she did not wish to be hampered by a marriage to a nobody, which was all Augustus was at the time. Augustus did not seem to mind the secrecy as long as he was not excluded from her bed when he desired to be there. That had to be accepted and was no hardship, he being a personable young man; but there followed the inevitable result which caused her a great deal of trouble. In spite of voluminous skirts these predicaments have a way of showing themselves and it soon became clear to Elizabeth that she would have to stage a little act. She would have to leave Court to take the air, she announced; there were smiles behind fans and whispers in corridors; much Elizabeth cared. She left Court and gave birth to a boy—christened Henry Augustus— and she put him out with a suitable family to be cared for. He did not live long, poor child, and she had soon forgotten him. She returned to Court, where acquaintances were inclined to make too tender enquiries after her health.

One pert young woman, and this in the presence of Lord Chesterfield, murmured that she had heard rumours and some had dared suggest that she had had twins. Elizabeth had turned to Chesterfield and demanded to know if he could believe such a thing.

Chesterfield who prided himself on being a wit replied: 'I never believe more than half I hear, Miss Chudleigh.' Which remark was noted down and reported and repeated throughout the Court as an illustration of the wit of the Earl of Chesterfield and the scandalous behaviour of Miss Chudleigh.

But she cared nothing for gossip and scandal. Let them chatter to their hearts' content. She was safe. No one knew she was married to Hervey—nor would they ever be sure of it, because even if he declared they were married she could deny it, for she had taken the precaution of forcing the parson to give her access to the register and had destroyed the certificate of marriage and torn the page from the register on which Mr. Annis, who had married them, had recorded the event.

Now the position had changed. The Earl of Bristol was very ill and Augustus was next in the line of succession to the Earldom. The Countess of Bristol was a very worthy title and she was wishing now that she had not destroyed the evidence of the marriage.

There was nothing to be done, she decided, but to go to Larnston and stay with her aunt and uncle, and when there she would bully little Mr. Annis into giving her another marriage certificate and rewriting the page in the register. It was a very simple matter.

So Miss Chudleigh had left Court 'to take a little country air, and in due course arrived at Winchester and from thence went to the home of her uncle and aunt in Larnston.

They were delighted to see their flamboyant relative from Court who was so beautiful, so dazzling, that everyone for miles round would envy them.

Miss Chudleigh accepted their homage and was graciously charming, explained that she wished to see Mr. Annis without delay for she had important business to discuss with him.

Oh dear, this was a sorry business. Mr. Annis was dangerously ill.

'All the more reason why I should see him without delay.'

'But the poor man is on his death-bed.'

'Then I certainly must see him before he expires.'

'In fact, his doctor has said he is to see no one.'

Miss Chudleigh smiled. She was not no one. Aunt and Uncle Merrill, country-folk though they were, should know that.

So into the death-chamber strode Elizabeth, vital, determined, in great contrast to the sick man on the bed. She must
speak with him alone; everyone must leave her; it was of the
utmost importance to the saving of his soul.

'Mr. Annis, can you hear me Mr. Annis?' His eyes were
glassy, but he must live until he had done his task. 'Mr. Annis,
it was a wicked thing you did to destroy that page from the
church register. How can you face your Maker, Mr. Annis, with
such a sin on your conscience? I have come to save you. You
must put back that page before you die.'

Mr. Annis remembered her. Who would ever forget her?

Often he remembered what he had allowed her to do. It was
an offence, was it not, a criminal offence to destroy part of the
church register.

'I heard how ill you were and I could not allow you to go
before your Maker until you had put this matter right. Do you
hear me, Mr. Annis?'

He did hear. He did remember his sin.

'Now you must give me the keys which open the cupboard or
wherever it is the books and certificates are kept. You married
me to the Honourable Augustus John Hervey, did you not?
Then you must write me another certificate and you must put
that page back in the register ... somehow. It is the only way to
salvation, Mr. Annis.'

Poor Mr. Annis! The sheer will to save his soul kept him
alive. In the death-chamber he listened to Elizabeth; he gave
her the keys and it was she who guided his hand.

And when he had done as she asked, he lay back on his
pillows and died.

An example she told herself of what can be achieved if one
only has the will to do it.

Poor old Annis! Let him rest in peace. He had done his
duty; and now if the old Earl of Bristol died tomorrow no one
could deny that Elizabeth Chudleigh was the Countess.

* * *

The Earl stubbornly and most unaccommodatingly clung to

life and Elizabeth returned to Court so that she might be close at hand to hear of his demise when it occurred. In the meantime she had to make the facts of her marriage known and the first person she must tell should be the Dowager Princess.

She would have to break the news gently, for Augusta would not be pleased with a maid of honour who married without her consent and kept the marriage secret for some years. It was most unconventional behaviour and Elizabeth had already offended the Dowager Princess with her manners.

Not that the Princess cared to reprimand her. Elizabeth was aware of matters which she would rather not have mentioned. Of course Elizabeth must never forget that although the Princess might not want to offend her she was the most powerful member of her own Court and she could take action which might be inconvenient to Elizabeth. She might even call her bluff and let her do her worst, which could be inconvenient. Now, if there was a little blackmail going on between them it was pleasant courtly blackmail; and that was really how Elizabeth wanted it to remain.

So she must act with care.

By good fortune—for her—she encountered the Prince of Wales when he was alone and was immediately struck by the change in him.

Our Prince has turned into a very serious young man, she thought. Something has happened.

Elizabeth must naturally find out what without delay.

She dropped a charming curtsy.

'What pleasure to see Your Highness looking so well. It is long since that pleasure was mine.'

'You have been away from Court, I believe, Miss Chudleigh?'

'Yes, I had to pay a duty call on my aunt and uncle in the country and I used that opportunity to take a little air.'

'You are looking well for the change.'

'How gracious is Your Highness.' She took a step nearer. 'Oh, this is presumptuous of me ... but it is out of my deep regard for Your Highness. I ... I trust all is well?'

'All is well, Miss Chudleigh.'

'I was thinking of ... that dear friend of us both.'

The Prince coloured. 'She ... she is better, thank you.'

'So she has been ill?'

He looked at her steadily for a few moments; her lovely face was suffused with tender affection. Much as he loved Hannah he could always be deeply affected by a beautiful woman, and there was something motherly about Elizabeth at that moment.

He longed to confide in someone; he was deeply worried. He had done something which he knew his mother would consider disastrous. Only that day she and Lord Bute had talked about the day he would marry; they had talked complacently as though they were looking forward to it. He had made an effort to tell them, but he could not bring himself to do it. Lord Bute had been saying that the people might like their King to have an English bride, but his mother said that he must have a royal Queen and that his ancestors had always taken their wives from Germany.

It was painful to listen to such talk and yet he could not bring himself to stop them, to explain to them. He had wanted to, but he knew—and he was realizing this more and more every day—what a shock it would be to them when they heard of his marriage to Hannah.

Therefore it would be comforting to explain to someone who would be sympathetic and he knew she would because she always had been.

'Miss Chudleigh,' he said quietly, 'I wish to confide in you.'

'Yes, Your Highness.' She tried not to sound too eager.

'You were so kind to me ... and to Hannah.'

'Your Highness, it is my duty to serve you with any power I have. As to Hannah ... I look upon her as a very dear friend. If I could do anything ... just anything ... to make you two happier, I beg of you, I implore you, to let me know what it is.'

'Miss Chudleigh, I have married Hannah.'

She caught her breath. It was incredible. Fresh from her own adventure with the church register of Larnston it still seemed fantastic. The future King of England married to a little Quaker girl—the niece of a linen-draper! Oh no. It couldn't be true. It simply could not.

He was watching her eagerly, so she forced her features into an expression of deepest sympathy.

'It seemed to me the only possible action, Miss Chudleigh.'

'I understand.'

'I knew you would. Oh ... I knew you would. So you are not shocked.'

'I think you have done a brave and noble thing.' She forced the tears into her eyes; it was not easy, but she had taught herself this trick and in any case she was so surprised that it was not so difficult as usual.

'Oh, Miss Chudleigh, I feel much better having confided in you.'

'I am glad Your Highness so honoured me. Have you ... told any others?'

'Only my sister Elizabeth and Edward ... my brother. Edward was our witness.'

'And who married you?'

'Dr. Wilmot. I commanded it. They cannot blame him.'

'Your Highness is your own master and will ere long, I doubt not, be the master of us all. So ... no one else knows.'

He shook his head. 'It is a great relief, Miss Chudleigh, to share this burden. I want to explain. Hannah is ill ... she fears she may not live. It was necessary, you see. She could not die with this sin ... on her soul. I had to do this, Miss Chudleigh. It was the only way.'

'I understand. I am sure you were right. It was good and noble. I am sure of it. And Mr. Axford...?'

'The marriage to Mr. Axford was no real marriage. It took place at the marriage mill, which is illegal. Mr. Axford himself believes this, for he has recently married a Miss Bartlett. Dr. Wilmot helped me discover the truth of this and there is no doubt of it.'

'So ... there is a Princess of Wales,' murmured Elizabeth.

'I do not know whether Hannah would wish to be so described ... nor that my grandfather...'

Elizabeth nodded. Here was excitement. This made her little adventure seem like a nursery prank. The Prince married —and the King in ignorance of it. And the Princess and old Bute...! She wanted to laugh, but she smiled benignly, sympathetically and affectionately.

'Your Highness, may I dare to advise you ...?'

'Oh, Miss Chudleigh, please do.'

'Say nothing of this to anyone ... who does not know already.'

'I certainly will not. And thank you for your kindness.'

'Your Highness, you must not thank me. I have done nothing ... though I wish you to know that I will do anything to serve you now and at any time.'

The Prince went to his apartments considerably comforted by the encounter; and Elizabeth went to hers in a state of great excitement.

*　*　*

Elizabeth presented herself to the Dowager Princess. Augusta forced herself to smile. She wished the woman had stayed in the country. There was something quite brazen about her; and when one thought how much she knew of that unfortunate affair of George and the Quaker it was really quite disconcerting.

'So you have returned,' said Augusta.

Elizabeth swept a demure curtsy. 'And have come to ask Your Highness's pardon.'

The Princess raised her eyebrows.

'Have I Your Highness's permission to proceed?'

'Pray do.'

'I have to confess, Your Highness, that I am married.'

'And when did this occur?'

'Some years ago, Your Highness.'

'I see, so you have been posing at my Court as a single woman.'

'That is so, Your Highness.'

'I find this distasteful.'

'Your Highness, I fear there is much going on that is distasteful.' The beautiful wide-open eyes met those of the Princess Dowager and the Princess felt her own colour rise. A reference to herself and Lord Bute. The insolence of the creature. She would not have her at the Court. Could this clandestine marriage be used as a means of getting rid of her?

'The name of your husband?'

'The Honourable Augustus John Hervey.'

'Bristol's grandson ... and heir.' Light was beginning to dawn on the Princess. Bristol was very ill, close to death, she had heard. Now she knew why Elizabeth Chudleigh was anxious to announce her marriage. She was looking forward to being Countess of Bristol. The woman was shameless, a schemer, unscrupulous.

Yes, in spite of Lord Bute's warnings she was going to get rid of her.

'I trust Your Highness is not displeased.'

'I am very displeased. I do not care for this secrecy. I find it ... discourteous. I trust you enjoyed your stay in the country. Where was it?'

'Larnston, Your Highness, not far from Winchester.'

'A pleasant part of the country, I believe. You should enjoy staying there.'

Elizabeth was startled. Was that a command?

'Now you may leave me.'

Elizabeth was alarmed. She knew what would happen. She had seen it before. She would retire to her apartments, and in a very short time a messenger would come to her with the news that there was no longer a place for her in the Princess's household and she would be expected to leave within a few hours. And once out it would be hard to come back. The King? He was getting old and tired. He might have forgotten that he had once found her attractive.

She must act quickly. She had always been impulsive; it was

one of her great faults; but this was definitely an occasion when prompt action was necessary.

'Your Highness ... certain information has come to me which my loyalty to you demands I pass on ... without delay.'

'What?'

'Madam, I scarcely know how to tell you. I fear it will be a great shock. It is a matter of the utmost gravity ...'

'What are you trying to say to me?'

'It concerns the Prince.'

The Princess Dowager's attitude had changed. She had suddenly realized that they were no longer discussing a maid of honour's trivial misdemeanour, and she was a frightened woman.

Dare I? Elizabeth asked herself. But it was the only way. She must not tell him that I told ... I must prevent that. And if she did? Well, then she could go to him when the storm had abated and tell him she had done it for the sake of the crown, the throne, the country.

She must create a diversion *now* ... she must show that she could be useful to the Princess ... otherwise a greater calamity than the Prince's marriage would occur: Elizabeth Chudleigh would be expelled from Court.

She had made up her mind.

'Your Highness, the Prince is married.'

The Princess Dowager had risen; she was speechless and reached blindly for the arm of her chair to steady herself.

'I am sorry it is I who must give Your Highness such news.'

'It is not possible ...' stammered the Princess, for this was the only state of affairs she could possibly tolerate.

'Alas ... Your Highness.'

'How? When? To whom?'

'A short while ago, Madam. He did not tell me the date. But he was married by Dr. Wilmot in Curzon Street to Hannah Lightfoot.'

'The ... the Quaker woman?'

'Yes, Your Highness.'

'I do not believe it. It is some fabrication. It is quite untrue. It would not be possible.'

'Would Your Highness wish me to summon one of the maids to bring you some ... stimulant. Your Highness seems in need...'

'Summon no one. Is the door shut? Make sure that no one is near.'

'Yes, Your Highness.'

'Now ... who has told you this ... ridiculous falsehood?'

'His Highness, the Prince.'

'*He* has told *you* this?'

'He confides in me, Madam. He finds me sympathetic. You will remember how useful I was able to be to Your Highness when he began this connection ... because he himself had confided in me.'

The Princess picked up her fan absently and began to fan herself. She felt faint. It is not true, she kept telling herself. It could not possibly be true. I am dreaming, of course. This is a nightmare. I must wake up because this idea is intolerable ... even in a dream.

'He would never do such a thing,' she said flatly.

Elizabeth was silent. If the Princess thought that she did not know her son. It was just the idiotic senseless chivalrous idealistic manner in which George would act.

'He felt he owed marriage to the lady in view of their relationship, Your Highness. The lady is sick ... and fears herself to be near death ... she was in great mental torment because of this ... relationship and the Prince believed that the only way to bring her peace of mind was to marry her.'

'He has told you this ...?'

'Yes, Your Highness.'

Oh, George, you fool ... you madman! thought his mother. Not only do you do this dreadful thing but you confide in this woman ... this unscrupulous creature who is a born schemer and intriguer, not above a little blackmail. George, you are mad ... quite mad. What are we going to do?

'You had better tell me all you know.'

'Your Highness, I have nothing more to tell you. All His Highness has told me is that the marriage has taken place.'

'Has he told anyone else of this marriage?'

'I think very few people know, Your Highness. His brother Edward . . .'

'Edward!'

'Who acted as a witness, Your Highness.'

'Oh, my God!'

'Then, of course, there is Dr. Wilmot. He did not mention any other.'

'Of course I cannot believe such a story.'

'But Your Highness will wish to find out whether there is any truth in it.'

'Such silly rumours should always be proved false.'

Elizabeth could almost feel sorry for the woman. She was really shaken; and the more she protested her disbelief the more plausible the story seemed to her.

'Your Highness at least believes in my good faith.'

'Your good faith?'

'That I would not be so false or so foolish as to tell you that His Highness himself confessed this to me if he had not done so?'

The Princess was silent.

'And may I ask Your Highness not to mention to His Highness that I have told you this?'

The insolence of this woman was past all bearing. But she must be careful. One must always be careful with blackmailers, and Elizabeth Chudleigh was an extremely subtle one; moreover, the information she had to hide was such which could make the kingdom rock.

'If His Highness knew that I had told you he would no longer confide in me. I would wish to be loyal to His Highness and I have pondered on this; I have come to the conclusion that I can best serve His Highness by making this known to Your Highness, for I know that you will bring the discretion to settling this affair which is necessary to His Highness and the nation.'

The Princess did not answer.

'Your Highness knows that I am entirely at your service,' went on Elizabeth. 'If in the action you will take you should need me to act for Your Highness in any way ... if there is something which I may be able to discover ...'

'Yes, yes,' said the Princess. 'Leave me now and send to me ...'

'My Lord Bute?' asked Elizabeth with a hint of mischief in her eyes.

But the Princess Dowager was too shaken to notice it.

*   *   *

She threw herself into his arms. 'What are we to do? I cannot believe it ... and yet I must. How could this have happened? Without telling us! He tells that ... *creature* ... and not us! Can you believe it?'

Lord Bute looked stunned. It certainly was disconcerting. The Prince, to whom he had believed himself to be so close, to have acted in this way and not told him!

But that was a small matter compared with the tremendous implication of all this.

'Oh, John, do you think my son is mad?'

'He is a fool,' replied Bute savagely.

'What are we going to do?'

'We must think about it ... clearly ... calmly.'

'Oh, my darling, what a comfort you are! I know you will understand how to deal with this matter. Should we send for him?'

'By no means. That woman is right. We will say nothing to him.'

'I could storm at him ... whip him with my own hands.'

'He is too big for that, Augusta ... and he is the Prince of Wales. I fear of late I have made him realize the importance of his position. Perhaps I have been wrong. I have tried to make him into a King ... which he may well be at any moment ... and as a result he thinks he can act as he wishes without consulting me ... us. Who would have believed he could have done this thing? But first we must prove that he has.'

'He told her ... Elizabeth Chudleigh ... himself, John.'

'And to tell that woman! What next? One act of folly on top of another!'

'Could he have been joking, John?' asked the Princess, piteously hopeful.

'Have you ever known him to joke? He doesn't know what a joke is. But we are wasting time. We have got to think of how to act.'

'How can we act? Think of it, John! That woman ... that merchant's daughter or whatever she is, is the Princess of Wales. She could tomorrow be Queen of England. Oh, what can we do?'

'We must stop it. That much I know.'

'How?'

'That's what we must discover.'

'Can you see a way?'

'Not at the moment. But it's there, of course. There's always a way.'

'John, you don't think we ought to advise Mr. Pitt or Newcastle.'

'Never. No, no ... no one must know of this. It has to be our secret ... and, a curse on her, that woman Chudleigh.'

'So we say nothing ... not even to George?'

'Most of all not to George.'

'I do not know how I shall contain myself in his presence. I think I shall plead a slight indisposition so that I do not have to see him.'

'Perhaps that would be advisable. It is a terrible ordeal, my love. But will you leave this to me?'

'Oh, my dearest, most willingly.'

'I will have some plan of action, you may be sure.'

'I am convinced of it.'

'In the meantime, I must see this Dr. Wilmot. I must get the truth from him, threaten him with dire consequences if this leaks out through him; and then I must find some means of severing this impossible connection.'

'My darling, do you think you can do it?'

'Have you ever known me fail you?'

'Never,' she cried fervently.

*   *   *

Lord Bute suggested that the Prince of Wales should accompany him to Kew where they would stay for a while.

'There we can find more solitude,' he explained, 'and I have much to say to Your Highness.'

George had always had a particular liking for Kew; the palace was unpretentious; he liked the river and he had taken a great dislike to Hampton since his grandfather had slapped his face there.

'I want you to get a real grasp of affairs,' Bute had told him. 'The country is moving forward at a great rate. In the last few years the change has been significant. You must see in every aspect this country of which you will one day be King.'

George was eager to learn. He was a little worried every now and then when he remembered his marriage. At first it had seemed so right and noble; but now that he was a little farther from the event he was beginning to realize what significant action he had taken. He would do the same again, he assured himself; but he did realize that when the news was out it was going to be a very great shock to the people he cared about— such as his mother and Lord Bute.

Hannah might say that she was prepared to live in retirement, but a Queen could not do that however much she wished it; and could Hannah ever act as a Queen of England? And if she did not, if they forced him to take another Queen ... then the children would be illegitimate. How could an illegitimate son be the next King of England?

What a web he was caught up in!

There were times when he considered confessing everything to Lord Bute, but he never reached the point. He could not find the courage and Lord Bute had, it seemed to him, actually turned the subject to something quite different when he had been on the point of broaching it.

So a little rest at Kew was very desirable. A little respite, the Prince called it. Perhaps in a few weeks time he would be able to see the position more clearly and then make the right decision.

One thing he continued to tell himself: 'I don't regret it. I would do the same again.'

They rode every morning at Kew. It was so pleasant along by the river and people came out of their cottages to curtsy as he rode by. Some called: 'Long live the Prince of Wales!' And he was gratified because they seemed to like him.

'The King is growing very unpopular,' Bute told him. 'The people are eager for you to ascend the throne.'

'It seems wrong to talk of Grandfather's death so constantly.'

'People will talk so of Kings. They consider their Kings their property.'

George shivered a little, though the sunshine was warm.

'There is something . . .'

But Lord Bute was smiling at a little group on the roadside.

'Give them a pleasant smile. They expect it.'

So he smiled and inclined his head in acknowledgment of the cheers and he told himself that when he was King he would work for the good of the people; he would be Good King George—that was what he wanted.

And before his reign he had made a secret marriage . . . he had children who were born before his marriage. Little John was the real heir to the throne. No, he was not . . . because then Hannah had been married to Axford and not to him. But had she been married to Axford? Was it a true marriage? And the sons born before marriage were illegitimate . . . unless marriage later to their mother legitimized them. It was indeed a tangled web and he was too ignorant to sort it out. Lord Bute would be able to. His dear friend was capable of understanding everything.

Lord Bute now began to talk about the successful campaigns. There was victory on all sides. Parades were common in the streets of London when the heroes returned from the scenes of their triumph.

'You should share in these triumphs. The King should give you a command in the army.'

A command in the army! An escape from the problems at home! It seemed a wonderful solution. He could shelve the problem of his marriage until he returned from the wars; and while he was away perhaps he could see the position more clearly.

'I can see that the idea appeals to Your Highness.'

'It is what I desire.'

Bute was a little surprised, knowing that the Prince disliked any form of bloodshed. Did he imagine that he could escape that by going to war? He had thought that the young man would have to be persuaded to it. It must mean that George was anxious about this terrible situation in which he had become involved. That was to the good. The more he realized the extent of his folly the more likely he would be to accept the solution.

Bute was aware that the Prince was on the point of confiding in him; he must steer him clear of that. It was Bute's intention to know nothing of the matter—ostensibly—until it was all over. Therefore he wanted no confidences from the Prince about a matter on which he had made sure he was already fully informed.

'You should perhaps write to the King and tell him that you would welcome a military appointment. After all, it is only natural that the heir to the throne should want to have a share in the country's triumphs.'

'I will do so without delay.'

'Would Your Highness care for my assistance in drafting the letter.'

'I should, of course, welcome it.'

They rode back to the palace and occupied themselves with writing the letter and when it was ready a messenger was despatched with it to Kensington Palace where the King was in residence.

The Prince and Bute then settled down to study maps and talk of war; and Bute was pleased to notice that in this new interest the Prince seemed to have lost a little of his apprehension, which Bute construed as meaning he was not so deeply obsessed by his marriage and the Quaker as he had been.

* * *

When the King read his grandson's letter he tossed it across the room.

'Puppy!' was his comment.

He would have torn it into pieces but he had to remember that it was, after all, a request from the Prince of Wales and that since his grandson held that position and was of age even he could not ignore him.

When Pitt and Newcastle called on him he showed them the letter.

'Put up to this,' was his comment, 'by his mother and that Scottish stallion. A nice figure he would cut in the field. I hear he doesn't like the sight of blood, but he'll be a soldier because Mamma says he should.'

'Your Majesty will, of course, reply in diplomatic terms to His Highness.'

'I shall tell the puppy the answer is No.'

'It is a reasonable enough request,' suggested Newcastle. 'One understands that the Prince wishes to serve the country at such a time.'

'It's made to embarrass us,' said the King. 'She doesn't want to lose her baby. She wants to keep him at her side ... making sure nobody is going to whisper in his ear but herself. I tell you this: she knows the answer is No. That's why he's been advised to make his request.'

Pitt was inclined to agree. It was the Leicester House set, who were trying to form a Prince of Wales's Party, seeking a chance to play the Prince off against the King, and, counting on the Prince's popularity with the people, hoping to make an issue of this.

Pitt shrugged the matter aside; but on his advice and that of

Newcastle the King wrote politely enough that the Prince of Wales could not be spared to leave the country.

'Insolent puppy!' growled the King as he passed the letter over for sealing.

'He is determined to insult me,' murmured the Prince as he read his grandfather's letter.

It's taking his mind off the Quaker, was Bute's mental note; and after all, that was the most important issue at the moment.

* * *

The Prince and Bute returned to Leicester House for the Prince's birthday. His popularity was clearly growing, for the people of their own accord decorated the streets and prepared to make this a great occasion.

There were crowds outside Leicester House and loud cheers when the Prince appeared; and all that day and night the citizens of London celebrated the occasion.

The Prince was gratified. It was soothing to his vanity after the King had so snubbed him. What did the approval of that irascible old man mean to him while the people loved him?

His mother had recovered from her slight indisposition and was almost herself again, although he was anxious to see that she was still a little wan.

He had had no time to visit Tottenham but he would go there soon. Perhaps he would talk over his predicament with Hannah; they would pray together and she would give him her opinion.

He might then arrive at some course of action.

He felt relaxed. Perhaps it was not as bad as he had feared. The people loved him; he was sure they would be ready to accept his bride as their Queen solely because he loved her and asked them to.

* * *

A carriage had drawn up before the house. Hannah was at the window watching. At first she had thought it was the Prince for it was long since he had come, but the carriage had not come by the private drive which he had always used.

A man alighted, tall, elegant. Her heart began to beat uncomfortably; instinctively she sensed some doom.

He approached the door; and she heard the knock echoing through the house—like clods falling on a coffin.

She turned from the window and sat in her high chair, her hand to her throat where a pulse was hammering under her lavender silk gown.

A scratching at the door.

'Madam, a gentleman begs to be allowed to see you.'

'Who is he?'

'He gives no name, Madam.'

'Bring him in.'

He came. He was of the Court she knew at once by his bearing and manners.

'I trust you will forgive the intrusion, Madam.'

'I pray you, sir, sit down.'

'Thank you.'

He sat and looked at her kindly. He was a very handsome man. He said: 'I come on behalf of His Highness, the Prince of Wales.'

'Yes.'

'That does not surprise you, I see.'

'No.' She had never been able to dissimulate.

The visitor seemed relieved. It was as though he had made up his mind that he had to deal with a sensible woman.

'You had been expecting someone to call?'

'Yes. May I know your name?'

'I cannot tell you that. Is it enough that I am a friend of the Prince of Wales?'

'It is enough if he sent you to me.'

'No,' he said. 'He does not know that I have come.'

She nodded and smiled faintly.

'I see you are a lady of good sense. I know that you are—or were—a member of the Society of Friends which is a great comfort to those who wish well to the Prince, for we believe that you are a good and religious woman who will be prepared to do your duty.'

'I shall try to do that,' she said.

'Let us be open and frank with each other. The Prince has contracted a marriage with you. You realize that this marriage can never be recognized.'

'I do not understand that. But whether or not it is recognized it is a marriage.'

'You yourself were married before to an Isaac Axford. Therefore it could be called a bigamous marriage and no marriage at all.'

'I did not count myself married to Isaac Axford,' she answered.

'And you do to the Prince of Wales?'

She nodded.

'You are devoted to His Highness, I believe?'

'I would do anything for his happiness.'

Now the visitor's relief was apparent. 'Then I am sure that when you have heard what I tell you, you will agree to what I have to say.'

Hannah listened to what she was told and as she listened she felt her life crumbling into ruins about her.

It was true what she heard. She had always known it. He had made his sacrifice for her knowing all this; she must not fail him. Now was the time to make hers for him.

* * *

In his closed carriage the Prince set out for Tottenham. It was some weeks since he had seen Hannah, but she would understand. Matters of state were increasingly taking more and more of his time and she had agreed that this would become more and more inevitable as time went on.

He reached the house. He was going to tell her how glad he was that their union was at last sanctified. He would discuss with her the advisability of making the matter known ... first, he thought, to Lord Bute, who had always been his friend and never showed any impatience. He reminded himself even when his father was alive—much as he had loved him—it was Lord Bute to whom he had taken his troubles.

The carriage turned in at the private drive. He alighted and looked with tenderness up at the window where she invariably watched for him. He believed that she was listening all the time for the sound of his carriage, for she always seemed to be there when he arrived. She would lift her hand in greeting as he alighted, and then run down to greet him.

On this day he stood looking up at the window. The curtains remained still. He had caught her today! She had not heard him.

He took out his key and let himself in by the door which he always used. She was not waiting for him, and he was suddenly aware of the silence of the house. It was strange. He had never noticed that before. Of course he had not, because she would be running down to meet him.

He went to the hall and called her name. He looked up the stairs.

'Hannah? Where are you, Hannah?'

Now it was really strange, for she did not appear on the stairs.

She was ill. Something had happened. He took the stairs two at a time, calling her name. Where were the servants? Why did they not come out to receive him?

A sudden panic came to him. He was alone ... alone in this house.

'Hannah! Hannah!' He scarcely recognized his own voice. Where could she be! There was nowhere for her to hide. He went into the room with the tall windows in which Reynolds had painted her picture. She was not there. He looked at the wall and stared, for where the picture had hung there was an empty space.

'Oh God,' he whispered. 'What does it mean?'

He ran to the nursery. The little beds were there ... neat and empty. The children were gone.

'Hannah! Hannah!' he called.

There was a cold sweat on his brow; his mind felt sluggish, unable to supply the answer he was demanding of it.

'Hannah, where are you? Come out ... if you are hiding. If

this is a joke ... Enough ... Enough...' He whispered her name; he shouted her name; but there was no answer. Only his own voice echoing through the empty house.

He ran through the rooms; there was no sign of her, no sign of the children, no sign of life. He would not believe it. They could not have gone.

'Where to?' he demanded of the emptiness.

The children? She could not have gone back to St. James's Market and taken the children with her ... his children? How would that have been possible?

But she had disappeared. She had been spirited away.

He would not leave the house; he went from top to bottom, searching, calling her name, through the empty rooms which he already knew were empty because he had examined them before.

He stood in the hall looking about him.

But she was gone.

He had lost her and he could not understand how.

Dazed, bewildered, he returned to the carriage and gave orders to be driven back to Kew.

*   *   *

Lord Bute was waiting for him when he returned to the Palace.

'Some business to discuss with Your Highness ... Good God! what has happened? Your Highness ... looks ... Your Highness has had a shock?'

'I want to talk to you. I must talk to you without delay.'

'Come into my private apartments. We shall be quite alone there.'

Lord Bute shut the door and looked at the Prince earnestly. He was taking it badly. Well, it was to be expected.

'Tell me what has happened to upset you.'

'I do not know what has happened. It's a mystery ... a terribly mystery. I do not understand what it means.'

'Pray tell me everything.'

So the Prince told—of his life with Hannah, of the children.

Lord Bute listened nodding gravely; but when the Prince came to the marriage he opened his eyes wide and exclaimed with horror.

'I had to do it. It meant so much to her. She feared death ... and the sin ...'

'Ah, I understand,' said Lord Bute. 'And you decided that at all costs to yourself you must relieve her of that.'

'I knew you would understand.'

'Certainly ... certainly. There will be difficulties. Your mother had decided on a German Princess for you.'

'What I have discovered today is what has reduced me to this state. She has gone.'

'Gone ... Gone where?'

'That I do not know. I went to visit her and I found the house empty ... I found her disappeared. Everything is gone ... The children ... herself ... There is nothing there. It is an empty house. Yet ... how could they have gone without telling me.'

'Are you sure?'

'I went through the house ... every room ... the nursery, the kitchen ... everywhere. There is no one there at all. And the picture has gone.'

'Picture?'

'Reynolds painted it. I wanted a picture of her.'

'So you sent Reynolds to ... er ... this ... er ... house to paint her?'

The Prince nodded. So there is another in the secret, thought Bute uneasily.

'You ... told him who she was?'

'No, no. I merely arranged that he should be commissioned to paint a picture of Mrs. Axford.'

'I see.'

'But what can I do. Where is she? Can you explain?'

'There is an explanation, obviously.'

'But what? I can think of none.'

'Nor I just at present. But if Your Highness will give me every detail of this affair I will do my best to find it.'

'Oh, please do. I shall not rest until Hannah is safe.'

'You said she was ill, did you not? That was the reason for the marriage?'

'Yes, there was a change in her. After the birth of our boy she was not so well and before the second boy was born she grew very frail. It was then ...'

'Ah yes, Your Highness told me. Now you will give me leave to set about this matter in the way I think fit?'

'Oh yes, please do.'

'First Your Highness must tell me everything ... everything remember. And then I will see what can be done.'

* * *

In a few days time Lord Bute solemnly presented himself to the Prince of Wales.

'Your Highness should prepare himself for a shock.'

The Prince grew pale, his lips sagged and his blue eyes looked as though they would fall out of his head.

'It is very sad. Your fair Quakeress is dead.'

'It cannot be.'

'Alas, it is so. You know that she was ill ... it was for this reason that you married.'

'Yes, she had a premonition ... but I thought she recovered a little after the birth of the child.'

'Perhaps knowing how anxious you were she kept the truth from you. She allowed you to marry her which perhaps had she not known she was going to die, she would not have done.'

'Why? Why?' George beat his fist on the table and his blue eyes were full of tears.

'Because she loved you and she knew how difficult marriage with her would make your life. She knew you would be King of England soon and she knew that she could have no place in public life. She knew she would always have to live in the shadows as she had been doing all these years. Do you think that if she had not known she was going to die she would have allowed you to marry her?'

'She was so happy when we were married. She said she knew

how Christian felt when his burden of sin fell from his shoulders. She seemed so happy.'

'That was because you had done the right thing by her ... and she by you.'

George covered his face with his hands—and Bute allowed him a few minutes of silence.

Then George said: 'The children ...?'

'I have discovered where they are. They are being well cared for.'

'But who ... who has done this?'

'She had an uncle. Did she never speak to you of him?'

'Was it someone named Pearne?'

'Why yes ... I believe it was.'

'I had heard her mention an uncle. He left her a little money some years ago. Forty pounds a year it was...'

'It must be a member of his family.'

'You have seen him?'

'No, but I have seen a man whom I can trust. A priest—a chaplain to the King at one time: Zachary Brooke.'

'Zachary Brooke. I do not know him.'

'He has a living at Islington. Apparently his help was called and he was present at Hannah's death. He has buried her in his churchyard.'

'But why ...'

'He cannot tell me details, he says. He has been sworn to secrecy. Presumably the lady's relations made these arrangements.'

'And the children? What of the children?'

'They are safe in the household of a very worthy gentleman in Surrey. John and Sarah MacKelcan will take good care of them and bring them up as their own. Your Highness can visit them whenever you wish. You can watch over them in the future. The only thing, of course, is that they will be known as MacKelcan, and it will be wise, of course, if they remain so.'

'Everything seems to have been so efficiently taken care of,' stammered George.

'I doubt not this is due to that relative of the lady's. This uncle must have had her good at heart to leave her this money.'

'It seems so strange ... I cannot believe it. Hannah to die like that ... and myself not to be there.'

Lord Bute laid his hand on the Prince's arm. 'This is a strange affair from beginning to end. You must try to forget it.'

'I shall never forget her. I can't take this in. I can't believe it. I shall never believe it. It's so strange. Why did she not send for me? A message would have brought me to her bedside. *I* should have arranged these matters ... not this relation.'

'She had her reasons.'

'I can't understand.'

'I can,' said Lord Bute softly.

'I feel bewildered. There is so much I want to know.'

'There is one thing of which Your Highness can have no doubt. That is my affection for you, my desire to protect you from trouble.'

'Oh yes ... yes, I know.'

'Then this is my advice. Plead a little sickness. I will have the doctor prepare a sedative for you ... something which will make you sleep. You have had a terrible shock. When you awake tomorrow you will feel refreshed and you will be able to see these things in a new light.'

'I shall never see Hannah's loss in any other way than the bitterest misfortune of my life.'

'My dear Highness, believe me, time helps. In a few months time the pain will be less acute. I can assure you of this. Pray do as I tell you. Rest now ... and rely on me. I shall be with you. And when you are in any dilemma, any need of help ... I beg of you trust me.'

George nodded blindly and allowed Lord Bute to send for the doctor. His lordship explained that a mild sedative was all the Prince needed and when it was administered he helped the Prince to bed and sat in his room until he slept.

•   •   •

'How did he take it?' asked the Princess Dowager.

'As I expected. He can't grasp it, of course.'

'At times I think he is such a fool.'

'Poor boy! He is too innocent for this world.'

'When I think of what this could have led to, I shiver with fear and shudder with mortification.'

'Let us be grateful that we learned of it in time.'

'Do you think this will be an end of the matter?'

Lord Bute shrugged his shoulders and looked melancholy.

'At least,' he said, 'now we are out of the dark. We can take care of him now.'

'It's clearly time he married.'

'Clearly time. But this will mean that there must necessarily be some delay. He has to recover from his broken heart.'

The Princess made an impatient sound.

'Poor George!' sighed Bute. 'But the sooner we have found a suitable wife for him the more comfortable we shall feel.'

The Princess grimaced. And what would be the effect of a wife on George? If a simple little Quakeress could lead him to such heights of folly what could a Princess, probably brought up to be a Queen, do?

Whatever happened they must keep a firm grip on their young Prince; and it was shattering to both to know that such a calamity could have occurred without their knowledge.

George should be carefully watched in future.

It was clearly very necessary with such a simple honest young man.

* * *

George could not believe that Hannah was dead. The more he thought of the extraordinary story Lord Bute had discovered, the more incredible it seemed.

'Why,' he cried again and again, 'I am sure she would have sent for me. She would have wanted to say goodbye. She would have wanted to hand the children to me; she would have wanted assurances that I would care for them.'

'She knew you would care for them,' Bute pointed out.

And George at least agreed that that was so.

'I must see this man . . . what is his name? This priest . . .'

'This . . . er . . . Zachary Brooke.'

'Yes. You have seen him. I must do the same. I must hear the story from his lips.'

'Your Highness cannot doubt my word?'

'Oh . . . no . . . no! But I must see him. I want to hear how it happened. I want to see her tomb. I want to pray there. Don't you understand?'

'Certainly I understand.'

'Well, then, I will go and see him.'

'Would Your Highness like me to accompany you?'

'Oh yes, please. And today . . .'

'I'm afraid that would not be possible. It will be necessary to find out when the Reverend Brooke can see us.'

'When he can see *us*!'

'You will not go as the Prince of Wales, remember. I do not think he is aware . . . At least I am not sure of that. Your Highness, now that this dear lady is dead, there can be no point in raising scandal. You see that, I am sure. No good can be served by making this matter public. You have your duty to the crown . . .'

'Yes, I see that. I must do my duty. That at least is left to me.'

'A high and noble destiny. You will find it will be your consolation, your solace. Allow me to investigate this matter and in a day or so we will go to Islington to see the Reverend Zachary Brooke.'

* * *

The Reverend Zachary Brooke received his distinguished guests with many expressions of respect, and it was clear that, in spite of Lord Bute's comments, he was aware who his visitors were.

'It is no use attempting to hide our identity,' said Lord Bute, smiling at the Prince. 'Your face has become too well known.'

The Reverend Zachary Brooke declared that it was his pleasure and duty to serve his future King in any capacity in which he was called upon to do so.

'The lady you buried here . . .'

'Ah yes. So young and beautiful.'

'You were with her at the end?'

'I was called to her.'

'Who called you?'

'I believe she had asked for me. The gentleman who was dealing with her affairs sent for me.'

'Who was this gentleman? What was his name?'

The Reverend Zachary Brooke wrinkled his brows. 'It slips my memory . . .'

'Was it Pearne?'

'It could well have been. Now Your Highness mentions it, I believe it was.'

'I see,' said the Prince. 'Take me to her grave.'

He and Lord Bute were led into the churchyard to a grave above which a stone had been erected. It was clearly a very new stone and as the Prince examined it he gave a cry of dismay because the name on it was not that of Hannah but Rebecca Powell.

'This is not the grave.'

The priest nodded. 'Yes, Your Highness.'

'But that name . . .'

'Will your lordship explain?'

Lord Bute assured him that he would.

'This is the grave,' he said. 'There are reasons why the name on the stone is not that of the lady who is buried here. I will talk to you on the way back. But at the moment rest assured that you are standing at the grave you have come to see.'

It was too bewildering, thought the Prince; it was like a nightmare that was made up of one fantastic scene after another. No sooner had he entered that empty silent house than the phantasmagoria had begun and it went on and on growing wilder and more macabre with every fresh image.

Oh, Hannah, Hannah, he thought, are you indeed under that stone? Is it true that I shall never see you again?

Lord Bute touched the priest's arm and they left him there.

*　　*　　*

On the way back to Kew, Lord Bute talked of the future. A King's life belonged to his people. He knew that the Prince was a man who would take his duties seriously. He must put the past behind him. He must forget this episode. It was sad in the extreme; it was regrettable. But had the Prince thought of what would happen if Hannah had lived?

He was the Prince of Wales, shortly to become the King of England. His marriage was a solemn affair. Did he not realize this?

Could he have presented a lady of the people—however accomplished, however good and charming—to his people and said: 'Here is my Queen. We have several children already, born before wedlock and although we have lived together for five . . . six . . . or was it seven years? . . . we have only just sought the benefit of clergy on our union.'

Oh no. That was not the way for a King to treat his people.

He must think first always of the good of his people. He must never for one moment act without considering them. This was one of the penalties of kingship. There were blessings; but a King's duty to his people came before anything else.

Lord Bute believed that when the Prince had grown away from this tragedy, when he saw it in its right perspective he would begin to see God's hand in this; and he would cease to mourn as bitterly as now he could not help doing.

'Hannah would have made a great Queen,' said George.

'There is no doubt of it,' soothed Lord Bute. 'But it was not the will of God.'

And that was something George had to accept.

A Sad Farewell

ALL through the summer months George mourned his loss. Sometimes he would awake from a dream in which he had heard Hannah, calling for him. Sometimes he dreamed of a grave in an Islington churchyard ... of a new stone on which the words Rebecca Powell had changed to Hannah's name. There was one nightmare which recurred now, in which he was digging up the grave; in this dream he exposed the coffin; he tore off the lid and there smiling at him was a woman who was not Hannah.

That dream was the most disturbing of all.

He never mentioned his dreams to Lord Bute. It was not that his dearest friend was not sympathetic; it was not that he murmured one reproach; but George himself felt a certain guilt because he had never confided in his friend, who had been everything a father could to him.

The one person to whom he could most easily talk was his sister Elizabeth and he went to her room as much as possible. She was spending almost the whole time in bed, for she was more easily fatigued than ever. When he expressed anxiety over this she would smile and say: 'It's my miserable old body,

George. But never mind. Such as I have to live for the spirit.'

And what a spirit she had. She never complained; her face would light up with joy when he visited her, as though he were conferring an honour; he felt humble in her presence and at the same time completely at ease.

He could tell her of the dreams. She listened with rapt attention. 'As time passes they will cease to haunt you,' she assured him.

Once she told him—this was some time after that visit to Islington when he had ceased to think of Hannah every moment of the day: 'George, perhaps it was for the best.'

'For the best!' He was aghast.

'Oh, my dearest brother,' she begged, 'imagine it. You, the Prince of Wales ... to have married in this way. The people would never have accepted her.'

'If you had known Hannah ... She was so good ... so gentle...'

'I know, George, but they expect a Prince ... a King ... to marry a Princess, and do you think Hannah would have been happy ... as a Queen! Imagine all the scandal, the intrigue. It was no life for her. No, George, I think she would have been unhappy, and you would have been unhappy to see her so. I know it seems hard to accept now, but I do believe that everything has happened for the best. The children are well cared for. You have seen them?'

'Yes,' said George. 'They seem to have accepted their new parents without question.'

'Children do. Thank God that they are so young. And perhaps in time you will come to thank Him for the way everything has turned out.'

'Never,' cried George.

But Elizabeth was sure; and she knew something which he did not; he was already growing away from the tragedy. If, she thought, he could have said goodbye to her, if he could have given her that last embrace at her death-bed, if the affair could have been neatly labelled Finished, it would have been easier to forget.

Mysteries have long lives, thought Elizabeth.

* * *

Elizabeth Chudleigh was in a quandary. She had very successfully skated over the thin ice of her relations with the Princess Dowager. The Princess avoided her as much as possible, but when they did encounter each other was coolly affable. I am safe there, thought Elizabeth grimly.

But her luck was out—or was it? She could not make sure. Clever people never waited for luck to come their way; they find a means of making it do so. That was the way she had always worked.

She had her certificate of marriage; the entry was safe in the register; but that irritating old man the Earl of Bristol refused to die. In fact he had recovered and looked as though he would continue to survive for several more years.

'And I do not grow younger!' sighed Elizabeth. She had to admit she was well past her first youth. While one remained in the lower thirties one could, if one were clever enough, continue to be young, but when one hurried towards forty ... ugh! And she still had not the title she longed for.

A complication had arisen from another direction. A certain gentleman had been casting his eyes on her and she had no doubt that he was becoming definitely dazzled. This was amazing, for he was not young and was scholarly, not the kind to indulge in riotous living; yet he was definitely interested in her—and she in him ... he because she was one of the most unusual women at Court, one of the most beautiful—most people would admit that—and one of the most outrageous. And she because of his exciting title. He was Evelyn Pierrepont, Duke of Kingston.

But she had told the Princess Dowager of her marriage to Hervey. She had gone to Larnston and forged the certificate and made that old man Annis reinstate that page in the register. What bad luck. If only the Duke of Kingston had come into her life before she had done that.

Now what? Old Bristol clinging tenaciously to life and

seeming to be good for years yet; and in the horizon the most glittering prize—the Duchess of Kingston.

She admired her bold adventuring spirit, but she had always admitted that there was one quality which had brought her trouble more than once: her impulsiveness.

She must curb that. Then she would not mention her marriage to anyone else. She would imply to the Princess Dowager that she wished it kept a secret; and that lady must obey because she, clever Elizabeth Chudleigh, knew so much that the Princess would not wish to be brought to light. Then she would very gradually enslave the Duke of Kingston—being reluctant at first, but not too reluctant—leading him on, yet holding him off. She had summed him up. He was not accustomed to women—not women such as herself, in any case. Perhaps she would become his mistress ... in due course. And once she had done that she would make herself so necessary to him that he would wish for marriage.

The Duchess of Kingston! It was a pleasant title. She preferred it to the Countess of Bristol. It would have to be fought for, but then, she had always enjoyed a fight. And the dear silly young Prince had put all the trump cards into her hand, so she had all the advantages. All she had to do was curb her recklessness and the game was hers.

*   *   *

September had come. George was at Kew a great deal in the company of Lord Bute; they rode together and constantly they talked of the future. In this way, contemplating his great destiny, George thought less of Hannah. He was beginning to realize, although he would not admit this even to himself, that Elizabeth was right when she had said that Hannah would not have been happy at Court. More and more he understood that. When he considered how much he had to learn—he who had lived all his life at Court—he saw at once that Hannah would never have fitted in.

But he could not bring himself to admit that everything had

turned out in the best way possible. Bute had hinted at it once or twice.

'There will always be Jacobites,' he had said, on one occasion. 'One of the most dangerous blows that can be struck at a crown is to have more than one claimant. And if a family divides as yours did when James II was turned from the throne by his nephew William of Orange and his daughter Mary, there is sure to be trouble. Remember the '45. It is not so far back. Then your grandfather might so easily have had to retire to Hanover, leaving England in the hands of the Stuart.'

'James II deserved his fate, I believe. He would not conform to the wishes of the people.'

'Ah, I see Your Highness has learned his lessons. One must strive to keep the goodwill of the people. One must never put oneself in the position of earning their disapproval. It is so easily done. One false step . . .'

George flushed and patted his horse's head. He knew what Lord Bute meant. The marriage with Hannah could have been as fatal to the crown as James II's religion. One had to be careful.

He wanted to be a good King. It was strange how accustomed to the idea of kingship he had grown. At one time the prospect had terrified him. He had even wished he had been born a younger brother . . . or perhaps of another branch of the family . . . perhaps not royal at all. Lord Bute's son. That would have been pleasant. But then, Lord Bute spent more time with him than he did with any of his own family.

Now, however, with every day he was becoming more and more accustomed to the prospect of ascending the throne. And during that summer and early autumn he found that he was dedicating himself to an ideal; it gave a new meaning to life. It was the best possible means of forgetting Hannah.

*　　*　　*

A message was brought to him that his sister Elizabeth wished to see him without delay.

He hurried to her and found her in bed, wan, frail and in pain.

'My dearest sister, what is wrong?'

'Oh, George, how glad I am that you have come. I am in great pain ... and I believe I am about to die.'

'This is nonsense. Where are the doctors?'

'They are in the anteroom. I told everyone that I wished to be alone with you.'

'Then we will be together, but do not talk of dying because that is something I cannot endure.'

'We have always been good friends, have we not, George?'

'The best. You are going to be well. I shall see that you are. I shall be with you ... night and day. Nothing will induce me to leave you.'

'My dearest of brothers, my greatest regret is to leave *you*.'

'Stop! You are not leaving me.'

'I am in such pain, George. They say it is an inflammation of the bowels ... but I do not know.'

'Can they do nothing?'

She shook her head. 'I believe they have given me up.'

'This cannot be. Not you ... too ... Elizabeth.'

'You still mourn for her, George?'

He nodded.

'Please, try not to be too sad, brother. Life is too short for sadness. Mine was. I am eighteen and you are three years older. It is young to die ... but I am not sorry to go. It was a poor body, mine. It gave me no pleasure to look at it. My soul is glad to leave it. Poor humped miserable flesh and bone.'

'Do not talk so, Elizabeth.'

'I wish to cheer you, brother. I want you to know that nothing is entirely bad. I am leaving this life, but although I shall be lost to those I love—and particularly you, George, I leave this malformed body of mine. I shall be free. I shall be as a bird which has just found her wings. Think of that, George, and do not be too sad. You have a great destiny before you. You will be King of England. And you will be a good king because you are a good man. Perhaps I shall be looking down on you from Heaven. Oh, George, if it were in my power to guide you, to help you ... I should do it. Now you are weeping. You grieve to see me go. But do not grieve for me, George, and do not grieve for Hannah. It is for the best, I assure you it is for the best ... everything that has happened.'

'Do not talk. You tire yourself.'

'I *must* talk, George. There is little time left. Promise me that there shall be no autopsy on my body. When I am gone let it rest in peace.'

'I promise,' said George.

'Our mother may wish it ... but I have your promise and you will not allow it.'

'I swear it, dearest Elizabeth.'

'Now give me your hand, George. Know this: I die happy. There is only one thing I regret, brother, which is that I shall not live to see you King. One more promise. Promise to be happy. Promise to put the past behind you. Marry, George. Raise a family. Have no secrets from the nation. Oh, George, if only I could be with you ...'

He sat by the bed. Why should this happen? Why should she, who was only eighteen years old, be chosen to die? Why had he lost Hannah?

Why ... why? There seemed no justice in life. The young to die so early ... the aged to go on and on wishing for death which eluded them like a mischievous child they were trying to catch.

The tears silently fell from his eyes and when Lord Bute came into the room he found him sitting thus beside the body of his dead sister.

* * *

'An autopsy?' said the Princess Dowager. 'Of course there must be an autopsy. Elizabeth died so suddenly. Three days ago she was well ... as well as she normally was, that is. There must be an autopsy.'

'It was her wish that there should not be,' said George.

'Nonsense,' retorted his mother. 'She was too ill to be reasonable. It is expected.'

The Prince glanced at Lord Bute. 'I promised my sister,' he said. 'I shall keep my promise. She did not wish it.'

'And the King?' asked his mother. 'Is he going to allow this ... this ... lapse?'

Lord Bute said: 'The King is getting too old to concern himself with such matters.' He smiled at George. 'It is the Prince's wish that he should keep his word to his sister and I am sure, Madam, that when you escape a little from your grief you will agree with His Highness that the Princess Elizabeth's wishes should be respected in this matter.'

How wonderful he was! thought George. So good, so kind. Did a man ever have such a friend! His mother shrugged her shoulders.

'I suppose you are right...'

How easily she accepted Lord Bute's decisions, although she still treated him, the Prince of Wales, as a child.

When I am King it will be different, thought George. And everything will be all right if Lord Bute is beside me when I ascend the throne.

Later he thanked his friend for his assistance.

'I had promised her. I was determined to see that her wishes were carried out, no matter what the objection.'

'I could see it. And I was determined to do all I could to see that your wishes—and those of the Princess—were respected.'

A stubborn streak in our George, Bute was thinking. I must warn Augusta.

'Our mother bears our common loss surprisingly well,' said George.

A reproach. Augusta would have to be a little more careful. George was a man of twenty-one and surely he had shown them how he could act on his own initiative in that disastrous affair of the Quakeress. Pray God they have heard the last of it. But Bute was not altogether certain of that.

What they *had* learned was that they must keep a closer watch on the Prince of Wales—and without appearing to do so. Yes, he must warn Augusta to remember constantly that they were no longer dealing with a child. And when they had a King to consider, the dangers would be greater.

'Thank you ... thank you once again,' George was saying. 'I know you understand. I cannot stop thinking of her. I have been trying to read this morning and find it impossible. She meant a great deal to me and we always planned we should be together for the rest of our lives. You see, she always said no one would wish to marry her and she counted that a blessing because it meant she would stay at home with me. And now she is gone.'

Bute nodded.

'I understand your sorrow, but I tell you now as I did on that other recent and so sad occasion, it is your preoccupation with your destiny which will place you above these early sorrows.'

'You will always be beside me ... to help me?'

'As long as you need me ... so help me God.'

George smiled. He had lost Hannah; he had lost Elizabeth; but he still had his dear friend, Lord Bute.

George, the King

ONE could not mourn for ever, particularly if one were a Prince, continually in the public eye. Elizabeth had not been a well-known figure at Court because her physical disability had kept her to her own apartments; therefore her passing was scarcely noticed. The Princess agreed that there should be no autopsy and as the King was scarcely aware of the death in the family, George had no difficulty in seeing that his sister's wishes were respected.

The Prince must attend levees and banquets which, Lord Bute was the first to point out to him, were actually given in his honour and if he failed to attend, those who had gone to such trouble to prepare such entertainments would consider their efforts wasted. So sighing George allowed himself to be dressed in his rich garments and he appeared at these functions where everyone was ready to pay him homage; for not only was he Prince of Wales, but he was young, and the people adored him and believed it would be a great day for England when he ascended the throne. He was not ill-tempered like his grandfather; he spoke English like a native; he was gracious, even modest, and with his fair skin and blue eyes was almost handsome, for when he smiled the heavy sullen Hanoverian jaw was scarcely visible and as his expression was invariably pleasant he was voted a veritable Prince Charming.

Life was becoming tolerable. Occasionally he visited the children, but those visits were becoming more rare. As Bute pointed out it was not wise to venture into Surrey too often because he was under continual surveillance. It might be discovered where he went and he must realize that the affair of the Quakeress had come to an end. It was a true marriage and he would never love anyone as he loved Hannah—that was understood—but as a man of the world he would understand that it was best to behave as though it never happened.

But he would never forget, George reiterated.

In time! Bute promised him. And Bute—that oracle of wisdom—was always right.

George knew that his mother and Lord Bute were concerned to find a bride for him. Perhaps that would be as well. He would marry and have children ... it would be pleasant to have a family which he did not have to hide away.

His friend Elizabeth Chudleigh was giving lavish parties and she always declared that, for her at least, they were spoilt unless he attended. She would throw him languishing glances and he would find her invitations irresistible. The rather solemn old Duke of Kingston was her very good friend and they were always seen together. Many said that she was his mistress, but there were always people to whisper unkind things about Elizabeth. He knew her for a kind and sympathetic friend. And she was so beautiful. He was discovering how much he liked beautiful women.

When he thought of women now he no longer saw Hannah's lovely but rather melancholy face. He saw brilliant Elizabeth Chudleigh's or that other Elizabeth who was the Countess of Pembroke. Her husband, the tenth Earl, was his groom of the Bedchamber and had been for some years, which meant that George was able to see a great deal of the Countess. There was a woman he could have been very fond of. She was older than he was, but so had Hannah been and he liked older women.

The Countess had recently given birth to a son and he had been congratulating them warmly. But sometimes the Countess was a little sad. He hoped the Earl was kind to her; he was not sure that he was. There were rumours that he was unfaithful. Poor Elizabeth Pembroke! He would be ready to comfort her if she needed his comfort. In fact, he often thought of himself comforting lovely Elizabeth Pembroke. It was a pleasant reverie.

And then something very startling happened, something which a few months before he would not have believed possible.

At one of his levees he was confronted by the most beautiful girl he had ever seen. He gasped. She was so enchanting; her skin was so fine, her dark hair abundant; her eyes perfectly shaped and her teeth showed white and even, when she smiled. It was difficult to know why she could be so lovely; it was not so much a beauty of feature but of expression, animation ... colouring ... he did not know what; he only knew that he was looking at the loveliest girl in the world and that the prospect excited him.

'Who is that beautiful creature?' he demanded of the man who stood next to him.

'Lady Sarah Lennox, Your Highness,' was the answer.

'Who ... who is she?'

'The Duke of Richmond's sister, Sir. Just returned to London from Ireland where she has been living for some time.'

'Why did she live in Ireland?'

'I believe she is an orphan.'

'And she is no longer living in Ireland? Where now does she live?'

'At Holland House, Sir. Her eldest sister married Henry Fox and she lives with them.'

'I see. That is very interesting.'

'Your Highness wishes her to be presented to you?'

'No ... no,' said the Prince uneasily.

It was enough to look.

*   *   *

He went on looking for her on every occasion. She seemed to become more beautiful every time he saw her. Looking at her, thinking of her, he forgot all his grief over Hannah. Hannah could never have compared with this gay vital girl who danced and chattered and now and then would glance in the direction of the Prince of Wales, rather invitingly and just a little piqued because he made no attempt to speak to her.

She is beautiful, thought George. One day I will speak to her.

He became obsessed by her. He forgot Hannah and to mourn for Elizabeth for he could not be unhappy in a world which contained Lady Sarah Lennox.

His eyes were always on her. One day he approached her.

'I know who you are,' he told her. 'You are Lady Sarah Lennox.'

'How discerning of Your Highness! I also know who you are, but that is not very clever of me, is it? Since everyone knows Your Highness.'

'I am sure *you* would be clever.'

'Oh, does Your Highness think so? It is more than some people do.'

'What people?'

'Oh ... one's family.'

He was very grave. 'I hope your family appreciates you.'

'About as much as yours do, I expect. You know what families are.' She laughed and he found the conversation scintillating. She was a little arch, having known for some time of the effect she had on him and being amused to find a Prince of Wales so shy in the company of a girl who although the sister of the Duke of Richmond, and more important still the sister-in-law of Henry Fox, was of little real significance in the exalted company of the Prince of Wales.

'Oh yes,' he said, laughing with her. 'I know. I have watched you dancing ... often.'

'Yes, I know. I have seen you watching.' And she laughed, and he laughed with her. 'Your Highness does not care for dancing?'

'Oh, I would not say that.'

'I have not seen you dance.'

'What was the dance I saw you dancing a few moments ago?'

'The Betty Blue—surely Your Highness knows it?'

'I confess I do not.'

'Why, la! It is the latest fashion.'

'I have never danced it.'

'Your Highness should. It is highly diverting.'

'One needs to be skilful.'

'Nonsense. Oh...' She put the slenderest of fingers to the prettiest of mouths. 'Now you will be angry. It's *lèse majesté* or something. I told the Prince of Wales he was speaking nonsense.'

'It does not matter. I ... I am sure you are right.'

'Is Your Highness sure?' Her lovely eyes were wide open. What he was uncertain of was whether she were serious or not. 'Your Highness is not going to send me to the Tower?'

'Not unless you allow me to come with you.'

She laughed again. Nobody ever laughed as she did, he was sure. So gay, so spontaneous, so joyous. It made him want to laugh too.

'And there,' she went on, 'I would teach you the Betty Blue.'

'It is not necessary to go to the Tower to teach me that.'

'Your Highness means that I should teach you here?'

'Would you ... would you object to that?'

'Why, if Your Highness *commanded* I could not object.'

'I would not wish to command you.'

'Then, sir, I will say it would give me the greatest pleasure to teach you the steps of the Betty Blue.'

So she taught him—touching hands, coming close; parting and coming together again. It was bliss, thought the Prince of Wales.

He had never been so happy in his life ... except with Hannah, he hastily told himself. But he must be truthful. With Hannah there had always been the sense of guilt. There was none of that with Sarah. He could dance with her, talk with her, laugh with her—and people looked on smiling at them.

Yes, this was sheer bliss.

*   *   *

At first the morning of the 25th October of the year 1760 seemed like any other in the King's apartments at Kensington. The King had slept well and on the stroke of six precisely rose from his bed; as usual he asked his valet in which direction the wind was blowing. The valet always had the answer ready, for the King would be testy if he had not. And it must be correct. Then he would look at his watch and compare it with all the clocks in the apartment. There were several, for time was one of the most important factors of the King's life.

He sat in his chair and waited for his cup of chocolate. It must arrive exactly to the minute; and it must be neither too hot nor too cold. His servants knew how to please him and he rarely had cause to complain, although when he was in a bad mood he could find many reasons. Schroder, his German valet, understood him well. 'Germans make the best servants,' he was apt to say; just as he said: 'Germans are the best cooks, the best soldiers, the best friends...'

'So the weather is good this morning, Schroder,' he said as the dish of chocolate was handed to him and he had heard the report on the wind.

'Yes, Sire. Some sun and pleasant for walking.'

'I shall take a walk in the gardens. Plenty of exercise, Schroder, and never guzzling at the table.'

'Yes, Sire.'

'That's the way to prevent getting too fat. I used to tease the Queen about her weight. Oh, she loved her chocolate, Schroder. Could not resist it. And she was a woman wise in every other way. I was always telling her she should eat less. There's a tendency to run to fat in the family, Schroder.'

'Oh yes, Sire.'

'That clock is almost a minute slow.'

'Is it, Sire? I will speak to the clock winder without delay.'

The King nodded.

But he was feeling in a jovial mood, not inclined to be angry about the clock. He was thinking of Caroline, sitting at breakfast with the family, and Lord Hervey hovering. An amusing fellow, Hervey, and a great favourite with Caroline. And all the children there. Not many of them left now. Fred had gone ... no loss. And William his only other son a disappointment to him. Emily a sour old spinster. They ought to have let her marry. Just those two left to him, William and Emily ... both unmarried. He couldn't count Mary who'd married the Landgrave of Hesse-Cassel. She was too far away. Not much of a family, then. And the boy ... George! He would be all right if he could cut loose from his mother's apron strings and free himself from the Scotsman.

It would have been different if Caroline had lived. He always thought of Caroline in the mornings; in the evenings he devoted himself to the Countess of Yarmouth. She was a good woman and he was glad he had brought her from Hanover. Caroline would be pleased, he told himself. She was always fond of those who were fond of me.

He looked at the clock, drained off his chocolate and rose to go into the closet. It was a quarter past seven.

He shut the door and suddenly he felt a dizziness; he put out his hand to the bureau to steady himself, and as he did so he fell to the floor.

*   *   *

Schroder had heard the fall and ran into the closet; he saw the King lying on the floor, and that he had cut his head on the side of the bureau.

'Your Majesty, are you all right?'

There was no answer. He knelt down and cried: *'Mein Gott!'*

Then he called to the other servants.

'His Majesty ...' he stammered; and they lifted the King and laid him on the bed.

'Call the physicians,' cried Schroder; and at that moment Lady Yarmouth came running in.

'Schroder. What has happened? Where is the King? Oh my God!'

'His Majesty fell, while in his closet,' Schroder told her. 'I have sent for the doctors.'

Lady Yarmouth knelt by the bed murmuring: *'Mein Gott! Mein Gott!'*

When the doctors came they said they would bleed the King without delay, for it was certain that he had had a stroke. But when they tried to bleed him, no blood came.

Schroder knew what that meant. The King was dead.

Schroder also knew his duty. He had been primed in it by Lord Bute and although he served the King loyally he was not such a fool as to believe that he must ignore the masters of tomorrow for the rulers of the day.

Lord Bute had said: 'It is imperative that if anything should happen to the King—and he is in his seventy-seventh year so it's not unlikely—the first to know should be the Prince of Wales. It is your duty, Schroder, to see that is done. So in this unhappy event send a message immediately to His Highness and do not say "The King is dead". Write that he has had an accident ... an accident will mean that he is dying; a bad accident will imply that he is dead.'

Those orders were clear enough and it was also clear to a man of Schroder's intelligence where the orders would come from now on.

So while the doctors busied themselves about the bed and Lady Yarmouth knelt by the bed in a state of dazed apprehension, Schroder wrote on the first piece of paper he could find that the King had had a bad accident and he despatched a messenger with it to Kew, with the instructions that it was to be put in no hands except those of the Prince of Wales.

*   *   *

George was taking his morning ride in the gardens at Kew

when he saw the messenger in the King's livery riding towards him.

He pulled up and waited. His heart had begun to beat faster. He guessed, of course. They had been waiting for it so long; it had to come sooner or later and there could be no denying that here it was when he read Schroder's scrawl: 'Your Highness, the King has met with a serious accident.'

In those first seconds George was aware of a terrible sense of isolation. This brisk October morning was different from any other in his life. He had changed. He was not the same man he had been yesterday. He had become a King.

He shivered a little. He had visualized this so many times, but nothing is quite the same in the imagination as in reality.

There was such a mingling of emotion—fear and pleasure, pride and apprehension; a sense of power and of inadequacy.

But there was one he needed; and it was of him he first thought.

He told the messenger he might return whence he had come and turning to his groom he said: 'Take the horses back to the stables and say one has gone lame. You have seen the messenger from the King. Tell no one you have seen this ... if you value your employment.'

'Yes, Your Highness.'

The Prince dismounted and made his way to the apartments of Lord Bute.

His lordship was at breakfast and as soon as he saw George he knew what had happened.

He hastily dismissed his servants and, kneeling, kissed George's hands.

'Long live the King!' he cried. 'And a blessing on Your Majesty.'

'Whose first command will be to hold you to your promise, my lord.'

'My life is at Your Majesty's service.'

'Now,' said George, 'I feel competent to mount the throne.'

*   *   *

While the new King and Lord Bute were preparing to leave for London, a letter arrived for George in the hand of his Aunt Amelia.

George took it and read it. It formally announced the death of her father and begged George to come to London with all speed.

Bute watched his protégé sign the receipt for the letter, boldly and without hesitation: G.R. A King of twenty-two, thought Lord Bute. That could be an alarming state of affairs —but not with George, innocent malleable George.

'Your Majesty is ready?' he asked when the messenger had gone.

George answered: 'Let us leave.'

There was certainly a new purpose about him. The lessons had been taken to heart. How different it would have been if that extraordinary affair of the Quaker had not been satisfactorily settled. Bute grew cold at the thought. That had been a narrow escape from disaster, brought about just in time.

On the road from Kew they discussed the new position. George would have to be firm; he would be surrounded by some very ambitious men; and the most formidable of them was, of course, Mr. Pitt.

The sound of horses' hooves made Bute put his head out of the carriage window.

He sank back in his seat grimacing. 'As I thought. They have lost little time. Mr. Pitt is on his way to Kew.'

Mr. Pitt's splendid equipage with his postilions in blue and silver livery and his carriage drawn by six fine horses had pulled up beside the royal coach. Mr. Pitt alighted—perfectly groomed, his tie wig set neatly on his little head, his hawk's eyes veiled but glittering.

'At Your Majesty's service.'

'You are kind, Mr. Pitt,' said George.

'As soon as the news was brought to me I set out for Kew to offer my condolences for the loss of your grandfather and my congratulations on Your Majesty's elevation to the throne.

There are certain immediate formalities and I have come prepared to advise Your Majesty on the way to London.'

Pitt was ignoring Bute as though he were some menial attendant. Bute could say nothing in the presence of the King, but his fury was rising. George, however, had indeed been well trained.

'Thank you, Mr. Pitt,' he said, 'but I shall give my own orders and am on my way to London to do so. I suggest that you get into your carriage and follow us.'

Pitt was amazed. He had expected to ride with the King into London. He had thought the young man would naturally have turned to him for guidance. Moreover, it was the custom for the King's ministers to advise the King; and here was this boy —twenty-two and young for his years—telling the Great Commoner himself that he had no need of his services.

For once Pitt was at a loss for words. He bowed; got into his carriage and while the King and his dear friend Lord Bute rode on towards London, Mr. Pitt had no help for it but to get into his carriage and follow.

Bute was laughing with glee as they rode along.

'I fancy Mr. Pitt is very surprised. He thought Your Majesty would almost fall on your knees before him. He has to be shown his place.'

'We will show him,' said George.'

'His position is not exactly a happy one,' smiled Bute, 'for although he has taken power into his hands it is still that dolt Newcastle who is the nominal head of the government. That will make it easier. Your Majesty should summon Newcastle ... not Pitt. Then our arrogant gentleman will realize that Your Majesty has no intention of being ruled by him.'

Indeed not! thought George. He would not be ruled by anyone. He was King. It was what he had been born for ... reared for ... and now he had reached that high eminence.

He looked at the countryside with tears in his eyes. His land! These people whom he saw here and there, did not know it yet, but they had a King who was going to concern himself only with their welfare. He was going to make this a great and happy country. He and his Queen would set an example of morality which would take the place of all the profligacy which had darkened the country before.

His Queen. He saw her clearly beside him. The loveliest girl in the kingdom—who but the Lady Sarah Lennox?

* * *

Pitt, regarding the new King's strange behaviour on the road as youthful arrogance and uncertainty, arranged for the first meeting of the Privy Council to be held at Savile House. Meanwhile George, under Lord Bute's direction, had sent for the Duke of Newcastle to wait on him at Leicester House.

There the new King told Newcastle that he had always had a good opinion of him and he knew his zeal for his grandfather and he believed that zeal would be extended to him.

Newcastle expressed his pleasure and was looking forward to telling Pitt that their fears regarding the new King were unfounded, when George said: 'My Lord Bute is your good friend. He will tell you my thoughts.'

Newcastle was bewildered. He had always known of the young King's fondness for Bute, but he could not believe it would be carried as far as this. He might regard the Scotsman as a parent, but surely he realized the heights to which Pitt had carried the country.

He left the King's presence and went to see Pitt to impart his misgivings to him.

Pitt agreed that the King's conduct was extraordinary.

'But we must not forget,' he reminded Newcastle, 'that he has been ill-prepared for his destiny. When he is made aware of the position he will be easy enough to handle. I have prepared the speech he is to make to the Council and was about to leave to see him now.'

'I will await your return with some misgivings,' the Duke told him.

* * *

Pitt bowed before the King.

He smiled and went on to say that he doubted not the King

knew the procedure on occasions such as the present—'of which, Your Majesty, there have been many in our history'.

'I am acquainted with the procedure,' said George coolly, for Bute had told him that the only way to deal with Mr. Pitt was to refuse to see him as the great man Mr. Pitt believed himself to be. Pitt was the King's minister and he had to be made to see that he was not the King. 'A misapprehension,' added Lord Bute, 'that his manner would suggest he deludes himself into believing.'

'I guessed Your Majesty would be, and I have prepared your speech. Perhaps you would look over it and give it your approval?'

George replied as Bute had suggested he should, because Bute had known that Pitt would present himself and his speech at the earliest possible moment. In fact Bute had already prepared the speech, so George had no need of Mr. Pitt's literary efforts.

'I have already viewed this subject with attention,' said the King, 'and have prepared what I shall say at the Council table.'

Pitt was astonished. Ministers had grown accustomed to the indifference of Hanoverian kings to the traditions of English monarchy. And here was a boy—twenty-two years old—flying in the face of custom.

'Your Majesty would no doubt allow me to glance over what you intend to say.'

George hesitated. Bute had not advised him on this point. He said: 'Er ... yes, Mr. Pitt. You may see it.' And going to a drawer he produced the speech.

Mr. Pitt cast his eyes over it and when he came to the phrase '... and as I mount the throne in the midst of a bloody and expensive war I shall endeavour to prosecute it in the manner most likely to bring an honourable peace ...' Mr. Pitt paused; his eyes opened wide and a look of horror spread over his face.

'Your Majesty, this cannot be said.'

George was alarmed, but he endeavoured to follow Bute's instructions and preserve an aloof coldness.

'Sire, this war is necessary to our country's well-being. Our conquests have raised us from a country of no importance to a world power. I recall Lord Bute's writing to me a few years ago when he deplored the state of our country in which he saw the wreck of the crown. Lord Bute was right then, Sire. Later he was congratulating me on our successes and thanking God that I was at the helm. I venture to think his lordship cannot have changed his mind since his hopes in my endeavours have not proved in vain. This war is bloody, Sire. All wars are bloody. It is not unduly expensive, for in spite of its outlay in men and money it is bringing in such rewards, Sire, as England never possessed before. You will not be a King merely; you will be an Emperor ... when India and America are yours. And believe me, Sire, there is untold wealth, untold glory, to come your way. So I beg of you do not rail in your first speech as King against a bloody and expensive war.' George was about to speak, but Pitt held up a hand and without Lord Bute at his side to guide him George could only listen. 'One thing more. I am sure Your Majesty has overlooked. You have allies. Are you going to make a peace without consulting them? Believe me, Sire, that if you use these words in your first speech to your Council you will do irreparable harm to yourself and your country.'

'You are very vehement, Mr. Pitt.'

'Not more so, Sire, than the occasion requires. Now, will you allow me to advise you on this one sentence. The rest of your speech stands as it is written. It is well enough. But this sentence must be adjusted. Now allow me ... Instead of "bloody and expensive war which I shall endeavour to prosecute in the manner most likely to bring an honourable peace..." we will say "...an expensive but just and necessary war. I shall endeavour to prosecute it in a manner most likely to bring an honourable and lasting peace, in concert with my allies." Now, will Your Majesty agree?'

George hesitated. He saw the point. It was true that Mr. Pitt was leading the country to a position it had never before attained. But Lord Bute had said they must do without Mr.

Pitt because Mr. Pitt would not be content to work under their direction. Mr. Pitt would want to rule and lead them. All the same, there was something about the man which made it impossible to rebuff him.

'I will consider it,' said George haughtily.

Mr. Pitt bowed and left.

It is the Scotsman who was trying to influence the King, thought Pitt. We shall have to delegate him to some position with a high-sounding name to hide its insignificance.

Without that evil genius George might be moulded into a fair shape of a King.

*　　*　　*

In a room at Carlton House the Archbishop of Canterbury received the members of the Privy Council when he solemnly informed them of an event which they already knew had taken place: George II was dead and they were assembled here to greet the new King, George III.

George, who had been in an antechamber waiting to be summoned, then came in.

In his hand he carried the speech he would deliver—his first as King of England. As he came to the Council Chamber his eyes met those of Mr. Pitt. The minister's were steely; he was wondering whether George would take his advice and change the speech which Bute had written. When he had been with the King he had been sure he would; but after speaking to Newcastle and talking together of the influence Bute had on the new King—and on his mother who also wielded great influence with the young man—he was a little uneasy.

He felt that what happened in the next few moments would be an indication and he would be able to plan accordingly.

Of one thing Pitt was certain; Bute would have to be relegated to the background, and the sooner the better.

George addressed his Council. At least, thought Pitt, they have taught him to speak. The new King enunciated perfectly —trained by actors. How different from his grandfather with his comical English, and his great-grandfather who couldn't speak a word of the language!

There were great possibilities in George, Pitt decided. A young King could be an asset, providing he were malleable and had good ministers. This was a situation which Mr. Pitt was sure prevailed but unfortunately there was Lord Bute ... like a black shadow, an evil genius to undo all the good the auguries promised without him.

The King had started to speak:

'The loss that I and the nation have sustained by the death of my grandfather would have been severely felt at any time; but coming at so critical a juncture and so unexpectedly, it is by many circumstances augmented, and the weight now falling on me much increased. I feel my own insufficiency to support it as I wish; but animated by the tenderest affection for my native country, and by depending upon the advice, experience and abilities of your lordships; on the support of every honest man; I enter with cheerfulness into the arduous situation, and shall make it the business of my life to promote in every thing, the glory and happiness of these kingdoms, to preserve and strengthen the constitution in both church and state; and as I mount the throne in the midst of an *expensive, but just and necessary war I shall endeavour to prosecute it in a manner most likely to bring an honourable and lasting peace, in concert with my allies.*'

Listening intently, Mr. Pitt permitted himself a slow smile of triumph.

* * *

In the streets the people were still rejoicing. The old man was dead, and in his place was a young and handsome boy, who had been born and bred in England—a real Englishman this time, said the people. This was an end of the Germans.

There was feasting in the eating houses and drinking in the taverns and dancing round the bonfires in the streets. They knew what this meant. A coronation; that meant a holiday and a real chance to celebrate. And then there'd be a marriage, for the King was a young man and would need a wife.

This was a change, when for so long the only excitements had been the victory parades. It was stimulating to sing *Rule Britannia*, but wars meant something besides victories. They meant taxation, and men lost to the battle. But a coronation, a royal wedding . . . they were good fun. Dancing, singing, drinking . . . free wine doubtless . . . and sly jokes about the young married pair.

Now the people had their King they wanted a bride for him.

Pitt was congratulating himself over the matter of the speech. Bute would be an encumbrance; they would have to deal tactfully with him, but they would manage.

It was a shock when the day after George had been proclaimed King at Savile House, Charing Cross, Temple Bar, Cheapside and the Royal Exchange, to learn that the new King's first act was to appoint his brother Edward and Lord Bute Privy Councillors.

'There will be trouble,' said Pitt. 'Bute is going to make a bid for power. But I can handle him. The only thing I fear is that the King, through that fool Bute, will try to interfere with my conduct of the war.'

The war! It was Pitt's chief concern. As long as everything went well on the battle-front, as long as he could succeed in his plans for building an Empire, events at home could take care of themselves.

*　　*　　*

At seven o'clock in the evening of a dark November day George II was buried in Henry VII's chapel at Westminster.

The chamber was hung with purple, and silver lamps had been placed at intervals to disperse the gloom. Under a canopy of purple velvet stood the coffin. Six silver chandeliers had been placed about it and the effect was impressive.

The procession to the chapel was accompanied by muffled drums and fifes and the bells tolled continuously. The horse-guards wore crêpe sashes and as their horses slowly walked through the crowds their riders drew their sabres and a hush fell on all those who watched.

Perhaps the most sincere mourner was William, Duke of Cumberland. He was in a sad state himself, for soon after he had lost the command of the army he had had a stroke of the palsy which had affected his features. Newcastle was beside him—a contrast with his plump figure and ruddy good looks. He was pretending to be deeply affected, but was in fact considering what effect the King's very obvious devotion to Lord Bute was going to have on his career.

He wept ostentatiously—or pretended to—and as soon as he entered the Chapel groped his way to one of the stalls, implying that he was overcome by his grief; but he was soon watching the people through his quizzing glass to see who had come, until feeling the chill of the chapel he began to fret that he might catch cold.

'The cold strikes right through one's feet,' he whispered to Pitt who was beside him.

Pitt did not answer; he was thinking how unfortunate it was that the old King had not lived a year or so longer to give him the security of tenure he needed. But it was absurd to fear; no one could oust Pitt from his position. Whatever Bute said the King would realize the impossibility of that. The people would never allow it for one thing. No, he had nothing to fear.

There was the young King, looking almost handsome in candle light. Tall and upstanding, and that open countenance which was appealing. The King was honest enough, there was no denying that. The point was how much had that mother of his and her paramour got him under their thumbs?

The King was thinking: Poor Grandfather! So this is the end to all your posturings and pretence and all your anger. You will never be angry with me again, never hit me as you did in Hampton.

I will do everything you wished. I have heard that *you* burned your father's will and that he burned his wife's, but I shall carry out *your* wishes to the letter. Lady Yarmouth shall have what you wished her to. I want to be a good King, Grandfather. Perhaps you did too. But you cared too much for

Germany, and a King of England's first care should be England.

Poor Uncle William! How ill he looked. It was sad when one recalled his coming to the nursery in the old days and talking about the '45. That was the highlight of his life, poor Uncle William; that terrible battle of Culloden had been his glory. And then he had lost his power and after that his illness had come, and now—although he was not very old when compared with his father the dead King—he was a very sick man. Yet he stood erect, indifferent to his own disabilities, and if one did not see how distorted his face was, which was possible in this dim candle-light, he looked a fine figure of a man in his long black cloak, the train of which must be all of five yards long.

The Duke of Newcastle was bustling about. Dear Lord Bute was right. That man was a fool and no use to them at all. If only he could be as sure that they should rid themselves of Mr. Pitt! There stood Newcastle, crying one moment, looking round to bow to someone the next, shivering with cold and whispering that he would be the next one they were burying, for there was no place more likely for catching one's death than at a funeral, and the Chapel of Henry VII must be the coldest place on Earth.

George saw Newcastle surreptitiously step on to his uncle's long cloak in order, the King supposed, to preserve his feet from the chill of the chapel.

Then his uncle was bemused as to what was restricting him and turning found it was the burly Duke standing on his train.

And at last the late King's coffin was placed where he had wished it to be—beside that of his Queen, that, he had said, they might lie side by side for ever.

George hoped that his grandfather was happy wherever he was. His wishes had been carried out and he was laid to rest beside the wife whom he had bullied during his lifetime, to whom he had been constantly unfaithful, but whom he had loved next best to himself.

'I shall hope,' prayed George, 'to be a better King than my

grandfather and when I marry to be truly faithful to my wife for the rest of my life.'

Marriage was a pleasant thought, for even in this sombre chapel he could not think of it without thinking also of the dazzling beauty of Lady Sarah Lennox.

* * *

George scrupulously carried out the last King's wishes. It was surprising that George II had left only £30,000 when he had always been so careful. This he had declared was to be shared between his three surviving children—Cumberland and his two sisters. Cumberland agreed to forego his share to the advantage of his sisters for he was a generous man and rich enough, he declared. For Lady Yarmouth there was an envelope in the King's bureau which was found to contain £6,000 in banknotes.

George made a point of seeing that these fell into her hands and added £2,000 of his own.

The King's honesty was noted and doubly admired when his grandfather's lack of it was remembered, for it was recalled how George II had destroyed his father's will. Everyone applauded it, and none more than Mr. Pitt.

If the King would put himself into his minister's hands there would be nothing to fear. Mr. Pitt would like to see the King presiding over social occasions; he would like to hear the people cheering their young Monarch. But he wanted to make sure that the young Sovereign did not interfere with the conduct of the country's affairs.

How far was Bute influencing him? And what of that other menacing shadow; the King's mother? The Princess Augusta would consider herself of very great importance now that her son had ascended the throne.

The sooner the position is clarified the better, thought Pitt.

Some light was thrown on it when the Parliament assembled to hear the Speech from the throne. These occasions in the past had gone according to pattern. A speech was prepared and the King delivered it.

It soon became clear that the speech the King was making in that very musical and well-modulated voice of his was *not* the one which had been written for him.

'Born and educated in this country I glory in the name of Britain ...'

Britain! Why not England? It could only be that the King was associating himself with the country across the Border, the breeding-ground of Jacobites, the land which had rebelled, which had harboured Bonnie Prince Charlie ... *and* was the birthplace of Lord Bute!

That was it. They knew who had substituted that word for England. Lord Bute! He was tampering with the speeches which the King's ministers had written for him. He was telling the King that Scotland was as important as England. And why? Because Bute was a Scottish peer. That was the reason. And had not Pitt pointed out to him before the death of the last King that one of the reasons why he could not be given high office was because he *was* a Scottish peer?

So this was Bute's answer.

Pitt wondered whether to challenge in debate the origin of those words. Perhaps it was unwise. He did not want to antagonize the King ... nor the people. The King was new and new Kings were often popular, more so if they were young and tolerably good-looking. No, he would leave it, but he would have to be very watchful of my Lord Bute.

Perhaps it was time the King was married. If he married the right woman she could help to wean the King from this most unfortunate friendship.

*　　*　　*

The Princess Augusta was of the same idea.

'The King should marry,' she told Bute.

Bute agreed but hesitantly. Like Pitt he saw the possible effect of a wife.

'He must begin producing heirs and cannot start too soon.'

Bute agreed with that.

'You hesitate, my love.'

'It is because I feel that if he married a woman who became possessive, she might be jealous of your influence with him and seek to lessen it.'

'We must choose the right woman.'

'Ah yes, and be very careful.'

'She must be German,' said the Princess. 'German women are properly brought up. They are taught to respect their husbands, to obey them and to know their place. Take, for instance, my mother-in-law.'

'Yet one has always heard she ruled the King.'

'She was an exceptionally clever woman. We must not find a *clever* woman for our George. But even Caroline who was so much cleverer than her husband, never let him know it. And there are not many Carolines.'

'There is also an Augusta,' said Lord Bute playfully.

'When Fred was alive I never meddled. I would have thought it most ... improper. It was only after he was dead that I saw the need to care for my children and I deliberately set out to protect them.'

'You are right as usual. It must be a German Princess for George and one of your choosing.'

She smiled at him tenderly. As usual they were of one mind.

*   *   *

The King was also thinking of marriage. Now the funeral was over and he was indeed King he would have to have a coronation. When he was crowned he wanted her to be crowned too.

He dreamed of her beside him. She would look so beautiful in a crown. She would have to be serious for once, he would tell her indulgently, and she would laugh at him and say: 'Yes, of course. I am really always serious where you are concerned.' And it would be true. She liked to tease and banter, but underneath that she was serious.

He was the King, so therefore he could choose his own wife. Why not? It was not as though he were asking to marry a linen-

draper's ... He flushed hotly and tried not to think of St.
James's Market and Hannah's sitting there in the window.
That had been impossible. He saw it all so clearly. Yet then it
had seemed so right.

But it was over. Thank God it had worked out as it did.

He would always remember her. He had loved her dearly. I
still do, he told himself defiantly. I shall always love Hannah.
But a man cannot go on mourning for ever, especially if he is a
King. She would understand that. She had always understood.

Of course she would. That was why she was always so
anxious, why she was always aware of the enormity of their
action. She had been far more aware than he had. That was
why he had always had to comfort her.

But it was over ... and he must forget it ... outwardly, of
course. Never in truth, Hannah, he whispered. I shall always
remember. But it is over and a King must marry.

He had made his peace with Hannah, now he could think of
Sarah. Sarah laughing, teasing, dancing that absurd dance, the
Betty Blue.

He would no longer delay. The first one he must tell would
be his dear friend Lord Bute who would advise him how best
to deal with this matter of marriage.

He took up his pen and wrote to that very dear friend:

'What I now lay before you I never intended to communicate to anyone. The truth is this: The Duke of Richmond's
sister arrived from Ireland towards the middle of last
November. I was struck with her appearance at St. James's
and my passion has been increasing every time I have since
beheld her. Her voice is sweet. She seems sensible ... In short
she is everything I can form to myself as lovely.'

He sat dreaming of her as he wrote; then he sealed the letter
and had it sent to Lord Bute.

The King's Courtship

LADY SARAH LENNOX was amused. She was a very high-spirited girl, not yet seventeen, and it was highly diverting to know that the King was in love with her. Sarah was living at the time at Holland House, the home of her brother-in-law, Henry Fox; and her closest friend Lady Susan Fox-Strangways, a niece of Henry Fox, was staying there. In Sarah's bedroom the two girls could giggle and chatter together and be as frivolous as they pleased.

Susan was more serious than Sarah. She was the daughter of the Earl of Ilchester and her family were perhaps not quite so prominent as Sarah's, whose brother was now the third Duke of Richmond and whose great-grandfather had been Charles II and great-grandmother Louise de Keroualle. There was, Susan often thought, something of the Stuart charm in Sarah. She was certainly attractive and yet when one studied her face one wondered why. Her eyes were too small, her mouth too large; but that was of little importance, for when Sarah laughed or chattered or merely entered a room, to the majority she was the most exciting female in that room.

Charm! thought Susan wistfully. And it will doubtless bring her a throne.

Sarah was saying: 'But he's so shy. Do you know, Susan, he *stammers*. He is really afraid of offending me. Fancy that. The King goes in awe of Sarah Lennox!'

'Oh, that is what is called courting. When and if you married him it would be very different.'

'And why should it be, pray?'

'Because that is the way of the world.'

'Don't look so wise, Susan. You know nothing about it. It is entirely in one's own hands and it would be in mine. If I married him I would keep him as he is today.'

'Sarah ... think of it! Queen! A coronation! And Mr. Pitt bowing to you and waiting on your judgments. And Mr. Fox doing the same.'

'Mr. Fox would always remember that I am his sister-in-law. He loves me, I know, but he would never bow to my superior wisdom, I do assure you. He thinks I am a bundle of inconsequent frivolity. I heard him tell my sister Caroline so the other day.'

'Sisters-in-laws may be that, but Queens would not be.'

'Oh, you don't know Henry. He has as high an opinion of himself as Mr. Pitt has of himself ... or my Lord Bute, of whom, I don't mind telling you, my dear Susan, they are constantly talking. It's my belief that they are more afraid of Lord Bute than anyone in this kingdom. I have seen a certain look in brother Henry's eyes when they rest on me. I think he is weighing me up against Lord Bute. He feels that if I married the King I could then help to break his infatuation for that man—for infatuation it is. He is devoted to him.' Sarah pouted. 'I think he is almost as fond of him as he is of me.'

'Sarah, be serious a moment. Are you in love with George?'

Sarah put her head on one side and appeared to consider. 'Well, I fancy a crown would look rather well on my head.'

'Don't be silly. What about Newbattle? I thought you were in love with him.'

Sarah's expression softened a little. 'I was, Susan,' she admitted.

'It seems to me, Sarah, that you do fall in and out of love rather easily.'

'That is wiser than falling in too deeply, don't you think?'

'It seemed hardly worth while taking him from Caroline Russell if you are just going to abandon him for the King.'

Sarah laughed. 'Can you imagine Newbattle ... deserted? He will soon find someone ready to give consolation.'

'Caroline would not have him back.'

'Caroline would not have been allowed to marry him in any case, I feel sure. Her people want the Duke of Marlborough for her.'

'But she wanted Newbattle, Sarah ... and you deliberately set out to attract him.'

'Oh, stop preaching, Susan. I wanted him, too, and he is not a parcel of goods to be handed about. He makes his own decisions, you know.'

'And what does he say now that he knows of the King's intentions?'

'If he knows of the King's intentions he knows more than most of us, Susan. Because the rest of us are not sure.'

'But he knows that the King is attracted by you.'

Sarah giggled. 'Poor George does make that a little obvious does he not?'

'He is rather charming,' said Susan wistfully. 'He is innocent and inexperienced.'

'I like that in him,' agreed Sarah. 'When he talks to me he says the most idiotic things ... and he keeps saying the same things over and over again.'

'It is because he is bemused. It shows how deep his feelings go for you. I heard it said that at the Council meeting and in Parliament he spoke with great firmness.'

'Ah!' laughed Sarah delightedly. 'So it is just in my presence. He's very different from my lord Newbattle.'

'I believe you have a strong fancy for that man.'

'I won't deny it.'

'You are in love with him?'

'Well, perhaps a little.'

'Because of himself or because he left Lady Caroline Russell so easily when you beckoned? Which is it, Sarah?'

'A little of both, perhaps.'

'That is not good enough.'

'Oh indeed, Madam Schoolmarm?'

'You are old enough to be married, Sarah, and your family will do everything in their power to make you Queen of England.'

'Queen of England. I like the sound of that.'

'Better than you like George?'

'Well, it is impossible to separate the two.'

'So it is a matter of choosing between two titles: Queen of England or Marchioness of Lothian, for Newbattle will one day be the Marquis.'

'The Queen sounds better, Susan. You must admit it.'

Sarah jumped up and rummaging in her jewel box brought out a golden bangle which she placed on her head. She sat in her chair, her arms folded, inclining her head regally until the bangle fell off and rolled across the floor.

'You are absurd, Sarah,' cried Susan. 'I don't think you realize how serious a matter this is.'

'I do. It's marriage, my dear Susan, a state into which our families insist we must all enter ... if they can find suitable matches for us.'

'Your family would never want you to accept Newbattle when there was a chance of George.'

'My sister Caroline ran away and married Henry Fox. The family knew nothing about it until it was *fait accompli*.'

'You would run away and marry John Newbattle?'

'If I wished to. But I don't think it would be necessary. His family would be delighted to have me. Don't forget I have royal blood in my veins.'

'Wrong side of the blanket,' Susan reminded her.

'Don't be coarse, Susan.'

'Certainly not. Only factual. The royal blood is there, but must be recognized for what it is.'

'Well, suppose I decided on George?'

'Then there might be some who do not consider you worthy.'

'What nonsense!'

'His Mamma, for instance. I heard that she wants a German Queen.'

'George would decide surely, and Henry says the people would be on his side.'

'And what about all those ambitious gentlemen around the King. They wouldn't want to see the power of the Richmonds and Foxes increased through having a Queen in the family. They would much rather have a German woman whom the King didn't love and who would take years to learn the language.'

'Ah, but my dear Susan, it will not rest with them, but with George ... and with me.'

'You are very sure of yourself.'

Sarah retrieved the bangle from the floor and put it on her head.

'Be careful, my lady, how you address the Queen.'

'Yes, I see you fancy the title, but I can't help feeling you have a hankering for Newbattle.'

'Shall I say,' said Sarah haughtily, 'that I have not yet made up my mind.'

*   *   *

Meanwhile Lord Bute was laying the letter the King had written him before the Princess Augusta who grew scarlet with rage as she read it.

'Lady Sarah Lennox! That silly little girl he has been eyeing. I thought he wanted to make her his mistress.'

'That would have been well enough,' agreed Bute. 'It would have been good for him to have a mistress. Her family would not have been pleased, though.'

'And why not? It's a tradition in that family, is it not? Their great boast is that they are descended from royalty through a King's mistress. Why should not Lady Sarah keep up the tradition?'

'Brother-in-law Fox is as cunning as his name.'

'I don't doubt it. But this affair shall be stopped.'

'I agree with you, my love. But we must go carefully.'

'Do you think we should send for George and explain? Really, I do believe that his innocence is worse than depravity. First he gets himself involved with a nobody ... a linen-draper's daughter—or niece—and marries her. And now he falls in love ... almost as unsuitably.'

'Oh come, my love, this is a different affair from that other which praise be to God we have most happily settled. This is the sister of the Duke of Richmond and say what we may the royal blood is there. Of course, I am in complete agreement with you that we must stop this, but I do not feel that at this stage we should attempt to command George. We must not forget that these last weeks have taught him that he is the King. The attitude of men has changed towards him. He has become aware of his position. If he feels strongly about this girl he will not be commanded.'

'But he must be made to *see* ...'

'It will be easier to persuade than command. I would be afraid of that last. One never knows when he is going to break away.'

'Break away from us, John? You ... his dearest friend and from me ... his Mother?'

'Don't forget the affair of the Quakeress—conducted in the dark without our knowledge.'

'I shall never forget that ... the fear ... the despair ...'

'All settled now, my love.'

She seized his arm suddenly and cried: 'Oh, John, it is? It is?'

'Yes, my love, it is,' he replied firmly. 'Now we have to think of George's future. I should like to see him married suitably ... and soon.'

'Although a marriage could come between us and him.'

'Not if we choose with care.'

'A German Princess ... docile, without friends ... coming into a strange country. That is what we need. Not an English bride surrounded by scheming relations.'

'Exactly, exactly. But I think we should find the bride without fail. George needs to be married and this I know of him,

once he is, he will be a loyal faithful husband. If we marry him
quickly I believe we shall have little to fear from the influence
of scheming women. He is by nature innocent and idealistic.
When he takes his marriage vows he will mean them. Our
George is at heart a very respectable man. So let us marry him
as soon as possible to the right woman. Then there will be an
end of this affair of the Lennox girl.'

'You think it is as simple as that, John dear?'

'My dearest, it is simple because we are dealing with a very
simple man.'

'Shall we send for him and tell him we propose to look for a
wife for him?'

'I think not. That would drive him to declaring his affection
for Sarah Lennox and his intention of marrying her. No. I
have to answer this letter. I must do it with the utmost caution.
I will write my answer now ... we will do it together ... and
when we feel it is the right one we will despatch it to him. But
I think we should act without delay, for promptness could be
of vital importance in an affair like this.'

So Lord Bute sat down at the Princess's writing-table and
with her at his side answered the King's letter:

'My dear Prince's kind confidential letter is of too great consequence to return an immediate answer; not but God
knows, my dear Sir, I with the utmost grief tell it you, the
case admits not of the smallest doubt. However, I will carry
your letter with me to the country, weigh every circum-
stance, and then like an honest man, a most devoted servant,
and a faithful friend, lay the whole before you. Think, Sir,
in the meantime, who you are, what is your birthright, what
you wish to be, and prepare your mind with a resolution to
hear the voice of truth, for such alone shall come from me,
however painful the office, duty and friendship and a thousand other ties command me, and I will obey though death
looked me in the face...'

Bute looked up from the letter into the anxious face of the
Princess.

'It is beautifully expressed, my dearest,' she said. 'And so ... cautious...'

'It will prepare him for my answer which will distress him greatly.'

'And you feel you should go to the country?'

'For a few days only. I fear if I stay here he will talk to me of this matter, having broken the ice, and that I should show myself unsympathetic which would be the surest way to lose his confidence. No, I will send this letter, and go away for a few days. When I return I shall have decided on the best way of dealing with this matter. And while I am away, my love, you should set enquiries in motion. We must find that suitable Princess for him. The matter is urgent.'

'What if he marries this girl ... secretly as he did ...'

Bute shook his head. 'Her family would not wish that. They will want a royal wedding and a shared coronation. You can depend upon it. Secret marriages are always suspect.'

'I often think about that...'

'No, no, my love. Do not even mention her name. It is best forgotten.'

She nodded slowly. 'Do not be away long, John. I am lost without you.'

He kissed her tenderly.

What a pleasant state of affairs when the King and the Princess Dowager could not do without him.

He would certainly do everything in his very considerable power to keep things as they were in that respect.

*   *   *

George read Lord Bute's letter and smiling put it into a drawer. Of course his dear friend did not understand the depth of his affection. When he did he would see that marriage with Sarah was the only solution.

He would persuade Lord Bute ... and his mother. And if they did not agree?

Well, he told himself, you are the King, you know.

Today he would go to his levee and she would be there. She

was often there. He believed her family knew how delighted he was to see her and that was why they always brought her with them. Sometimes he spoke to her; sometimes he contented himself with looking at her. He was a little embarrassed when face to face with her and never quite sure what to say. There was a look of mischief in her eyes which while it delighted him disconcerted him. She was serious beneath, he was sure of that; she was everything a Queen ought to be, but she liked to laugh and tease. That could be very amusing and exciting between two people when they were alone, he believed; but it was a little alarming in public.

She was very different from Hannah. No one could be more different. Perhaps that was why he found her so entrancing. Perhaps he wanted to forget Hannah had ever existed. Memories were so painful and whenever he thought of her now he thought of what would have happened if Hannah had lived and he had had to make known his secret marriage to his ministers. He shivered at the thought. He could imagine Mr. Pitt's reactions; and Newcastle, fool that he was, was at least a politician. He could imagine the talk in the streets ... the gossip, the scandal. It would have been insupportable. Lord Bute had told him once when he had brought up the subject that it would have shaken the throne. A king must always think very carefully before he took an important step. He owed it to his throne and his people.

Well, he must not think of Hannah. It was all over. Hannah lay beneath that tombstone under the name of Rebecca Powell. And her children? He felt a pang of uneasiness when he remembered them. But they were well cared for. He had made sure of that. He received reports on their well-being. And he had seen them once or twice. But Lord Bute had pointed out the folly of visiting them because as they grew older they would recognize him. His features were so well known, particularly now that he was King.

'Content yourself with knowing they are well cared for,' advised that dear friend and mentor. 'And when they are of age you can see that they are well placed in the world. Their mother would ask no more of you than that, because it is the best thing possible for all concerned. And now there is only one thing to do. Forget it ever happened. Forget ... forget ...'

That was exactly what he wanted to do, and on those occasions when he remembered he must quickly push those thoughts out of his head.

And the best one to make him forget was Sarah ... who was as different from Hannah as any woman could be.

Sarah, enchanting, frivolous, gay, teasing, tempting, and with royal blood in her veins.

She was at his levee. All the time he was receiving he could see her on the other side of the room with her sister Lady Caroline Fox, and kept taking surreptitious looks at her. Oh, she was lovely. She seemed more beautiful every time he saw her. Perhaps he would speak to her. What should he say? He wished he could think of brilliant witty things. But he was going to marry her. He had decided in that moment. Nothing would satisfy him but marriage with Lady Sarah.

Lady Susan Fox-Strangways was being presented to him by her sister, Anne, who was married to the Earl of Albemarle. A pleasant-looking girl. He liked her; he would have thought her very pretty if he had not been aware all the time of the dazzling perfections of Lady Sarah.

He signed to Lady Susan to sit down and sat beside her. She had a special attraction for him because he knew that she was a very close friend of Sarah's and he found it easy to talk to her of Sarah than to Sarah herself. Moreover, Sarah was on the other side of the room with her sister and he could keep glancing her way.

He said rather haltingly that it pleased him to see Lady Susan at his levee. He wished she was present more often but he believed her home was in Somerset.

'That is so, Sire.'

'Somerset. It is I believe a very pleasant county.'

'Very pleasant, Your Majesty.'

'And my lord Ilchester's seat very ... very ... pleasant.'

'Oh yes, Sire, my father's house is very pleasant.'

'You will be going there, I suppose.'

'Yes, Sire, for the summer.'

'And nothing will bring you back ... before the winter?'

'I don't know of anything.'

The King was silent and Susan was growing more and more embarrassed. One could not broach a subject to the King and must content oneself with answering, but how boring it was. Moreover, she was aware of Sarah's eyes on her from across the room. Sarah was looking sly; she was going to accuse her of trying to snatch the King from her as she herself had snatched Newbattle from Caroline Russell.

'Would you ... would you come back to see a coronation?' asked the King.

'Oh yes, Sire, I should hope to come back to see that.'

'I have put off my coronation for a while. I have a reason.'

'I am sure Your Majesty has.'

'I thought that a coronation with a Queen would be a much finer sight than one without.'

'That is surely so, Sire.'

The King looked at her so intently that Lady Susan was alarmed. Good heavens, she thought, is he proposing to *me*? Has it all been a mistake. Am I the one ... not Sarah ...

She dared not look at the King and lifting her eyes she saw Sarah glaring at her. Sarah would want a detailed account of this conversation.

'I have had a great many applications from abroad,' said the King. 'Foreign Princesses. I don't like the idea much.'

'No, Your Majesty.'

He looked wistful. 'I have had none from at home.' He leaned towards her. 'I should like it better if I had.'

Lady Susan began to tremble. It must be. A proposal of marriage from the King. Oh no! It could not happen in this way. It would have to be a formal approach through her parents. She was dreaming surely ... Or the King was mad.

He too was looking across the room at Sarah, which was a relief since he could not see her, Susan's, discomfiture.

'What do you think of your friend? You know who I mean.'

He was smiling at Sarah.

'Oh ... oh yes, Sire.'

'Don't you think she is the fittest?'

'Think, Sire?'

He did not seem to hear her. He said firmly: '*I* think none so fit.' Then he turned to Susan. 'Come with me,' he said. 'I wish to speak to your friend.'

Susan rose and together they crossed the room. Sarah swept an enchanting curtsy.

'I have been talking to your friend,' he told her.

'I have observed Your Majesty,' she answered pertly.

'So you were ... aware of me?'

'Sire, everyone is aware of the King.'

He chuckled. 'Will you ask your friend Lady Susan what I have been saying to her?'

'If it is your wish, Sire.'

'It is my wish. Yes, it is my wish. Ask her to tell you and make her tell you *all* I said to her. Will you promise me to that?'

'I promise, Sire.'

George seemed overcome by mirth and emotion. He left the girls and went and joined Lady Pembroke, an old friend of his.

Sarah looked at Susan interrogatively. 'I'll tell you when we're alone. It's too fantastic.'

* * *

Susan had repeated every word the King had said not only to Sarah but to the whole of Sarah's family.

She must go through it all when she returned to Holland House. Lady Caroline questioned her, so did Mr. Fox.

'Now, Susan, are you sure? He said he thought none so fit. Are you sure of that?'

'Absolutely sure. I remember every word.'

'And then he took you over to Sarah and said you were to tell her what he had said.'

'Yes ... it all happened exactly as I have explained.'

'You could have misconstrued.'

'No, I'm sure I didn't. It was all so simple ... so straightforward ... and so fantastic. Of course I haven't made up anything.'

The Duke of Richmond called at Holland House, and Susan had to repeat the story to him.

There was a long family conference.

'It is tantamount to a proposal,' was the verdict.

'But,' said the astute Mr. Fox, 'we must have it made in the correct manner—as soon as possible.'

*   *   *

Lady Sarah was in tears. Lady Susan going to her room found her on her bed, face buried in the pillows.

'What on earth is wrong?' cried Susan. 'I thought you were the heroine of the hour.'

Sarah sat up, dabbing at her eyes. 'That's just the point. All this fuss has shown me my true feelings. I love John Newbattle. He's the one I really want and now that the King has proposed through you I'll never be allowed to accept him.'

'You could run away from home and marry him ... like your sister did Mr. Fox.'

'It's a possibility I've been thinking of.'

'Sarah, after the King has expressed his desire to marry you!'

'What a way to do it. To tell *you* because he hadn't the courage to tell me himself.'

'*I* think it rather charming,' said Susan.

'Because he talked to you? I'll swear you thought he was proposing to you when he started that rigmarole. Oh, you're blushing. So you did.'

'Of course not. It's not the way Kings propose in any case.'

'This one did.'

'You can hardly call it a proposal. He was only saying what he would like, that's all. Perhaps he has no intention of asking you properly.'

'Nonsense! He said all that about the coronation. My family are sure he wants to marry me. What they've got to do is bring him to the point.' She sighed. 'But there is my dear John...'

'I don't think he loves you as devotedly as the King does, Sarah,'

'What nonsense! He adores me. He told me so.'

'His affection has grown now he knows the King wants to marry you.'

'Well, why shouldn't it?'

'It doesn't seem the right reason.'

'It's not the only reason, idiot. I'll tell you something. He has written to me.'

'Who ... the King.'

'No, John. He wants me to meet him in the Park tonight. He has something important to say to me.'

'You shouldn't go, Sarah.'

'Don't be ridiculous, Susan! Of course I must go. I have to choose between them, don't I, and how am I going to do that if I refuse to see them?'

'The King is considering marrying you and you are going out by night to see another man! You are mad.'

'And you are very prim, Susan. In any case, I am going.'

'You have very quickly dried your eyes.'

'Yes, because I thought they were going to force me to marry George. I have made up my mind that I shall decide. So I am going to meet John tonight in the Park and see what he has to say to me. He has written such a letter. I must show it to you. One moment. It's in this drawer. No it's not. Oh, where did I put it? It must be somewhere.'

'You should be careful where you leave letters like that ... particularly as...'

'"The King is considering marrying you,"' chanted Sarah. 'Now, listen, Susan. I am the one who is doing the considering and I am not so sure that it is so wonderful being a Queen after all. There are tiresome duties and levees; there are ministers to receive and horrible visiting royalty. I've been thinking that it might be more fun to be a little distant from the throne than actually sitting on it. And it is a matter of whether I prefer gay and amusing John Newbattle to shy

George. I think I know, Susan, and tonight I am going to find out.'

*　　*　　*

Lord Bute, returned from country, went at once to Kensington to see the King. A very interesting little matter had arisen during his absence. He had always made sure that he had people situated in the right positions to bring him information; and Mr. Fox's house was a terrain he had not neglected. The news which had been brought to him did not concern that famous politician this time, but it did concern someone who was—temporarily he hoped—of more interest still: Lady Sarah Lennox.

A very interesting piece of news. Lady Sarah was inclined to be haughty and was by no means certain that she intended to accept the King's proposal. She had another string to her bow—that bold and flirtatious young man, son of the Earl of Ancram and grandson of the Marquis of Lothian—John William Newbattle. It seemed that Madam Sarah was inclined to favour that young man in spite of his reputation for fickleness rather than steady King George.

Interesting, and what was more than interesting was the fact that the young lady had agreed to meet John Newbattle in the grounds of Holland House after dark—surely something no young lady should do, particularly one who had a chance of being Queen.

The letter from John Newbattle had actually been delivered into his hands. He carried it in his pocket now as he rode to Kensington to see the King.

George was delighted to receive his dear friend.

'It seems you have been long away. I know it is only a few days, but your absences always seem long.'

'Your Majesty is so gracious to me. I am unable to express the pleasure your kindness gives me. I can only say that you, Sire, cannot be so pleased to see me as I am to see you.'

These expressions of affection over, Bute immediately mentioned the matter which was uppermost in his mind.

'Sire, I have given great thought to your problem.'

'Ah, I knew you would. I have been thinking of her since I spoke to Lady Susan . . . in fact, thinking of nothing else.'

Since he spoke to Lady Susan! Bute knew to what he was referring. Everyone knew what he had said to Lady Susan. The news was fast spreading through the Court and London.

'Has Your Majesty considered what a marriage of this nature would mean?'

'I have considered everything.'

'Of course, the Lady Sarah is a charming girl.'

'I knew you would think so.'

'Young . . . very young. She is not yet seventeen, I believe.'

'There is no harm in being young, surely.'

'No harm at all. Of course, it has been the custom for the Kings to marry royal persons.'

'Sarah *is* royal. Her great-grandfather was Charles II!'

'Yes, but through a not very creditable union, shall we say. I mean the people look to their Kings to marry Princesses, usually from abroad.'

'Germans!' said George. 'I do not think the people are really very fond of the Germans.'

'Still . . . a Princess.'

'I see, my dearest friend, you have no real objections to offer. Then I do not see why I should not be formally betrothed to Lady Sarah. If I wish it and she wishes it . . .'

'Indeed not,' said Bute quickly, noting the King's firmness. He put his hand into his pocket and touched Newbattle's note. He had been wondering whether to show it to the King and would have preferred not to. It would have been so much better to have been able to persuade him of the folly of this obsession. But he could see that the King was set on marrying the girl, and the King could be a very stubborn young man.

There was no help for it, then.

'Sire, I have to pass on to you something which may cause you some displeasure. I have been debating within myself whether to withold it, but I realize that I could not be your true friend if I did so.'

'What is this?' asked George, and as always on such occasions his thoughts turned to Hannah. Something had come to light. This thought was always at the back of his mind ready to spring forward at the least alarm.

'I feel, Sire, that you should be absolutely sure that this lady is worthy of you.'

George was relieved. 'I am absolutely sure. In fact it is really a question of whether I am worthy of her.'

'The King of England worthy of a little...' Bute stopped himself in time. 'If you can prove she is worthy, then I do not see why we should not fight all the opposition—and it will be considerable—to your union with her.'

'I knew you would be on my side.'

'Have I not always been?'

'Always,' declared George fervently. 'But what was making you anxious.'

'Lady Sarah is in love with someone else.'

George grew pale. 'I ... I can't believe it.'

'This note has been brought to me by someone who wishes to serve you.'

'Note ... note? What note?'

'Here. Read it. It is a love letter and you will see it is from Lord Newbattle to Lady Sarah.'

George's face was scarlet, his blue eyes more prominent than usual, his jaw slacker as he read.

'So ... he asks her to meet him in Holland Park ... tonight! What a scoundrel! What of her reputation?'

'He would have had encouragement to write such a note.'

'She ... she will not go.'

'Is your Majesty sure of that?'

'Yes. I know she would not go.'

'I am going to make a suggestion, Your Majesty. Perhaps it will be distasteful to you and if so, you must forgive me. You know full well that in the past every action of mine has been taken with your good in mind. That will always be so. That is why I come to you now with this letter and risk your displeasure.'

'I could never never be displeased with such a true friend. But you are wrong about Lady Sarah.'

'I am sure I am wrong.'

'I am happy again, then.'

'But I am concerned for Your Majesty's welfare. There was that unfortunate affair of . . .'

'Yes,' said George sobered, and even forgetting the perfections of Sarah temporarily.

'I would not wish to see Your Majesty similarly involved.'

'Similarly. It is quite different.'

'Quite different, Your Majesty, that is true. But if this young girl were not all you think her to be a marriage could be disastrous.'

'But I know her to be . . .'

'Then you will bear with my suspicions and know that they are only the fears of one who loves you better than his own life. Your Majesty, if I were convinced that this girl truly loved you and was worthy to be your Queen I should be beside you. And you do not doubt, do you, that together we could not overcome all opposition.'

'Of course we could.'

'But I must be convinced myself. I am going to ask Your Majesty's permission to do something of which you might not approve.'

'What is that?'

'I am going to witness this meeting. I am going to see what happens for myself. And if I am convinced . . .'

'Yes?'

'That she is just an impulsive girl. If she goes to this rendezvous with a friend and tells this young man that she wants no more to do with him—then I shall be with Your Majesty. I would say that although the Lady Sarah was a little indiscreet to make such an assignation she is after all an innocent girl and since Your Majesty has such regard for her I would be ready to say that Your Majesty should go ahead with your plans.'

'I am sure it will happen just as you say.'

'But I shall be there to witness it. I must satisfy myself. I had thought that perhaps Your Majesty . . .'

George was silent, staring at Bute.

'. . . perhaps Your Majesty would wish to accompany me?'

* * *

Lord Bute was delighted. He called at once on the Dowager Princess to give her the good news.

'I think all will be well,' he informed her, and proceeded to tell her of his great good fortune in securing the note which Newbattle had written to Lady Sarah, giving details of the rendezvous in Holland Park.

'But you are a . . . genius!'

'I would not say that, my dear. But my entire life is given to you and the King, as you know. It is only natural that such devotion should bring results. And this was better than I hoped. I did not ask the King outright to accompany me but I guessed he would be unable to resist coming. And I was right.'

'And you saw this meeting?'

'Yes. The lady was, however, accompanied by Lord George Lennox who, you may remember, is married to Newbattle's sister. I was a little dashed when I saw this, for I believe that flighty young woman capable of real indiscretion. *But* . . . there was no doubt that she is on very affectionate terms with New-battle and was certainly not repulsing his advances. I do believe that as far as I can see they were making some arrangements and what could those possibly be with Lord George present? Only this: Newbattle is going to ask his father's consent to his marriage with Sarah Lennox. Well, the sooner we see that mischievous young woman safely settled into matrimony with master Newbattle, the happier I shall be.'

'And George—how was he affected by all this?'

'Very deeply. He is in a state of great melancholy and while I am pleased that he has seen the girl for what she is I am disturbed because it shows how deeply his affection for her goes.'

'He is a very affectionate young man, I fear. He was really quite cut up over ...'

Lord Bute placed his hands playfully over the Princess's lips. 'Don't let us even mention her name.'

'I often think ...'

Lord Bute kissed the lips his finger had touched.

'Then you must not, my dearest. And our problem at this moment is the Lady Sarah Lennox. Tell me this: What news from abroad?'

'Colonel Graeme left as you suggested and is now at Mecklenburg-Strelitz. I have not yet had his report on the Princess Charlotte but I am sure when it comes we shall be pleased with it.'

'That is good. Trust a Scotsman to get on with the job. Let us hope that his report will be good, for we have to act very promptly.'

'But what he saw in the Park ...'

'Our King is in love. I am sure if my lady Sarah gave him a good account of what she was doing there he would be ready to believe all she told him. We must be prepared.'

Augusta nodded.

'Colonel Graeme is well aware of the urgency of the situation.'

* * *

Sarah could not believe her eyes. She read the letter several times. It was impossible. The Earl and Countess of Ancram could not give their consent to their son's marriage with the Lady Sarah Lennox.

It was an insult. And worse still, her lover's attitude to the affair was despicable.

'In view of my parents' views we must perforce end this matter. It is with the deepest regret ...'

'Regret!' cried Sarah. 'What a coward he is! Why did I ever think I loved such a man?'

She threw herself on to her bed and wept bitterly. She was weeping—on and off—all through the morning and her sister,

Lady Caroline, came to her room to see what was wrong with her.

'Good Heavens,' cried Caroline. 'What a sight you look! And you have to attend the King's levee this afternoon.'

'I shall not go.'

'Don't be a fool,' retorted Caroline. 'Of course you will go. The King expects you.'

'I don't want to see the King. I don't want to see anyone.'

Lady Caroline summoned the maids and told them that the Lady Sarah was suffering from a cold. She must attend a levee this afternoon and Lady Caroline suggested that her face should be bathed and pads of witch-hazel put over her eyes. She was to lie flat on her back for an hour in this state, by the end of which time she should look more like herself. Lady Caroline would choose what gown she was to wear.

'And you will stop being foolish this instant,' she hissed.

Lady Sarah lay on her bed and thought about Newbattle's letter and his so-called love for her which had been forgotten at the first sign of opposition. George was different, she told herself. But she did not want George.

I don't want either of them! she murmured. And if I don't want them, I won't have them.

She was sullen when it was time to dress for the levee; but Lady Caroline declared that she was passable. She was, in fact, so pretty that nothing seemed to hide that prettiness. So the party set out.

George was watching for her eagerly when she arrived and he was debating with himself whether or not he would speak to her. He told himself that Lady Susan had probably forgotten to say anything to Sarah and that was why she had gone to meet Newbattle. She surely would not have gone if she knew what he had said.

Yes, he told himself, that is it. She was waiting for some declaration and despairing of ever getting it she went to meet Newbattle in the Park. After all, her brother was with her. There was nothing wrong ... just a little immodest perhaps, but then Sarah was so young she would not realize that.

Once he had heard that she did not know what he had said
to Susan he would say it to her himself, and what joy it would
be to watch her pleasure!

He went to her.

'Have you seen your friend Lady Susan lately?' he asked.

'Yes.'

That bewildered him. But then she had seen the girl, who
had not told her. That was it.

'Has she told you what I said to her?'

'Yes.'

He was astonished. Then why was she looking so miserable?
This was something he had not considered.

'Did she tell you all?'

'Yes, *all.*'

'And ... do you approve?'

Sarah turned her head away. How could she say to the
King: I don't want you. I'm in love with Lord Newbattle who
has decided to forget all about me because his parents tell him
to.

George was astounded and mortified. There was nothing he
could do but walk away.

＊　　＊　　＊

Her family were furious. What had she done? She had
ruined her chances.

'I don't care. I don't care. I am tired of them ... both.'

'Oh, so this is pique on account of Newbattle, is it?'

'What if it is?'

'Oh, Sarah, you fool, you fool. You have thrown away the
greatest chance that ever came to a woman.'

'And a good thing, too.'

'Everyone could see that the King was most hurt. I doubt he
will ever want to speak to you again.'

'Then I'm glad.'

'You silly creature.'

'I don't want to stay here to see ... Lord Newbattle. I want
to go away for a while.'

'It's a pity you didn't leave with Susan and stay in Ilchester for a while.'

'Yes, a great pity. I wish I had.'

'Well, I think it would be a good idea if you left town for a while. Go to Goodwood and stay there until you are in a better mood. Don't stay too long, for if you do the King may have forgotten you.'

The next day Lady Sarah left for Goodwood.

*   *   *

On the road to Goodwood, Sarah's carriage was overtaken by another and when she saw who was in it she cried out in delight, for it was Lord Newbattle.

He left his carriage and came into hers.

'So you are off to Goodwood,' he said.

'How did you know, and it is no affair of yours.'

'I learn everything about you and it is my affair. I always make it my business to find out where you are.'

'Have you Papa's permission to do so?'

'You didn't think that letter was important, did you?'

'What else should I think of it?'

'I wrote it because they stood over me and expected me to. I didn't mean it, of course.'

'You didn't mean it!'

'Of course not. What a simpleton you are, Sarah. Of course I didn't. We'll be married, and when the deed is done we'll tell them and they'll have to accept it. That's the way it's done. You ask your sister and Mr. Fox.'

Sarah was laughing.

'Still,' she pouted. 'You should not have written such a letter. I cried over it, and then I was very sullen with the King.'

'Serve him right,' said Newbattle. 'That's what I like to hear. I shall be a constant visitor to Goodwood.'

He left her, and the carriages, one behind the other, rattled on to Goodwood—which was only two days ride from London.

Sarah was looking forward to a very pleasant time. She had made up her mind. Lord Newbattle was the man she really loved. It must be so because he only had to appear to make her happy; besides it was because she was so angry with Lord Newbattle that she had snubbed the King.

*   *   *

When the Foxes and Richmonds heard that Newbattle was visiting Sarah at Goodwood they were incensed and they decided that she should not stay there. Lord Ilchester suggested that she should go to his estate at Bruton in Somerset and as his daughter Susan was already there, Sarah agreed.

When she told him she was going, Newbattle was annoyed.

'That is too far for me to come and see you. You must refuse to go.'

'Too far. So I am not worth such a journey?'

Newbattle yawned. Lady Sarah was certainly capricious and it had been quite enough to ride out to Goodwood. He was certainly not going all the way to Somerset to see her. There were many other young ladies who found him fascinating; and although Sarah was the prettiest of them—and admired by the King—he was inclined to think she took him for granted. In fact, although Sarah was attractive he wished her to realize that he was equally so, and he was certainly not going to Somerset to see her.

Sarah retorted: 'Very well, stay away.' But in her heart she did not believe he would, for had he not written that letter cancelling their betrothal and then told her he had not meant it. No, with such an attractive young man as Newbattle, who was so very much aware of his charms, it was necessary to show him that he could not hope to hold her affections unless he made an effort to do so.

She was determined to go to Somerset.

*   *   *

Lady Susan was there and that was fun. Each day Sarah waited for Lord Newbattle to arrive, but he did not come; and she began to think that he had meant what he said.

Then one day when she and Susan were riding, Sarah fell

from her horse and broke her leg. She had to be carried back to Bruton and there the leg was set and news sent to London of what had happened.

When the King heard he was stricken with grief.

'I must go and see her,' he declared; but Lord Bute pointed out to him that he could not possibly travel so far. He must remember that he was a King and Kings could not travel without an entourage. It would take a long time to get ready and everyone would know where he was going and why. It was simply impossible. He must realize that.

George, growing more and more sensible of his position, did realize the truth of this.

'But,' he said, 'I shall write to her. She must know that I am thinking of her at such a time.'

Bute was disturbed.

'He does not appear to have recovered from this infatuation,' he told the Princess Augusta. 'She so rudely snubbed him and yet he is deeply concerned because the tiresome creature has broken a leg.'

'Perhaps we shall soon be having some good news from Colonel Graeme.'

'I fervently hope so.'

Mr. Fox and Lady Caroline travelled down to Somerset accompanied by their son, Charles James, and the Duke and Duchess of Richmond.

Sarah was very amused to see them. She had, in fact, been a good patient and as long as Susan was there to talk to her she did not appear to mind being incapacitated.

'You see,' she said to Susan, 'what an important person I have become.'

Every day she waited in vain for a visit from Newbattle, and Lady Caroline told her rather maliciously that Lord Newbattle had been informed of the accident.

'And what did he say? What did he do?'

'He took it very calmly,' replied Lady Caroline. 'In fact his remark is being whispered round the Court.'

'Oh?' Sarah dimpled. 'What was it?'

'Simply that it would do no great harm, for your legs were ugly enough before.'

'I don't believe it.'

'Now don't excite yourself. It's time you learned what sort of man he is. He cares nothing for you. He is amusing himself. He thinks it extremely amusing that you could be such a little fool as to throw away the chance of a lifetime . . . for nothing.'

Sarah's lips began to quiver. How could he be so cruel, first not to bother to visit her, then not to care that she had broken her leg? And most heartless of all, to say such cruel things about her!

'Don't be so silly,' said Lady Caroline. 'You are coming back to London as soon as your leg is well enough for you to travel. Then perhaps you will show the King how honoured you are by his attentions.'

Talking it over with Susan, Sarah admitted that her sister was right.

George was the better man—and he was a King. It was characteristic of Sarah that now the decision had been made for her she should turn all her enthusiasm towards it and behave as though what she wanted more than anything on Earth was to marry George.

During her convalescence she and Susan discussed at length the excitement of being a Queen.

And as soon as she was well enough to travel she returned to London.

*   *   *

It was May when she arrived. As soon as George knew she was back he became excited, and Bute. mournfully told the Princess that he was as infatuated as ever.

Hearing that Lady Sarah was going to the play—her first engagement on returning to her brother-in-law's house— George announced his intentions of going too and everyone noticed that he spent the time looking at Lady Sarah rather than at the performance on the stage. All attention was focused on them. It seemed certain that George had decided to marry her.

The following Sunday when she attended his Drawing Room as soon as he saw her he was at her side and he talked to her during the whole of the session. She was very different from the coquettish girl who had flouted him before she had gone to the country; she smiled and showed quite clearly how his attention delighted her. In such a mood Sarah was more charming than ever and people remarked that they made a very handsome couple. Soon, thought the Princess uneasily, the people in the streets would hear of this; they would cheer them when they went out, for nothing would please them more than for the King to marry a commoner—and an Englishwoman at that. They would much prefer such a match to a German one.

The Princess Dowager was frantic.

She sent for her eldest daughter Augusta and told her that she must try to prevent the King's reaching Sarah Lennox at any function. Augusta, who was a rather short young woman, by no means handsome but possessing the family's clear complexion, fair hair and blue eyes, was envious of the undoubted beauty of Sarah Lennox. She had no love for her mother, who had shown little interest in her—or indeed any of the family, all her attentions being concentrated on George—but Augusta liked to meddle in Court affairs and this gave her an excellent opportunity, so she decided to do what she could to foil the match George was trying to make with Sarah Lennox. Lady Bute, who had been coming to Court recently, for both her husband and the Princess agreed that she could not be shut out indefinitely, appeared to accept her husband's relationship with the Princess with no pangs of jealousy. She was wise enough to realize what great advantages came to her and her children through his close relationship with the royal family, for it was not only the Princess who adored him but the King as well. Bute had in March become Secretary of State at the King's express wish, and Lady Bute understood even more fully that she would be foolish to protest about anything that touched on her husband's advancement at Court. Therefore she was a staunch ally of the Princess and her husband, and would certainly play her part in spoiling the Lennox girl's hopes.

Lady Susan Stewart, the Princess's bedchamber woman was told she must help too, and the three of them could make a circle about Lady Sarah and fend off the King that way, for George was too polite to ignore them if they stood in the way of his reaching the young lady.

This was small comfort, the Princess agreed; but at least it was something and the situation was so desperate that they could not afford to ignore any help.

News would soon arrive from Germany and then she trusted the King could be persuaded to do his duty.

* * *

On the 4th of June there was a ball to celebrate the King's birthday and Sarah attended this. Her leg, however, not being completely well, prevented her from dancing, so she was obliged to sit out while the others danced. This gave the King some opportunity to speak to her and made it very difficult for the bodyguard to prevent his doing so.

Sarah was clearly enjoying the situation—sitting there looking more beautiful than anyone at the ball, conscious all the time of the King's adoring glances which she returned, partly because she had made up her mind that she would be Queen of England, partly to foil the bodyguard whose purpose she knew too well.

When she thought of the casual treatment of Lord Newbattle she felt furious; and that alone, she told herself, would make her love George, who was so different. She sat dreaming of being the Queen and governing him as she was sure she could. He would be a good and faithful husband, always ready to please his wife. Very different from Lord Newbattle!

The King's sister, Princess Augusta, had come to speak to her accompanied by Lady Bute and Lady Susan Stewart.

How maddening! They surrounded her and shut out the sight of the King.

How was she? How sad that she could not dance! And had

she enjoyed her stay in the country ... apart from the time
when she had been incapacitated? That must have been most
annoying, and painful too. Oh, she was very brave to come to
the ball. Should she not have stayed in the country until she
was quite ... quite better. But perhaps she felt she *must* come.
Life in the country was perhaps a little *dull*.

Oh, be silent, thought Lady Sarah, while she smiled at them
and answered their silly questions. Do you think I don't know
what you are doing? You are trying to keep the King away
from me and you won't succeed.

Nor did they, for here was George unable to endure the
separation any longer.

'Augusta,' he said to his sister, 'I should like to see you dance
the Betty Blue.'

Augusta looked startled, but the King did not seem to
notice; he was smiling at Sarah.

'It is a dance that you are acquainted with. I am very fond of
it because it was taught to me by a lady.'

'Was it, Your Majesty?' She was smiling up at him bewitch-
ingly, more for the benefit of the watching ladies—whom she
was sure were grinding their teeth with rage—than for him.

'Do you not know what lady?' he asked.

'No, Sire.'

'Well, I will tell you. It was taught me by a very pretty lady
who came from Ireland, a year last November.'

Sarah put her head on one side pretending to consider,
which delighted the King.

'I am talking to her now,' prompted George. 'She taught it to
me at the ball on Twelfth Night.'

Sarah laughed, watching the sick looks on the faces of the
three women. 'In truth, Your Majesty, I did not remember
until you reminded me.'

'Perhaps you did not. But *I* have a very good memory for
what relates to that lady. I had a pretty new country dance of
my own, which should have been danced on the late King's
birthday ... if he had lived. What do you think I named it?'

'I have no idea, Sire.'

'The 25th of February. That is a very important date to me. Do you know why?'

She pretended to be confused and stammered: 'I ... I cannot think, Sire. I know it is my birthday.'

He laughed triumphantly. 'That is why.'

The Princess Augusta groaned inwardly at this conversation which the King seemed to find sparkling with wit, and which showed, thought the Princess, how deeply in love he was if he could mistake such puerile utterings for conversation even.

She would report what had been said to her mother— and it seemed that others would be reporting it all over the place because there was no doubt that many had their ears cocked.

So the King stayed at the side of Lady Sarah during most of the evening, now and then being forced, reluctantly it was obvious, to do his duty and dance. But he lost no time in returning to her chair. In fact, so absorbed was he that he remained talking to her until one o'clock, quite forgetting that the dancers were waiting for him to end the ball.

No one was in any doubt after that birthday ball of the King's feelings for Sarah Lennox.

There was jubilation at Holland House.

'The King,' said Lady Caroline, 'is surely on the brink of a declaration.'

* * *

The Princess Augusta was sighing with relief. She sent at once for Lord Bute. Colonel Graeme had reported that a marriage of the King of England and his sister Charlotte Sophia would be very acceptable to the Duke of Mecklenburg-Strelitz and also to Charlotte Sophia's mother the Dowager Grand Duchess. The Colonel described the Princess's appearance as pleasant (which implied that she was no beauty) and added that in his opinion she appeared to be a bride in every way suitable for His Majesty.

'There must now be no delay,' said the Princess. 'We must talk to George.'

Bute agreed and Augusta asked her son if he would call on her as she had something of great importance to say to him.

George arrived, having no notion of what was to be discussed, but Augusta did not leave him long in doubt.

'My son,' she said, 'it is time you were married.'

George smiled happily. 'I myself have been thinking that.'

'There has as yet been no coronation,' went on the Princess.

'No. I wished my Queen to share in it.'

'That will be excellent and we have found a very suitable bride for you.'

George was silent, and the Princess glanced at Bute who said quietly: 'Colonel Graeme reports from Mecklenburg-Strelitz that the Princess Charlotte Sophia will be an ideal bride for you and she and her family are eager for the marriage.'

'This . . . is impossible.'

'It is highly suitable,' said his mother sharply.

'You do not understand,' said the King. 'I have already decided.'

'Then I trust you will think again, for this is of the utmost importance.'

'I have pondered a great deal on this matter. I love the Lady Sarah Lennox and she loves me.'

'Are you sure of that, Sire?' asked Bute gently.

'Sure of it! I am never more sure of anything.'

The Princess was about to speak but Bute looked at her and she nodded, implying that he must direct the way this painful interview should go.

'Sire,' said Bute in his kindest and most tender voice, 'a little while ago that young lady was making it very clear that she preferred another gentleman to you.'

'That was not so. She was merely . . . amusing herself.'

'Amusing herself? When the King had shown preference for her?'

'I did not wish her to regard me as a King but as a man.'

'She clearly did neither,' retorted the Princess tartly. 'She treated you like a foolish boy and I must say that you have behaved like one—to allow her to flout you, use you to attract this young . . . young rake . . . and then beckon you when she finds he has done with her!'

'This ... this is not so.'

'The King is clearly deeply affected by Lady Sarah,' said Bute gently.

George turned to him. Best of friends! Always reliable! He would understand and help him to explain.

'And in that case,' said George, 'since we love each other would it not be desirable for us to marry?'

'I fear,' Bute reminded him, still in the same kind voice, 'it would not be desirable from the nation's point of view. You see, Sire, you are a King. You are young and have not until now been brought face to face with your obligations. Your marriage is not your own affair. It is the nation's. Every King or Queen has to face this problem. It rarely happens that what they desire is what the nation needs. It is the sad side of a ruler's life. Self-sacrifice. Again and again he must pass by what he desires to give his country what it needs.'

George was beginning to lose his confidence. 'But why should the nation not want Sarah?'

'A King's sons and daughters must be royal,' said the Princess. 'They should have royal blood on both sides.'

'Sarah is royal,' cried George eagerly.

The Princess laughed. 'Yes, descended from a whore!'

George flushed as though he had been struck. 'I beg of you, Madam, do not say such a thing.'

'I am concerned with the truth,' retorted his mother. 'We all know where the Richmonds got their title. Through Louise de Keroualle, sent from France by the King of that country to be his spy and the King of England's mistress. That at least is common knowledge.'

'You ... can scarcely blame Sarah.'

'I do not blame her. I merely say she is unfit to be Queen of England. George, be reasonable. The people of this country are waiting for an announcement of your marriage. They expect you to marry. They are growing impatient. And they expect you to make the right marriage.'

'I am sure I am the best judge...'

The Princess said hotly: 'As you were the best judge in that disastrous matter of the Quaker girl.'

George caught his breath in horror. He could not bear to think of Hannah. When he did so he was overcome by feelings of remorse and inadequacy.

Lord Bute was at his side, laying a gentle hand on his arm.

'Your Majesty,' he said softly, 'that affair is done with. May I speak frankly?'

George nodded.

'Your Majesty should not feel remorse over that affair. It was true there were difficulties ... but there need not have been. Had you consulted me in the beginning, I could have arranged matters satisfactorily for you and there would have been no trouble. Your Majesty is good and honest and my heart rejoices to see it—but the world is full of scheming men and women ...'

'Sarah is not scheming.'

'Indeed no. She is an enchanting young girl, unsure of her mind, it is true, flitting from one to the other, unable to come to a decision ... a delightful creature. But she is surrounded by ambitious men and women who will seek to guide you through her and separate you from your true friends.'

'You mean yourself ...'

'Myself and Her Highness, your mother.'

'No one would ever do that.'

'I am sure Your Majesty would not allow it, but they would attempt it. In the interests of the country, Your Majesty should accept the Princess Charlotte Sophia ... and ...'

'And Sarah?' whispered George.

'If she truly loved you she would consent to become your mistress. Other women have had to take a similar decision. It would be a test of her love.'

'I should not ask her to. I should not care for such an association. When I marry I intend to be a faithful husband. I intend to set an example to my people.'

'Noble sentiments, and they do Your Majesty credit. You can set the pattern of your Court and I know you will do it. Profligacy, so rife in the last reign, will disappear and it will be due to our King. That is magnificent. But you must have a woman who will help you in this. There must be no uncertainty after marriage. No wandering out by night to confer with other men . . . nothing of that sort.'

'It was only mischief.'

'There must be no mischief. Your Majesty, I beg of you listen to Her Highness, your mother. You never had, and never will have, a better friend in the world.'

'Yes, listen to me and listen to my Lord Bute. When have we ever failed you?'

'Never, but . . .'

'Then heed our words now,' pleaded Bute. 'The country needs this marriage with the Princess Charlotte, and you must give the country what it needs.'

'No,' said the King. 'I have heard enough. I am going to marry Sarah.'

He bowed abruptly and left them.

The Princess was in despair, but Bute was not so despondent.

'Our words have had some effect,' he said.

'What if he goes to Holland House and actually asks for her hand?'

'I do not think he will act so rashly. I shall stay close with him during the next days. I shall bring him to see where his duty lies.'

Augusta felt faintly relieved. Her confidence in Lord Bute never wavered.

          *   *   *

When the King rode out from Kensington Palace he passed Holland House in the grounds of which Sarah, looking delightful as a country girl in a sunbonnet, was helping to make the hay.

He stopped and spoke to her. How enchanting she was! How wonderful it would have been if he had been a country squire and she the daughter of a neighbour! He could fancy that, on a morning like this.

She looked expectant. Was she hoping he would ask her to marry him?

'I shall,' he told himself a little too defiantly.

He rode on past Holland House. A King had his duties to his people. Hannah had said that. No one had realized that more than she had. She had wanted to keep in the background so that she did not embarrass him.

Hannah had been different—a Quakeress and niece of a linen-draper. Sarah had royal blood in her veins and they could say what they liked, it was royal blood by whatever means it had got there.

I shall not listen to them, George insisted. I am going to marry Sarah.

Not listen to Lord Bute, his best friend, whose advice he constantly sought? Lord Bute was so certain that it would be wrong to marry Sarah.

This was one instance where Lord Bute was wrong.

But Lord Bute had never been wrong ... until now.

It was noticed that the King looked very melancholy as he rode along.

*   *   *

Bute came to the King's apartment, his manner grave.

'Your Majesty, I have just heard news which disturbs me.'

'What. Is it Sarah?'

Bute shook his head. 'A man named Green was arrested at Westminster for making disloyal comments about Your Majesty.'

'I'll dareswear he is not the only one. There were disloyal comments enough about my grandfather. Why should I escape?'

'These, Your Majesty, were directed against your relationships with ... a Quakeress.'

'What?' cried the King turning pale.

'I heard that this man had talked of your enticing the Quakeress from her home and setting her up in a house where you visited her.'

'Is that ... so?'

'Your Majesty will see how unhealthy it is that such rumours should be allowed to grow.'

'But ... will they grow?'

'Yes, Your Majesty, unless you marry and show the people that you live respectably with your Queen.'

'It is what I intend to do.'

'There would be a scandal if you did not marry the bride who has been selected for you. Colonel Graeme is already negotiating. If you married the Lady Sarah all this scandal about the Quakeress would be revived.'

'I do not see why.'

'This man,' Bute went on, 'was fined and allowed to go free with a warning. But there will be others to chatter. We must stop this gossip without fail. And the only way is to marry the Princess who has been chosen for you.'

'No,' said George. 'I will marry Lady Sarah.'

But Lord Bute was sure that the King's resolution was weakening.

*   *   *

George could not sleep. All night he had been thinking, Hannah! Sarah! They were together in his thoughts. He could hear their voices in his imagination quite clearly, 'If you really love me,' said Sarah's, 'you will marry me. You are the King. You have but to say the word and none can stop you.' Hannah's said: 'Think, George. Thou thought thou lovest me once. Remember thy vows. Thou wanted to make me Princess of Wales, Queen to be. And now ... thou hast forgotten. Thou wouldst have risked thy crown for the sake of a love that was so ephemeral. See how mistaken thou wert.'

It was true. He had believed he would love Hannah for ever and now he scarcely remembered her—only to shiver with horror to contemplate the folly he might have committed. Yet Hannah had borne his children ... he had married Hannah. The thought made him go cold with fear.

Hannah, he thought, you are dead and buried but you will live with me for ever.

And her voice seemed to come out of the darkness: 'Art thou sure that I am dead and buried, George?'

He faced the truth, the dreadful uncertainty. No. He was not sure. The new gravestone rose up clear in his mind as he had seen it on that day. Rebecca Powell. Who was Rebecca Powell? He had never found out. Why, because even then he had preferred not to know what it was better not to know.

Lord Bute had advised him then. His dearest friend was right. When had he not been right? He was beside him to guide him through all the difficulties which lay ahead. He should trust his friend, and his friend said: 'You cannot marry Sarah.'

Of course they were right. Kings married the women who were chosen for them. They did not marry the nieces of linen-drapers; they did not even marry the daughters of noblemen. But they did. Henry VIII had done it. Anne Boleyn, Katherine Howard. Two heads without bodies laughed at him in the darkness. Yes, and look what became of us. Edward IV had married Elizabeth Woodville for love. He could hear the voices of her little boys crying in the Tower as they were done to death.

It was folly to think of these events in connection with himself. He was a man of gentle nature; he only wanted to live an upright life, to live in harmony with the woman he loved and the family they would raise; he wanted to set a good example to his people, to be happy and make them happy.

That was the crux of the matter as Lord Bute would say. A King must not think of his own desires but of the nation he governed.

'I made a great sacrifice for thee,' a voice seemed to say. 'George, thou must make this sacrifice for thy country.'

'What sacrifice?' he whispered. 'What sacrifice did you make?'

But he knew. He had suspected and had not wished to know. But in his heart he knew.

She was haunting him. Perhaps she did not want to see him happy with Sarah. Oh no, that could not be said of one who had made such a sacrifice as Hannah had made. But he was imagining this. What was he thinking of? Even now he did not know and he would not seek the truth because he did not want to face it.

All through that night he wrestled with his problem, and Hannah was constantly in his thoughts.

By the morning she had convinced him. He must sacrifice his own desires for the sake of the country.

When he went riding he passed Holland House and there was Sarah in her sunbonnet making hay. He stopped to talk to her and she was very gay and inviting; but when he had talked for a while he rode on.

He believed his heart was broken.

*　　　*　　　*

The Dowager Princess was as ever delighted by my Lord Bute's brilliance and devotion.

'You have turned failure into success,' she cried, 'I must confess that I was in great fear. And you did it through gentleness and reason.'

'It is the only way to manage George. We must, though, have the public announcement made as soon as possible. I confess I shall not feel easy in my mind until it is made.'

'The Privy Councillors should be summoned at once and George himself must make the announcement. I agree with you and shall tremble until he has done so.'

'He will do it,' Bute assured her. 'George's goodness is our salvation. He is a young man who is determined to do his duty. Would there were more in the world like him. It would be a different place then.'

'Ah yes, a good boy,' sighed his mother. 'What a pity that he should have to be stupid as well.'

*　　　*　　　*

George summoned the Privy Council to hear a matter of urgent and important business. The notifications were marked 'absolute secret', and the councillors arrived expecting that the King had decided to make peace or had come to some such momentous decision.

When they arrived he faced them, looking stern and pale, and he appeared to have lost that look of boyish innocence.

He stood up boldly and even as he did so he had a strong inclination to disband the meeting, to tell them all it was a great mistake.

But Lord Bute was there smiling at him encouragingly, anxious for him, wishing him to know that he could help him. 'You can make her your mistress,' said Bute, like a fond parent offering a child a sweetmeat to take with the medicine. But that was not George's way.

'Be a King,' said his mother; and she was right. Before he was a lover, he must be a King.

He began to speak a little falteringly at first but his voice strengthened as he proceeded:

'Having nothing so much at heart as to procure the welfare and happiness of my people, and to render the same stable and permanent to posterity, I have, ever since my accession to the throne, turned my thoughts towards the choice of a Princess for my consort; and now with great satisfaction acquaint you that after the fullest information and mature deliberation, I am come to a resolution to demand in marriage the Princess Charlotte of Mecklenburg-Strelitz, a Princess distinguished by every eminent virtue and amiable endowment, whose illustrious line has constantly shown the firmest zeal for the Protestant religion and a particular attachment to my family. I have judged proper to communicate to you these my intentions, in order that you may be fully appraised of a matter so highly important to me and to my kingdoms and which, I persuade myself, will be most acceptable to all my loving subjects.'

Lord Bute could scarcely hide his triumph, but his expression was one of deepest compassion and admiration as he met the King's gaze.

As soon as possible he was with the Princess Augusta.

'We must be prompt. There must be no delay. Betrothals have come to nothing before. This marriage must now take place at the earliest possible moment. Only then can we rest. Do you agree?'

'I am in complete accord.'

'Then I propose sending Lord Harcourt—a man I can trust —to Strelitz without delay. The Princess Charlotte must come to England at once.'

'Let it be done, my dear.'

*   *   *

Lady Sarah could not believe the news. It was impossible. How could he have talked to her as he had when all the time he must have been making arrangements to marry the Princess Charlotte? She could have believed Newbattle capable of such duplicity, but not George.

Lady Caroline Fox was furious. She stamped up and down the apartment.

'You have been a fool. You have thrown away the biggest chance you will ever get! It was all that folly in the beginning with Newbattle.'

Lady Sarah wept; but Mr. Fox came in and shook his head over her. 'It is a great calamity,' he said. 'When I consider all the good you might have brought to the family and all the disappointment you have brought us, I am speechless.'

'I wish you would be,' cried Sarah. 'The whole lot of you.'

Then she threw her head into the pillows and put her fingers in her ears and refused either to look or listen to them.

When they left her she rose from her bed and looked at herself in the mirror. She *was* pretty. No one she knew was as pretty. And he had thought so. Why had he done this? Why had he insulted her . . . so publicly. It was not revenge for the way she had treated him over Newbattle. She was sure of that. And he had been so timorous . . . so eager to please her. He had behaved as though he really loved her.

'And now . . . jilted,' she said dramatically.

She was angry not so much because she had lost Goerge—or rather a crown—but because he had made everyone think that he was going to ask her to marry him and then had, without warning, asked someone else. Everyone would be talking about the King's engagement and when they did that they would talk about her. Poor Sarah Lennox, they would say. Newbattle would laugh. It was not really very pleasant.

She wished Susan were here. She would have had something to say about this and Susan was always good to talk to.

She could not talk to Susan, so it might be a comfort to write to her.

She took up her pen.

'Even last Thursday the day the news came out, the hypocrite had the face to come up and speak to me with all the good humour in the world. He must have sent to that woman before you went out of town. Then what business had he to begin again? In short, his behaviour is that of a man who has neither sense, good nature nor honesty.'

There was some comfort in setting her feelings on paper, but nothing could alter the fact that the Lady Sarah Lennox had been jilted—and in the most public manner imaginable.

The Face in the Crowd

BY September of that year—two months after George had made up his mind to accept the Princess Charlotte, he was married to her.

George was reconciled; he was quite convinced that his duty to his crown must come before any personal desires. His heart had sunk when he had first seen his bride for she was no beauty and he could not stop thinking of the gay vitality of Lady Sarah, the haunting beauty of Hannah Lightfoot. The Princess was very different; she was small and thin, although he was pleased to see, not deformed; she was pale and what could be kindly called homely, with a flat nose and a very big mouth.

He gave no sign of his disappointment and welcomed her with warm affection. He had made up his mind that he would be a good husband to her and never, whatever the temptation he might be called upon to face, be unfaithful to her.

He must forget Sarah; he must stop Hannah from continually intruding on his thoughts.

*　　*　　*

Lady Sarah had given up thinking about the King. I had not really wanted him, she assured herself. I would have said No right away if the family had not persuaded me. I'd rather have had Newbattle ... but I don't want him either.

Her pet squirrel was not well and that was a matter of much graver concern to her, she told her sister, then the silly King's wedding.

Lady Caroline, tired of telling her what a little fool she was, left her alone with her squirrel.

She did, however, write to Lady Susan:

'I shall take care to show that I am not in the least mortified. Luckily, I did not love him, nor did I care very much for the title. But I am angry to have been made to look a fool. Please don't tell anyone what I have written to you. I expect George will hate me and the family for ever, for one generally hates people that one is in the wrong with, and who know one has acted wrongly ...'

Then she shrugged her shoulders. She was really worried about her squirrel.

*   *   *

It was a different matter when the bridesmaids to appear at the King's wedding were selected. These were to be eleven young ladies from the highest families in the land and because of her age and position it was inevitable that Sarah should be one of them.

When the invitation came Lady Caroline was furious.

'This is an added insult,' she declared.

'It's not a command,' pointed out her husband, 'and it can be refused.'

'I shall go,' replied Sarah.

'You don't know what you are saying!'

'I know full well. If I don't go it will be said that I was moping at home. Everyone will know I have been invited. No. I shall go and ... discountenance him. *He* shall be sorry I am there ... not I.'

The day before the wedding she was discovered weeping and her sister sought to comfort her.

She must not brood. Her own folly was partly to blame, but

she had learned a valuable lesson. Not that she could hope for such an opportunity again. Still her rank and beauty would enable her to make a very good match.

'Match!' cried Sarah. 'What are you talking about? My little squirrel is dead!'

'You're nothing but a child!' cried Lady Caroline in disgust.

And so it seemed, for the very next day Sarah found an injured hedgehog in the grounds of Holland House. She brought it in and believed she could make it well.

The prospect made her radiant with joy.

*   *   *

At nine o'clock the marriage took place in the Chapel Royal at St. James's. The bride looked very small in her white and silver gown and her mantle of purple velvet fastened by a cluster of enormous pearls. The diamonds in her tiara were said to be worth a fortune.

George was very much aware of Lady Sarah; he kept thinking how different it would have been had she been standing beside him instead of this strange woman. How happy he would have been! And how ironical it was that she, Sarah, beautiful and desired, should be standing so close to him at this moment.

'Dearly beloved, we are gathered together...' began the Archbishop; but George was thinking. If only I had insisted. Why did I not? I am the King. But he had made an oath to serve his country, to care for nothing but his duty. And this was his duty. He must never allow this plain little woman at his side to doubt his affection for her. He must learn to love her. He must never let his thoughts turn to any other woman. He had sinned enough. Even now he could not stop thinking of that other ceremony. Was there no escape from Hannah?

'Look, O Lord, mercifully upon them from Heaven and bless them as Thou did send Thy blessing upon Abraham and Sarah...'

Sarah. He felt the hot blood rush into his face. Everyone was watching. He could not resist looking in Sarah's direction. She met his gaze coolly, contemptuously.

Hastily he looked away. Oh God, he prayed, help me to do my duty.

And now the words were spoken which united him with Charlotte.

This strange, plain little woman was his wife.

* * *

On the way back to the Palace he saw a face in the crowd. It was there for a second and it was gone. But it brought back memories ... of the house in Tottenham, the private carriage drive, of looking up and seeing that face at the window. Then, the entry into the house, the hasty embrace.

'So thou hast come and I am happy to see thee.'

It could not have been. Imagination played strange tricks, and he had been thinking of her almost continuously ... of her and Sarah.

He had imagined the whole thing. How could it have been; she was dead and buried under a gravestone marked Rebecca Powell.

Lord Bute was beside him.

'Your Majesty looks shaken. It was an ordeal, but you came through it magnificently. You always will ...'

'I must speak to you ... in private ... soon.'

'Yes, yes. Of course.'

In the Palace the bride sang for the company and gave them an opportunity to admire her skill on the harpsichord. Supper was announced and the company led by the King and the new Queen went into the banqueting hall.

When they had eaten the King and the Queen would retire to the nuptial chamber, but the King had said that he would have none of the usual ceremony in the bedchamber which he considered both vulgar and obscene. He and his bride would go to bed in private.

He ate little. Bute, watching him, thought he was regretting the loss of Sarah. But it is too late now, thought Bute triumphantly. He was surprised a little later when he had the opportunity of being alone with the King to discover it was not the thought of Sarah which tortured him but of Hannah.

'I wanted to speak to you,' said the King quietly. 'I thought I saw Hannah in the crowd.'

'Impossible. She is dead.'

'Are you sure?'

Bute was taken off his guard; he had come to talk of Sarah and now he was confronted with Hannah.

'But Your Majesty saw the grave...'

'I saw *a* grave.'

'But we were told...'

'The name above the grave was not even hers. I have a feeling that she is not dead.'

'But I was told...'

'I know. But you might not have been told the truth.'

'Why should I not have been?'

'Because Hannah wanted to disappear. She wanted to make everything easy for me and that was the only way she could do it.'

'She left her children, then, you think?'

'No. She would not do that. The children are with good parents. Why should she not visit them ... even be near them. She might be in the household where they are. How can we know? I believe it was Hannah I saw in the crowd.'

'You have been thinking a great deal of her lately, have you not?'

'Yes, that's true.'

'Then it would be so easy to imagine you saw her. A Quaker habit ... In similar dress people look alike.'

'I knew her well ... very well.'

'That is so. But Your Highness imagined you saw her. Please, Sire, it is better that way.'

'I married her. If she still lives was I married today?'

'She does not live and she was already married to Isaac Axford. It was a mock marriage you went through with her.'

'I ... am not sure.'

'Your Majesty torments yourself unnecessarily.'

'That lady ... the Queen will bear my children. They will be the heirs of this country ... but perhaps it is Hannah's children...'

'Your Majesty is, if you will forgive my saying so, tormenting himself with impossible nightmares.'

'I want to see who lies under that stone.'

'Impossible. It is too long. Oh no ... no ... It would be dreadful.'

'I shall never be sure. I shall be haunted by doubts ... for the rest of my life.'

'Your Majesty, there are some occasions when Kings who have the good of the people to consider should think of nothing but their duty.'

'And the truth?'

'Duty, where Kings are concerned, takes precedence over truth.'

'Then you think...'

'I think she is dead. I think that unhappy affair is at an end. I think we have a young and good King who will lead his country to greatness. Today he has united himself with a good Queen who will bear him sons to the glorification of this land.'

The King stared at his dear friend.

'You have always been right,' he said. 'I cannot believe that you could be wrong.'

'I was never more right than I am at this time. I rejoice in Your Majesty's goodness; in Your Majesty's marriage; in Your Majesty's heritage. Sire, there are experiences in all our lives over which we would wish to draw a veil. The thicker that veil very often the better. We make our biggest mistakes when we look back and draw it aside. The past is done with. No good can come by going back ... even in thought. Go forward. Long live the King! I say. I trust that this time next year I shall be saying "Long live the Prince of Wales!"'

'You convince me, my dear friend, as you always have done.'

Bute embraced the King and for a moment George clung to him as he had when he was a child and this man had come to the schoolroom to help extricate him from some small mis-demeanour.

'You are right,' he said firmly. 'My dear friend, you are right. There is no going back. The past must be forgotten. I have my duty to my country and my Queen.'

'She will be missing you,' said Bute, smiling.

And George left him and returned to his Queen.